WOMEN OF THE MEAN STREETS

edited by

J.M. Redmann & Greg Herren

A Division of Bold Strokes Books

2011

CREDITS
EDITORS: J.M. REDMANN, GREG HERREN, AND STACIA SEAMAN
PRODUCTION DESIGN: STACIA SEAMAN
COVER DESIGN BY SHERI (GRAPHICARTIST2020@HOTMAIL.COM)

Dedication

To my fabulous co-editor Greg Herren.
Long may his red pen rule.

Acknowledgments

I need to thank the talented group of writers who were willing to contribute stories and endure my editorial suggestions—"but it's not dark enough—channel Barbara Stanwyck, please." This is a great bunch of writers, talented in myriad ways and a pleasure to work with. I also need to thank my co-editor Greg Herren, for making this so easy and fun—okay, let's be real, we didn't kill each other and the rest of the wounds will heal. Also big thanks to Rad for making Bold Strokes what it is. Stacia and Cindy, for all their hard work behind the scenes, and everyone at BSB for being the best little publishing house in the world.

CONTENTS

INTRODUCTION   1

A.R.M. AND THE WOMAN
    Laura Lippman   3

DEN OF INIQUITY
    Lori L. Lake   15

BOOMERANG
    Carsen Taite   25

THE ECONOMICS OF DESIRE: A CAUTIONARY TALE
    Jeane Harris   51

SOME KIND OF KILLING
    Miranda Kent   61

ANYTHING FOR THE THEATER
    Clifford Henderson   91

SOCIAL WORK
    Kendra Sennett   107

DEVIL IN TRAINING
    Ali Vali   131

THE DARKEST NIGHT OF THE YEAR
    Victoria A. Brownworth   145

LOST
    J.M. Redmann   157

CHASING ATHENA
    Diane Anderson-Minshall   187

LUCKY THIRTEEN
    Anne Laughlin   215

FEEDBACK
    Lindy Cameron   229

CONTRIBUTORS   273

INTRODUCTION

"For neither life nor nature cares if justice is ever done or not."
—Patricia Highsmith

Women. Crime. Justice—or what can be found in the far reaches of a dim streetlight or deserted road. A hasty kiss when the clouds cover the moon. A tryst in someone else's bed. On the mean streets, the back alleys, the sinister corners. The dark unleashes sex and violence in a way that just won't do in a cozy mystery or happy romance.

Why do we want to look into the shadowed alleys, behind the heavy curtains of the house on the corner? What is the fascination with the mean streets? Is it the adrenaline rush of a life we want to live? Or more likely, a place we don't want our daily journey to take us, not really, not where the stench of garbage fills our nostrils, the lone footsteps could be coming after us, and the consequences are more than just turning the next page. Perhaps we read these stories as cautionary tales, worlds we want to view only through a glass darkly.

Early stories about the mean streets—aided and needed by the rise of the paperback—started out as a men's club—men interested in women, that is. It took a few decades—and some major changes in society, with women's liberation and LGBTQ activism—but the bookshelves made room for woman, then men who liked men and women who liked women.

This evolution in who could write what led to there being authors like the ones you'll find in these pages, enough to create an anthology like this one. (With many more authors in other books still waiting on the bookshelves.) I am fortunate to know many in the literary community, so when I asked some of my friends and acquaintances, "Hey, can you write a dark, twisted story—in addition to everything else you're doing?" the ensuing chorus of "yes" was quite gratifying. Included in these pages are some of the top crime writers practicing today, with a long list of award winners and authors you probably know or should know.

These are stories of tough women in hard places. The nights are long, the women are fast, and danger is always a short block or quick minute away. Love can be fleeting or deceiving or the wrong woman in the wrong place or the right woman and the wrong time, a jumble that doesn't promise happily ever after, only that, in true hardboiled fashion, hot sex is better than no sex and right here, right now feels good, the morning after be damned.

These stories take us from small-town Kansas to an Australia far away not only in distance, but in time. New Orleans, the dark lady at the end of the Mississippi, features in three of the stories, but they take us from the West Coast to Europe, from the darkest night to the height of folly. The talented authors take us backstage and back home, from an ironic shrug to desperation at the common horrors of life. A criminal comes into her own, and some detectives lose their cases. Love is found and lost and lost again.

So sit back, get comfortable, and strap yourself in. It's going to be a bumpy ride.

J.M. Redmann
New Orleans, 2011

A.R.M. AND THE WOMAN
LAURA LIPPMAN

Sally Holt was seldom the prettiest woman in the room, but for three decades now she had consistently been one of the most sought-after for one simple fact: She was a wonderful listener. Whether it was her eight-year-old son or her eighty-year-old neighbor or some male in-between, Sally rested her chin in her palm and leaned forward, expression rapt, soft laugh at the ready—but not *too* ready, which gave the speaker a feeling of power when the shy, sweet sound finally bubbled forth, almost in spite of itself. In the northwest corner of Washington, DC, where overtly decorative women were seen as suspect if not out-and-out tacky, a charm like Sally's was much prized. It had served her well, too, helping her glide into the perfect marriage to her college sweetheart, a dermatologist, then allowing her to become one of northwest Washington's best hostesses, albeit in the amateur division. Sally and her husband, Peter, did not move in and did not aspire to the more rarefied social whirl, the one dominated by embassy parties and pink-faced journalists who competed to shout pithy things over one another on cable television shows. They lived in a quieter, in some ways more exclusive world, a charming, old-fashioned neighborhood comprising middle-class houses that now required upper-class incomes to own and maintain.

And if, on occasion, in a dark corner at one of the endless parties Sally and Peter hosted and attended, her unwavering attention was mistaken for affection, she managed to deflect the ensuing pass with a graceful shake of her auburn curls. "You wouldn't want me," she told the briefly smitten men. "I'm just another soccer mom." The husbands backed away, sheepish and relieved, confiding in each other what a lucky son of a bitch Peter Holt was. Sally Holt had kept her figure, hadn't allowed herself to thicken into that androgynous khaki-trousered—let's be honest, downright dykish—mom so common in the area, which did have a lot of former field hockey players gone to seed. Plus, she was so great to talk to, interested in the world, not forever prattling about her children and their school.

Sally's secret was that she didn't actually hear a word her admirers said, just nodded and laughed at the right moments, cued by their inflections as to how to react. Meanwhile, deep inside her head, she was mapping out the logistics of her next day. *Just a soccer mom, indeed.* To be a stay-at-home mother in Northwest D.C. was to be nothing less than a general, the Patton of the carpool, the Eisenhower of the HOV-lane. Sally spent most of her afternoons behind the wheel of a Porsche SUV, moving her children and other people's children from school to lessons, from lessons to games, from games to home. She was ruthlessly efficient with her time and motion, her radio always tuned to WTOP to catch the traffic on the eights, her brain filled with alternative routes and illegal shortcuts, her gaze at the ready to thaw the nastiest traffic cop. She could envision her section of the city in a three-dimensional grid in her head, her house on Morrison and the Dutton School off Nebraska the two fixed stars in her universe. Given all she had to do, you really couldn't blame her for not listening to the men who bent her ear, a figure of speech that struck her as particularly apt. If she allowed all those words into her head, her ears would be bent—as crimped, tattered, and chewed-up looking as the old tomcat she had owned as a child, a cat who could not avoid brawls even after he was neutered.

But when Peter came to her in the seventeenth year of their marriage and said he wanted out, she heard him loud and clear. And when his lawyer said their house, mortgaged for a mere $400,000, was now worth $1.8 million, which meant she needed $700,000 to buy Peter's equity stake, she heard that, too. For as much time as she spent behind the wheel of her car, Sally was her house, her house was Sally. The 1920s stucco two-story was tasteful and individual, with a kind of perfection that a decorator could never have achieved. She was determined to keep the house at all costs, and when *her* lawyer proposed a way it could be done, without sacrificing anything in child support or her share of Peter's retirement funds, she had approved it instantly and then, as was her habit, glazed over as the details were explained.

"What do you mean, I owe a million dollars on the house?" she asked her accountant, Kenny, three years later.

"You refinanced your house with an interest-only balloon mortgage to buy Peter out of his share. Now it's come due."

"But I don't have a million dollars," Sally said, as if Kenny didn't know this fact better than anyone. It was April, he had her tax return in front of him.

"No biggie. You get a new mortgage. Unfortunately, your timing sucks. Interest rates are up. Your monthly payment is going to be a lot bigger—just as the alimony is ending. Another bit of bad timing."

Kenny relayed all this information with zero lack of emotion. After all, it didn't affect his bottom line. It occurred to Sally that an accountant should have a much more serious name. What was she doing, trusting someone named Kenny with her money?

"What about the equity I've built up in the past three years?"

"It was an interest-only loan, Sally. There is no additional equity." Kenny, a square-jawed man who bore a regrettable resemblance to Frankenstein, sighed. "Your lawyer did you no favors, steering you into this deal. Did you know the mortgage broker he referred you to was his brother-in-law? And that your lawyer is a partner in the title company? He even stuck you with PMI."

Sally was beginning to feel as if they were discussing sexually transmitted diseases instead of basic financial transactions.

"I thought I got an adjustable rate mortgage. ARMs have conversion rates, don't they? And caps? What does any of this have to do with PMI?"

"ARMs do. But you got a balloon, and balloons come due. All at once, in a big lump. Hence the name. You had a three-year grace period, in which you had an artificially low rate of 3.25 percent, with Peter's three thousand in rehabilitative alimony giving you a big cushion. Now it's over. In today's market, I recommend a thirty-year fixed, but even that's not the deal it was two years ago. According to today's rates, the best you can do is—"

Frankennystein used an old-fashioned adding machine, the kind with a paper roll, an affectation Sally had once found charming. He punched the keys and the paper churned out, delivering its noisy verdict.

"A million financed at thirty-year fixed rates—you're looking at seven thousand a month, before taxes."

It was an increase of almost four thousand dollars a month over what she had been paying for the last three years, and that didn't take into account the alimony she was about to lose.

"I can't cover that, not with what I get in child support. Not and pay my share of the private school tuition, which we split fifty-fifty."

"You could sell. But after closing costs and paying the real estate agent's fee, you'd walk away with a lot less cash than you might think. Maybe eight hundred thousand."

Eight hundred thousand dollars. She couldn't buy a decent three-bedroom for that amount, not in the neighborhood, not even in the suburbs. There, the schools would be free at least, but the Dutton School probably mattered more to Sally than it did to the children. It had become the center of her social life since Peter had left, a place where she was made to feel essential. Essential and adored, one of the parents who helped out without becoming a fearsome buttinsky or know-it-all.

"How long do I have to figure this out?" she asked Kenny.

"The balloon comes due in four months. But the way things are going, you'll be better off locking in sooner rather than later. Greenspan looked funny the last time the Fed met."

"Funny?"

"Constipated, like. As if his sphincter was the only thing keeping the rates down."

"Kenny," she said with mock reproach, her instinctive reaction to a man's crude joke, no matter how dull and silly. Already, her mind was miles away, flying through the streets of her neighborhood, trying to think who might help her. There was a father who came to Sam's baseball games, often straight from work, only to end up on his cell, rattling off percentages. He must be in real estate.

❖

"I own a title company," Alan Mason said. "Which, I have to say, is like owning a mint these days. The money just keeps coming. Even with the housing supply tight as it is, people always want to refinance."

"If only I had thought to talk to you three years ago," Sally said, twisting the stalk of a gone-to-seed dandelion in her hand. They were standing along the first base line, the better to see both their sons—Sam, adorable if inept in right field, and Alan's Duncan, a wiry first baseman who pounded his glove with great authority, although he had yet to catch a single throw to the bag.

"The thing is—" Alan stopped as the batter made contact with the ball, driving it toward the second baseman, who tossed it to Duncan for the out. There was a moment of suspense as Duncan bobbled it a bit, but he held on.

"Good play, son!" Alan said and clapped, then looked around. "I didn't violate the vocalization rule, did I?"

"You were perfect," Sally assured him. The league in which their sons played did, in fact, have strict rules about parents' behavior, including guidelines on how to cheer properly—with enthusiasm, but without aggression. It was a fine line.

"Where was I? Oh, your dilemma. The thing is, I can hook you up with someone who can help you find the best deal, but you might want to consider taking action against your lawyer. He could be disbarred for what he did, or at least reprimanded. Clearly a conflict of interest."

"True, but that won't help me in the long run." She sighed, then exhaled on the dandelion head, blowing away the fluff.

"Did you make a wish?" Alan asked. He wasn't handsome, not even close. He looked like Ichabod Crane, tall and thin, with a pointy nose and no chin.

"I did," Sally said with mock solemnity.

"For what?"

"Ah, if you tell, they don't come true." She met his eyes, just for a moment, let Alan Mason think that he was her heart's desire. Later that night, her children asleep, a glass of white wine at her side, she plugged figures into various mortgage calculators on the Internet, as if a different site might come up with a different answer. She charted her budget on Quicken—*if* she traded the Porsche for a Prius, *if* she stopped buying organic produce at Whole Foods, *if* she persuaded Molly to drop ballet. But there were not enough sacrifices in the world to cover the looming shortfall in their monthly bills. They would have to give up everything to keep the house—eating, driving, heat and electricity.

And even if she did find the money, found a way to make it work, her world was still shrinking around her. When Peter first left, it had been almost a relief to be free of him, grouchy and cruel as he had become in midlife. She had been glad for an excuse to avoid parties as well. Now that she was divorced, the husbands steered clear of her as if a suddenly single woman was the most unstable molecule of all in their social set. But Alan Moore's gaze, beady as it was, had reminded her how nice it was to be admired, how she had enjoyed being everyone's favorite confidante once upon a time, how she had liked the hands pressed to her bare spine, the friendly pinch on her ass.

She should marry again. It was simple as that. She left the Internet's mortgage calculators for its even more numerous matchmakers, but the world she glimpsed was terrifying, worse than the porn she had once found cached on Peter's laptop. She was so *old* by the standards enumerated in these online wish lists. Worse, she had children, and ad after ad specified that would just not do. She looked at the balding, pudgy men, read their demands—no kids, no fatties, no over-forties—and realized they held the power to dictate the terms. No, she would not subject herself to such humiliation. Besides, Internet matches required writing, not listening. In a forum where she could not nod and laugh and gaze sympathetically, Sally was at a disadvantage. Typing "LOL" in a chat room simply didn't have the same impact.

Now a man with his own children, that would be ideal. A widower or a divorcé who happened to have custody, rare as that was. She mentally ran through the Dutton School directory, then pulled it from the shelf and skimmed it. No, no, no—all the families she knew were disgustingly intact, the divorced and reblended ones even tighter than those who had stayed with their original mates. Didn't anyone die anymore? Couldn't the killers and drug dealers who kept the rest of Washington in the upper tier of homicide rates come up to Northwest every now and then, take out a housewife or two?

Why not?

❖

In a school renowned for dowdy mothers, Lynette Moore was one of the dowdiest, gone to seed in the way only a truly preppy woman can. She had leathery skin and a Prince Valiant haircut, which she sheered back from her face with a grosgrain ribbon headband. Her laugh was a loud, annoying bray and if someone failed to join in her merriment, she clapped the person on the back as if trying to dislodge a lump of food. On this particular Thursday afternoon, Lynette stood on the sidewalk, speaking animatedly to one of the teachers, punching the poor woman at intervals. Sally, waiting her turn in the carpool lane, thought how easily a foot could slip, how an accelerator could jam. The SUV would surge forward, Lynette would be pinned against the column by the school's front door. So sad, but no one's fault, right?

No, Sally loved the school too much to do that. Besides, an accident would take out Ms. Grayson as well, and she was an irreplaceable resource when it came to getting Dutton's graduates into the best colleges.

Three months, according to her accountant. She had three months. Maybe Peter would die; he carried enough life insurance to pay off the mortgage, with plenty left over for the children's education. No, she would never get that lucky. Stymied, she continued to make small talk with Alan Moore at baseball games, but began to befriend Lynette as well, lavishing even more attention on her in order to deflect any suspicions she might harbor about Sally's kindness to Alan. Lynette was almost pathetically grateful for Sally's attention, adopting her with the fervor that adolescent girls bring to new friendships. Women appreciate good listeners, too, and Sally nodded and smiled over tea and, once five o'clock came around, glasses of wine. Lynette had quite a bit to say, the usual litany of complaints. Alan worked all the time. There was zero romance in their marriage. She might as well be a single mom—"Not that a single mom is a bad thing to be," she squealed, clapping a palm over her large, unlipsticked mouth.

"You're a single mom without any of the advantages," Sally said, pouring her another glass of wine. *Drive home drunk. What do I care?*

"There are advantages, aren't there?" Lynette leaned forward and lowered her voice, although Molly was at a friend's and Sam was up in his room with Lynette's Duncan, playing The Sims. "No one ever says that, but it's true."

"Sure. As long as you have the money to sustain the standard of living you had, being single is great."

"How do you do that?" Asked with specificity, as if Lynette believed that Sally had managed just that trick. Sally, who had long ago learned the value of the non-reply, raised her eyebrows and smiled serenely, secretly.

"I think Alan cheats on me," Lynette blurted out.

"I would leave a man who did that to me."

Lynette shook her head. "Not until the kids are grown and gone. Maybe then. But I'll be so old. Who would want me then?"

Who would want you now?

"Do what you have to do." Another meaningless response, perfected over the years. Yet no one ever seemed to notice how empty Sally's sentiments were, how vapid. She had thought it was just men who were fooled so easily, but it was turning out that women were equally foolish.

"Alan and I never have sex anymore."

"That's not uncommon," Sally said. "All marriages have their ups and downs."

"I love your house." Logical sequences of thought had never been Lynette's strength, but this conversation was abrupt and odd even by her standards. "I love you."

Lynette put a short stubby hand over Sally's, who fought the instinctive impulse to yank her own away. Instead, it was Lynette who pulled back in misery and confusion.

"I don't mean *that* way," she said, staring into her wineglass, already half empty.

Sally took a deep breath. "Why not?"

Lynette put her hand back over Sally's. "You mean—?"

Sally thought quickly. No matter how far Sam and Duncan disappeared into their computer world, she could not risk taking Lynette to the master bedroom. She had a hunch that Lynette would be loud. But she also believed that this was her only opportunity. In fact, Lynette would shun her after today. She would cut Sally off completely, ruining any chance Sally had of luring Alan away from her. She would have to see this through, or start over with another couple.

"There's a room, over our garage. It used to be Peter's office."

She grabbed the bottle of wine and her glass. She was going to need to be a little drunk, too, to get through this. Then again, who was less attractive in the large scheme of things, Alan or Lynette? Who would be more grateful, more giving? Who would be more easily controlled? She was about to find out.

❖

Lynette may not have been in love when she blurted out that sentiment in Sally's kitchen, but she was within a week. Lynette being Lynette, it was a loud, unsubtle love, both behind closed doors and out in public, and Sally had to chide her about the latter, school her in the basics of covert behavior, remind her not to stare with those cow-like eyes, or try to monopolize Sally at public events, especially when Alan was present. They dropped their children at school at 8:30 and Lynette showed up at Sally's house promptly at 8:45, bearing skim milk lattes and scones. Lynette's idea of the perfect day, as it turned out, was to share a quick latte upon arriving, then bury her head between Sally's legs until 11 a.m., when she surfaced for the Hot Topics segment on *The View*. Then it was back to devouring Sally, with time-outs for back rubs and baths. Sally's large, eager mouth turned out to have its uses. Plus, she asked for only the most token attention in return, which Sally provided largely through a hand-held massage tool from the Sharper Image.

Best of all, Lynette insisted that as much as she loved Sally, she could never, ever leave Alan, not until the children were grown and out of school. She warned Sally of this repeatedly, and Sally would nod sadly, resignedly. "I'll settle for the little bit I can have," she said, stroking Lynette's Prince Valiant bob.

"If Alan ever finds out—" Lynette said glumly.

"He won't," Sally assured her. "Not if we're careful. There. No— *there*." Just as her attention drifted away in conversation, she found it drifting now, floating toward an idea, only to be distracted by Lynette's insistent touch. Later. She would figure everything out later.

❖

"You're not going to believe this," Sally told Lynette at the beginning of their third week together, during one of the commercial breaks on *The View*. "Peter found out about us."

"Ohmigod!" Lynette said. "How?"

"I'm not sure. But he knows. He knows everything. He's threatening to take the children away from me."

"Ohmigod."

"And—" She turned her face to the side, not trusting herself to tell this part. "And he's threatening to go to Alan."

"Shit." In her panic, Lynette got up and began putting on her clothes, as if Peter and Alan were outside the door at this very moment.

"He hasn't yet," Sally said quickly. "But he will, if I fight the change in the custody order. He's given me a week to decide. I give up the children or he goes to Alan."

"You can't tell. You *can't*."

"I don't want to, but—how can I give up my children?"

Lynette understood, as only another mother could. They couldn't tell the truth, but she couldn't expect Sally to live with the consequences of keeping the secret. Lynette would keep her life while Sally would lose hers. No woman could make peace with such blatant unfairness.

"Would he really do this?"

"He would. Peter—he's not the nice man everyone thinks he is. Why do you think we got divorced? And the thing is, if he gets the kids—well, it was one thing for him to do the things he did to me. But if ever treated Molly or Sam that way..."

"What way?"

"I don't want to talk about it. But if it should happen—I'd have to kill him."

"The *pervert*." Lynette was at once repelled and fascinated. The dark side of Sally's life was proving as seductive to her as Sally had been.

"I know. If he had done what he did to a stranger, he'd be in prison for life. But in a marriage, such things are legal. I'm stuck, Lynette. I won't ruin your life for anything. You told me from the first that this had to be a secret."

"There has to be a way..."

"There isn't. Not as long as Peter is a free man."

"Not as long as he's *alive*."

"You can't mean—"

Lynette put a finger to Sally's lips. These had been the hardest moments to fake, the face-to-face encounters. Kissing was the worst. But it was essential not to flinch, not to let her distaste show. She was so close to getting what she wanted.

"Trust me," Lynette said.

Sally wanted to. But she had to be sure of one thing. "Don't try to hire someone. It seems like every time someone like us tries to find someone, it's always an undercover cop. Remember Ruth Ann Aron." A politician from the Maryland suburbs, she had done just that. But her husband had forgiven her, even testified on her behalf during the trial. She had been found guilty anyway.

"Trust me," Lynette repeated.

"I do, sweetheart. I absolutely do."

❖

Dr. Peter Holt was hit by a Jeep Cherokee, an Eddie Bauer limited edition, as he crossed Connecticut Avenue on his way to Fancy Japanese Restaurant, a place where he ate lobster pad thai every Thursday evening. The driver told police that her children had been bickering in the backseat over what to watch on the DVD player and she turned her head, just a moment, to scold them. Distracted, she had seen Holt and tried to stop, but hit the accelerator instead. Then, as her children screamed for real, she had driven another hundred yards in panic and hysteria. If the dermatologist wasn't dead on impact, he was definitely dead when the SUV finally stopped. But the only substance in her blood was caffeine, and while it was a tragic, regrettable accident, it was clearly an accident. Really, investigators told Holt's stunned survivors, his ex-wife and two children, it was surprising that such things didn't happen more often, given the congestion in D.C., the unwieldy SUVs, the mothers' frayed nerves, the nature of dusk, with its tricky gray-green light. It was a macabre coincidence, their children being classmates and all, the parents being superficial friends on the sidelines of their sons' baseball games. But this part of D.C. was like a village unto itself, and the accident had happened only a mile from the school.

At Peter's memorial service, Lynette Mason sought a private moment with Sally Holt, and those who watched from a distance marveled at the bereaved woman's composure and poise, the way she comforted her ex-husband's killer. No one was close enough to hear what they said.

"I'm sorry," Lynette said. "It didn't occur to me that after—well, I guess we can't see each other anymore."

"No," Sally lied. "It didn't occur to me, either. You've sacrificed so much for me. For Molly and Sam, really. I'm in your debt, forever. It will always be our secret."

And she patted Lynette gently on the arm, the last time the two would ever touch.

Peter's estate went to the children—but in trust to Sally, of course. She determined that it would be in the children's best interest to pay off the balloon mortgage in cash, and his brother, the executor, agreed. Peter would have wanted the children to have the safety and sanctity of home, given the emotional trauma they had endured.

No longer needy, armored with a widow's prerogatives, Sally found herself invited to parties again, where solicitous friends attempted to fix her up with the rare single men in their circles. Now that she didn't care about men, they flocked around her and Sally did what she had always done. She listened and she laughed, she laughed and she listened, but she never really heard anything—unless the subject was money. Then she paid close attention, even writing down the advice she was given. The stock market was so turgid, everyone complained. The smart money was in real estate.

Sally nodded.

DEN OF INIQUITY
LORI L. LAKE

After she recognized Gordon Chasney, Ava Tanner spent weeks trying to figure out a way to kill him and get away with it. Shooting? Stabbing? Poisoning? Mow him down with her car? Her favorite method involved crushing him. She imagined him in a giant vise, screaming as bones cracked and blood spurted. The vision was so ruthless that she shuddered and felt nauseated even while she maintained a fascination for every murderous idea she teased into being.

But murder would be too quick. What she really wanted was to hurt him, make his pain last, humiliate him the way he'd shamed and abused her. Most of all, she wanted to relish the fact that he'd know who she was and be aware, before the end, that he was paying for what he'd done.

But she couldn't think of a single way to accomplish this. He was well over six feet tall, built like a lumberjack, and had physical power and agility she could only dream of. Though only five-two, she possessed an unexpected wiry strength, but she knew her 125 pounds was no match for him.

Ava had finally tabled her dreams of murder and brainstormed for another solution...which was why she broke into Gordon's house. If you could call it breaking in when no breaking was involved. She was amazed at how casual he was about security. Her own doors were never left unlocked, and the windows in her small apartment didn't open far enough to allow anyone over two years old to wriggle in. Not so at Gordon's.

She'd watched him off and on for weeks. One day, while he mowed the backyard, which was nicely secluded by tall hedges in which she was hidden, his mower ran out of gas. He walked off toward the gas station four blocks away, red can in hand. Ava waltzed right through the back door into Gordon's unlocked kingdom.

The house smelled of stale beer and burnt meat. On the stove, a pair of wizened bratwurst sausages surrounded by a heap of dead sauerkraut lay in a black frying pan, burnt almost beyond recognition. From the spatter around the pan, it was clear they'd been there a few days.

Wrinkling her nose, Ava passed through the kitchen, then hastened through the living room and down a hallway where the smell wasn't so strong. The crappy-brown shag rug cushioned her every step. Somebody had probably paid big money a couple of decades earlier to lay this expanse of carpet throughout the house.

A pair of crooked shades blocked the morning sun, but she could still make out stray socks and little clumps of underwear here and there. What was it with him? Didn't he see anything below knee level? Items on his dresser top—watch, pen, pocket change, penknife, checkbook—sat in orderly fashion, and in the bathroom, he'd lined up his shaving cream, razor, aftershave, deodorant, and toothbrush holder in a row on the counter. But she had seen dustballs scattered liberally throughout the house, and she nearly kicked over more than one empty beer can sitting next to furniture.

The next room, instead of being a second bedroom, looked like a cross between a sportsman's paradise and a home office. A den of iniquity, she thought. An eight-point deer head mounted on the wall was flanked by two fish so shiny they appeared to have just leapt out of a lake and suddenly found themselves attached to ovals of decorative wood.

Gordon's desk bulged. Paper, envelopes, old phone books, and other junk overloaded every drawer. A stack of receipts and a three-ring binder, obviously from the auto parts store where he was employed, were piled on the computer desk on top of random slips of paper and a handful of music CD jewel cases. The corner of a photo peeked out from under a pile. Ava hastily donned a pair of latex gloves she used when she changed toner in her printer and lifted the papers on top. Gordon had printed out a picture of a naked woman, her breasts pendulous and her private parts splayed open for all to see. Feeling queasy, Ava covered the photo, careful not to let any of the paper pile cascade to the floor.

She forced herself to stop focusing on the stacks of junk and the wildlife rotting on the walls, and moved to the computer, which she was delighted to find was humming away. One touch brought up the screen. Still standing, she opened a browser, typed in an address, downloaded and installed a program, and closed the browser.

How long had she been inside? Ninety seconds? More? She calculated that it would take Gordon six or eight minutes round-trip to the gas station. To be on the safe side, she set her watch timer for three more minutes. She swiftly examined his computer applications and files.

Within thirty seconds, she found his cache of dirty pictures. She didn't bother to open the multitude of video files, but she clicked on the first in a series of photos. With a gasp, she plopped into the desk chair, feeling light-headed. There was no doubt—Gordon Chasney was the one. Shots of naked women and frightened-looking teenage girls— beaten, bound, and sexually used—made her so sick to her stomach that her breakfast rose up in her throat.

"Not here, not now," she said aloud, then looked around, shocked that she'd spoken. Even though she still had another minute, she'd seen enough. Now if she could only find his keys. She took a deep breath to center herself, closed the photo files, and hustled from the room.

He made it easy for her. A key rack hung next to the front entryway. She hunted through all the dangling metal, searching for a key to the back door. She took his ring and several individual keys to the kitchen door and started fitting them in the lock. Voilà. Not only was there a backdoor key on his ring, but also a spare, which she tucked in her pocket.

Her watch alarm went off, and she silenced it. She returned the keys to the rack and headed for the back exit, noting an open door she'd missed before. She saw it led to the downstairs level and to the tuck-under garage.

She had barely slipped into the hedge when Gordon rounded the corner of the house. Oh, shit, she thought. That was a lot closer than I intended. As he filled the gas tank, she tried to calm down. Once he had cranked up the mower, she moved through the hedge and away from Gordon Chasney's den of iniquity.

That was the start of it.

❖

Over the next weeks, Ava came to believe Gordon was the most obvious man she'd ever known, so why didn't anyone else see it? All you had to do was watch him closely, and it was clear there was something off about him. Had he been this obvious during her childhood when he'd stalked her, gained her trust, and then molested her? She wished she could remember the details better, but she couldn't. Whenever she thought of that day—being grabbed, held down, the relentless probing—her stomach clenched and sometimes she very nearly passed out. All she knew for sure was that he'd initially been very smooth. He'd had to be, or even at age ten she would have seen his true intent.

She watched him now as he walked briskly around the neighborhood park, his eyes glinting with interest as he surreptitiously glanced toward little girls on the swings, on the slide, twirling on the merry-go-round. Ava wanted to scream at the parents in the park. People, she wanted to say, can't you see him? He's a sexual predator!

But she had no proof, and he looked completely innocent as he kept to the sidewalk, hands in his Windbreaker pockets, smiling and nodding pleasantly. Couldn't anyone else see how his eyes followed the children like a voracious grizzly seeking flesh to devour?

She couldn't waste another moment worrying about perfecting a plan. He was on the prowl again, and she needed to act. If she couldn't kill him and get away with it, there had to be another way to stop him. Luckily, her self-employment as a website designer gave her time and flexibility. Tuesday nights Gordon bowled in an eight p.m. league at the Leapfrog Lanes. No more dithering. She needed to get back in his house and take care of business.

❖

The program Ava had installed during her first foray into Gordon's domain yielded all sorts of good information. Every time he typed something, the spyware monitored where he surfed and what he searched for, and every keystroke he made was transmitted over the Internet to her. She knew his home and work computer passwords, banking information, credit card details, and what he'd bought online. If she wanted to, she could install a program that would allow her to update his computer remotely…but she didn't dare use that for what she had in mind.

Tuesday night she dressed in a long-sleeved gray shirt, black slacks, tennis shoes, and a baseball cap. When it was sufficiently dark, she drove to the side street near Gordon's house and waited until she saw his truck turn the corner and pass her car. Show time. She gathered her courage, picked up a clipboard, and got out. She strode into his backyard as though she had every right to be there. Had anyone seen? She stood on his back porch stoop, hardly breathing, expecting someone to call out. A dog barked in the distance. Over the hedge she could see the second-story windows lit up in the house behind Gordon's, but no one seemed to have noticed her.

She pressed the back doorbell and heard the muffled ringing inside. The house stayed dark, and no one came to the door. After waiting one sweat-filled, oxygen-deprived moment, she put on her gloves, inserted the stolen key, and was surprised to find that Gordon hadn't locked up when he left. She giggled nervously. All that work to get his keys, and he doesn't even bother with security. What an arrogant man.

Ava slipped into the house and turned on a penlight to find her way through the kitchen. He'd left a light on by the front door, and for a moment that worried her. What if he came home unexpectedly? When he parked in the garage underneath the house, she thought she'd hear the door go up and know to get out. But what if he parked on the street and came in the front door?

In all the time she'd watched him, he'd never parked on the street, so she had to assume he'd do exactly what he always did.

The computer was on. Did he ever turn it off? Didn't he know that hijackers could put all kinds of spyware on his computer much more easily when he left it on? Since he went to porn sites, his computer would likely be stuffed full of bots and malware. She checked his cookie file. Sure enough, he had all sorts of problems festering. This pleased her.

Now it was time to do the one distasteful thing she'd been avoiding. She entered keywords that she hoped would bring up kiddie porn chat lists. She knew they'd be difficult to find, that they were well hidden. But with some persistence, she expected to at least come across some Internet groups where she could advertise her plan.

She should have set her watch alarm. So deep was she in her searching and inquiring that when she felt a strange rumble beneath her, she didn't pay attention at first. Then far away, below, a car door slammed, and she came to her senses. She leapt from the chair, grabbed her clipboard, and tiptoed toward the kitchen.

She heard him coming up the back stairs. Quick course correction. She ran to the front door, opened it, and pushed at the screen door. A light came on behind her. She stepped out to the porch as she peeled off her gloves. Over her shoulder, she saw Gordon's foot as he came up into the kitchen.

She whipped around, between the front door and the open screen, the gloves balled up in one hand. His eyes met hers, a surprised look on his face. She froze.

"Can I help you?" he asked.

"Cable company, sir." She looked down at her clipboard. "I got the call that you're having trouble with your TV reception and Internet." She pulled down the brim of her cap and hoped it shrouded her face.

He moved to stand in the hallway only a few feet away, wearing a puzzled look. "Isn't nine thirty kind of late for repair work?"

She glanced at her watch. "Dispatch said this was an emergency, and that no matter what, I was to get in and fix the problem. We work till ten, so here I am."

He rested a big, meaty hand against the edge of the door. His eyes looked glassy, his face relaxed. "I didn't call."

She smelled beer on his breath. Maybe he wasn't so with it after all. Heart beating fast, she lifted a page on her clipboard. "Twelve eighty-nine Birch, cable and Internet out."

He made a snorting sound. "Look, lady, this is twelve eighty-nine Franklin. Birch is a couple blocks thataway." He gestured behind him with a big thumb. "Better get your ass moving if you want to fix 'em up before ten."

Ava stepped back and let the screen door flutter closed. "Thanks, mister." She stumbled off the porch feeling giddy and amazed. Oh, my God. Had that really happened? She'd almost been caught. Unbelievable.

She was hunting for a parking place in front of her apartment when she realized she'd left her penlight behind.

❖

Ava spent the next week alternating between feeling triumphant and trying not to melt into a puddle of stress. She made herself focus on her work with her Internet accounts, but she couldn't help thinking that her entire plan was in danger due to a damned penlight. How could she have been so stupid?

The next Tuesday night she repeated her preparations, though every time she realized what she was contemplating, she shook, and just before she left her house, she threw up. Still, she forged on. When Gordon departed for the bowling alley, she entered the house quickly. This time he had locked the back door. Maybe he was educable after all.

She didn't have the penlight to guide her, but she crept through the house to the den of iniquity. A touch of her gloved hand brought up the computer screen, and it shed enough light for her to search by. She moved piles carefully and looked under the new detritus.

The penlight wasn't on the desk.

On a hunch, she knelt and felt around the carpet, wincing at how dusty and crud-flecked the shag was. She had almost given up when she saw a glint of silver along the front of the desk pedestal and found the penlight half-hidden in the long fibers.

Ava pocketed the light and checked her watch. She had a lot to do, but in order to complete the transactions, she had to wait until Gordon would be on his way home. The timing would be maddeningly close, but she wouldn't be taken unawares again.

Over the next hour she prepared to set up a merchant account using Gordon's credit card, built a bare-bones Internet storefront and got it ready to post, then created his very own e-mail address— gordyluvsgrrls—at a popular free service.

The worst part was finding and downloading online photos of degraded women and girls and writing disgusting comments to advertise what was for sale in each of the packets she created to sell at the storefront. She felt guilty about using the pictures, even though justice would ultimately be done. If she had any way of knowing who the women were, she would apologize, but of course each was as anonymous as the abusers who raped and hurt them.

Ava had just enough time to send out an advertisement to a few pervert lists before her watch alarm sounded. She went to the front window and peeked out the edge of the closed curtains. When she saw Gordon's truck come to a halt at the stop sign down the block, she ran back to the den, sent all her creations, and waited during maddening seconds for them to be approved. The sound of the garage door cranking open set her heart into overdrive, and she mashed her lips together to stop their trembling. When the approvals to flashed on the screen, she quickly closed each program and ran to the front door before Gordon even got out of the truck. She was in her car driving away, penlight in pocket, before another minute passed.

The next week Ava went back to Gordon's house to field orders off his merchant account. She was disgusted to see 412 orders from all over the world, totaling in excess of four thousand dollars.

She selected U.S. customers only and used Gordon's equipment to print out smutty photos and type up envelopes from his desk in which she enclosed photos of children, girls, and women. Before he arrived home, she had prepared thirty orders. She drove directly to a mailbox in a neighborhood far from her own and dropped in the first makeshift packets, knowing that the recipients would be furious upon receipt. They'd paid $9.95 for poor quality photos on regular laser paper. It was only a matter of time before her carefully contrived plan would blow up in Gordon's face.

The next Tuesday night in Gordon Chasney's house, Ava managed to mock up fifty-one packets and transfer $11,074.35 to his savings account. His gordyluvsgrrls e-mail account also had eighteen messages from outraged customers. The noose was tightening.

She deleted her original key-logger program and other traces that she'd been on his computer. When she heard the garage door, she got away, headed to the mailbox, then went home and had her best night of sleep in years.

❖

The following Monday, Ava opened the newspaper to see the headline she'd longed for: *Local Man Arrested for Running Kiddie Porn Racket.* She scanned the article. Multiple counts of mail fraud… illegal possession of child pornography…possibility of decades of imprisonment if convicted…more charges to come.

"Aha! Gotcha, Gordy-O. You're toast. Woo hoo!" She danced around the house, laughing with unbridled glee. Her level of elation was so great that she skipped breakfast, put on a sweat suit, and went outside to jog.

The sun shone down upon her, and the chilly breeze wasn't cool enough to penetrate. She quickly worked up a light sweat in a two-mile loop, and by the time she came back past the neighborhood park, her muscles were pleasantly fatigued. She stopped at a bench to stretch, and that's when she saw him.

Square-shouldered and beefy, the man had a hard face and predatory eyes. He strolled along the sidewalk, glancing periodically at the children frolicking on the playground equipment. He seemed particularly interested in one tiny girl who lay on her stomach over a swing, legs dangling, arms wrapped around the swing's wood slat. Her long, golden hair nearly touched the ground as she sang a little song and periodically stuck a foot down to keep the swing moving. Ava watched the man with growing alarm.

She wondered how long it would take to find out where he lived.

BOOMERANG
CARSEN TAITE

If I hadn't been so hungry, I might've asked the right questions. It wasn't the first time my appetite clouded my common sense. The grainy photo only hinted at her beauty. Full blond waves tumbled down her shoulders. Bare shoulders. The sleeveless red blouse dipped low at the neck, and the row of numbers marching across her chest only partially obscured what I imagined was pure perfection. I traced a finger over the numbers as if I could erase them with my touch, and pinch the luscious breasts beneath. I felt a rush of heat between my legs and my own nipples tightened. First time a jumper turned me on. Hunger of a different kind made my mouth water. I would have this one. Without a doubt.

"Luca, are you listening?"

I mouthed the name on the photo before replying to the man waving a hand in my face. *Diamond Collier.* I rolled the name over my tongue, tasting the salty edge of anticipation.

I tore my eyes away from Diamond and faced my potential employer. In his flannel shirt, hunting vest, and John Deere cap, Hardin Jones looked more like a cross-country trucker than one of the most successful businessmen in Dallas. I didn't care what he looked like. He had a job for me when no one else was calling.

"How much?" I asked.

"Bounty's fifty grand."

I would've been happy with a couple of thousand and Diamond as a bonus. Hot broad like her? Figured she ran up some poor soul's credit card, maybe a few too many cosmos behind the wheel, but fifty grand meant she was in deep. One more way she wasn't your typical jumper. I hadn't cared before, but now I needed to know. "What's the charge?"

"Murder. Bond set at half a mil. She missed her first court date, and I'm not in the mood to be charitable. Surety's not either. Find her in a week and the fee's yours."

His unspoken words rang loud. After a week, I'd lose my shot and Hardin would pass the case along to another agent. I wondered why I had a shot in the first place. No one had reached out to me in weeks. Luca Bennett was persona non grata, surrounded by a cloud of suspicion, and bondsmen hated being in the spotlight. I'm a big fan of the direct approach, so I asked. "Why me?"

"You doing anything else?"

No need for me to answer. Hardin, along with everyone else, knew I was hurting. And too hungry to be particular. I reached for the file in his hand, and he gave it up. "All the info's here."

I nodded, but kept the file closed. I'd seen all I needed to know I could do this job. Diamond Collier would be mine within the week.

❖

I slid into a booth and waited for Maggie to notice. Seconds passed before her loud voice rang out.

"Hey, Luca, that's a four top. I got real customers that can fill those seats. Get your ass up here to the bar where you belong."

I made a show of looking around the mostly empty bar, and blew her a kiss. "Love you, too, Maggie." I ignored her hands-on-hips, evil-eye expression and arranged the half dozen sheets from the file on the table in front of me. Maggie's scrawny frame, stage show makeup, and blazing bottle-red hair caused some folks not to take her seriously. I always took her seriously, but I also knew I could take her. At six foot and a hundred and eighty pounds, I was Amazon to her pixie. I smiled to soften her mood. "How 'bout a beer?"

"You paying tonight?"

I pointed at the spread in front of me. "Put it on my tab. I got a good hand here."

"Sure you do, Luca. Sure you do." Maggie shook her head and pulled a glass of her cheapest pilsner. I focused on the papers in front of me. Once I brought Diamond in, I could buy a round of the best brew for the house.

"She looks like trouble."

I glanced up and accepted the glass Maggie offered. "You got that right."

"So, you got some real work? That's good." Maggie fingered the photo, squinting into Diamond's eyes. I resisted a possessive urge to grab it from her. I hadn't even begun my week with Diamond, and I wasn't ready to give her up.

"She looks familiar."

"Seen her around?"

"Not here, but I've seen a picture of her." Maggie tapped Diamond's mug shot against the edge of the table in time with her thoughts. "Can't place her right now, but I'll let you know if I remember. Hungry?"

I shifted easily with her non sequitur, and nodded. I was hungry, but mostly I just wanted her to let go of my photo. She released the picture and headed to the kitchen, barking out an order along the way. She didn't ask me what I wanted, but I'd eat whatever she brought. I always did.

I set the photo on the far inside corner of the table and focused on the rest of the paperwork. I passed over the standard court notice and the warrant for failure to appear. I'd need them when I turned her in, but they wouldn't tell me anything about where to find her. The only other paper in the file was the multipage form Diamond and the surety had signed to spring her in the first place. Hardin's big bold handwriting in the middle of the typewritten form jumped off the page. The bond amount: five hundred thousand dollars. Next to Diamond's flowing signature at the bottom, someone had scrawled her last known address. I flicked a glance at the name of the surety, curious about who had a half a million in collateral to spare. I sucked in a breath. Yuri Pretov.

A plate clattered onto the table. "Now I remember where I've seen that woman," Maggie declared. I already knew what she was going to say. I didn't remember seeing Diamond's picture or hearing her name, but like everyone else in Dallas, I'd read about the infamous murder of Pretov's rival, Leo Kaminsky, and the arrest of Pretov's woman while she was still standing over his body with a freshly fired gun in her hand. Maggie reached for the photo again, and I smacked her away. She slid into the booth across from me and shoved the plate toward me. "Eat."

I tore rough bites, barely chewing. I needed the sustenance, but

I wanted to go home. Fire up the computer. Fill in the blanks about Diamond Collier. Figure out why her man cared more about the fee he'd paid Hardin than the woman who'd murdered for him.

❖

I waited impatiently for the laptop to fire up, mentally adding a new computer to the long list of things I'd buy when I collected on Diamond. Food and beer topped the list. Except for a couple of bottles of long neglected condiments, my refrigerator appropriately reflected my bank balance—empty. I hadn't worked in over a month, and my funds had run out a couple of weeks ago. Thank you, state of Texas. I could hear my old man's voice echo his annoying refrain: "Should've stayed with the force. Steady pay, benefits, good retirement." All the things he never had.

Whatever. I'd given police work a shot, but I didn't last long on the job. Everything about it was too black and white. The cars, the rules, the money. Besides, people like me don't live to retirement. My last gig was proof I was looking at a short lifespan. I'd leapt out of a second-story window when the brother of the jumper I was trying to apprehend pumped shotgun shells my way. I had been working a righteous lead that the jumper was in the house, but by the time the boys in blue showed up, all I had to show for my trouble was a sprained ankle and a pissed-off homeowner.

Now, my license was "under investigation" while bureaucrats sorted out the facts. Fact one: I broke into the house, square against the rules. Fact two: Homeowners in Texas have a right to shoot the hell out of anyone in their castle. The only fact in my favor was the jumper's brother, who'd done his level best to kill me, had a rap sheet and wasn't allowed to have a firearm. So I was merely under investigation with a red flag on my license for the next six months.

The paper pushers in Austin considered it a slap on the hand, but my status paralyzed me. Bondsmen expect the bounty hunters they hire to do whatever it takes to bring in a bail jumper. Sure, there are rules, but we're supposed to know them so well that breaking them is easy work. Word got around quick that I was under a bureaucratic microscope, and every one of my previous employers figured I couldn't or wouldn't push boundaries anymore. They blacklisted me as a result.

Why Hardin suddenly tossed me a big case was a mystery, but I wasn't in the business of solving mysteries. Find the jumper, collect the bounty. Those were my goals.

I opened the Internet browser and selected my neighbor's wireless network to sign on. After dollars became too scarce to pay for my own connection, I'd spent a valuable hour figuring out that his password was the name of his incessantly barking mutt, Fluffy. Stealing a few minutes online was my revenge for too many sleepless nights.

Diamond and Yuri had made the news several times before Diamond killed Leo, but always society pages, never the metro section. Yuri was a mob boss, but like all good bosses, he made a show of being human by contributing to charities. He cut ribbons with the best of them, and Diamond stood behind her man on every occasion, dressed to the nines. The high-resolution glamour on the screen made the attraction I felt in response to the mug shot seem like a schoolgirl crush. I was in full-on aching arousal mode now. I'd channel the surges. Use the energy to hunt her down and collect my fee. With fifty grand in my bank account, surely I'd a way to take off the edge. In the meantime, craving was a great motivator.

A few clicks later, I'd exhausted my online search. I had a list of notes, but no real clue where a bail-jumping pseudo socialite might be hiding out. Especially not one who had just offed a major player on the Dallas crime scene. Her main squeeze, Yuri, had posted her bond. He might want to cut ties now, and he could afford to pay the full amount at risk, but it wasn't chump change—even to him. What had Diamond done to piss Yuri off? After all, she'd killed his main rival. What more could a man want from his woman?

I pulled back the shade on the window by my desk. It was dark outside. I touched the glass. Cold, too. I strode to my closet and waved through my wardrobe. One of the things I'd hated about being a cop was wearing a uniform. Funny, since my choices consisted of three clothing items: jeans, T-shirts—long- and short-sleeved, and boots. I reached for my worn black leather jacket and tugged it on. Moments later, I slid behind the wheel of my 1991 Ford Bronco and drove to Yuri Pretov's house.

❖

"Mr. Pretov is not seeing visitors."

I stared down the uniformed gate monkey. "I'm not a visitor. I have business with Mr. Pretov. Tell him Hardin Jones sent me."

The exaggeration got me through the gate, which meant Pretov was curious. I was curious too, so that made us even. We could both satisfy that urge in a moment. Mansions in Dallas proper didn't have enough real estate to accommodate long, winding driveways. I was parked and out of the car in moments. A beefy beast, taller than me, held the front door open a foot while he assessed my threat potential.

"Leave your weapon in the car."

My forty-five long Colt wasn't easily concealed, but I'd worn the big gun as a message. "No."

"Then go."

Never hurts to bluff. I wasn't there to shoot anyone. Yuri and I were on the same side, but I knew I'd lose this battle. He hadn't become a captain in the Russian mafia by letting armed strangers in his house. I stood my ground for a full ten seconds to show I wasn't a pansy before I gave in.

The beast led me to a suite on the second floor. Our path was crammed with massive, ornate wood furniture, jeweled vases and curios, and giant gold gilt frames surrounding dark and gloomy oil paintings of the Motherland. I felt like I was in a mini-museum of Old World culture. I imagined Diamond, as a voluptuous nude, reclining on a chaise, her blond waves fanned out against the silk brocade. An authentic beauty in this knock-off palace.

Yuri didn't rise when I entered. I wasn't sure if that was because I wasn't worth a formal greeting, or whether he was being considerate of the woman whose head rested in his lap. He waved me to a chair and motioned Beast to a corner, all the while stroking his love kitten. Whatever Diamond had meant to him in the past, Yuri had moved on.

"Mr. Jones, he sent you?"

I read a hint of irritation, and covered. The last thing I needed was to piss Hardin off. "No, he didn't send me. He gave me a job to do, and I thought you might be able to help."

"I see." He steepled his fingers and waited. The woman stirred at the absence of his stroking hand, then nestled back against his thighs. She was beautiful, but nothing compared to Diamond. Had Diamond spent hours curled on the floor at the feet of her master? I wanted to know as much as I didn't.

"I'm a recovery agent. I—"

"I know who you are. Isn't the term you people use 'bounty hunter'?"

I ignored the question and focused on his first statement. I wanted to ask how he knew me, but I didn't want to reveal my curiosity. I'd ask Hardin. In the meantime, I countered his blunt approach with subtlety.

"I'd like to help you *recover* the assets you placed as collateral for Diamond Collier."

"Yes, please do. I am extremely concerned about all of my assets, especially the one you seek."

As he spoke I noticed a faint stirring from the opposite side of the room from where Beast stood sentry. A uniformed young man stood next to a large serving cart lined with rows of dome-covered dishes. Apparently, I'd interrupted Mr. Pretov's mealtime. I glanced back at the master of the house. With a beauty in his lap, surrounded by wealth and security, he didn't appear to be concerned about anything. I, however, was very concerned about how I was going to pay for my next meal. And rent. And phone service. Pesky but necessary stuff that led me to be brash. "I'll find her. Quickly. Anything you can tell me about her habits would help."

"Habits?" He laughed and called to the Beast. "Did our Diamond have any special habits?" He laughed again and gestured at the woman resting on his thigh. "Other than those our new friend, Charity, has to offer?" Charity stirred slightly at the sound of her name. She cast a hazy glance my way, and her full lips formed a sated smile that lingered after her eyelids eased shut again. She wore a cobalt silk robe, which was striking against her ivory skin, and I was willing to bet she wore nothing underneath. *Focus, Luca, focus.*

I looked up to catch Yuri watching me watching her. Time to move this along. He didn't seem too keen on offering any information about Diamond, and what I really wanted to know—why he wanted to turn in the woman who'd gunned down his rival instead of using his considerable resources to spirit her away—I didn't plan to ask. Not without a loaded gun in my hand and a getaway plan.

Since it was expected, I thanked Yuri for the audience and waited for the Beast to escort me back downstairs. As I reached the door, Yuri spoke. "Our friend came from humble roots, similar to sweet Charity." He paused and fixed me with a stare. "I'll be watching you. You do a good job, and I'll have more work for you, Ms. Bennett."

❖

I'd been leaning against her car for fifteen minutes before Detective Jessica Chase finally emerged from her apartment. She didn't look happy to see me. It was early morning, so I wasn't happy either.

"Beat it, Bennett."

"Is that any way to greet an old friend?"

"Key word 'old.' I hear you're still under investigation. No favors until you're clear."

"I don't need a favor," I lied. "Just some conversation. Over coffee. I'll buy."

"I'm late."

"For what? John's not expecting you for another hour." Her partner had answered the phone when I called the station and conveniently gave up Jess's morning schedule.

I'd spent the balance of the night before surfing for clues, but my Internet searches were running dry. Diamond Collier was a news story and not much more. She'd been born in North Carolina, had a Texas driver's license, and that was about it.

I'd gone to the address on her license late the night before. The only thing there was a strip club, closed on Mondays, as if horny men needed a day of rest after spending the Sabbath getting lap dances. I planned to go back later when the club opened, but in the meantime, I needed inside intel. The kind the law can get quicker than folks like me.

I hadn't seen Jess for a while, but we often went months between favors. She'd been the last one to ask, when a particularly bad murder scene had her on my doorstep at three in the morning. I was happy to indulge and we fucked until dawn, countering the inevitability of death with an endless parade of life-affirming orgasms. It would be bad taste for me to mention who owed who a favor, so I waited patiently for Jess to figure it out.

She didn't take long. "Good coffee, not that diner swill you drink."

I nodded. "I'll follow you."

Ten minutes later, we were seated in the back corner of some upscale coffee shop. I had a mug of black joe, and Jess sipped a triple tall, extra-dry cappuccino. Ordering coffee shouldn't take more than three words, and the tiny cups they used shouldn't cost more than a gallon of high test fuel. I suppressed a grumble and paid with my last ten-dollar bill.

I got right to the point since the change from my ten wouldn't cover a refill. "I need to find Diamond Collier."

Jess took a sip from her fancy drink, swallowed, and took another.

"Did you hear what I said?"

She put her cup down. "Oh, I heard you. I'm ignoring you."

"Seriously, Jess, I just need a little intel."

"Stay away from that case."

"I'm not working a case. I'm recovering a bail jumper. I just need a lead. So far, all trails to Diamond dead-end."

"That's appropriate. I imagine lots of people want her dead. Maybe she's already been found."

I shook my head. Hardin would've known, and I would've gotten a hint from Yuri. I sensed Yuri was keeping something from me, but I didn't think Diamond's death was his secret. Something he said had stuck with me. Made me think he'd met Diamond and Charity in the same place.

"Where does Yuri meet his women?"

"Not my case. I don't know."

"But you could find out."

"I could do a lot of things."

"Yep. You *are* multitalented."

She stiffened, and her face reddened slightly. Our last encounter was great for me, but it had been nothing more than stress relief for her. Bad taste for me to bring it up. I groveled. "I need this, Jess. Can you drop me a crumb?"

Her eyes pierced through me. She knew I didn't display weakness for anyone else. I barely did for her, and then only when naked. Hard times make it easier to be humble. After a few beats, she rewarded my vulnerability. "I hear the Slice of Heaven is his current stable. Eddie Haster owns the place. At least a few of his girls are guaranteed to have outstanding warrants at any given time. I'll text you some names. Use that for leverage, and he may talk to you." She drained the rest of her expensive brew and stood. "Be careful, Bennett. Money's no good if you're not alive to spend it."

It was the nicest thing she'd ever said to me.

❖

When the club opened, I paid my cover and strode through the door. Haster had probably been there all day, but I figured my threats would carry more weight if the girls were on-site. I left the hefty Colt in the car, since it was illegal to carry in the bar, but I had a smaller Sig Sauer tucked under my jacket. I didn't mind breaking the law. I just didn't want to get caught.

I asked one of the cocktail waitresses where I could find Vixen aka Mary Sellers. She pointed to a door in the back marked "Office." I ignored the center stage show and strode to the back. The door wasn't locked. Eddie obviously didn't care who saw him getting a lap dance. He groaned as I entered, but I couldn't tell if his reaction was in response to my presence or the gyrations of the naked redhead. Even in her pretend throes of arousal, she looked like her mug shot. I flashed a sheaf of papers under the stripper's nose and introduced myself as a recovery agent.

"Are you Mary Sellers?"

She looked frazzled, but Eddie held her in place as he rubbed himself against her crotch. She was done, but he wasn't quite there yet. Warrantus interruptus. This would be fun.

"Mary Sellers, I have a warrant for your arrest."

She sprang out of the chair. "That's not me."

I shrugged. "Sorry. *Vixen*, I have a warrant for your arrest." I flashed a shiny pair of handcuffs. She backed away, stumbling over the chair where Eddie sat, moaning the sudden loss of sensation.

He managed to pull himself together long enough to ask, "Who the hell are you?"

"I'm a recovery agent. I'm here to arrest Ms. Sellers a.k.a. Ms.

Vixen." I made a show of consulting the papers in my hand. "Oh, and a few of your other employees." Vixen's eyes darted around, and I positioned myself to block the door. I opened my jacket just enough to let them both see the Sig.

"Tell you what, Haster, I have a business proposition for you. If you would see fit to answer a few questions for me about another matter, I think I could see fit to overlook this business." I waved the papers to indicate what "this business" meant.

Eddie nodded. I stepped aside, and he hissed "get out" to Vixen. She grabbed a g-string from the desk and ran out the door.

I sat on the desk and propped my boots on Eddie's chair. If I'd had more time and money, I would've spent a few nights in the place, asking casual questions of the girls over cocktails, until I'd gathered enough information to get a lead on Diamond. Pumping Eddie wouldn't be as much fun, but it would yield faster results.

I cut right to the chase. "My name's Bennett. Yuri Pretov hired me to find his ex-girlfriend, Diamond Collier. He said she used to work here."

Eddie nodded, confirming my belief that a good lie is often the shortest path to the truth. I kept at it. "He said for you to cooperate with me. She failed to appear for court. He's worried about her. Wants me to find her before the law, so she'll have an opportunity to explain her situation on her own terms. Any assistance you can provide would be considered a debt owed by Mr. Pretov." This is the part where, if I were telling the truth, I would have flashed some good faith money. Thankfully, my gun was enough collateral to assure Eddie's cooperation.

"She came by here yesterday. Talked to a few of the girls. I don't know anything else about where she might be. Talk to Roxy." He looked me up and down. "Have her take you to a private room if you want. She'll be happy to cooperate." His eager tone turned my stomach, and I almost punched him for tricking his girls so he could suck up to an asshole like Pretov, but he wasn't worth getting my hands dirty.

According to the announcer, Roxy was the next act. Eddie escorted me to one of the VIP booths, stage right. I settled in to wait, waving off the friendly waitress who offered me a shot of tequila from her cleavage. She left in a huff, probably concerned Eddie would scold her for failing to please a favored customer.

Roxy strutted onto the stage, an agile tiger hunting her prey. She worked the pole like an athlete and teased the audience with well-timed clothing tosses. It was quite a show, but it didn't do anything for me. I tuned out halfway through, and imagined Diamond in her place, her voluptuous curves hugging the pole like a hungry lover. Did Pretov sit in this very seat and watch her dance? What had he seen that caused him to take one of these usually disposable girls and doll her up for public appearances? Whatever it was, I could sense it myself, just from the grainy photo I'd gotten from Hardin. Diamond had something Roxy and the other girls were missing—an edge in her gaze that said this place wasn't the end of the road.

I didn't notice the music end. If not for Eddie, I would've missed my chance to talk to Roxy. The crowd clamored for her, waving tens and fives to signal their love, but Eddie waved her over to us. She slid into my side of the booth, still panting from her show.

Eddie leaned across the table and pointed at me. "Talk to her about Diamond. Whatever she wants to know." He leaned back and crossed his arms. Roxy opened her mouth to speak, but I placed a finger on her lips and glared at Eddie. He raised his shoulders. "What?"

"Why don't you go ask the waitress to get Roxy a drink while I talk to her?" He remained seated, oblivious to subtlety. I tried again. "Eddie, beat it. I need to talk to Roxy alone." I touched my jacket to remind him I could back up my demand.

"Whatever." He crawled from the booth and stomped away.

"You pissed him off. We'll all pay for that later." Roxy's voice was silky smooth.

"I'm sorry." I was. "Why do you put up with him?"

"Don't you really mean why do I make my living taking off my clothes?"

"Maybe."

"Why not? I'm good at it. What do you do for a living?"

"I look for people."

She yawned. "Sounds boring. You make much money doing that?"

"Sometimes."

"I do better than sometimes."

I stroked her with my eyes. "I bet you do."

She leaned closer and slipped a hand between my legs. "You like what you see?"

I inched away. "I'm not here for that."

"People come here for all sorts of things."

"I'm here for information." I paused to allow her to absorb the fact I wasn't a customer, but her hand stayed between my legs. I let it. "I'm looking for Diamond Collier. Word is you talked to her recently."

Roxy pulled her hand back. "What do you want with her?"

"It's private."

She started to get up. "Then so is anything I may happen to know."

I placed a hand on her arm, gentle, but insistent. "Please."

"Eddie said you work for the Russian."

I resisted the urge to point out there was more than one Russian in the world. "I work for myself."

She shook her head. "She's in deep trouble."

Yeah, most people facing murder charges are. I sensed Roxy's words carried a deeper meaning, so I pretended to know what she meant. I took a shot in the dark. "I know. That's why I need to find her. Before *they* do."

I don't know whether it was my sincere expression or the urgent tone in my voice, but she sighed deeply and spilled her guts. "Two of the girls, Angel and Porsche, were there the night it happened. Diamond came by to talk to them yesterday. They've disappeared."

"It" had to be the night Leo was murdered. I nodded, urging her to continue.

"I don't know anything, personally, but Diamond, she thinks they saw it all go down."

"So, do you think she had something to do with their sudden unavailability?"

She looked at me like I was thick. "She wanted to find them so they could testify for her. Prove she didn't do it."

Sure she did. I played along. "If she didn't shoot Leo, who did?"

She crawled into my lap, grinding her sex against the buttons on my fly, her tits swaying in time to the music. I was startled, confused, and slightly aroused by her nonverbal answer to my query. While I contemplated how to rephrase the question, she slid forward and pressed her breasts tight against my chest. We rocked together, cheek to cheek, and for a minute I forgot my question. She didn't. Her voice was low, and her breath was warm. "The Russian's brother. That's who."

❖

I climbed into the Bronco and waited for the engine to warm up. I was already warm. Roxy's lap dance had tickled me into wanting more. I contemplated calling Chance for a drive-by, but she'd already repaid her favor, and I wasn't in the mood to sink deeper into debt. Instead I focused my energy on the information Roxy had provided. What was Diamond up to? Were her questions designed to deflect attention from herself? If she hadn't killed Leo Kaminsky, her poking around was only going to get her killed. She'd be better off back in custody if this was how she handled freedom. I'd be better off, too. Bondsman don't pay bounties for dead bodies.

Leads were scarce. I pulled a crumpled cocktail napkin from my pocket. Roxy had scrawled the name of a bar Diamond frequented and the address of the place Angel and Porsche stayed at before they disappeared. She'd gifted it to me during one of her particularly forceful grinding maneuvers. I recognized the name of the bar. Straps was a leather bar on Maple. A seedy one. I tried hard, but couldn't conjure an image of Diamond sipping a drink amidst a crowd of guys dressed in buttless chaps who were cruising each other for rough sex.

I glanced at my watch. Nine o'clock, still early by leather bar standards. I didn't hold out much hope the former address of a couple of strippers would yield any clues, but I was a day behind Diamond and I needed a break. If, by some wild stroke of luck, Angel and Porsche had resurfaced, they might have some info to offer, especially if Diamond had been by to see them the night before. I steered the Bronco out of the parking lot and drove toward downtown.

The apartment complex was a step above the projects. A short, crumbling step. The walkways reeked of old booze and fresh urine. Month-old trash littered the path to the apartment. The only window I could see was covered with a sheet. I heard a voice from inside, and I leaned against the door. The voice was female, but I couldn't make out the words. I reached down to test the lock, but before I could turn the knob, someone jerked my arm and twisted it behind my back. I whirled and slammed a fist forward, but my assailant spun with me and I only connected with the air by his face. I reached into my jacket, but before I could draw my gun, the bastard kicked me square in the knee and I dropped hard.

Big mistake. I was pissed off now. I gave up on the gun since he was too close for me to get off a good shot. In two swift movements, I grabbed a knife from my boot and slashed at the leg that had taken me down. Blood spurted, and I heard a loud grunt, but the asshole kept coming. I stabbed again, aiming higher this time. He fell to the ground with a heavy thud. I stood and surveyed the damage. He looked vaguely familiar. Surprise was the only reason he'd been able to take me down, since I was taller and outweighed his skinny frame by at least thirty pounds. I found a big gun inside his jacket. Little guy like him needed a big gun.

He was covered in blood, but didn't cry out. He'd talk, though. I'd make sure of that. I reached down and grabbed the collar of his once white shirt.

"Who are you?"

A solid grunt was his only response. I nudged the handle of my knife against one of his still bleeding wounds. Last chance.

"Who. Are. You?"

He didn't cry out, but I saw him glance behind me and his expression flashed from defiance to worry. I heard a door slam shut, and I turned in the direction of his gaze. I nearly dropped my knife in surprise as I watched the backside of a blonde in heels and a trench coat run out of the apartment complex. She looked over her shoulder, but didn't slow her pace. I had a split second to place her. *Diamond.*

I gave the wounded guy one last look before I took off running. When I rounded the corner, Diamond was nowhere in sight, but a car peeled out of the lot squealing its brakes. I froze the license plate number in my memory. I couldn't tell if she was in the car, but it was the only clue I had. I wasted a few minutes searching the bushes and knocking on nearby doors just in case the car was a red herring. Nothing. Frustrated, I returned to the apartment doorway and looked down at a pool of blood. Wounded guy was gone, and the trail of blood led in the opposite direction of my hundred-yard Diamond dash. *Shit.*

I stood and stared as if I could conjure him back. It didn't work, but my focused energy did resurface a memory, and I realized where I'd seen him before. He'd been standing behind a serving cart in Yuri Pretov's drawing room. *Double shit.*

❖

Maggie shoved a full plate and a frosted beer, not the cheap brand, across the bar. "You look like hell."

I didn't have the energy to protest the truth. Knives were always messier than guns. Not as efficient either. A well-placed shot would have rendered wounded guy immobile, and then I could have used the knife to facilitate our question-and-answer session. Now all I had were blood-spattered clothes and unanswered questions.

I wasn't surprised Diamond was being tracked. Her questions about Kaminsky's death likely telegraphed to someone that she needed a visit, but I would've expected the visitor to be someone from Kaminsky's camp. Then again, if she had a mind to pin the murder on Dimitri's brother, Andrei, then Yuri had a vested interest in shutting her up. The big question was why Hardin hired me if Yuri was going to send his own men to hunt Diamond down. Hell, they were probably using me to find her. They didn't need me to bring her in because they had other plans once she turned up. Time to give Hardin a call and let him know his client was trying to kill off his jumper.

"Maggie, I need to use your office phone." I wanted privacy and I might as well conserve my cell phone battery while I was at it. She pointed a finger at my plate, wagging it until I picked up the juicy burger and took two big bites. Satisfied, she waved me to the back.

My first call was to Jess. I started by talking dirty before resorting to begging. She finally agreed to run the plate number. I was racking up quite a tab. Next, I dialed Hardin's cell. He answered on the first ring and I jumped right in.

"I think your client's trying to sabotage me. Do you want Diamond brought in or not?" I was talking smack. For all I knew, Wounded Guy was Pretov's idea of insurance, a backup plan in case I sucked, which currently I did. Yet the guy wasn't Pretov's typical muscle. His only means of persuasion was the big gun, and judging by the way I was able to take him down, he wasn't quick to use it.

"Pretov has a vested interest. He brings her in, everyone wins." Hardin didn't have to voice the obvious. If Pretov turned Diamond in, Hardin wouldn't owe a bounty.

I rolled his statement around in my head for a minute. Something Pretov had said earlier had been itching at me, and it finally surfaced. "Why did you hire me?"

"You need the work, don't you?"

"Yep, and no one else will touch me. So why you?"

"Pretov asked for you. Said you were the best. Find her, Luca." And he was gone.

I was the best, even if I was a little off my game. At least I'd finally spotted her, and I had another lead to follow. I glanced at the beer-stained Coors clock over the bar. Eleven thirty. Time to head to Straps.

❖

I wore my jacket zipped to cover the blood spatters from Petrov's lackey. At least I was dressed appropriately, not that anyone in this joint was interested in me. I think my imposing size was the only reason the bouncer had even let me in the door. They might as well post a sign— "No Women Allowed." Only one of the reasons I wondered why this was Diamond's haunt. I didn't rule out the possibility Roxy had sent me on a wild goose chase after I'd only tipped her three dollars for the best lap dance I'd ever had. I'd given her everything I had, but it wasn't enough. Story of my life.

I stood in the back, near the pool tables. The joint was packed, and I was the only one without a drink or someone else's body part in my hand. Ten minutes in and I was ready to call it a night. I cut through the crowd, tired and frustrated. My right knee, where Wounded Guy had kicked me, hurt like a sonofabitch. Time to go home, ice up, and make a new plan. I was five feet from the door when I felt her heat, up against my neck. Her voice, every bit as sultry as I imagined it would be.

"I need you to stop following me."

I turned slowly. She was practically on top of me. Diamond Collier and fifty thousand dollars were mine. I leaned in close and whispered in her ear while I fished a pair of handcuffs from my belt. "But I want you." As I spoke the last word, I reached around her waist, out of her sight, to secure my catch. Before I could clip one of the cuffs around her wrist, the pair was yanked out of my hand.

Wounded Guy stepped out from behind Diamond and held up the shiny cuffs with a grin. I shot out a hand to reclaim my stolen property—hadn't we already established who would win in a fight? A cold, hard nudge against my ribs told me I was outnumbered. The gun pointer was my size. I was confident I could take them both, but I couldn't guarantee there wouldn't be bloodshed in the process, possibly mine. Getting shot in a leather bar wasn't how I saw this scene ending, so I raised my hands slightly in surrender. If I could buy some time, I'd come up with a plan that didn't involve leaving pieces of my own flesh on the floor.

Diamond motioned for me to follow her. I didn't hesitate. Neither did the two guys in her entourage. We wove through the crowd to the row of private rooms in the rear of the club. If the front of the house at Straps was seedy, then the back was a cesspool. All I could think about was how many times I'd have to scrub the bottom of my boots before all traces of jizz would be gone. I probably should've given some thought to why one of Petrov's men was hanging tight with his ex-girlfriend.

Gun Pointer shut the door and stood guard while Wounded Guy patted me down. He laid my Sig, wallet, and phone on the only piece of furniture in the room, a leather-covered spanking bench.

The guys had the firepower, but Diamond was in charge. She circled me as she assessed her prey. She was dressed for the part in tight jeans and a leather bustier, those silky bare shoulders from the jail photo back to tease me once again. It was fifty outside. My sensible side wondered if she would catch cold in her current attire, while I burned to ash in response to the heat that came off her in waves.

She repeated her earlier words. "I need you to stop following me."

If she wanted me to stop, she better put on some more clothes, ugly herself up a bit. Her beauty brought out my bravado. "Is that so?"

"It is."

I stared deep in her eyes. She didn't act like a typical jumper—fidgety, paranoid, disheveled. No, she was brazen and bold. "You're a fugitive."

She laughed at my statement of the obvious. "I'm a lot of things." She strode closer. "*If* I come in, it will be on my own terms. Understood?"

I couldn't help it, I licked my lips. She was close enough to wrestle to the ground, bind, gag, and kiss. I was tempted to do all three before I remembered the gun trained in my direction. The gun wasn't the only thing that interrupted my thoughts. My phone rang loudly in the small room. Diamond glanced at the screen. "Who's J. Chance?"

Perfect timing, Jess. She was probably calling back about the plate number I'd asked her to run. No point now, I knew where Diamond was—for all the good it would do me. "Nobody."

"And that's what I am to you. Nobody." She punctuated the words with finger jabs to my chest. The surge I felt in response to each touch told me she was dead wrong. Diamond Collier was somebody. Somebody special indeed.

Within seconds she was gone. Wounded Guy trailed after her. I watched him limp away with a sense of satisfaction. The big guy with the gun stayed behind and kept me in place for several minutes. Then he picked up my phone and my gun and left the room without a word.

Perfect. I had a slew of other guns in the Bronco, but only one phone. I counted to ten and then made myself walk casually through the bar. I knew it was crazy, but maybe Diamond was still out there. There was no sign of her or her friends in the steamy crowd. I started to feel claustrophobic, so I stepped outside. As I made my way to the Bronco, I heard a low rumble and I recognized the sound of the muscle car from earlier in the evening. I couldn't get all the numbers as it tore past me, but I had no doubt Diamond was inside. I tore open the door to the Bronco and scrambled to fit the key in the ignition. Her demand that I do nothing was motivation enough to do the opposite.

I swung into the driver's seat and jumped when I felt something hard and metal jab me in the ass. My Sig and my cell. I didn't pause to wonder why Gun Pointer returned them, but I did murmur a quick "thanks." As I raced through the streets, hoping to catch a glimpse of Diamond's car, I punched the button to check my voice mail.

Jess's voice was low and urgent. "Something's off, Bennett. The plate you asked me to run? It's in the system, but I can't get any info on it. Nothing. You understand? Call off the chase and call me."

So, Jess's information source was fallible. I was surprised, but strangely satisfied to have to rely on my own instincts. I'd call her later. Right now I was in hot pursuit. The easy apprehension of a stripper turned socialite was fast becoming a more complicated pursuit, but I was up for the challenge.

❖

I wondered if the car behind me wanted me to know I had a tail. I hadn't been paying attention when I left Straps, but within three blocks I realized I was being followed. Probably Petrov's men hot on Diamond's trail, but once again they were a step behind. Losing them took an extra thirty minutes. Thirty minutes I wasn't in the mood to spare. When I finally arrived back at Angel and Porsche's apartment, I was satisfied they were headed in the opposite direction. For now, anyway.

The blood trail had faded. I listened at the door, but this time I kept a close watch on my own backside. I could easily smash in the thin door, but decided on the safer route and picked the lock. Hard to prove I had broken in when there was nothing broken.

I wielded the Colt for this trip. I wanted anyone I ran into to know I was capable of blasting a huge hole through them, no real aim required.

The place was a complete dive. Cigarette butts, razor blades, and once-shiny surfaces with faint shadows of white powder were the only real evidence that anyone had ever lived here. No clothes, no food, nothing personal. I tried to imagine Diamond in this dump, smoking long skinny menthols, snorting coke up her nose. I remembered her breath, whiskey sweet, and her gaze, hard and focused. Diamond didn't belong here. She didn't belong with Pretov either, resting her head in his lap, waiting for business to be done so she could please her master. Maybe she had killed Kaminsky as a way to prove her real worth.

Or maybe she was being set up. Apparently, that's what she thought. I just needed to think like her and follow the trail. I knew exactly what I'd do first. I'd confront the son of a bitch who set me up to take the fall. I'd already been to Yuri's house. On my own, I didn't have the muscle or the firepower to get him to talk. Time to pay a visit to his baby brother.

❖

I made a pit stop at my place to fire up the Toshiba and get an address for the Russian's brother. I debated calling it a night—I was only two days into my week, after all, but a strongly worded note from my landlord taped to the door convinced me to push through the night. I'd rather confront an angry Russian than an unpaid landlord any day of the week. I rushed to get the address and didn't bother changing. Ten minutes later I was back in the Bronco, headed uptown.

It didn't take me long to realize I was being tailed again. The car was bigger, the driver more practiced, but once we reached Andrei's neighborhood, I had no doubt. Cars didn't circle the streets in this high-priced neighborhood without drawing too much attention from the highly paid, highly vigilant local police force. I purposely dragged out the journey, but I couldn't shake him. I spotted a home with a circular front drive and decided it was time for a game of chicken. I whipped into the drive and sped back in the opposite direction. Within seconds I closed the distance between us and my bumper kissed his. I couldn't see his expression through the tinted window, but I knew if I were in his position my next move would've been to stride over and put a gun against my window. I waited for the confrontation with the long Colt in my lap.

The sedan's engine roared to life. I raised the gun. The car lurched slightly forward, then took off in reverse, screaming backward down the street. I'd won, but my victory was short-lived. Porch lights flickered on, and I registered I only had a few minutes before cops showed up. I whipped back through the drive and took off the in the opposite direction.

The distraction messed with my sense of geography, but I roughly calculated Andrei's house was two blocks away. I parked the Bronco at the end of a close-by but still dark street and doubled back on foot. I did my best to keep out of sight. Not an easy feat, especially when my cell phone rang at the loudest setting. I ducked into a tall row of bushes and glanced at the screen. Jess again. I flipped it open and answered on the move. "What?"

"Why are you whispering?"

"Why are you stalking me?"

"Excuse me for trying to save you from yourself. I think you've bit off more than you can handle with this job."

"Yeah, maybe." I was barely listening. My long strides had me almost to Andrei's house. I could tell from the outside Andrei Pretov didn't live as good as his brother, but it was a damn sight better than my digs. Doubt he had a landlord hovering with an eviction notice. Time to kill this call and get to business, whatever that was. This time I wasn't checking my firepower at the door.

"Luca, are you there?"

I perked up. Jess didn't call me Luca unless we were naked, and then only when she was about to come. "Seriously, Chance, what do you want?"

"Where are you?"

Her tone was urgent. Maybe she was ready to for me to repay my earlier favor. After I paid Andrei a visit, a romp with Jess would be a great way to burn up some of the adrenaline from the evening. "Andrei Petrov's, but I can swing by after. Maybe we can—"

"Shit. Don't go in. Do you hear me?"

I did hear her, but what I saw outside Andrei's house kept me silent. I recognized the herd of black-vested men gathering across the street for what they were. I didn't need a SWAT team overhearing my conversation. I clicked the phone shut and shoved it in my pocket, not wanting to risk even a text for fear they'd spot the light from my cell. I'd follow Jess's advice for once and get the hell out.

I figured more of them might be gathering in back, so I ducked into the neighbor's bushes. I'd wait until they made it into the house, then double back to the Bronco and call it a night.

At least that was the plan.

I watched the front door, anxious for the raid to get started. At the twenty-minute mark, my sore knee and the damp chill in the air almost had me convinced to call it a night. I tossed a mental coin, but a loud creak and a steady whir interrupted my game of chance. Andrei's garage door was opening.

I couldn't see the driveway from where I was, but something drew me to it. I bent in half and dashed back over to Andrei's side of the property. Smashed up against the bricks, I slid along the wall until I could make out the car pulling into the garage. I only caught the backside, but I knew the plate number by heart now. Was she inside? Only one way to find out. I didn't give it another thought before I stepped into the shadows of the oversized garage.

Clean garages make crappy hiding places. I stood taller than anything in the place, and even the forty-watt in the fixture above would be enough to reveal my presence as soon as the passengers stepped out from behind the tinted windows. Timing was the only thing on my side. The moment I heard the car door click, I hunkered down. Diamond and her entourage exited the car. She was still dressed in the black leather bustier. I stopped breathing, only partly to keep from making noise.

Diamond and friends whispered quietly and then entered the house. I didn't even consider my options. With a raid poised outside, this would be my only chance. If the cops got her first, there'd be no bounty for me. I tested the knob on the door from the garage to the house and breathed a sigh of relief when it turned in my grasp. I pushed it open and eased into the pitch-black space. My ears picked up the sound of whispered voices before my eyes could adjust to the dark.

"...front window...on my signal...we need him alive..."

Footfalls faded and the voices grew distant. I leaned forward, straining to hear more, and my still-sore knee smacked metal. Hard. I smothered a yelp, but I couldn't haul back the resounding crash. I fumbled for the doorknob, figuring my best bet was to get back to the garage, but stopped short when I felt the press of cold metal in my ribs for the second time that night.

I took my time considering my options. If my knee held up, I had a decent chance of getting off the first shot with a quick turnaround. Of course, the blast from the Colt would echo down the block and the cops would bust in for sure. Problematic, sure, but whoever was holding a gun on me faced the same issue. If it was Diamond's friend, he might not know there was a SWAT welcome committee out front.

I decided to give diplomacy a try before blowing a hole in this guy. "The place is surrounded by cops."

"Is that so?" Her voice was quiet, but cocky. I heard a slight smile.

"It is." If I didn't have a gun in my side, I would've laughed at the echo of our earlier conversation.

"My friend here's going to take your gun. Don't fight him or I'll shoot you. Do you understand?"

This was ridiculous. I couldn't count on one hand the number of times I'd been bested in a fight, but this luscious blonde had managed to get my gun from me twice in one night. I gave it up, stalling for time. I could take the three of them, hand to hand, if I got the chance and a fist fight wouldn't be as noisy. It suddenly occurred to me the cops weren't the only ones we should keep quiet for—if Andrei were in the house, surely he'd be showing up soon.

"Turn around."

I did. My eyes had finally adjusted and I saw Diamond and Wounded Guy. The way Diamond held the Glock in her hand told me her résumé hadn't been fully revealed. I glanced around, but didn't see anyone else. Their friend must have gone to round up Andrei. If I could get Diamond alone, I'd narrow my odds. "I was serious about the cops outside."

Worked like a charm. She nodded to wounded guy. "Change of plans. I'm going in. I need three minutes' lead time, then give the signal." He didn't move, obviously reluctant to follow her cryptic instructions. Her tone was firmer the second time. "Go. Now." He shook his head, then headed back into the house.

Signal? Going in? My curiosity threatened to distract. "What now?" I asked.

"Where's your car?"

"Couple of blocks away."

"Let's go."

Perfect. I'd have five minutes, ten tops, to work out a plan. As soon as we put some distance between us and the house, I'd make a move. Once I had her in cuffs, it'd be a ten-minute drive to the jail.

I was a purposely docile captive, and we made good time. We were steps away from the Bronco when I heard a shout. "Stop. Police."

I knew the voice, but wasn't used to obeying the speaker. I silently cursed myself for telling Jess where I had been. No doubt she'd headed right over when I disconnected the line. I wondered why, but cared more about the fact she was messing with my business. Diamond's gun nudged against me, but I risked speaking. "It's okay, Chance. I got this one."

"Sure, Bennett, I can tell you have the situation completely under control."

She had a point. I still held out hope, though. I'd used the steps from the house to plot out my strategy, which involved concealed firearms in the Bronco and lots of luck. Jess's sudden appearance signaled luck was in short supply. I started to respond, but Diamond cut in. "Officer, I strongly suggest you let us go on our way. Maybe you can be of some assistance at Mr. Petrov's house."

Jess wasn't easily dissuaded. "I think I'll stay here. I know who you are, and I *strongly suggest* you put your gun down."

"If you know who I am, then you know I won't do that. I won't hurt her. She's going to help me out, and then she'll be free to go."

I didn't like being the object of a discussion I didn't understand. "What the hell are you two talking about?"

They continued their debate as if I wasn't there, but neither was willing to give in. Finally, Jess directed a comment my way. "Bennett, remember what I told you about that plate you asked me to run?"

"Yeah."

"I followed up on it. Got a call from a fed who told me to butt my nose out of places it doesn't belong."

Jessica and I had a common trait. We hate to be told not to do something. She wouldn't have let that go. I tried not to dwell on the fact I was surrounded by women with guns, and asked, "So, what else did you find out?"

Jess shot me an apologetic look. "Sorry, Bennett. I don't think you're going to get much for this one. Is she, Agent Collier?"

Agent Collier? A rush of images flooded my brain. Some real, some imagined. Diamond in couture, posing beside Yuri Petrov in the society pages. Diamond in a g-string, pole-dancing for a dollar-waving crowd. Diamond with a hard edge in her eye, standing close enough to kiss. Not a single one of these pictures jived with the title "Agent Collier."

"If she's a federal agent, why are you holding a gun on her?" It was the only thing I could think to say, but Jess looked at me like I was too stupid for words. She shifted her gaze to Diamond's gun, still shoved up against my ribs. *Duh.* My next question was directed at Diamond and it was much more intelligent. "If you're a federal agent, why are you holding a gun on *me?*"

She let her hand drop, and Jess lowered her gun. Diamond spoke first, and her question was directed to me. "You want that bounty or not?"

I started to point out she was answering a question with a question, a trait that usually annoyed the hell out of me. It seemed petty to be irritated in the face of a fifty-thousand-dollar haul. It also seemed stupid to question her motives. I gave the only answer that made sense. "Sure."

We both looked at Jess. She shrugged and holstered her gun. She waited until we were in the Bronco before she turned and walked away.

I leaned forward to place the key in the ignition, but Diamond's hand on my arm stopped me. "We need this to look like the real thing." She slid her hand inside my jacket and roved around. Her soft hand brushed my breast before she found the handcuffs she was looking for. She fastened her seat belt, then clicked the cuffs on her wrists.

I drove slowly. Tomorrow, I would collect my fee from Hardin. Tonight, I would pay myself a little bonus.

THE ECONOMICS OF DESIRE: A CAUTIONARY TALE
JEANE HARRIS

I.

"I call it the Lesbian Starter Kit."

"Cute. What's in it?"

"Everything the budding young lesbian needs to acquaint herself with our culture."

"Which is?"

"Okay, we got your *Changer and the Changed* CD, *Rubyfruit Jungle*, an 'Amazon' button, a pair of women's symbol earrings, and a 'See You Next Year' bumper sticker from Michigan. Pretty cool, huh?"

"You can sure tell you're a seventies dyke, Flynn."

"Fuck you, Dee. I'm a sixties dyke."

"Get real, you're an old dyke—and if you're trying to impress this sweet young wanna-be lesbian—what's her name?"

"Stefanie."

"Stefanie, then you better wise up—nobody listens to Cris Williamson anymore, no one reads *Rubyfruit Jungle* either."

"Well, if they don't, they should. The young ones need to remember our herstory."

"God, listen to you. 'Herstory'? Nobody says herstory anymore. It's so eighties."

"Well, at least I've moved up a few decades. Anyway, it doesn't matter. She doesn't know anything about lesbian culture."

"Ah, but she will—eventually she'll meet other lesbians, go to bars, parties, festivals, and then she'll realize how clueless you really are."

"Fine. What should I buy her?"

"That's a good question—one I bet you'll be asking yourself a lot over the next four or five years."

"What are you talking about—four or five years?"

"That's usually how long your relationships last."

"Not this time. Stephanie's perfect for me. We never fight. In fact, I get along with her better than I've ever gotten along with anyone. Except you."

"Where did you get the idea that we get along? You know, Flynn, I swear you're getting a Southern accent. We've got to get you out of Memphis before you actually start to like fried okra."

"Gotta go where FedEx sends me, Dee, and Memphis is the headquarters. Anyway, what's wrong with fried okra?"

"If you have to be told what's wrong with it, you're beyond hope. Look, if you feel compelled to buy this woman something, get her a Melissa Etheridge album—the first one. It's got a lot of lesbian *angst*. Buy her a lesbian novel written in the last decade. Hell, get her a tattoo or an eyebrow ring. Better yet, give her a dildo."

"Oh, that's perfect. She's dumping her boyfriend to be with me, and I give her something shaped like a penis."

"Give her one that looks like a dolphin if she's that sensitive about phalluses—is it phalluses or phalli?"

"Would you shut up about penises, please?"

"That's what hip young lesbians are into these days. Not dried-up lesbians like Cris Williamson or Rita Mae Brown."

"God, Dee, the Lesbian Starter Kit could turn out to be expensive. All that stuff—it could run me fifty or sixty bucks."

"Honey, in a few months fifty or sixty bucks will sound like a bargain to you."

"What do you mean?"

"She's young, right? Still in school? Doesn't have a job yet?"

"She doesn't know what she wants to do. Maybe go to art school. Maybe start her own business."

"And didn't you just get that big promotion?"

"You know I did."

"So you'll help her out financially?"

"Sure."

"Sucker."

"C'mon, Dee. It's not about money."

"Not now. But it will be. You've already spent a lot of money on her, haven't you?"

"I don't know what you're talking about."

"I heard you two went to Hawaii."

"So?"

"Who paid for the plane tickets and hotel and food?"

"What's your point?"

"You did, didn't you?"

"What if I did? What's wrong with that?"

"Not a thing."

"I can't believe you're doggin' me like this, Dee. Don't you want me to be happy and have somebody in my life?"

"In your life, Flynn. Not in your bank account."

"Look, never mind, okay? Just forget I mentioned her to you."

"No, I'm sorry. You're right. It's none of my business. I just don't want to see you get hurt."

"Why is everyone so convinced that she's going to hurt me?"

"Aha, so I'm not the only one. Who else?"

"Never mind, Dee. Let's not talk about it, okay?"

"Okay by me. Forget it."

"Fine, it's forgotten. Let's just move on to some other topic."

"So—you gonna market these Starter Kit things?"

"Why?"

"You could package them, sell them on the Internet. I bet you could make some money."

"You really think so?"

"Not really. But with this new girlfriend, you're going to need a lot of money."

II.

"Nora's doing *what?*"

"Selling her RV."

"What the hell for?"

"To buy a ring. Actually two rings—one for her, one for what's-her-name."

"Nora's selling her RV to buy a couple of *rings*?"

"Yeah."

"I can't believe it—she saved up for ten years to buy that thing. I've never known her to want anything like she wanted that RV."

"I told her that. She said, 'Yeah, and you and Jennie bitched about how stupid it was for me to buy it. So now I want something more than the RV. I want'—oh, whatever her name is—Camille? I can't remember."

"So? She can have her. Just don't sell the RV to buy a goddamned *ring*."

"Nora said, 'What do I need that hunk of junk for anyway? I never use it.'"

"What?"

"Yeah. I said, 'You've traveled all over North America in that hunk of junk. You're a travel writer.'"

"To which she responded?"

"She said, 'Not anymore. I quit the travel desk.'"

"What the *fuck*, Lila? She's wanted that job all her life. Why?"

"Guess?"

"So she wouldn't have to travel so much and be away from what's-her-name."

"Bingo."

"Her name is Bingo?"

"No, her name is *not* Bingo. It's—shit—my memory is so gone."

"It's probably Buffy or something—you know how these society people name their children stupid names, but I'd never heard Bingo before."

"Would you forget about Bingo? Her name isn't Bingo."

"Okay, okay. Well, what's Nora going to write for? The society page?"

"How'd you know?"

"Now you're kidding. She knows as much about society as I know about astrophysics."

"So what? What's-her-name's folks are really, really rich. They own half of downtown Houston, including the paper where Nora works."

"Aha."

"Indeed. So, they love their baby girl, and she wants her new girlfriend to stay home. Bingo! Nora gets the society page."

"I thought you said her name *wasn't* Bingo. Make up your mind, would you?"

"Oh, for God's sake, would you just forget about it…it's just an expression…never mind…clearly Nora's having a mid-life crisis. Or a mental breakdown. I told her that. She said, 'Bullshit.'"

"That's all? 'Bullshit'?"

"Yeah, I know. So I said, "'Nora, remember who you're talking to here. It's me, Lila. Your best friend since junior high school.'"

"Wait a minute. How old is this woman?"

"You know, I asked her that very question. She said, 'What do you mean "this woman"? You know what her name is. Call her by her name.'"

"God, she is *such* a child. What's the woman's name again?"

"I told you already. I can't remember. Something like—Candella?"

"I think it's kind of sweet in a way."

"Guess how old she is?"

"I cannot imagine."

"Twenty-nine."

"She's five years younger than Nora's youngest child!"

"I pointed that out to her. She said, very sarcastically: 'Lila, you know what your problem is? You're ageist.'"

"What's that mean? Is that one of those politically correct words?"

"Right. Like sexist. Only ageist. She said that you and I need to go out more. She said, "You two never go out—you're insulated, cut off from the community, new ideas—you need to meet younger lesbians.'"

"Like her new girlfriend?"

"I suppose so."

"Hmmmm…how much is she asking for the RV?"

"Nine thousand—that's what the dealer said she could probably get. She's putting an ad in the paper this weekend."

"She paid over thirty thousand dollars for that thing. It's worth a lot more than nine thousand."

"Yeah."

"So—you wanna buy it?"

"It would serve her right if we did. Then when Carmen dumps her—"

"You'd sell it back to her."

"Probably."

"Did you see the rings?"

"Yeah."

"Are they gorgeous?"

"Custom made. Diamonds, emeralds, and sapphires."

"Did you ask her why she's doing this crazy thing?"

"She says she wants to show this woman how much she loves her—how wonderful her life's been since she met her."

"Yeah, well, it sounds like a disaster in the making to me. Giving up the job she's always wanted, selling her beloved RV—"

"I pointed that out. She said it's called 'change,' which we would know if we ever left the house. She said all we do is sit on our patio and barbecue."

"We do so change. We went to San Francisco last year instead of Provincetown. That's change."

"I don't know. It is kind of sweet that she's selling her RV to buy the woman a ring."

"I assume they're having some kind of lame union ceremony?"

"The invitations are in the mail."

"Do we have to go?"

"Don't be ridiculous. Of course we're going."

"Oh, God, I hate those things. All those flakey, New-Age vows they write themselves…"

"Then forget them halfway through?"

"And the guitar player who's had two lessons on the Internet singing some sappy love song."

"Yeah, yeah. Still…it is sweet, in a way. You never sold anything of yours to buy me a diamond ring."

"Ha! I sold my soul to the devil for you, sweetheart."

"You did not."

"Did too. It was positively Faustian. I promised if only you would break up with Barbara, I'd give him my soul."

"Oh, God."

"I tried God first. He didn't respond. So I tried the devil. It worked."

"That is sick, Jennie. I can't believe you're telling me this. After all these years?"

"C'mon, honey…I'm kidding."

"No, you're not. I know when you're kidding."

III.

"Oh, no. Oh, I'm so sorry, Flynn."

"Yeah, well, that's life, huh?"

"When did you find out?"

"I went to St. Louis to visit her for a couple weeks—you know, over spring break. There were some suspicious phone calls, people giving me funny looks—"

"What do you mean—funny looks?"

"I don't how to describe it, I just started feeling weird vibes."

"And?"

"And there was a party and I noticed this one woman—Melissa—looking at Stef—I can't explain how I knew. You know? It was just a feeling."

"And you were right?"

"Yeah."

"Don't make me torture you to get the details, Flynn."

"I found some letters, okay?"

"Found?"

"Okay, I ransacked her room and found them in the bottom of an old trunk. I'm not proud of it, but I was desperate."

"The letters were from Melissa?"

"There were some from her—yeah."

"Some? You're implying there were others? She slept with somebody *besides* Melissa?"

"Oh, yeah. A bunch."

"How many are in a bunch?"

"A dozen?"

"Oh, Flynn. God, how awful. You must feel terrible. Anybody I know?"

"Do you know my friend Babs who lives in Key West? Stef and I went down there last Christmas to visit."

"Yeah, I remember you talking about her. Oh, for Christ's sake, she didn't sleep with Babs?"

"No, she slept with Babs's lover, Dana."

"That tramp! When?"

"While we were there. Dana and Stef got real chummy, and Babs and I thought it was so sweet that they were being friends. They went off dancing to a club a few times. Apparently after the first time, they skipped the dancing and just went to a hotel downtown. They wrote each other, and Dana visited her when she was in St. Louis on business."

"Good grief. Does Babs know?"

"I don't know. I haven't talked to her."

"I know you must feel terrible, sweetie."

"Well, I'd feel better if I had back all the money I spent on the little shit over the last five years."

"So—what happened?"

"Nothing, I never told Stef about the letters. I didn't say anything to her really."

"You haven't told her you know?"

"I told her I knew about Melissa a couple months ago. But I'd already started seeing a woman that I met—you'll love this. I met her at the Garden Club."

"I thought only little old ladies belonged to Garden Clubs."

"Hey, I *am* a little old lady. So is Iris."

"Hold on. Her name is Iris, and she belongs to the Garden Club?"

"Yeah, everybody makes jokes about it. Anyway, she's great. A little older than me—fiftyish. We have a lot in common and—here's the good part—she's rich!"

"How rich?"

"Well, she's an antique dealer. She has her own shop down on Overton Square—very posh. Anyway, we started seeing each other in July."

"Have you told Stefanie about Iris?"

"Yeah, I told her last week."

"What was her reaction?"

"That was kind of weird, actually. She got really mad. Threw things—broke all those dishes I bought for her birthday last year."

"Wow."

"Anyway, I wanted to call and fill you in. I'm going away with Iris for a few weeks. We're going to Mexico first and then to Barbados."

"Who's paying for all this?"

"Well, she has a house in Baja. We're going to stay there for a week or so. But she offered to pay—just as well. I'm broke!"

IV.

"Just give me the highlights of the conversation, okay? I don't think I have the stomach for the sordid details."

"Nora's selling the house."

"Why? What for?"

"She said it's too big for just her. Candy took the dogs. Nora said she doesn't have the energy to take care of the yard, and the hot tub and the pool. I know those things cost a fortune to heat and clean. I believe it was me who tried to tell her that before Candy talked her into buying that stuff. Now Nora says every time she looks out the window, it reminds her of Candy. Frankly, I don't think she can afford to live there anymore."

"Well, where's she going?"

"She's going to live in her parents' garage apartment."

"Oh, come on. That apartment is the size of one of her closets."

"Not to mention having to listen to your parents say, 'I told you so.' But she can live there for free, and she says she doesn't need much room."

"Her mother will drive her crazy."

"Her mother drives *me* crazy. I told her that if she needed money that you and I would help."

"I bet that went over big."

"She really bristled. 'No need for that, Lila. I'm not destitute. I'm healthy and I've got a good job.'"

"Sounds like her. I bet she wishes she had her RV back now. It's bigger than her parents' garage apartment."

"Right...then get this—she asked me—didn't I think Candy had loved her—in her own way."

"You're kidding."

"No, I'm not. She talked about how Candy took care of her."

"Took care of Nora?"

"Yeah, get this. She asked me if I'd ever noticed how Candy always filled up her iced tea glass and was always asking if she needed anything."

"That's so pathetic."

"Even now, she's more worried that everybody will hate Candy and ostracize her."

"Ostracize her? I'd like to drown her in a sack."

"Well, if you do, don't do it in their pool. That would definitely lower the resale value, and Nora needs every cent she can get."

SOME KIND OF KILLING
MIRANDA KENT

I was thirteen when it happened. Thirteen is one of those ages where everything changes. Yesterday you were a kid, today you are a teenager, which is almost an adult. Which means some people get confused about the lines between kid and adult. Thirteen is where everything gets blurry and indistinct, like looking out a car window when it rains and someone's driving really fast. And that's when stuff goes wrong—really, really wrong.

That's what happened to me. Stuff went wrong. It wasn't just because I turned thirteen. Stuff had been going wrong for me for a long time. If I thought about it, it had been going wrong as far back as I could remember.

It's hard growing up with crazy people. Sure, everyone uses the word *crazy* or *insane* all the time. Just like they say "I'm *starving*," when they're really just hungry. But not *really* starving. Not like people in Africa starving. So when people say, "She's *crazy*," or "That's *insane*," it's just hyperbole—you know, exaggeration. Except I'm not exaggerating. I grew up with crazy people, and it was hard. *Really* hard. Like *really* crazy and *really* starving. And it's why everything started to go so wrong so early.

No one ever expects to see someone get killed, let alone kill somebody. That's what I think, anyway. And no one expects to go to prison or have someone they know go to prison. That stuff happens on TV and in the movies, in books and in graphic novels, but not to real people. Except when you watch the news. It happens to people there. That's why it's news—because when it happens, it's not normal, it's crazy, it's something that doesn't happen to just anyone.

We were those people. The people on the news. The story where they show the house and almost whisper the news story to the camera because it's *so awful* and *so tragic* and *none of the neighbors had any idea* and *someone said they kept to themselves.*

We were *that* story. *I* was that story.

In the beginning there were seven of us. Two parents, two grandparents, three kids, some cats. Then some of us disappeared, some of us died.

When you see those stories on the news, the stories about murder or other grisly things, everything usually looks pretty normal from the outside, where the cameras are. Every once in a while the house itself looks crazy—shutters falling off the hinges and cars jacked up with no tires and all kinds of junk and stuff piled up in the yard and scattered all around on the front porch with hungry, mean-looking dogs on chains jumping and barking and looking like they would tear you to shreds if they got loose. But most of the time what strikes you is how ordinary and just *normal* everything seems. Then the reporter explains how dozens of cats were found dead in the house after neighbors complained about a foul odor. Or that a man had been living with his mummified parents for years. Or that a kidnapped girl was found living chained in a basement. Or that a woman had smothered first one, then two, then five babies as she gave birth to them and buried them in her own backyard.

I would watch those stories on the news without any emotion. What was I supposed to feel? *Horror? Shame? Sadness? Disbelief?* Maybe. But mostly I felt relief. That night's news story was not *our* story. No one had looked beyond the empty porch, the yard in which no dogs were chained, where there was no barking to alert anyone to something being wrong on the other side of the front door with the big brass knocker on it. No one had come up the walkway lined with tidy little bushes that kept themselves. No foul odor emanated from the house. Everything looked normal.

Even if it wasn't.

It's hard to explain *crazy* to people who haven't experienced it. It's like it's hard to explain pain. You can tell someone "That's going to *hurt*," but if they've never gotten hurt, they won't know what you mean.

Everything and everyone in my house was crazy. Everything that happened on the other side of the front door was nuts, insane, out of control, swirling in the kind of chaos and vortex that happens when you slip through a portal into another world. It was Tolkien and Rowling and Larsson all rolled into one, but without any of the good stuff—no comforting little owls or other creatures, no friendly professors, no old people full of wisdom to make everything better.

At first, that was as bad as it ever was: *crazy*. But then, when I turned thirteen, everything changed. And then *crazy* turned to something I didn't know how to name.

Did I say we had a dog? I know I mentioned the cats. Because the cats never left. Well, some did, because some died because of the crazy. But we had a dog. Not for long, though. It got hit by a car one afternoon in front of the house. It just ran out of the front yard and across the street and we lived on a hill and a car came up suddenly and it got hit.

It was winter and there was snow everywhere and I sat on the sidewalk in the snow with the dog—I don't feel like saying his name— in my school uniform and it took a long time before anyone took him to the animal hospital and he never came back.

Memory is a vivid thing. Even if your memories are wrong, they are vivid. Like a bright color or a slap in the face. My memory of the dog dying was vivid. The day was gray and very cold. The snow was white in places and dirty in others because it had been around for a while and no one came to help for a long time and the horizon began to blur between the white-gray sky and the white-gray snow.

Vivid.

The other memories are like that, too. Vivid. Like a bright red pool of blood or a bright red slap mark on the side of a child's face.

I'd like to tell this story from the beginning—that's always the best way to unravel a mystery, to put the pieces in their logical and chronological order. But I'm not sure when the beginning was, exactly. And I'm not certain that where I am now is the end. Maybe telling the bits and pieces of the story will make it clear—give it a beginning, middle, and especially, an end.

❖

Blood is a strange thing. If you eat meat, you see it run onto your dinner plate all the time. But you never think: *blood*. And (unless you're a vegetarian like I am) you never think: *killing*. You just eat what's on the plate and think maybe, *delicious* or *tasty* or *overcooked* or *underdone* or *needs salt* or something like that. You don't think about what the meat was before it was on your plate. You don't think about the blood running out of the animal onto the floor of the abattoir and down into the French drains they have all over the meat-processing plants. You don't think about the fact that yesterday the cow or the chicken or the pig was running around in a yard or in a pasture and now it's on your plate. You just don't think about the killing. Or why there's blood on the plate. And that you're eating it. But there's some kind of killing every time you eat an animal. Something has to die.

We see blood a lot, every day, and we don't really think about it. Cut your finger on a knife in the kitchen, or the scissors slip, or the paper runs through your hands too fast, or you fall off your bike, or you trip on the stairs and there's blood. Somewhere, every day, there's blood.

There was blood in our house. It took a long time before anyone saw it. It took a long time before anyone said *so tragic* or *they kept to themselves* or *how awful*.

❖

When I turned thirteen, my grandfather died. It wasn't the first death in the family but it was, for me, the only one that mattered because he was the only person I was sure I loved. And then he was dead.

He died the way a lot of children see grown-ups die: He just disappeared. One day he was there and the next there was a phone call from a hospital and the word *aneurysm* and then he was gone and I never saw him again. There was no good-bye scene like there is in the movies, no letter like there is in books. Just nothing—the page turns and the next one is blank.

He died on the day before Halloween, so I kept thinking that there would be a ghost, a real ghost, that would hover near us, that I could see. But there wasn't. There was just blank space. There was nothing to protect us. Nothing to protect *me*.

I didn't cry. I'm not sure why. Crying was forbidden in the crazy house—crying was for babies, crying was for those who were weak, and crying was something to be ashamed of. *Don't do it. Don't cry. I'll give you something to cry about.*

When you watch a TV show with murders—especially more than

one—some psychologist always comes in and talks about triggers. "Well, *that* must have been the trigger." Because the trigger is the thing that goes off—the cocking of the gun or the pulling back of the arrow and then…

My grandfather's death was a trigger. He died. Then the dog died. Then my mother went very, very crazy. My brother stopped talking and didn't go back to school after Christmas. My father disappeared. The baby… And then someone else went to the woods and tried to hang herself, except a man came along with a dog that wasn't dead and cut her down.

That was me.

Mysteries almost never have suicides. There's the body that is set up to look like a suicide, but it always turns out to be murder. The killer forgets something specific, like kicking the chair over in the right direction, or using the left hand for the prints on the gun, or remembering how neat and tidy the victim was, or typing out the note and not signing it, because nobody does that.

It was easy to tell the man with the dog that someone else had done it—strung me up with the rope and left me. *I think he went that way!* And then I escaped, because the woods were my second home and I knew where to hide from the man and even the dog, because when you live in a crazy house, animal instinct is something you know very well. So I crawled behind the waterfall into the crevice of rock where I used to sit in the summer and read because it was cool and the sound of the water was soothing and the big spiders as big as your hand that moved delicately over the wet rock didn't bother me. I crawled there and waited. Waited until I realized that perhaps the way out was simply not to go back.

I didn't explain why I was there in the woods with the rope, using my Girl Scout training to tie a slipknot that would hold my thirteen-year-old self. I didn't explain why I thought this was the best answer to the question of what lay behind the door with the big brass knocker.

I went to the woods to hang myself because that afternoon when I came home from school there was blood. Lots of blood. There were bits and pieces of flesh and a smell like metal and rotting meat and when I saw everything that was there, I decided I didn't ever want to see anything else again. I got the rope from the shed out back and I went down to the woods, made the knot, tossed the rope over the limb of the tree, and tried to figure out exactly how to swing myself down from the big rock to the left of the trunk so that my neck would snap quickly and I would die.

Without any blood.

But then the man came and he was screaming and the dog was barking and running around in a circle. It was almost dusk and very cold and I wasn't exactly sure if I was conscious or not. I remember the feel of the rope on my neck, bristly and rough, and how it cut into the flesh like hundreds of tiny teeth. I remember the rock was dull and gray and there was moss on one side and that my left foot slipped when I was trying to position everything the way I thought it should be before I jumped off.

And then there was screaming and barking and a man who kept saying a rush of words that came like the sound of the waterfall at the mouth of the creek nearby.

"Who did this to you? What kind of monster... Can you hear me? Wake up, come back to us. Just a slip of a girl, a slip of a girl..."

That was me, the slip of a girl. I had slipped the rope over my head, then slipped on the rock, and now I would slip through the truth into a lie, because lies came easily and readily to me because when you grow up with crazy, you learn that the truth isn't something anyone really wants to hear.

And so I lay on the leaves and pine needles, smelling the loamy smell of the woodsy earth and the smell of the dog barking near my head and the smell of the man's hands as he slapped my face lightly, his hands were surprisingly warm and my face was cold and his hands stung my cheeks. And then I sat up slowly and I was dizzy and so cold and I looked at the man and the dog and for a second I thought I might cry and then I raised my hand and pointed away from the waterfall and toward the old mill house road that led out of the woods and said, "I think he went that way!"

The man looked toward the mill house and then at me and the dog had stopped barking and was looking at me like it knew I was lying, but couldn't say anything and I thought for a moment about our dog, our dead dog, our dog who no one came to help until nothing could be done, and I wanted to hug the dog and leave with the man. But instead I just pointed again, mutely, my eyes glistening with tears, and the man said, "You stay here, I'll be right back and we'll get you seen to." And then he took off at quite a clip and the dog looked around once and then I slipped behind the waterfall and I never saw the man or the dog again.

It was almost dark when I realized it was too cold to stay in the woods and I would have to go back home. Home to the blood and the carnage and the things I wish I had never seen.

As I crawled back out and over the rocks and up the embankment to where the rope still lay like a thick chalk outline of a young girl's body on the floor of the forest, I wondered what I would do when I got home. Would I call someone—who would I call? Would I clean everything up? I wasn't sure how I could clean up what I had seen. I wasn't sure if anyone could clean up what lay behind the door with the big brass knocker.

The door was still unlocked when I got back to the house. I went around turning on lights, careful where I stepped. In the back hall near the kitchen I saw one of the cats lapping at blood on the floor and I tried to remember that this was just like blood on the plate at dinner for the cat and that it shouldn't make me want to vomit.

I went upstairs and went into my grandmother's bathroom and ran the water in the sink and started to wash my face. There was a ring of red and purple around my neck and one of my eyes was black and blue, the white a bright red, like someone had stuck a pin in it. There were leaves in my hair and on the shoulder of my sweater and there was dirt on my cheek.

I took all my clothes off and got in the shower and stood there under the water like I had stood behind the waterfall—for a long time. Then I got out and wrapped myself in several towels and went to my room and shut the door. My clothes were still in a pile on the floor of the bathroom.

I put on a T-shirt, then a sweatshirt, and a pair of jeans and got under the quilt. I was shaking with cold and the house was really quiet. I don't ever remember it being so quiet. It was quiet enough to think, but I couldn't think. I didn't know what to think. I was going to try to sleep, then I was going to get up and feed the cats and try and figure out what to do. Because I knew I had to do something. I just wasn't at all sure what that something was. And I was so tired. I had to sleep. I had to sleep and pray I wouldn't dream.

When you go to sleep with all the lights on but it's dark, it's disorienting when you wake up. *Is it night or day? Where am I? What time is it? What day is it?* I lay in my bed under the quilt trying to remember.

And then I remembered.

❖

I got home from school at 3:15 in the afternoon. It was cold. Very cold. When you live in a crazy house, things are always one of two ways: very quiet or very loud. In our house, all the doors to all the rooms were always shut. It was like a rooming house where everyone has their own space and then there are common areas like the kitchen and dining room and living room for people to congregate in. Except there was no congregating in the crazy house. My mother never left her room. My father never came home. My grandmother lived in her own rooms—a sitting room, a bathroom, a bedroom—like a little apartment in our house after my grandfather died. My brother and the baby slept in the same room because they were both boys. And I had my own room up in the attic, which had started out creepy, but then got comfortable, like the place behind the waterfall in the woods. The windows in my room had ivy growing over half of them and at night there would sometimes be glowing eyes peering in—there were raccoons who climbed down from the roof and they always looked in my room first. They were the only things that ever checked on me there. Well, not the only things.

It was usually quiet in our house unless my mother was screaming. But she screamed a lot. And the screaming could go on for a very long time. The screaming could go on until you would do almost anything to make it stop. Your hands over your ears or a pillow over your head was never enough. Sometimes I would find a way to slip out the back door and ride my bike to church and just sit in there, because it was quiet and peaceful and Jesus didn't ask anything of me. Other times I would walk down to the woods and just sit there on one of the rocks by the creek and imagine that when I went home it would all be different and better and no longer crazy.

On this afternoon, there was no screaming. There was just quiet. And cold. So cold my teeth started to chatter. And there was blood. So much blood.

It's hard to know why people do the things that they do. You're in a situation and you just think, *I'll do this.* But it isn't always the right choice. I decided to go to the woods with the rope. It wasn't the right choice. And then I came back home—because I didn't know where else to go—and that wasn't the right choice, either.

When you smell gas, they tell you to leave the house and call 911. But sometimes there's still an explosion. Flip a light switch and the whole block can go up in flames, everything blown to smithereens. I saw that on the news one night. Someone made the wrong decision and bad things happened. That's just how it is sometimes. There's no way of knowing that things will go so wrong.

❖

Nothing prepares you for blood. Not really. Sure, we got "the talk" at school and the little package of things to prepare us for our first period. Yet the first time there's blood on your underwear, you get scared and you can't help thinking you must be dying. And then it just seems normal after that. You know you won't die. You know the bleeding eventually stops. But there's still something off about the whole thing that you can't quite explain. It's unsettling. And it doesn't prepare you for more blood, just for *that* blood.

I wasn't prepared for *this* blood. For the blood on the stairs and on the walls and in the sink and on a chair and on the beds and in the crib. I wasn't prepared for how blood looks when it's matted into hair or running down a cheek like a tear or dripping slowly down fingers onto a rug. I wasn't prepared for how blood spreads like tendrils of hair across a quilt or soaks into a pillow. I wasn't prepared for blood spattered onto the fur of a cat or sprayed across a table top or swirling at the bottom of a coffee cup.

It was just so *much* blood. Which is why I had to try and get the images out of my head. *Forever.*

The decision I made was to just keep going. The man and the dog had saved me. I wasn't part of the blood and the meat-like bits strewn through the house that had once been but no longer looked anything like the people I had seen that morning before I left for school.

Thirteen is that blurry, indistinct time. You think maybe you're grown-up enough to live like an adult. But then you decide to do stuff that really proves that you aren't. I decided to just go back to my house. And then I decided to act like everything was okay. That's the kind of thing a kid thinks can work. Because thirteen really is still a kid. No matter what that kid has done or seen or had happen to her. Thirteen isn't as blurry as anyone ever thinks.

❖

When I woke up and I didn't know if it was day or night, I went through the house and decided that I could just close the doors. One by one. Shut out the blood and the smells and the other things that I can't even explain. Close the doors. Because one of the things about the house that had always been true was that the doors were always shut. And so if the doors were shut now, then it would all seem the same as it had before the blood, before there had been some kind of killing in all those rooms, with all those people.

I got the cats out of the rooms. I didn't look at any of it anymore—I just closed the doors. I went to the thermostat and turned the heat down because I had seen enough *CSI* episodes and read enough mysteries to know that heat makes bodies decompose faster. So I kept it as cold as it could be without the pipes freezing or me and the cats freezing.

I pretended none of it was there and that I was just in the quiet house, not the screaming house, and that my only chores now were to feed the cats and go to school and do that over and over again.

The cats pretended along with me. At first they scratched at the doors. Then they stopped.

I'm not sure exactly how it all unraveled. It may have had to do with money—in the movies and books money's usually the thing that's at the center of everything. That wasn't the case in my house—at least that wasn't why there was some kind of killing. But it was probably why everything fell apart afterward—because at thirteen you really don't know how much money it takes to live and eat. And you don't really know what to do when you don't have any money. You just know you have to get some.

Did I ask someone for money? Maybe I did. Or maybe I just went into the drawer where Sister Mary Margaret kept the petty cash from the recess candy sales and took that. And maybe someone saw me take it and said something. And maybe when the phone just rang and rang at my house, someone decided to go there. And maybe someone decided to open all the doors. And maybe a big buzzing of flies came out, even though it was still winter. And maybe you could see maggots crawling on places where there should have still been flesh. And maybe someone saw the cats run in and lap at the blood that had congealed to jelly on the floors. And maybe the quiet turned to screaming all over again.

I can't be sure. Because some memories are vivid and some are vague, but neither really seems to have a close connection to the truth. That's the really unsettling part. Like when they explained that you would bleed for a week but not die and you knew you had to believe it, but how could it be true? Or like when I was in the snow with my dog and everything turned that brutal grayish white and I could tell that my dog was dying and that there was nothing I could do to save him, even though I was praying really hard and I remember praying really hard and thinking that it had to work, because it was just an accident and accidents shouldn't have terrible consequences like when things are done on purpose. Or like the last time my mother slapped me so hard that my face stayed red the rest of the day and her hand was imprinted on my cheek, just like a stigmata on one of the saints I read about at school.

I remember all of these things really really vividly—so vividly that I can feel the cold wet numbness in my knees from kneeling in the snow next to my dog or the hot painful mark on my cheek. Yet I can't be sure how true the memories are, just because they are vivid. Because sometimes we tell ourselves things and make up new memories because what's wrong is so terrible that something less wrong feels better, somehow—a bad memory is better than a horrifying, terrible, make-you-wake-up-screaming memory. Like kneeling in the snow with your dying dog because it was hit by a car, not kneeling on the linoleum in the laundry room with your dying dog because someone slit its throat. Or…or all those other things that were more than a slap, more than a red mark on the face of a child.

❖

There were so many memories. I tried to explain this later, however much later it was—I can't be sure. Everything got very clouded by the flashes of the blood and the chunks of flesh and the meaty feel and smell and look of the bodies.

Someone asked me about the doors and I tried to explain that they were always shut, it was natural to shut them. And also that it made me want to vomit to see the cats licking up the blood. I remember a look of horror or terror or something I couldn't quite place on the face of the person I told this to. Or maybe that was someone on the news. I can't be sure. It's all a little blurry and indistinct.

People can draw the wrong conclusions so easily. Like when I took the money from Sister Mary Margaret's desk. It didn't feel like stealing because I needed it. I needed it for food and I didn't know how to ask for it. So when that girl, Georgiana, who I never liked anyway and who was always kind of a coward and prone to telling tales called me a thief, why wouldn't I slap her? People slapped me all the time. Slapping was part of life. Slapping is what happened when people said things someone didn't like or didn't agree with or sometimes just because you were passing by with a certain look on your face. *Wipe that look off your face, little girl, or I'll wipe it off for you.*

Probably if I hadn't slapped Georgiana, with her smug, mean smile, she wouldn't have started yelling and she wouldn't have gone to Sister and there wouldn't have been the calls to the house and everything would have gone on as it had been, with me and the cats and the closed doors. But that slap was like the thrown light switch—everything just blew up after that. And people drew the wrong conclusions.

Ever notice how on those news stories there's always someone who says, *They kept to themselves* or *We didn't really know them that well* or *She was always a little strange* or *We knew something like this would happen. It was only a matter of time. Only a matter of time…*

❖

Later, the thing the police got stuck on was that pile of clothes on the floor of the bathroom by the bathtub after I came home from trying to hang myself in the woods and they drew the wrong conclusions. They thought because I was only thirteen, I couldn't figure things out, that I just went on instinct, because children are just the smallest step

up from feral animals and go on instinct, rather than logic. They forgot
that thirteen is that blurry line between kid and adult. They forgot that
when you live in a crazy house, you grow up fast. Faster than all the
other kids your age. They forgot that you know things from living in a
crazy house that other people—adults—don't know. All they could see
was the blood and the clothes and the bathtub.

I'm not sure how that led them to the conclusion that *I* was the
killer, but it's where they stopped. Because I was the only one left
alive—just me and a few cats, although two of the cats were killed, too,
and all the others would have to be put down, according to the police,
because they had tasted human blood and now they might turn feral
and kill.

Like me.

❖

Police stations look very different on TV and in the movies than
they do in real life. I sat on a wooden chair next to a detective in a
room with flat fluorescent lights and a low dropped ceiling with patches
where leaks of something ugly had stained the pocked squares. There
was a loud buzzing in the room—the drone of computers and Xerox
machines and those fluorescent lights. Everything was gray or beige or
a washed-out green and everything was ugly.

I don't know how old the detective was. Older than my father. Not
as old as my grandfather. Older than the parish priest, but then he was
around the same age as my parents. But the detective leaned in toward
me, which made me want to lean back away from him, but I knew I
was supposed to stay still, so I didn't move. The detective told me he
had two daughters of his own and I sat and listened as he told me about
them. Two little girls just like me, he was saying. I was pretty sure that
the detective didn't live in a crazy house and that all the doors to all
the rooms were open and that his daughters and his wife all sat in the
living room together and watched TV or sat at the dining room table
and ate dinner together and that no one sat and waited while the food
got cold for the phone to ring but it never rang and that the detective,
the father, came home for dinner, even though he was a policeman and
his job was to open the doors on the rooms with the flies and maggots
and blood in them.

So I was pretty sure that his daughters were nothing like me. Because they weren't there, in the police station, with the detective, were they? They were home with a mother who wasn't crazy and where there was probably no screaming. And probably no creepy quiet, either. And definitely no blood.

I wasn't sure what I was supposed to feel when the detective was telling me his story and I was just sitting there, still and quiet and not moving and thinking how the nuns always said I was fidgety, but if they could see me now, they would be impressed and I would probably get a better grade than B- for self-control and obedience, which I don't think should be graded like history and religion and math anyway because they're what you call subjective. And the nuns didn't know how to be objective. When you're thirteen you're old enough to tell who is objective and who isn't, and almost no one is. Which is why there really isn't anyone to help like a friendly owl or a wise professor or a kindly wizard except in books. And those books are written just for kids like me, so we can think that maybe someone like that will turn up and everything will be different.

The nuns weren't those people. Neither was the detective.

I was certain the detective was trying to get me to say something— maybe anything—that would make him nod his head and type phrases in on his computer and make him think *now I get it, now I understand*, except no matter what I said, he wouldn't get it, he wouldn't understand. So why should I say anything? What was there to say, really? Things should have been said long before this, but just as I hadn't known who to call when I walked back from the woods rubbing my neck from where the rope had almost-but-not-quite killed me, I didn't know who to call when things were just *crazy*, before they switched over to that level of awfulness like when you have a really super-awful dream and it sticks with you when you first wake up and you think you are still in it.

I was still in it. I was in it before and I was in it now. This was the bad part of the books—the part where you aren't sure that someone is going to save the boy or the girl in the story. Except usually someone does. But the only person who might have saved me was dead. And even if the other people were alive, they wouldn't have saved me. They were why things were the way they were. They were why it was all so wrong. They were why thirteen wasn't a magic number or a special number but the number that people are afraid of, the number that has a special name—*triskaidekaphobia*—and why some buildings don't have a thirteenth floor, just a twelfth and a fourteenth, because no one wants to be on the thirteenth floor. No one wants to be near that number, thirteen. Because for some people it's something to be afraid of, something that makes people shudder and turn away and hide behind the easier, safer numbers, that don't have some ancient taint to them.

The detective seemed stuck on that number, too, just like the other police officers had been stuck on the pile of clothes. Because it seems that the law is as confused about thirteen as everyone else. Thirteen is blurry and indistinct—you could be a kid or you could be an adult. The detective was trying to explain that to me. Explain to me that without much effort on anyone's part, I could be an adult in the eyes of the law, that I could go to prison. Which didn't really mean much to me, since I didn't have anywhere else to go except back to the blood and the closed doors which had all been opened. There were no cats now—I had seen them taken away in carriers by some official looking people in coveralls. They looked scared. I hoped they would be all right. I hoped if they were killed that it would be quick and painless and that there would not be blood.

As I listened to the detective explaining things to me, I wanted to explain things back, but didn't. I wanted to tell him that the thing of it all was, I thought about killing all of them all the time. I thought about taking the knives in the kitchen and stabbing them in their sleep. Stabbing and stabbing and stabbing. I thought about turning on the gas and then leaving and hoping someone would flip that switch. I thought about setting fire to all the curtains in every room and then taking the cats and running. I thought about making dinner and putting something in the food, except I didn't know what to use. I thought about some kind of killing all the time. I thought about the rhyme we used to jump rope to: *Lizzie Borden took an axe and gave her mother forty whacks and when she saw what she had done she gave her father forty-one.* Except I had read a book that had said it was really only twenty-nine whacks and that there were a lot of mitigating circumstances, except I wasn't entirely sure I understood what that meant. But I had definitely thought about killing them like Lizzie Borden must have on that hot morning with the house smelling like the rotting meat in the kitchen with lots of flies and other terrible smells from the time before plumbing and fans and air fresheners. So yes, I had definitely wanted to take up my own axe. Because I was tired of the crazy house and my grandfather was dead and my dog was dead and the bad things just kept getting worse and worse and there was no one else I could count on, no one else I could trust, no one else who might say, "Don't do that to her, you know it's not right. Leave her alone."

But I had come home to the blood, it was already there. And I had left and gone to the woods with the rope. And they had found the rope, right where I said it was, but not the man and the dog, and besides, they decided the rope was just remorse, but not real remorse, that the deep mark around my neck was just an attempt, not a serious effort, because I was still alive and they were all dead. *Cut to bits*, said the detective. *You understand they were cut to bits? I want to be sure you understand what happened here.* He said this to me over and over, like I somehow hadn't been there, hadn't seen what was behind the doors before I closed them and hoped they would never be opened again.

A grisly, incomprehensible scene of carnage and mayhem, said the reporter on the news in that hushed voice they get when they can't quite believe what they are reporting. *Details are still unfolding.*

They weren't unfolding for me. I knew the details that the detective and the other adults did not. I knew why there was all the blood. I knew about the trigger. I knew things that no one else knew except the other people who lived in the crazy house and not even all of them knew but they were all dead now so it didn't matter what they knew. *But I still knew.*

We never used the word *secret* in my house. But we just knew that you didn't say certain things, tell certain things. There were things you could say and things you couldn't: *I tripped and fell on the stairs* not *My mother pushed me down the stairs*. Or *I hurt myself riding my bike* or *climbing a tree* or *getting over that fence* not *He comes into the room late at night when he's really drunk and my mother said I made it up, that I'm trying to steal him, that I'm just a little thief, just a pathological liar. Pathological. Liar. Thief. Pathological.*

No one used any of those words on the news. I sat watching story after story that was my story but not my story and still no one talked to me, no one asked me, and I was pretty sure no one would and even more sure that if they had, I wouldn't have said anything, anyway. Because secrets are secrets and it doesn't pay to tell. I learned that long before I was thirteen. Long before *crazy* turned to *mayhem*.

When I had first woken up from that dazed and unpleasant and nightmare-filled sleep, I had decided to call the police. I had. Really. But I was still disoriented from the sleeping and the trying to hang myself and all the other things. I had lain in my bed with one of the cats and I had been stroking her fur and she was purring and everything felt normal for a time and I held on to the cat as tight as I could without scaring her and I tried to smell nothing but her furry animal smell. But the smell—the other smell—was beginning to seep up into my room and it made me want to retch and I was sure that the smell would begin to permeate everything and that it would start to seep outside and someone else would notice and call the police and it seemed better if it was me, not them. Because I knew about those news stories where the neighbors say *And we had to call the police. The smell, you know. It was so awful. We had to call.*

I knew I should be the one to call. I knew it should be me.

When I punched in 9-1-1 on the keypad, I tried to remember the tone of each number. Somehow it seemed important—it was the first real sound I had heard since I had come back home. There was the shower and the purring and the sound of the tones of the numbers before they connected to the operator who said, "9-1-1, what is your emergency?" in a voice that was both surly and dismissive. She said *what* like *What could you possibly tell me that I haven't already heard a million times?*

So then I said, "Sorry—it's not really an emergency" and hung up. Because I knew then that everyone would have that same tone—surly, dismissive, not helpful at all. That there was not going to be any rescue—not for me. Not like in all the books I had read where someone finally comes and rescues the girl or the boy and takes them away and everything gets better, or you think it will get better, because the book ends before things get better but it's implied—you know it will happen. You know it will all be okay. You know that life will start to feel *normal*.

But there is never any normal in a crazy house and I knew as soon as I heard the operator's voice that there was probably not ever going to be any normal for me. That there just was no one to call. No one to help. That it was just me and the blood and the cats and I was going to have to figure it out on my own. Just like I always had done in the past.

I thought about what I would have said: That my family was dead, that there was so much blood. I imagined that the operator might be quiet for a time, that there might be an actual moment of silence, and that then she would ask me to repeat it, and that then I would say it again—that my family had been murdered and that someone should come. *Now.*

On TV, the operators always ask in that same toneless voice if anyone is still alive. If they had asked me that, I would have said no.

They always ask the young girl in the movie who calls 911 from the house where she's babysitting and a maniac is in the basement or the attic to stay on the phone until the police got there, but the girl always says she wants to go to the door and wait for the police and that she's going to hang up. And then she hangs up and someone comes up behind her and slits her throat or stabs her or puts something over her head and everybody screams.

❖

I could have called the police. I *should* have called the police. But I didn't. I didn't know what to say. I still didn't know what to say once I was at the police station *eleven days later*, as the news reports kept saying in an incredulous kind of way. *She continued to stay in the house with her murdered family for eleven days. Details are still unfolding.*

It didn't seem that long to me, eleven days, but I had kind of lost track of time. It was just me and the cats and that unpleasant smell, and eleven days is either a really short time or a really long time, depending on what you are waiting for or hoping for or dreading.

They weren't sure what to do with me, once the police took me in. Was I a killer or a victim, a lunatic or a survivor, satanic or saintly?

❖

The detective finally stopped talking to me. He decided he wasn't getting anywhere, that there probably wasn't anywhere he could get with me. Because I basically just sat there and didn't say much of anything and didn't cry or sob or scream or kick or act crazy or any of the things he seemed to expect from the thirteen-year-old girl who had been taken from a house with three murdered adults, two murdered children, and a couple of dead cats. *Cut to bits.*

But they didn't know what to do with me. Someone said I was obviously injured, *look at her eye, look at her neck*, so they took me to the hospital to be checked out. At the hospital a really nice doctor came in and talked to me and then they told me to take off my clothes and I wasn't really okay with that because the doctor was a man and it was making me kind of shaky, even with the nurse there, so they sent in two women who weren't doctors but social workers and they asked me if I would take off my clothes to be examined. And they were really nice and kind and their voices were low and soft but not with that creepy edge that you sometimes hear in adult voices when they get low and soft and you know something else is coming.

They told me they had to look at me naked, that the doctor had to do *a full exam.* So I took off my clothes and stood there and I saw the look, they both got it, although the one with the dark red hair, not the brunette, she tried to hide the look. And then one of them, the redhead, handed me a gown and a sheet—kind of shoved them at me, then kind of apologized in a kind of strangled way, and that one backed out of the room and went for the doctor while the other one just stood there and tried not to look at me funny but I could tell she wanted to run, too.

I knew what they saw, of course. They saw the marks. It's not like I could hide them. It's not like on gym day when I would wear the top of my gym uniform under my school uniform so that when we got undressed in the locker room there was nothing to see. Teresa did the same thing, because her family was so religious that they thought it was somehow perverted that we all had to undress together and put on our gym clothes because only God and your parents should ever see you naked. I used to think that maybe Teresa had the marks, too, but there was no way to find out for sure. It just made me feel better to think there was someone else with them. I think probably the saints felt that way, too, and that's how everyone started to get involved in flagellation as part of penance—because then you couldn't tell the real saints from the fake ones and everyone felt more equal in God's eyes. Or at least that's what I think caused it to happen. Because it just feels safer to know other people are going through what you're going through. Because then maybe it's not so crazy.

Maybe.

The other woman came back to the exam room and I could tell she had started to cry because her eyes were wet and glisten-y and the doctor had a different look on his face—a serious, concerned look, while before he had a kind and open look, like he was welcoming me into his house and ready to feed me dinner or tell me a bedtime story like I was small or something sweet like that.

Would you mind removing the gown? His voice was low and soft like the women's, who I now knew were from some child protective agency because the nurse said it when she came back in the room. There was a policeman outside the door, but no one mentioned him.

I sat on the edge of the examining table and closed my eyes and took off the gown and tried not to feel like I was in my room with the eyes of the raccoons glowing at me and the sound of the door creaking open late at night and the smell of the scotch and cigarettes seeping into the room. I tried to remember that was all over and that now I was in a hospital and the man coming over to me was wearing a white coat and had a stethoscope and was talking low and soft but not those kinds of words but normal things like *Tilt your head back, please* and *Open your mouth and stick out your tongue, please* and *Take a deep breath, please, and now let it out slowly. That's good, that's fine.*

But I still didn't open my eyes until he said, *I need you to open your eyes* and so I did. The woman with the red hair from the agency was standing right next to me, behind the exam table, and she said in the same soft voice everyone was using, *Can you tell us about these marks?*

❖

In a crazy house, no one ever asks you questions about *you*, they ask you questions about *them*. So it's *Do you want to tell me about this blood in your underwear?* and not *What happened to you, are you hurt?* Or *Who hurt you?*

So I wasn't really prepared for the question, and that may be why I started to scream.

I didn't mean to scream and I wasn't really sure why I started screaming or why I kept yelling *Stop stop stop* because no one was doing anything to me and I never had said that before no matter what was happening because you just didn't say anything or do anything because it only made things worse and it was easy to figure this out, even the baby seemed to get it pretty quickly. *Don't cry, don't talk back, don't complain, don't don't don't. Be still, be quiet. Don't.*

The doctor almost fell back away from me while the nurse moved close but didn't do anything. The women moved to the side but no one touched me or did anything or said anything. We just all kind of stayed in this bubble of sound where I was screaming and nothing else was happening except that. I wasn't moving. I wasn't flailing my arms or kicking my legs or doing any of the stuff that usually goes with screaming. I didn't get off the table and I didn't run to the door and try to escape. I didn't even shut my eyes. But I could hear my own voice ringing in my ears and it was so loud that it hurt my head and made my lips feel numb and my hands started to sweat and I was shaking and then I just suddenly was quiet and the sound stopped coming out of me.

I think the nurse wanted to give me a shot or something. She looked at the doctor and they did that eye communicating thing, but nothing happened. And then the doctor asked if I was all right and I said yes and then he asked if he could examine me and I said yes and he asked if I would be very still and I said yes and then he moved close to me and I just felt all the air go out of me and I fainted onto the table.

When you wake up after a really bad dream, it's hard to shake it. You feel like you are still in the place of the dream and you feel like you are in two worlds—the dream world and the awake world—and it is really unsettling and creepy and you just want to either be back asleep or really wide awake and not remembering the dream at all.

When I woke up, I was still in a different room from the exam room, but it was still the hospital and I was lying down and there was a thin tube in my arm taped to my hand and there was a blood pressure cuff around my upper arm and the sides of the bed were up and I was propped up on a pillow and the bed was halfway up, almost like I was sitting.

The woman with the red hair from the child protective services agency was sitting on a chair next to me and no one else was in the room. The blinds on the window on the door were shut and there was a TV on across the room but the sound was low, like a hum of voices from another room. I turned toward the woman and saw that her name tag read *Emily Denton, MSW.*

I wanted to ask her questions, but my mouth felt heavy and shut and the words stuck in my throat, all thick. She asked me if I wanted some water and I nodded my head yes and she got me a cup with a straw and ice and the water felt smooth and silken in my throat and made me feel like I could talk again.

Where am I? What happened? Where's the doctor? My voice was cracked sounding and I didn't recognize it and my throat hurt and I moved my hand to rub it and felt the rough marks the rope had made that were still there all these days later.

I had passed out from the screaming—too much oxygen going out and not enough coming in. Something like a panic attack, only different, Emily explained. They had given me a sedative and Dr. Blanchard had examined me. I had extensive trauma and would need to be hospitalized for a few days and have some more tests and this tube would stay in my arm because it was giving me fluids and drugs and I would stay calm and not get any infections and everything was going to be okay.

Emily's words came out in the quiet, urgent rush of an adult who wants a child to understand something very important and understand it right away.

I asked about the policeman outside the door and Emily said he was gone and that he wasn't going to be back. I told her that the detective said I was going to prison and she just looked at me. She shook her head so slightly that I almost didn't catch it.

Your case has changed.

Her voice had an edge to it and I must have flinched involuntarily because it was a tone I was familiar with, a tone my mother used all the time, and when she saw me pull back, she put her hand on my arm above the place where the needle was in my hand and she just laid it there, not moving it.

Your case has changed. There is new evidence. Her voice was steadier, without the edge, and now I knew that the edge wasn't about me at all, but about something else. Probably the marks.

She stood up and said she would be right back and left the room. I was waking up from whatever the latest nightmare was, but not all of it. My eyes focused on the TV and I saw a flash of my crazy house on the screen and the crawl at the bottom explaining news at 11 would have continuing details about the case of the murdered family. I closed my eyes and flashes of blood and flies and meaty bits flooded my head. I opened my eyes and Emily was coming back into the room. Behind her was the detective, Ruggiero, from the police station. He didn't look like he was going to tell me about his daughters or anything else about his house. He had a notebook in his hand and he had the same serious concerned look I remembered from the doctor's face. He said he had some new questions he hoped I could answer and that those answers would help him *piece things together*. And then I remembered that he had said over and over *they were cut to bits*, but I was sure that wasn't what he meant about piecing things together.

Emily said I didn't have to say anything I didn't want to say. She gave the detective a menacing kind of look and I wasn't really sure what that meant. Except she had told me before the detective came back that she was in charge of me now, that she was appointed by the court—she didn't say what court—to be sure I was treated fairly, that I was thirteen and not an adult at all, but a child.

Detective Ruggiero asked the questions and I answered them one at a time. I explained about my grandfather and my dog and about the raccoons at my bedroom window and the room filled with the smell of scotch and cigarettes and words and sounds I didn't like hearing. I explained about my mother's screaming. I tried to explain how between when my grandfather died and the dog died, my baby brother got really sick and turned blue and that my brother had held him for a long time and then he had just been quiet in the crib. I told him that my brother had stopped talking soon after Christmas, which was after my baby brother got so quiet, and that my mother kept him home from school and said he was just *learning at home for now*. I explained how the last time my father came in and the raccoons were there, my mother was there when he left, or maybe it was my brother, it was someone, and that I didn't see my father again after that. I had just gotten up and gone to school in the morning, like always. I hadn't seen anyone, actually—not my parents or brothers or grandmother. I had just gone to school, because it was what I was supposed to do. And then I came home from school and there was all the blood and I had gone to the woods and come back again.

After the detective left, Emily came back and sat next to me. I had heard her talking to the detective outside my door, but I hadn't been able to understand what she was saying. I saw her shake her head and I saw him put his hand on her shoulder. I saw her kind of shake herself, like the cats did sometimes. And then he went away and she came back in.

Emily told me there would be *another small surgical procedure* and then a few more days in the hospital. She told me that after I left the hospital I would not be going back to the crazy house, but to a different place that was sort of like a hospital where I would stay for a while. After that, she said, *We'll see.*

The reporter was standing out on the walkway in front of my house, her left foot right up against one of the little bushes. I recognized her from other stories. She had the same concerned face that everyone around me had now. *New details about the grisly murders here tell a story of brutality and abuse*, she explained. *The medical examiner has determined that the eleven-month-old infant boy may have been dead for some time of what appear to be natural causes and that the blood found on the body was not his but his brother's. Autopsy reports indicate that the father was the first victim, and that he was most likely killed while he slept. It has yet to be determined, however, whether the mother, who had experienced a psychotic break after some as yet undisclosed events, or the young boy, aged ten, was the killer, as tests are still pending. The grandmother was not the killer. The boy was,*

according to police sources, suffering from some kind of emotional collapse himself and had not been attending school for at least a month, possibly longer.

The sole survivor of the carnage, the thirteen-year-old girl who had been at school when the mayhem occurred and who had originally been in police custody as a person of interest, has been cleared of all involvement in the tragedy.

According to hospital officials, the girl suffered extensive physical trauma of an ongoing nature and has already had two surgeries since her hospitalization, although the nature of those procedures has not been released by the hospital. She has been sedated much of the time and a hospital spokesperson has said that her injuries are consistent with ongoing and severe child abuse. Sources tell me that she will be sent to a rehabilitation facility in the western part of the state which specializes in extreme trauma and in fact deals extensively with torture victims from Africa and the Middle East. The court has appointed a guardian for her, since all her family members are now apparently deceased. Officials at the girl's school declined comment when we asked why they hadn't noticed anything unusual in the girl's behavior or demeanor or what police say were visible physical injuries to her and why school officials had done nothing about the fact that her brother had not attended classes for a significant period of time or notified child protective services that the girl was obviously being abused.

Then the reporter turned toward the front porch and the door with the big brass knocker and waved her gloved hand in the direction of the house. A small puff of breath came out of her mouth as she said, *No one knew what went on behind this calm exterior.* Her voice slightly hushed, she added, *And in the days and weeks ahead, we can expect there will be more revelations and more disturbing findings. Stay tuned to Action News for continual updates on this tragic, tragic story.*

I continued to look at the TV long after the report had ended, but I don't remember what else was going on. I thought about how the reporter, who I had seen before reporting on other tragedies in other places, had been standing in front of my house this time, talking about my family, talking about me. Now that house was *news*, not *home*.

I lay in the bed staring at the screen, but not registering any new images. I spent a lot of time sleeping now, because of the drugs and what one of the doctors called "trauma deficit." The detective had been back and had asked some more questions and Emily spent a significant amount of time in my room every day. So did a court-appointed psychologist. But there was nothing else to tell them. Everything I had to say I had said that first time. I told them that.

The psychologist explained that I needed to give details and explore my feelings, he wanted me to discuss the marks and the *incident* as he called it, but I didn't really want to give more details and I didn't know what he meant by exploring my feelings. I told him that what I wanted most was to go back to my house, with just me and the cats and the quiet. But without the blood. I knew how things were there. I didn't know how they would be anywhere else. I didn't know how *I* would be anywhere else. When you live in a crazy house, you have to be kind of crazy yourself, I guess. He just shook his head when I said these things and wrote them down on the long yellow pad of paper he had. I heard him tell Emily that if I didn't talk I wouldn't get better and that *we will never get to the bottom of what really happened.*

❖

I knew what really happened. There was a trigger, and a gun went off. Not a real gun, but an emotional gun. What everyone wanted to know, of course, was who pulled that trigger. Was it my mother? My brother? Me?

When you live in a crazy house, you learn to make the line between the truth and not truth blurry and indistinct. You learn to say what's expected of you, not what really needs saying. You learn how to tell a story—or how not to tell. You learn that truth and memory aren't black and white because there are what the court calls *mitigating circumstances.*

The facts of the case came out after the investigation. According to those facts, my father was murdered in his sleep. My grandmother had her throat slit as she drank her morning coffee, which was why the blood swirled at the bottom of the cup. The cat who had been sitting on her lap had been stabbed once through the heart and killed dead right away. The baby had been dead for nearly a month—the report said *mummified remains of a suffocated infant.* What remained unclear, because the bodies were in the same place, was whether my brother or my mother committed the murders and which of them committed suicide.

I knew what really happened. I knew that my brother had the marks like I had. I knew there were probably handprints on my brother like there were on me. And the small round marks from the glowing eyes of the raccoons. There just weren't the other things. The things inside. Probably. Probably not.

I knew my brother had held the baby until the breath came out of him and that he never said anything again after that. I knew my mother never looked at the baby after that day and that we all acted like I did when I saw all the blood. Like we could just move forward and pretend it was all okay, all *normal.* Like no one would ever look beyond the door with the big brass knocker and no one would ever say *How awful* or *We had no way of knowing this was going on.*

The place where I am now is quiet and in the mornings I go to a classroom and each day I have a class in something—English, math, history. No religion. On Sundays Emily comes and takes me outside this place to Mass and then we go have lunch and she brings me back. She still wants to know what happened, but there's nothing I can say. Not if I want to leave here. Not if I want to move forward, as everyone keeps saying I must. I read a lot of books. I write in a journal like I am supposed to. I keep two journals—one with the memories I want to have, one with the memories I do have.

In the afternoons we sit in a group—there are kids and adults, it's all blurry and indistinct, the way we all have the same experiences. Some of the people are foreign, but some of them are from here. All of us have experienced some kind of killing. Some of us are murderers, all of us are victims. The doctor who runs the little group reminds us that victims who live are called survivors and that that is who we are and we must take pride in that. Like saints who were put on the stake but didn't burn.

Some people talk more than others in this group. I don't talk very much because there isn't really anything to say. I wasn't in a war. I wasn't in a gang. I was never a child soldier. I really don't think I belong here, but I never say that. Because I know what to say and what not to say.

Once a week, Detective Ruggiero comes to see me. Sometimes it's a Tuesday, sometimes it's a Friday. Once he came on a Saturday when we were all outside because it was sunny and getting warm, finally. He always asks me the same questions: He wants to put the file away, he says, he wants to close the case. But he needs more facts, he needs to know what else *I* know. He wants answers.

I have learned to tell him just a little bit. Just a little about the things that went on in the house with the big brass knocker. I have learned to tell him the words that were said to me and the color of the baby when he was blue and the smell of the cigarette that made the marks that will never go away. I have learned that these little bits of information are part of what Ruggiero calls *the puzzle* and that he has what I have learned is a *voyeuristic interest* in my case that is maybe just a little twisted up with thinking that something like what happened in my house could happen in his house. Except he has to really know it can't, it won't. Because he doesn't live in a place where there will ever be some kind of killing—not like where I lived. Not like where the people in this place lived. He always makes a kind of awkward gesture toward me when he leaves. He wants to hug me, but I know the doctors have told him that I am not supposed to be touched. Not until I am healed. Which may never happen. Just like Ruggiero may never have the answers to the questions he has. The answers that will somehow end the investigation into how three adults, two children, and two cats were killed and one girl survived. He's told me he's never had a case like this. And I believe him.

At night I have dreams about the blood and the maggots, the flies and the bits of flesh. At night I remember the raccoons and the glowing eyes and the end of the cigarette going into the flesh on my back and my chest and the hand over my mouth and the things inside. I remember the sizzling sound and the sucking sound and the sound of the knife going across the throat, the sound of the knife going into the flesh and coming out and going in again and again. I remember the smell of blood and I remember the cold and I remember the rope around my neck and I remember the big spiders running across my arms as I get behind the waterfall.

At night I sometimes wake up screaming and a nurse comes and gives me a shot and then everything is black and there are no dreams at all. And in the morning when I wake up, I don't remember the dreams. I only remember the soft feel of cats' fur and the sound of purring and I get dressed and go to breakfast and think that soon I will be able to go home, soon I will be back in the house with the big brass knocker and soon everything will be better and then there won't ever be any blood again. Soon I will wake up and I will get dressed and I will go to school and it will be as if none of this ever happened, as if this is the life I always had, without any of the sounds or smells or blood. I think that if I just keep going the way I am now, if I can make everyone know that I am okay now, that I am not like the people in the crazy house, it will happen. I will get to go home.

Which is why I can't tell them anything more about the crazy house or that day or all the days that came after. No one will ever have the answers to why there was some kind of killing there, at that house, because no one will know what came before.

No one, that is, but me.

ANYTHING FOR THE THEATER
CLIFFORD HENDERSON

I learned of Edna Powell's death at a production meeting for Blue
Moon Theater's upcoming play *The Diviners*. I was running
the meeting. It's my job as stage manager to make sure the director and
designers communicate. Not always an easy task. There's a joke about
the hierarchy of a production. Actors are at the bottom of the ladder,
next rung up are the designers, then comes the director, on top of that
is God, and the rung above that, well, that's me, the stage manager,
Hattie Parker. To meet me, you wouldn't know I wield such power.
Like most stage managers, I'm soft-spoken. But my actors never miss
their entrances or forget their props, and my light and sound board-
ops hit their cues dead on. I run a tight ship. When a director asks the
impossible, I make it happen.

In this one show I ran, the attractive female lead had ten seconds to
zip offstage and do a complete gender switch, from suit and tie to dress
and heels. The director wanted red lipstick, but no matter how many
times we rehearsed the change, ripping off the jacket with attached shirt
and tie, yanking on the Velcro-fastened dress, we could never get to
the lipstick, we just couldn't make the time. Then I came up with a
solution. I slathered lipstick on my own lips and kissed her right before
her entrance.

I'm not saying the job is without its perks.

The announcement of Edna Powell's death came while we were
discussing color palette. Douglas Trent stepped into the green room. He
looked shook up, his face pale, his hands fidgety. "Sorry to interrupt,"
he said, but he didn't have to apologize to us—or to anyone. Douglas
is president of the board, a.k.a. head fund-raiser. If it weren't for him,
there would be no Blue Moon Theater. "I just got a call from Edna

Powell's son." He pulled a hanky from his pocket and blew his nose. "She died in her sleep last night. Her cleaning lady found her in her bed this morning."

I was floored. Or maybe floored isn't the right word. Ultra creeped out might be a better choice. But that doesn't fully capture the feeling either, because along with ultra creeped out was a dash of excitement. Adrenaline. Could the pendulum of fortune for once have swung our way?

Rewind to the night before.

I was hanging out backstage with Edna. It was closing weekend of the premiere of *In Your Dreams*, a new play that just wasn't getting the audiences anyone expected. Too avant-garde, I suspect. Now, a box office bomb can either draw actors together in a kind of misunderstood-artist team-spirit thing or push them apart in mutual blame and loathing. In this case it was the latter. The actors wanted the embarrassment to be over.

Edna, playing the token old-lady role, was no exception. Her part was a minor one, meaning lots of backstage time, something she's never been fond of. I know because I've endured many a show with her. Edna's swimming in the money her mogul husband left her, and donates scads of it to the theater, so there's sort of this…obligation to cast her whenever possible. I say obligation because she's a pain in the ass to work with. She's a decent enough actor—uses her hands too much, mistakes volume for intensity, that sort of thing. The problem is she's an enormous prima donna. If another actor mistakenly steps on her line or upstages her, she throws a massive fit. I've heard tales of her younger days when she actually lobbed hand props at actors who crossed her. And while she's well past having the upper-arm strength to pull that off, her tongue is weapon enough. I can't tell you how many times she's caused one of my stagehands to break down in tears. Or quit. I wouldn't put up with it from any of my other actors, but when it's Edna Powell, well, you bite your tongue and remind yourself that she just donated a whopping chunk of change for new risers.

Edna was acting oddly that night. And I'm not the only one who thought so. My current stagehand and major crush, Maria Gonzales, did, too. Edna was sitting on a stool, wedged between the roll-on fireplace and the fake cow, scribbling furiously on a clipboard. The backstage lights are nothing more than clip lamps with blue bulbs, but

Edna had a little book light attached to the top of the clipboard, and she was really going at it. Generally, this would not warrant much note. I've seen actors do their homework backstage, write bills, what have you. But not Edna. She spends all her time backstage "preparing," which essentially means sitting stock still and glaring at anyone who walks through her "energy circle." Naturally, I was curious. Besides, it's my job to know what's going on with my actors. So I asked her what was up. I had to whisper. The play was in a quiet part, and a flimsy wall is the only thing between the dressing room and the stage.

She scrutinized me briefly, then whispered back, "I'm writing an addendum to my will."

My first thought was: Who's pissed her off now? Edna was always pulling stunts like this. Be a nice little puppet and she'd reward you, go against her in any way and she'd make sure you felt it. "Kind of a funny time to be working on your will," I said.

Maria, filling a brandy decanter with flat Coke, and looking super cute in her backstage blacks, gave me a look that let me know she was on the same page.

I squatted so I could get a look at Edna's face—harder than it sounds. Her milkmaid costume included a bonnet with a ridiculously large brim. But even in the shadows of that dim blue light, I could see that something was bothering her. I prayed it wasn't something we'd done to piss her off. Last thing the theater needed was for her to pull her money. "Is everything okay?"

"I don't want my son, Darrell, to know I'm doing this," she whispered.

"Why?"

She glanced briefly at Maria, whom Edna had recently decided to like, then signaled for the two of us to huddle around her. Maria placed the filled decanter onto the silver tray, then joined me squatting next to Edna. We were just minutes away from the next set change. I prayed Edna would make it quick.

"He's in town for a visit. Of course, he won't stay with me. Says I make his lady friends uncomfortable. His whores, is more like it. And now he's trying to convince me I'm incompetent to handle my financial affairs. Can you imagine? Me, Edna Powell. He's even got my lawyer on board."

"That doesn't sound good," Maria said diplomatically, but I'm sure she was thinking what I was. Edna *was* starting to get forgetful. The week prior she'd stormed into the theater and blamed the office manager for double-charging her Visa, which was not the case. There'd been other incidents, too.

Edna laid a blue-veined hand, slightly palsied, but nonetheless entitled, on Maria's shoulder. "Thank you, dear. I appreciate your support—everyone's here at the theater." She generously included me with a nod, then glanced around as if someone might be listening in. "Unlike my son, *you* appreciate me. That's why I'm going to bequeath the bulk of my estate to the theater. I've made up my mind. I'm just afraid if Darrell finds out, he'll try to stop me. He'll convince our lawyer that I'm being irrational."

Maria and I exchanged glances. The bulk of her estate? Wouldn't that be a boon for the theater! But I don't think either one of us took her too seriously. You couldn't. It would only hurt you in the end.

"Can't you get some kind of doctor's note," Maria whispered, "confirming you're of sound mind?"

"I plan to, dear. But in the meantime, I want Darrell to understand that he is no longer my beneficiary. I've had it." She thrust the clipboard at me. "So, if you wouldn't mind signing your name, I'd like you to witness my change."

It felt slimy taking the clipboard. Who knew what little trespass her son had committed to deserve this? But there was no time to dwell on it. We were coming up on our most complicated set change. I scrawled my name, then said into my headset, "Two-minute warning on sound cue thirteen. It's a visual. Watch for the actress to drop the vase."

"On standby," my sound and light op replied.

"Lights, prepare for fade to black."

"Ready," my light op said.

"He blames me for everything," Edna went on. "For his failures with women, his inability to make lasting friendships. Says I was too domineering. Can you believe?"

I handed her the clipboard, envisioning a day I might actually be able to pay my staff more than stipends, then told myself not too get too excited. This was Edna Powell we were talking about. "It's your money, Edna."

She passed the clipboard to Maria. "I believe I need two witnesses to make it legal."

Maria signed her name, then grabbed the broom and dustpan for the high-speed cleanup.

I got into place so I could see the actress as she held the vase above her head. "Genie! If you won't come out on your own free will," she roared, "I will make you come out!"

Smash!

"Music. Go," I said, then silently began counting: *One chimpanzee, two chimpanzee, three chimpanzee.* "Lights. Go."

Right before stepping onto the stage for the set change, I saw Edna take the will from the clipboard and slip it into her makeup box, a metal tackle box doubling as her footstool.

I didn't get a chance to talk with her afterward; there were always too many actors for the small backstage, and there was that minor disaster involving an actress's wig and a spilled soda. Maria and I were the last to leave. We had to refold the prop blankets that had been hastily stuffed onto the shelf so the actors could get to their night of partying.

"I'm kind of worried about her," Maria said.

I'll admit I was having trouble focusing on the conversation. Every time we completed a fold, she'd step in close to hand me her edge. "Who, Edna?"

"Hattie." She stopped not six inches from me. "Have you even heard a word I've said?"

I reached for her edge of the blanket.

She jerked it back. "Have you?"

What can I say? I get distracted in the presence of sublime beauty. "Sorry." I attempted a concerned look. "I'll check on her tomorrow. Give her a call." Worrying about Edna hadn't even occurred to me. But Maria cared, so I would, too. Then, the next morning, I slept in and had to race to pick up the bagels and cream cheese for the ten o'clock production meeting. I didn't give Edna a second thought. Not until Trent's announcement.

Everyone, of course, was shocked by the news of her death. And there were the logistics to figure out. Who'd finish out the run of the show, and could they get off book fast enough? I listened to my colleagues prattling on, but my mind was fixed on only one thing. Getting my hands on that will. I started imagining a soundboard with no pop, a set of blacks that weren't ripped from the negligent use of safety pins, a grid full of new lighting instruments. After an appropriately sensitive amount of time, I brought the meeting back to the production end of things. It's what I get all those tens of dollars for, to keep a show on schedule. But I couldn't get that will addendum out of my head. It was floating around somewhere—and needed to be found.

Before closing, I made it clear that at the next meeting I wanted to see a maquette, some costume renderings, and light plots. Then I hung around to pick up the coffee cups and bagel wrappings. Glamorous, I know. Oh yeah, and I had myself a good cry. I wasn't crying because Edna was gone. It was more about death in general. It's so…irreversible.

On the wall an old play poster for *The Gin Game* featured a photo of her with a quote from a local reviewer: "The Jessica Tandy of The Blue Moon Theater." I chuckled. The difference there was Jessica Tandy was *sweet*. But it couldn't be denied, Edna was our resident old lady, our crone, ol' biddy, hag, witch. She'd played them all, and that's how she'd be remembered.

The floor around the lighting designer's chair was covered in crumbs. The slob! I opened the utility closet to grab a dustpan and broom. Someone was bumping around in the dressing room. Figuring it was the sound designer checking out the headsets, I ignored it. Then the thumping grew frantic like someone was trashing the place. I dropped the broom and strode in, planning on chewing someone a new asshole. There was no one there, but the place was thrashed. Costumes were thrown to the floor. Prop boxes dumped. This pissed me off on so many levels. It also scared the crap out of me. Who would do this? I grabbed a prop fireplace poker and crept into the theater. The ghost light in the center of the stage cast eerie shadows over the sharp angles of the set. I edged my way over to the work lights and flicked them on. The stage was empty. Poker held high, I walked the center aisle up to the tech booth in case someone was hiding out there, but whoever it was, was gone.

The door to the outside slammed, startling the shit out of me.

Forcing my now shaking legs out into the foyer and to the door, I cracked it open. A group of laughing people stood outside the adjacent restaurant. A couple of guys walked out of the hardware store. Individuals strolled down the street minding their own business. I fiddled with the outside bulletin board trying to calm myself. Who had vandalized the dressing room? And why? Then I remembered the will. I bolted inside to the dressing room to see if her makeup box was in its usual spot on the shelf. It wasn't.

I unscrewed my thermos and poured myself a cup of coffee, then paced the length of the green room trying to decide what to do. I considered contacting the police, simply mentioning to them the conversation Edna and I had had the night before, but I couldn't get it out of my head that if I got the police involved, the will would get caught up in some kind of legal bullshit and the theater would never see that dough. There had to be another way.

Lest you find my fixation on the money shallow, let me say this in my defense. I believe theater to be sacred. On a good night, the connection between audience and players literally changes the molecules in the room. We are transformed, however briefly, into our highest selves. That said, funding for theater is at an all-time low. The Blue Moon Theater is the only surviving live theater in our area. We work our butts off to provide our community with a solid season every year, plus we do programs in the schools and offer internships for kids at risk. We sponsor events like the Rainbow Awards for gay teens and a reading series for emerging writers. But each year we question if we can go on. And this year has been the direst yet. We've actually had the ugly discussion about replacing staff with volunteers. A gift like Edna Powell's would be a godsend. And, more importantly, job security.

I stopped pacing. I had to get a hold of the will.

I pulled out my cell phone and dialed Maria. I'd wanted to call on her socially for weeks and could never find the right pretext. The fact that it took a possible crime for me to get up the guts tells you something about my courtship skills.

She picked up on the third ring. "Hattie?"

"Uh, yeah." I cursed my knotted tongue. Just once I was hoping to talk to a woman I was attracted to without sounding mentally challenged.

"Is something wrong?" Her voice was full of concern, like maybe she cared.

"Yeah. Could I meet you somewhere? I need to tell you in person."

"You're not throwing me off the crew because of Sandra's wig? I moved Blaze's soda from the makeup counter like three times. I even threatened to cut his hand off if he put it there again. But you know how spacey Blaze is."

"No. No." Her presumption made me feel like crap. Was I really that much of a taskmaster? "It has nothing to do with the show. It's about Edna"

"Edna?"

"Yes. She died last night."

"Died?"

"Uh-huh."

"That seems kind of…weird, doesn't it? I mean…after she had us—"

"We need to talk."

Forty-five minutes later we were sitting at a rickety table in a local coffee shop, me with a latte, her with a hot chocolate, and I'd filled her in on the situation. Oh yeah, and I'd paid for the drinks, if that makes me seem less pathetic.

It was my first time to see Maria outside the theater and I had to keep from gawking. She was stunning in her jeans and Fry boots, her long wavy black hair cascading over her shoulders. She was an amazing woman who had done a lot for theater-community relations, hosting an outreach mask-making class for the local Hispanic kids, for one thing. Over half of them were scholarships, meaning Maria let them take the class for free, using her own money for supplies. The way I saw it, it was our civic duty to get our hands on that makeup box before anyone else did.

Maria sucked a swirl of thick whipped cream from her fingertip. "It was probably her son. From the way she made it sound, he was the one with the most to lose."

"My thoughts exactly."

She giggled. "Too bad he doesn't know what I do. Last night when she was leaving, I helped her load the makeup box, and the will, into her car."

"So she didn't leave it here, then?"

"Nope."

I took a satisfied sip of latte. There was still hope. "Knowing her, she hid it somewhere." I flashed on an evening I'd recently spent at Edna's. I'd given her a ride home because her car was in the shop.

She'd invited me in for "a nip." *Darrell doesn't like it when I drink,* she'd said. *Says it makes me unsteady. But I've been having a drink before bed as long as I can remember.* She laughed. *It's all part of his plan to make me feel old and feeble.* She'd pulled a bottle of malt whiskey from a secret panel in the back of a rolltop desk.

"You got any plans tonight?" I asked Maria.

"I do now."

Five hours later we were driving down Edna's pretentious, hedge-lined circle driveway. Her Mercedes was parked out front. We parked behind it and got out for a look. Contents from the glove box were strewn all over the floor. The mess had a violent energy to it.

"Shit," I said.

"Yeah," she said.

The door to the car was unlocked, which I found strange—Edna was paranoid as hell—but I used the opportunity to rifle through what was left in the glove box and around the floorboards. I came up empty-handed save for some major second thoughts. Weren't there laws about breaking into dead people's cars? Homes? A fleeting hope that Maria might suggest we bag the break-and-enter routine tickled the edges of my brain, but Maria, seemingly undaunted, turned to face the palatial Craftsman-style house. "Shall we?"

"I…uh…figure we should knock first, just in case someone's here," I stammered.

"I thought you said she lived alone."

"She does—*did!*—but you never know." I reassured myself that whoever had ransacked her car was probably long gone and started making my way down the slate path.

The knocker on the large red door was in the shape of a gargoyle and about the size of my head. I gave it three loud raps.

We waited.

Maria tried peering through the frosted glass on the side window. "We should go around the back, see if we can find an open door or something."

"Sounds good."

A loud bumping sound came from inside the house. We both froze.

"Now what?" I mouthed.

Maria stepped back taking hold of the rail to keep from toppling off the low step.

The door swung open and we were face-to-face with a man who looked to be in his fifties, although he could have been older. His features were grotesquely distorted from too much plastic surgery; his skin barely looked real. A five o'clock shadow dusted a bizarrely chiseled jaw and cleft chin. He was dressed in designer jeans and a man-pink button down, an outfit I'm sure a personal dresser chose. He also was shitface drunk.

"Can I help you?" His upper lip twitched.

Hackles standing at attention, I plunged in. "I…we…were hoping to talk to you about Edna Powell."

He seemed to remember that he should appear bereft and hit us with a poor-me look. "Yes. Edna. My mother."

"Ah. You're Darrel, then. My name is Hattie and this is Maria." I thrust out my hand to kill some time. "We worked with your mother at the theater." What the hell were we doing?

Maria jumped in. "We were hoping that maybe when you write Edna's obituary, you might encourage people to give to the theater."

I marveled at her invention, adding, "In lieu of flowers. You know how people do." My heart was pounding so loudly in my chest I could barely hear myself.

"Obituary…" he repeated, his mind clawing through the inebriation.

"As a matter of fact," I went on, "knowing how consumed you must be with all the details of her death, we thought we might help you…write it."

"She was very popular in the theater community," Maria said.

"Yes. And people will expect you to mention some of her more prominent roles."

He didn't say anything, just stood there in his alcohol-induced haze, squinting into space as if there were a movie screen above our heads playing a particularly gruesome horror flick.

"Uh, Darrell," I said. "Could we come in? It'll just take a minute."

"Oh. Sure." He opened the door just wide enough for us to wriggle through.

The place was a mess. Coffee table books were tossed to the floor; a cedar chest gaped open with colorful throws draping out like octopus tentacles; the pillows of the couch and chairs were askew.

He glanced around nervously. "I was, um, packing up some of Mom's stuff."

I had the urge to bolt while the door was still open, but Maria strode over to the couch, straightened out the pillows, and sat. She looked small, vulnerable, under the vaulted ceiling and gaudy chandelier.

He shut the door warily then ran his fingers through his hair, obviously implants. He cleared his throat. "Could I get you ladies something to drink?" Although he'd used the word *ladies*, his sudden politeness was obviously aimed at Maria. He'd apparently sobered up enough to notice she's a knockout.

"How nice of you to offer," she said, primping her hair. "I'd love something. What have you got?"

He took the bait and swaggered toward her. "I have a lovely Chateau Ste Michelle or—"

"Sounds great." She flashed him a flirtatious smile. "I love a man who knows his wine."

He looked at me still standing by the foyer. "You?"

"Sure."

I staked a claim next to Maria on the couch. His leering made me nervous. Hell, everything about the scene was making me nervous.

Clearly unsteady on his feet, he took off down the hall for the kitchen.

"Where's the rolltop?" Maria whispered.

I pointed down the hall. "In the library."

"Shall we—"

"Not yet. It's too risky. He'll pass the library coming from the kitchen."

"So I'll follow him into the kitchen and stall him. Come on."

Before I knew it, she was up out of her seat and trailing after him. I took up the rear, whispering, "Maria! Maria!" But it was no use. She was a woman with a mission.

I slipped into the library just seconds before I heard her say, "I thought I'd give you a hand." She was pouring it on. Which bothered me. If he'd done what I was starting to suspect, he was more dangerous than he looked. I pictured Edna telling him about the will, taunting him until he was so angry he…

But there was no time to worry about that. I turned my attention to the library. The light from the hallway illuminated the otherwise dark room. I closed my eyes for a couple of seconds so they'd adjust. As in the living room, books were lying all over the floor. The top of the rolltop had been swept clean, pencils, photographs, and paperwork scattered all over the floor. I tiptoed through the mess and began feeling around the underside of the desk. I hadn't been totally paying attention when she opened the secret panel that other night and now prayed I could figure it out. And quickly.

The cork popped on the bottle of wine. Maria laughed at something Darrell said. I heard the sound of wine tinkling into high-dollar crystal. "Come on, come on," I whispered to the desk. I pushed lightly on the back panel and heard a click. I slid the panel to the side and felt around. Her bottle of scotch was still there. But was there anything else? My hand brushed against something that felt like a folded-up document. I plucked it from the hidey-hole. Then I heard Darrell ask in an accusing tone:

"Why don't you want me to walk down the hall?"

"It's not that I don't want you to," Maria said coyly. "I was just hoping—"

There was a loud smash that sounded like a wine bottle being hurled against the wall. "I get it! I know what you bitches are after!" he roared.

"Hattie!" Maria screamed. "Run!"

I stuffed the document in the back of my pants and sprinted for the library door, but smacked into Darrell. I stepped back just in time to miss having my face sliced open with a broken wine bottle.

"Darrell! No!" Maria appeared in the doorway, backlit so I could only see her silhouette.

He held the bottle by the neck, its jagged edges aimed at my jugular.

"Slow down, Darrell," I said, my hands raised to protect my throat. "You've had way too much to drink."

"Just put the bottle down," Maria said.

He spun around, almost tripping over a book, and took a swipe at Maria. "Fucking bitches. You're trying to trick me. Just like Mom."

"Put the bottle down," I repeated. "Your hand is bleeding. It needs a bandage."

"You don't know what it's like," he wheezed, "having an actress for a mother. She was always at rehearsals, in shows. Never gave a shit about me. *My* life. Noooo. She had to grab all the attention. It was always all about her."

"You feel cheated," Maria said.

"And Edna could be tough," I added.

"Oh. What? Are you psychoanalysts now? You don't know anything. I didn't do it because she didn't *love me*. I did it because she was fucking writing me out of her fucking will. I'm her fucking son. She fucking *owes* me."

In the shadowy light, I saw his hand loosening its grip on the bottle. Or I thought I did. Praying I was right, I lunged forward.

He stumbled back, tripping over a large black book. His head cracked against the door frame.

Maria and I watched as he slo-mo slid down the polished wood wainscoting.

For a moment we just stood there, waiting for the monster to rise again. In those moments, I actually felt sorry for him, in that weird Michael Jackson kind of way. Too much money and not enough love.

"Is he out?" Maria finally asked.

"Looks like it."

"Did he just confess to killing Edna?"

I peeled my attention away. An involuntary shiver shot up my spine. I noticed I was rubbing my jugular.

"You okay?" she asked.

"I guess." I flicked my attention back to Darrell, making sure he was still lying there like a good little murderer. "You?"

"I think so."

We gazed into each other's eyes, lone survivors on the battlefield.

"Did you find the will?" she asked.

I flicked on the light, pulled the document from my pants, and gave it a once-over. "Yeah. This is it."

The harsh light revealed the violence of Darrell's search: Two wingchairs were overturned, pages were torn out of books, a framed glossy of a gorgeous young Edna holding her new baby boy lay smashed on the floor.

I knelt by Darrell, fearful that he might lurch up and grab me by the throat, but he just lay there breathing loudly through his mouth. "What kind of sick fuck kills his mom?"

Maria didn't respond. She was messing with her iPhone.

"Don't call the police. We need to get our stories straight first."

She held up a finger. "I'm just checking to see if my video came out."

"You videoed that whole thing?"

"Yup. Let's see how much I got."

Watching Darrell's ghastly confession on the small screen was almost more terrifying than the actual event. He was such a loose cannon. Anything could have happened. "Think that'll be admissible in court?"

She shrugged. "Hard to say. He never actually says he killed her."

"And I don't know what the laws are surrounding video footage. Can they even be considered as evidence?"

"If not, I'll post it on YouTube."

I tried to laugh but it came out more of a cough. I was shaking.

She pulled me into a hug. "Hey. It's over."

Opportunist that I am, I wrapped my arms around her and breathed her in: cloves and amber. We stood that way for a few blissful seconds, but we were both too jumpy.

"We should call the police," she said.

She was right, of course. When this guy woke up, I wanted someone with a gun on hand. I pulled an extension cord off a lamp and started tying up his hands.

"I'll tell you one thing," she said, punching numbers in on her phone. "That's not the first time theater saved my life."

"Huh?"

"Back in my twenties, I was having a tough time, getting myself into some things that weren't good for me."

I nodded. So many of us in the theater have tales like these, about how theater found us at a low point in our lives. But why was she saying it saved her life now? Seemed like this time theater almost got her killed.

She nudged the book he'd tripped over with her boot. *The Collected Works of William Shakespeare.*

This girl was special, all right. Now if I could just get the nerve up to invite her on a real date.

"Hi. My name is Maria Gonzales and I'd like to report a murder."

I walked over to Edna's printer and made a copy of the addendum. The money was ours, fair and square.

SOCIAL WORK
KENDRA SENNETT

O f all the social work schools in the world, she had to walk into my class on Theory of Social Change and Community Practice. And sit right in front of me. She was tall, a little older than most of us, with thick hair a glossy shade just between red and brown and the kind of tan that said she spent a lot of time outdoors. Her lips were full, she had dimples when she effusively smiled and shimmering green eyes with flecks of gold in them. Her shoulders were broad and her arms strong, but also her breasts and hips left no doubt that she was a sensuous woman.

She smiled at me the first day, reached over the back of her chair to shake my hand, and said, "I'm Amanda. I'll need you to watch my back for the whole semester."

"I'm Megan. I'll be glad to watch your back." Only after I said it did I realize that she meant it literally—I was sitting behind her after all. But I was happy to watch her back; she had those muscled shoulders, and it was hot and she wore a tank top. I noticed a small scar on her shoulder blade.

The second day she offered me gum.

I was smitten.

The second week she asked if I wanted to join her and her friends for coffee. Most of them were older, so I felt happy for being included. I didn't say much as they had a fascinating discussion about social justice and oppression and how the suburbs increased man's inhumanity to man and how SUVs were really just phallic symbols.

That was the first time she hugged me, as we were leaving. She hugged all her friends, but included me, adding only to me, "You get home safe now, okay?"

The third week, she said to me, "Hey, want to do some real social work instead of this boring class stuff?"

Of course, I agreed. I didn't even ask what we would be doing.

She told me not to dress up, but I didn't want to look too dykey, at least not until I had a better idea of how cool she'd be about that, so I went with my medium-nice jeans and a pink sweatshirt that was slightly snug in the chest and my good black sneakers.

I looked at myself in the mirror. Okay, so I wasn't quite as tall as she was, but I wasn't a runt either. I have sort of dark brown hair; it looked sleek in bright sunshine, but in the dull fluorescents of the classroom, it came off as a black blob. Hazel eyes that looked squinty behind my glasses, but at night when it was dark I could call them green. I stuck my chest out, but even the pink sweatshirt didn't help bring out my girlish figure. The best thing to say about my looks was that I appeared smart and like I might be a good social worker.

I sighed and decided that at least I could be a good listener on the few occasions she and her older friends invited me out for coffee.

We met by the parking lot behind the school of social work.

Amanda took one look at my bike and said, "Leave that here. It won't work where we're going." Then she hopped into the front passenger's side of a big van and I just followed all the others as they crowded into the back. There were a couple other social work students and a few of Amanda's older friends. One of the guys, with a skanky beard and breath that smelled like he had spilled beer in it last night, was sitting a little too close to me. But I didn't let that bother me; the cause was too important.

It wasn't a long van ride, which was a good thing as I was starting to get queasy from skanky beard's beer and unwashed boy funk. We were under one of the interstate's overpasses. Of course I'd driven by here, but only on the fast highway with this area safely below my wheels. It was the kind of place better suited for police officers than social workers. I could tell from a few of my classmates' looks that they were feeling the same way I did.

But the back door of the van was flung open and Amanda was reaching out her hand to help me out and I couldn't say no to that.

Some other older guys, all with skanky beards, joined us. I wasn't close enough to notice if they smelled of beer as well. Then an older woman also appeared. She gave Amanda a hug, but no one else.

"Thanks for coming," she said to all of us, then to Amanda she added, "Thanks for rounding up the troops, we couldn't do this without you."

Then the older woman—she had to be in her thirties if not forties—gave us instructions. It turned out that our mission was to hand out sandwiches to the homeless who were living here under the highway. Some of the skanky beard guys pulled folding tables out of the van, and our first task was to slap peanut butter and jelly onto bread. It was disorganized at first, everyone trying to put a knife into the jelly jar at the same time, but I sorted my co-table workers into an assembly line—one person putting bread slices down, two putting peanut butter on them, two putting jelly, and the last person—me—putting two slices together and into a plastic bag. I'd worked at a fast food place during high school and was amused that it turned out I could use those skills in my social work career. Amanda saw what I was doing and gave an approving nod. I was in heaven.

One of my classmates looked at the white bread we were using and asked, "Shouldn't we be using something more nutritious? And a PB&J sandwich isn't all that great either."

A skanky beard guy sneered a reply, "You're from the suburbs, aren't you?"

She started to retort, but I stepped in. I didn't want my smooth-running team to fall apart in front of Amanda.

"Celeste," I said calmly, "it's one of those trade-offs we're going to have to make as social workers. You're right that there are other food choices that would be more healthy. But they cost more and we'd feed fewer people. Plus, if someone sticks one of these sandwiches in his bag for a day or two, it won't go bad like meat might."

I consider whether to point out to skanky beard that it might be better to educate than look down on and be sarcastic, but I didn't know him well enough for that, and he was one of Amanda's friends.

Once our sandwiches were made, we were assigned to teams to fan out and find the homeless. I was willing to go with Celeste, but the older woman insisted that there could be no all-female teams, so I ended up with one of the skanky beards.

He seemed nice enough until we were mostly through handing out the food, then as we crossed behind one of the huge concrete pillars, he pushed me against it and said, "Time for some fun, don't you think?" and tried to kiss me.

I guess my pink sweatshirt had an effect on someone, just not the right someone.

"Get your hands off me," I said forcefully. "I came here to do social work, not this. And you have mustard in your beard and that's disgusting."

He laughed and said, "It's probably snot." And tried to kiss me again.

I jerked my head away, but was starting to get worried. We'd gone quite a way from where the van let us off and I hadn't seen any of the other teams for at least ten minutes, even though we were supposed to keep in sight of each other. This guy was tall, the tallest of the skanky beards. I keep in shape with water aerobics, but even in a fair fight wasn't sure I could take him—and in this was a less than fair fight. He had me pinned against the concrete.

"C'mon, be nice. Just a quick blow job, 'kay?"

"No! Get your hands off me."

He shoved his knee between my legs. "I like girls who pretend they don't want it."

"I'm not pretending!" I tried to duck under his arms and wriggle out, but I didn't get away and he put his hand on the top of my head and was trying to push me down so that my face was… I didn't want to think about that. Instead I jerked and twisted any way I could in a desperate attempt to get free.

"What the hell, are you a dyke?" he taunted me.

"Yes!" I yelled as I tried to tear myself out of his grasp. But I only managed to turn so that I was facing the concrete barrier and to lose my glasses. I reached out and grasped one of the edges of the pillar and pulled, trying to get away from him.

"So you like in it the rear, huh?" he muttered evilly.

"Scott, what the hell is going on here?"

I was let go so suddenly that, like a rock in a slingshot, I slung into the older woman and ricocheted off her into Amanda. It was the older woman who had asked the question.

"Nothing, Marion, nothing. Just some horseplay," he answered.

"Nothing?" I sputtered. I was so outraged it was hard to speak. "He was just trying…just trying…to make me do something I didn't want to do."

"We were just handing out sandwiches. I thought you wanted to do that," he said, trying for a bland, innocent expression.

My outrage was so great that I didn't even notice at first that Amanda had kept her arm around my shoulder after catching me. That gave me the courage to speak. "We were just handing out sandwiches until you grabbed me without my permission, told me it was time to fool around, and demanded a blow job."

"In your dreams, kid. I can do far better than a flat-chested little thing like you. C'mon, Marion, you know me better than that."

"I know what I saw, Scott," she said tersely. "You go with Tom and Hank and finish handing out the sandwiches. I'll deal with this later."

He stalked off.

Amanda let go of me and retrieved my glasses. "Are you okay?" she asked as she handed them back to me.

Maybe a few bruises, but that didn't seem like much and I didn't want to whine in front of her, so I nodded.

We headed back to where the van was parked.

"He's an asshole," Amanda said over my head to Marion. "You need to let him go."

"You're probably right," she said. "I'll take it up with Joe."

I was silent for a moment, then said, "But what he did was wrong. Illegal. Shouldn't we—"

Marion cut me off, "Yes, but it's his word against yours. We saw five seconds of struggle, and a defense lawyer could easily argue that it was playing rough."

"She's right," Amanda said. "Consider it lucky that you're okay and that he'll lose his job."

They were older and wiser, and I had to admit they were probably right.

Amanda asked Marion for a ride back to the parking lot behind the social work school. She said it was because she didn't want to be stuck with a bunch of sweaty men, but I like to think it was because she knew I didn't want to get in the van with any of the skanky beards right now. I sat in the backseat and couldn't really be part of the conversation because Marion was listening to the radio pretty loud.

It was starting to get dark by the time we got back.

Amanda took one look at my bike and said, "Put that in my car. I'm giving you a ride home."

She had a nice car, had probably worked a real job before going to social work school. I took off my seat and both tires to fit it in her trunk. I didn't want to scratch the finish. She took a while to talk to Marion, lucky for me, so she wasn't waiting for me to pull my bike apart.

She and Marion had a long hug good-bye and then I was alone with Amanda in her car.

"Directions?" she asked.

"Directions where?"

"Your house?"

"Oh, right." I was glad of the dark so she couldn't see how embarrassed I was.

I lived fairly close, so didn't even have time for my blush to go away before we got to my place.

"You have a roommate?" Amanda asked as she turned off the car.

"Had. She lasted the first week of classes, then flaked out and went home. Her parents were nice enough to pay her rent for the rest of the semester. Guess they felt bad about her going crazy on me."

"Would it be okay if I came up and used your bathroom? It's been a while since the last pit stop."

I had cleaned up this morning, something I do every Saturday morning, a habit I was profoundly grateful for right now.

"Sure. Got new toilet paper and everything."

Amanda helped me get my bike out of her trunk, carrying my seat and front tire up the stairs for me.

I pointed her to the bathroom as I put my bike back together. I kind of liked that she had touched the seat that had touched my...

She came out of the bathroom. "Nice place you have here. Can I have some water? Or something to drink? I've been thirsty for the last hour but didn't dare drink anything since I already needed to pee."

I liked how direct and unpretentious she was.

She followed me to the kitchen area and peered over my shoulder as I opened the refrigerator. "You saving that beer for anything?" she asked, seeing a bottle in the door. It had been there for a while; the last girl I had dated had brought them over. Our one and only date. That had been several months ago.

"Nope, it's yours," I said as I handed it to her. Then remembered that I needed to find a bottle opener. "Uh, it might be old, it's been there for a while," I admitted while I rummaged in the junk drawer.

"You more a white wine type?" she asked.

I finally found the opener. She took it from me and opened her bottle. I hated to admit that I wasn't much of a drinking type, hadn't tried enough drinks to even know what I liked to drink. "Um, it depends, it varies with what's going on. As you can see, I don't have any white wine."

"Just old beer," she said, a slight smile playing on her lips as if she could see right through me. "You going to have anything?"

To prove I wasn't a total alcohol prude, I took the remaining beer for myself. I managed not to gag as I took my first swallow. It was either old or beer was not my drink.

Suddenly Amanda had a look of concern on her face. Maybe I wasn't as good a beer drinker as I thought I was.

She reached out and touched my cheek with her finger. "That looks like a bruise. I'm so sorry, I got distracted by my thirst and bathroom needs that I forgot you had a pretty rough outing today." She gently stroked my cheek.

I felt like I was on fire. "I'm okay," I managed to get out. I quickly took another swig of beer to hide what I was thinking. Except I wasn't even thinking, my brain was too much of a jumble to call it thinking, veering from "you have to stop now" to "don't ever stop."

"I know you're okay," Amanda said, "but that doesn't mean you didn't get a few bruises. Let me take a look. Pull off your shirt."

I must have looked like a dyke deer in headlights, because I didn't do anything for so long that Amanda put down her beer and grasped the hem of my sweatshirt. I only had time to set down my beer before she pulled it up and over my head. She put a hand on my shoulder and gently turned me around to look at my back.

I felt her finger on my shoulder blade. "One bruise here," she murmured. The finger trailed down to my bra strap. "One here." Then down my back to just at the waistband of my jeans. "Might be one here.

It's"—the finger hooked in my belt and tugged the jeans down—"hard to see for sure unless you take your pants off."

I hesitated. Goddess of all creatures great and small, did I want to take my pants off for her! Except that I was terrified to get any more naked than I already was. She was just being a good social worker and making sure I was okay, and I was wearing white panties and her finger at my waist was making it likely that the crotch area wasn't quite as white.

"Don't worry, I don't bite," she said. Then added close to my ear, "Unless I'm asked nicely."

She was standing very near me. I could feel her breath on my neck. I reminded myself not to read anything into it, remembering from class how different cultures viewed personal space differently.

"Are you cold?" she suddenly asked.

"Uh…no." I had no idea if I was hot or cold. Or both.

"Your nipples are very erect and huge. That's usually a sign of being cold. Or being…" She trailed off.

"I must be cold," I muttered. I had no clue if she was a lesbian or not, and I didn't want to be so gauche as to have erect nipples for a straight woman.

"It's my fault," she whispered in my ear.

I could smell her perfume overlaid with whiffs of peanut butter and grape jelly.

"I pulled your shirt off without ever considering how chilly it is," she continued.

"It's okay, I'm not really that cold," I stammered out.

"So why are your breasts so stiff?"

"I'm not really cold, but a little cold, between cold and chilly, more on the slightly chilly side than really cold. I'm sensitive to cold, well, a little chilly. At least certain parts of me, that is, I mean…" I ran out of things to say.

"So, I should pay no attention to your nipples?" She waited a moment for an answer, but I could come up with nothing. "And you're warm enough for me to go ahead and take your pants off, so we can check the rest of you for bruises?"

It didn't seem to really be a question as she didn't wait for an answer. Instead she reached around, undid my jeans, and started to pull them down. That galvanized me into action. I stumbled backward, my jeans around my knees tripping me up. Amanda grabbed me to keep me from falling.

"You must be a light drinker if two swigs of beers gets you this tipsy," she murmured to me.

"I'm not…I'm just not used to…I mean, two sips of beer…"

"Ah, I see, not used to getting naked this quickly." She laughed, then added in a more serious tone, "You have a girlfriend?"

"Girlfriend?"

"Someone you date on a regular basis?"

"Uh…no."

Amanda still had her arms around me. "You the kind who needs white wine and flowers?" Her hand moved down from my waist to the top of my underwear. "Tell me what you want," she whispered as she softly kissed my neck.

"For this not to be a dream," I blurted.

"Not a dream at all." She removed my glasses, then kissed me like I'd never been kissed before.

I know I like women, but more in spirit than in the flesh. I've slept with exactly two. Jessica was my first; we were Girl Scouts together and met up again one summer during college. First is stretching it because we never got much beyond a few shy kisses and a finger inside the panty boundaries. I couldn't even claim an orgasm from her. My second was Reba, in college, and she had an unfortunate overbite that made kissing her more like rock climbing. We got past just fingers, but that overbite made some things more risky than the benefit I was getting from the activity. My brain had been energetic, but my body, save for self-loving, not so much.

And now Amada was kissing me. She knew how to kiss, so much so that I worried if I was good enough for her. But she kept kissing me, her hands sliding up my back to unhook my bra. She didn't stop kissing me as she slid it off. Didn't stop kissing me as her hands covered my breasts, her fingers kneading my nipples.

Just as I was about to asphyxiate, she came up for air. "How about a shower? We both smell like peanut butter and homeless people."

We were in the bathroom. She was undressing. She was the most gorgeous woman I'd ever seen. No, I'd only seen two women; she was the most stunning woman I'd ever imagined. But I had to be honest, she'd find out soon enough. "Look, Amanda, I'm...well, I'm not...I haven't been with many..."

"It's okay. I like shy girls, girls who haven't done everything and are jaded and cynical." She softly kissed me. "Shush, don't worry. I'll guide you. As long as you want to be with me, it'll be okay."

"Be with you? There's nothing I want more."

We got in the shower and she kissed me under the streaming water, her hands roaming over my body, tweaking my nipples until I couldn't tell if it was pain or pleasure. But I didn't want her to stop.

"You've gone down on a woman, right?" she breathed into my ear.

"Yes," I breathed in return. Twice with Reba before I realized how dangerous her overbite was, so I couldn't risk that she would reciprocate.

Amanda's hands were on my shoulders, leading me down to my knees, and I willingly went. As promised, she guided me, telling me what she wanted, her hands keeping my head firmly in place. It was so wonderful, her breathing getting faster, her hips jerking, her wanting me to do this. She came so hard she knocked my head against the shower tile, but I didn't mind.

We ran out of hot water, so hastily toweled and went to my bedroom. She wasted no time; we were on my bed, she was on top of me and her hand was between my legs. Suddenly, her fingers were someplace fingers had never been before. I'd had fingers on my clit, but not this. It felt weird and it felt good. I must have grunted because she slowed down.

"Relax and spread your legs," she told me. "Anyone been inside you before?"

I hated to be so naïve and inexperienced. "It's, uh, been a while."

"A while?" A smile played on her face. She slowly pushed her fingers in, then did something inside me that sent shivers through me. "I'm not your first?"

"You are," I admitted. "Didn't want to seem..." She moved her fingers again, out and back into me, and part of me felt like I'd died and part of me felt like I'd gone to heaven.

"Good, I've always wanted to fuck a virgin." And then her thumb found my clit and I exploded. "And I'm going to fuck you like you've never been fucked before," she murmured as I thrashed under her.

When I finally stopped, I thought, now I'm a woman, now I know what sex is really about, it was about having Amanda's fingers in me, and using words like *fuck*, and her telling me how she was going to fuck me.

She had to leave, couldn't stay the night as she had somewhere she needed to be in the morning.

"We'll do this again, soon," she said as she kissed me good-bye.

But first we met again with her friends for coffee and she whispered "soon," in my ear as we hugged good-bye. I again helped hand out food to the homeless, and this time all teams that had women on them had three people.

I would do anything to be near Amanda. Even if we never had sex again, it would be enough just to see her and hear her.

Just when I was beginning to think that soon might turn into never, she caught me after class.

"You doing anything this evening?"

I had been planning to catch a water aerobics class, but quickly dismissed that and told her I had no plans.

"Want to come to my place?"

I wanted nothing more.

We barely got in her door when she kissed me hard, her tongue in my mouth. I just had time to get my glasses off. When she finally broke it off she said, "I've been thinking about this all day." She unzipped her pants and pushed down on my shoulder until I was kneeling in front of her. She shoved her jeans off, then cupped my head with her hands and pulled me into her. I licked and I sucked, trying to do everything and anything to please her.

Suddenly she said, "Get on the floor." She pushed me down on my back. "Ever done this before?" she asked as she lowered herself onto me. "It's called face sitting." She positioned my arms, then said, "Now, suck me right on my clit, not too hard."

It was tricky to breathe, but I so wanted to please her and did what she asked.

"Don't stop, baby, don't stop," she said as if she knew I was about to come up for air.

Then she came, gushing juices down my cheeks and onto my neck. My clothes are going to smell like her, I thought, and that made me happy. Amanda has soaked me good.

She finally rolled off me and looked at me with her lazy half smile.

"Strip," she ordered me. Once I was done, she said, "Now play with yourself, make your nipples hard."

I felt awkward having her watch me touch myself. But I did as I was told. I had a lot to learn, and Amanda was teaching me.

"Between your legs. Touch yourself there."

That was harder to do than my breasts. I had to close my eyes so I couldn't see her watching me.

"Make your clit hard," she whispered in my ear. Then I felt her mouth clamp over a nipple. She sucked it, finished with a nip that made me gasp, and said, "Get yourself really wet. I want to put three fingers in you this time."

I wasn't sure if I could have done that with just touching myself, but doing her had thoroughly soaked me.

"You are *so* not going to be a virgin when I'm done with you," Amanda told me. "Are you wet yet?" she asked as she licked a nipple. "Are you ready to be fucked?" She licked the other nipple.

"Yes! Yes!" I was aching for her to touch me.

"Keep playing with your clit. I want your hand down there while I'm fucking you."

Then her fingers were pushing inside me, pushing hard.

"Breathe out," she instructed. "Relax. Let me in."

Like I could relax with her touching me down there. I let her in; I kept my legs spread as wide as I could so she could do whatever she wanted to with me.

She was right, once I let go it started to feel good, real good. She buried her finger in me, her palm hard against my labia. "Make yourself come. I want to be deep inside you while you come."

Just her voice was enough. I bucked and screamed, obeying her.

She even let me spend the night, and we did it all again early in the morning before she had to leave.

I'm in love, I thought as I rode my bike home in the early morning fog.

Then it was another stretch of me sitting in the back with her friends at the coffee shop, handing out sandwiches to the homeless. I had to settle for her hand brushing mine as she passed out the peanut butter jars.

She did pull me aside briefly when the skanky beard guys were loading the tables into the van and say, "I hate this, but we should be discreet and act like nothing is going on while we're out here. Homeless work isn't always as cool about lesbianism as other areas of social work."

She was right, of course. So I acted like she was just another classmate of mine from school and nothing more. I had to not even look at her if I could help it because when I did look at her it was hard not to remember her smiling at me while she lay on top or how glorious she looked naked. I had to hide my love and desire for her. If it was what she wanted, I would do it.

It was almost two weeks of waiting and not being able to look at her before she made a point of catching up with me after class.

"Walk me to my car," she asked. She ambled slowly, letting the others leave.

When we got to her car, she said, "Megan, I need you to do me a really big favor." My eyes must have said yes, because she didn't wait for me to reply. "I need you to take something to where we usually park the van."

"On my bike?" I asked.

"Yeah, it's not that heavy. It's something the homeless population needs." I must not have hidden my worry quickly enough because she added, "It'll be safe, the cops just did a big sweep there and they're still out."

She removed a small blue duffel bag from her trunk.

"Go to right below the overpass and ask for Smiley. Give him this and tell him it's the usual deal. He'll know what it's for."

I nodded agreement. This was for social work and Amanda.

She hastily scanned the parking lot, but no one was near us. She quickly kissed me. "Don't go home, come to my place when you're done," she whispered.

I twined the straps of the duffel around my bike handlebars, balanced it, and then pedaled off into the afternoon.

Amanda was right about the police. I passed three cars on my way there. One cop even asked me what I was doing and I had to show him my social work school ID and let him know I was doing outreach to the homeless. He shook his head and told me it was dangerous out there. I was polite and didn't point out that social workers went places the police were afraid to go.

Finding Smiley was easy. He looked surprised to see me with the duffel bag, but quickly took it from me.

"Amanda says it's the usual deal," I remembered to say to him.

He muttered, "Yeah, right. See ya in the funny papers," and left immediately, getting into one of those big noisy cars.

Social workers came in all varieties.

I hurriedly biked to Amanda's place, desperately wanting to see her. I could almost taste her and feel her as I pumped my legs. Stop thinking these things, Megan, I had to admonish myself as I flew through a stop sign. It's not safe and you're going to ruin your nice leather bicycle seat.

When I got to Amanda's apartment, the door opened as if she was watching for me.

"Any problems?" she asked, pulling me inside and quickly kissing me before giving me a chance to answer.

"Nope, not a one. You were right about the police. There were a bunch of them out."

"Did any of them see you give the stuff to Smiley?"

"I don't think so. Not that I noticed. And he left pretty quickly. Does it matter? We weren't doing anything wrong."

"Of course not, but you know cops. They think homeless people are scum and sometimes they cause problems just because they can."

"Well, they didn't cause any problems this time," I assured her.

"Good. You're such a smart kid." And she kissed me again. "Hey, shower for you, you smell like you biked all over town."

She lovingly shoved me in the direction of the shower. "You're not joining me?" I asked when she didn't follow.

"I just showered earlier. And I've got to make some quick phone calls. Once you're done, I'll be ready and waiting for you." She gave me one of her radiant smiles, and my heart fluttered.

I tried to hurry though the shower, but wanted to make sure I was clean for Amanda, so scrubbed a couple of times between my legs.

Amanda was just getting off the phone when I came out of the shower.

She pulled the towel off me, then kissed me hard, her tongue filling my mouth and her hands roving over my body, rolling my nipples between her fingers, then brushing her palm against my thighs.

She pulled away, then grabbed one of my nipples with her fingers and used that to lead me to the bedroom. She pushed me down on the bed; I fell easily as I was too intoxicated with her to stand upright.

"Have you ever used one of these?" she asked as she threw something long and purple on the bed beside me. "Of course not," she answered her own question. "You were a virgin when you met me." She smiled at me.

"What is it?" I asked. It was some kind of deep purple rubber and it looked like—I looked closer—it looked like a man's thing.

"A dildo, a strap-on, a dyke dick."

"But why would you want to do that?" I asked, puzzled. "I like your fingers just fine."

"Because when I have this on, it rubs against my clit while I'm fucking you, so we both feel good." She was taking off her clothes and I watched, mesmerized. She was so beautiful. She looked right at me, her green eyes sparkling. "Hey, kiddo, I'm blowing your world, aren't I?"

"No. No, of course not. It's just that…just that…I'm new to…"

She was naked. As she slid in bed beside me she said, "We can go slow. Or even just do what we've been doing. I want to make this good for you." Her fingers gently circled my nipples. "Or we could try it. I'll have to make sure you're really hot and ready." Her mouth followed her fingers.

I didn't even answer; what she was doing was too distracting for me to form words. She even kissed me between the legs, a long soulful kiss that got me close to coming.

"Not yet, baby," she murmured when she stopped kissing me, "not until I'm inside you."

Yes, of course she could be inside me, Amanda could do anything she wanted to me. I didn't even need to say it; she could so easily see it on my face.

Then she was on top of me and something was entering me. It was big and compared to her warmth, cold. I felt stretched tight, but I could see in her face that she was enjoying herself.

She pushed deep into me, then said, "Your clit needs some attention, doesn't it? I'm being a selfish pig and enjoying how hot it feels to be this far in you and forgetting some important things." Her fingers slid down my side and she pulled out enough for her hand to get between us. Then she was kissing me and her fingers were rubbing right where it felt good.

I had to trust Amanda, know that she would take care of me, and I had to give her as much of myself as I could. I was quickly bucking and thrashing under her, breaking our kiss because I couldn't hold it.

"Come for me, c'mon, baby, come for me," she crooned in my ear and I exploded.

"I love when you come, you make me so hot, I need it now," and she was pushing in and out of me hard. It felt good and a little bit painful, but even if I wanted to protest, I was too spent from her making love to me to get a single word out. She grabbed my hands and held me down as she reared back and into me. Amanda was inside me and she was coming and I knew right then I would do anything to have her on top of me and taking her pleasure from me.

She finally pulled out and rolled off me. "You're amazing," she said. "Wow, there's a little bit of blood. You really are a virgin."

"It's okay," I brushed it off. "And I'm not one anymore."

She wrapped her arms around me and said, "You have to let me know if I ever hurt you, okay? Sometimes we can take more when we're in the midst of sex then at other times."

"I'm okay," I reassured her. "I liked it. I liked it a lot." There was nothing Amanda could ever do to hurt me.

She let me spend the night, neither of us had classes until the afternoon.

Next week Amanda let me deliver another bag for her. I was happy to help her in her important work. And again, after the delivery, she let me come home with her. That was the best part. She was such a goddess, at times I wondered what she saw in me. But clearly she liked what she saw as she kept inviting me back.

The next time I delivered the bag, Smiley told me that things had changed, that it would have to be half the usual as there were some difficulties. That didn't sound good, so I wasn't sure what he meant, but I delivered his message to Amanda.

"Half the—what the fuck?" was her response. "That slime ball. That fucking slime ball."

"What's the matter? Is there anything I can do?"

She gave me a quick smile. "No, just the usual social work hassles. You go shower and let me make some phone calls. I'm going to need some stress reduction in a few minutes."

I came out of the shower in time to hear the tail end of her conversation. "Yes, I know." A pause. "I know." Another pause. "I don't know, I'll think of something." A pause. "I understand. I'll take care of it." As she put the phone down she looked at me. "How much of that did you hear?"

"Not much. I just got out." I ruffled my hair to indicate how wet it still was.

"Okay, good." Then she added, "I don't want to worry you, you've been so good to me." She playfully ran her fingers through my hair. "Dripping wet, little girl." She grabbed me by the hips and pulled me to her. "Time to get some other things wet as well."

Then it was a flurry of her hands, kissing me, fondling me, a pinch, a lick. We finally slowed enough to make it to the bedroom.

"I really need to fuck you and fuck you hard. Is that okay?" Amanda asked.

"I like you fucking me," I told her, enjoying how easily I said the word.

She quickly fastened the harness, then looked at me and said, "Let's do something different. Turn over."

I rolled over onto my stomach. She knelt between my legs, then pulled me by the waist until I was on my knees. "We're going to do it from behind," she whispered in my ear. She grabbed a pillow and stuffed it under my stomach.

Her hands seized my thighs, then a rough massage up to my hips and butt cheeks.

"Ever been fucked in the ass?" she asked. I started to say no, but I was face-down and it came out as a muffled groan. However, she answered, "Of course not, you weren't even fucked in the cunt when I met you." I felt the cool rubber against my thigh, and she grabbed my ass cheeks and spread them open. "You've got a beautiful, tight little butthole. Someone should plow it for you."

"I don't think…" But she placed a hand on my back and using her weight, pushed me down.

"I like fucking virgins," she said in a low whisper.

Then she took her big dick and shoved it in me.

In my cunt.

I screamed, partly pleasure, mostly relief.

With the rhythm of her pumping she said, "It feels good because you were scared. Heightened emotions—done the right way—can make sex really good. I wouldn't shove a big cock in your ass." She buried herself in my cunt and wrapped her arms around me, cupping my breasts, and said in a seductive low voice, "That has to be done right, slowly. A small butt plug to open you up, working up to bigger ones until you're ready to be fucked. You're going to let me do that to you some day, aren't you?"

"Yes," I mumbled against the sheets.

"What? I can't hear you," she crooned in my ear.

"Yes! Yes! I love you so much you can do anything you want to me."

"Megan, you know I won't hurt you, maybe push your good-girl limits a bit, but I'll never hurt you," she said as her hand moved from my breast to between my legs and she took me to heaven. She even made me come again without stopping.

The next morning while pedaling to school, I was happier than I'd ever been. A few weeks ago, I had been a shy, nerdy girl, stuck with being smart because I couldn't be anything else. Now I was a ripe, sexually adventurous woman, one who could do things like get fucked in the cunt and even contemplate being fucked in the ass. I had the best girlfriend in the world.

We saw each other only in class for the rest of the week. She had asked me to be discreet and I obeyed. She didn't even go out to coffee with her friends, so I couldn't sit in a corner and steal glances at her when she said something funny or smart.

This will be over soon. Once she finishes her internship with the homeless she can move on to something that's more accepting and we wouldn't have to hide our love, I reminded myself on a lonely Friday night. I was home by myself, eating popcorn and watching something stupid on TV.

Just as I was getting ready to go to bed at around midnight, the phone rang. Expecting a wrong number I picked it up, but Amanda's voice greeted me.

"Megan, I really need your help."

"Where are you? What's wrong?" I asked.

"I don't have time to explain. Can you meet me in the school parking lot in fifteen minutes?"

"But what's going on?"

"Please, just trust me on this. I'll explain once this is over."

She hung up and I hurriedly dressed and sped to the social work school. It didn't feel right being out this late riding my bike. It's Amanda, I reminded myself. She needs me.

I got there in fourteen minutes.

She was already waiting for me.

"I told Smiley to meet us here," she said. "Park your bike over there so it's hidden."

I did as she instructed. When I returned to her, she opened the trunk of the car and took out one of the usual small duffels. And then she took out a gun.

"What do we need that for?" I asked. It seemed so out of place.

"Smiley isn't thinking, asking us to meet him at this hour," Amanda explained. "So we need something to scare people off. I just need you to hold this while I talk to him, then we'll go back to my place." She smiled at me.

I would do anything to go back to her place with her. I could already feel the pulse between my legs.

"I need you to hold this," she said as she handed me the gun. "Keep it hidden. I'll talk to Smiley. Only show the gun if I tell you to, okay?"

"Yes, of course," I replied, thinking it was a good thing that it was a little chilly and I was wearing a jacket. Amanda was cold enough to be wearing gloves. First checking to make sure the safety was on, I tucked it in the waistband of my pants. I'd been brought up with guns, being the youngest and only girl with four brothers and a father who liked nothing more than hunting.

Smiley's noisy car drowned out any further conversation. He really needed to have that muffler looked at. He pulled up right in front of us and got out.

"You wanted to talk?" he demanded of Amanda.

"Half the usual isn't good enough. And taking an extra month to get it to us isn't good either. We had a deal. You need to stick to your end of the bargain," she replied.

"I got other people breathing down my neck and they get taken care of first. Besides, what are you and your carpet muncher going to do about it? Now give me the bag and maybe I won't make you wait two months."

"If you don't keep your end of the bargain, I'm not going to keep mine," Amanda told him.

I wanted to say, "But what about the homeless people? They need this," but Amanda knew what she was doing so I needed to follow her lead.

Smiley spat on the ground. "Fuck this. I got better places to be." He took an envelope out of his jacket and threw it at her. "One quarter now, and if you behave I'll give you the rest next month. Now give me the bag."

"No. All or no deal."

He spat again, then muttered, "You bitch. You'll regret being this hard to deal with." He spun on his heel.

"Now, Megan!" I guess I didn't move fast enough because she said, "He's going for his gun!"

I pulled the pistol out and pointed it at him, just remembering to flick off the safety in case he did pull a gun.

Suddenly Amanda wrapped her hands around mine, taking control of the gun. Her finger covered mine on the trigger. The gun exploded and Smiley spun around, a look of surprise on his face.

"Damn, I was gonna pay you—" But the rest of his words were drowned out with three more shots.

He slumped over the hood of his car, then rolled down slapping against the pavement.

"You have to get out of here," Amanda told me. "I need you to be safe." She grabbed the blue duffel and stuffed the gun and the envelope that Smiley gave her and shoved it at me.

"We need to call the police," I said.

"I will. I'll take care of everything. I don't want you here. Take this," she pushed the bag into my arms, "and pedal away from here as fast as you can. You know I'll never hurt you. I'm trying to protect you. I need you to trust me on this. Please? We'll meet tomorrow. We'll spend the whole weekend together."

I nodded. Smiley made a weird farting sound. I had to trust Amanda.

I did as she told me, slung the bag over my shoulder and ran to my bike. As I pedaled away I saw that she was opening the trunk of Smiley's car. Probably looking for a first aid kit.

But I didn't dare look back after that. It was dark and these roads weren't well paved. I couldn't risk a bike wreck and disobeying Amanda.

After a few blocks I heard sirens. She had called an ambulance.

I made another block and saw a police car blazing by, its lights flashing a blinding blue.

It flashed away, only to be replaced by another strobing blue and red coming from behind me. That car passed me only to suddenly stop right in front of me, making me brake so quickly, I went down.

I started to untangle myself from the bike, but two police officers were pointing guns at me and telling me not to move.

I've never been in a situation like this before. I started to hyperventilate, then forced myself to think that Amanda would explain everything. I might have to endure a few hours in custody, but she'd come rescue me.

They roughly handcuffed me and shoved me into the backseat of their patrol car. I didn't even have time to ask them to lock my bike up.

It was hours before anyone really talked to me. I was left in a small, windowless room, still handcuffed. I was left for so long I finally had to bang on the door and ask for a bathroom break. Two deputies led me to the bathroom, the woman following me in. There were no doors and she watched me the entire time. I have a shy bladder and it was hard to go even though I really needed to.

Then they led me back and left me in the room again.

There must be some mistake, I thought. Amanda must have told the police what happened by now. Someone must know that I'm innocent, but somehow the message hadn't gotten here yet. I kept hoping that any minute the door would open and she could come in, demand they take the handcuffs off me and let me go.

But when the door finally opened, it was an older man and younger woman, both in regular clothes, but with badges.

"So, do you want to confess?" the older man said.

"Confess? To what? There has to be some mistake."

The woman spoke. "I'm Detective Bennett and he's Detective Halpern. We have some questions we need to ask you, but first let me read you your rights." Then she did that, just like they do on TV.

Once she finished the older man again said, "We have plenty of evidence against you, you might as well confess."

"What are you talking about?"

"The murder of Robinson 'Smiley' Jenkins," the woman said. She seemed much nicer than he was. "Someone fitting your description was at the scene. You were stopped with a duffel containing a pistol that's been recently fired, several hundred OxyContin, and about five thousand in cash."

"What? But that's not…that's not what happened. You need to talk to Amanda Waterfield. She was there with me."

"Yeah, right," the older man growled. "She was the one who called it in and said to be on the lookout for a young woman with glasses on a bike."

I suddenly felt cold and hot, like I was burning and freezing. "No! You're lying. Amanda is my girlfriend and she wouldn't do that to me!"

They exchanged a look.

The woman said gently, "Amanda Waterfield and her partner Marion Caldwell claimed that they've been together all night. They're social workers and were with an outreach to the homeless group, when Amanda saw you shoot Smiley Jenkins grab the bag, and then ride away."

"We know you murdered him. The only thing we don't know is what happened to the rest of the money. He had a couple of hundred thousand in the trunk of his car and it's not there now. What'd you do with it?"

I couldn't answer; I couldn't think. I was so cold and hot, I had to be sick, this had to be a dream.

No, a nightmare. In my head I could hear Amanda laughing at me, but that couldn't be true. She was my girlfriend. She said she'd never hurt me. We'd made love. She'd put her hand inside me, fucked me. Fucked me like I'd never been fucked before.

But the walls were cold and the light was harsh and I couldn't make myself wake up.

❖

Sally Ann looked up at the stunning woman walking into her school of public health class. She was the most beautiful woman Sally Ann had ever seen. She walked toward Sally, flashed her a big smile that revealed dazzling dimples, and took the seat right in front.

"Hi, I'm Amanda, and I'll need you to watch my back for the whole semester."

DEVIL IN TRAINING
ALI VALI

R emember you've got a big day tomorrow," Dalton Casey said to his daughter Derby Cain Casey as she put her leather jacket on.

Cain had finished her final exams at Tulane the week before and was planning a night of fun before her graduation the next day. The last four years had been enjoyable after the pointing and staring had calmed down whenever a professor checked names on the first day of class. Her last name and resemblance to her father were usually good for a long round of whispering and made her laugh because of people's fascination with organized crime.

The fact her father was the head of one of the most powerful crime families, not only in New Orleans but in the South, was probably why her social life had been so active. It was either that or the rumors she was next in line for the throne, as she liked to tease, but whatever it was, she had one more night to enjoy this part of her life. Once she collected her business diploma in the morning with the entire Casey clan watching, she'd get her own crew as her father's graduation gift. Since high school she'd worked with Dalton's most trusted man outside the family, Walt Kennedy, making deliveries and other tasks no one ever spoke of again. From her first day Walt hadn't treated her like Dalton's kid and had expected her to follow orders like the rest of his guys.

Every Casey started at the bottom, not only to toughen them up and make them learn their business, but to teach them every potential weak spot in the system. Working for Walt taught her the business, but sitting with her Da every night was where she got her true education.

"I promise to do you proud, Da, and not fall on my face before they hand me my diploma." She slipped Dalton's other gift into front pocket of her coat as he looked on. The switchblade was the only weapon she ever carried.

"You do that, and I won't be able to keep your mum from getting on that stage and picking you up by your ear and smacking you in the head," he said, laughing. "Billy's not going with you?"

"He said he'd meet up with me when he's done with Walt and the guys," she said, referring to her younger brother, who'd taken her place on Walt's crew.

"How about Lou?"

"Don't worry, it's only a few drinks with some of my classmates."

"Listen to your Da," said her mother, Therese. "You go out and something happens to you, and I'll put you over my knee as soon as I know you're okay."

Cain laughed at her parents' protective nature, but she wasn't about to argue. The world was a dangerous place for everyone, but in her position, going out unprotected wasn't a way to prove she was ready for more responsibility.

"You two ready?" she asked Lou Romano and Merrick Runyon. Lou she'd known all her life, and Merrick had been with Dalton for two years. They were unquestionably loyal, equally vicious when needed, and her first recruits.

"Let's enjoy tonight, because Mr. Dalton said the bikes are being retired after this," Lou said. "Your promotion means sedans from now on."

"I guess getting what you want doesn't mean getting *everything* you want."

"Beats the hell out of any entry-level position your friends will be starting next week," Merrick said, making her and Lou laugh before the Harleys drowned her out.

❖

Their first stop was a bar Cain felt better suited for her parents, but her classmates had wanted to meet somewhere quiet so they could plan out their night. There were enough people engaged in conversations in the Royal Orleans Oak Bar to cause a din, but it was still subdued compared to some of their neighbors on Bourbon Street.

"You guys want to get a head start on trying to act grown up," Cain said when she saw the five martini glasses, each still containing an olive. "Make sure you get that first paycheck before you start pickling your livers."

"You should be thrilled, considering I hear your family's business revolves around liquor, so don't make fun of us," the newest male member to their group said, not to Cain's amusement. "You won't have to schlep from place to place trying to find something that'll at least pay the rent."

"I'm sure Cain will have other concerns once she starts working for her father," Nicolette Blanc said, changing Cain's mind about leaving right away. She was the only exchange student Cain had befriended and the main reason she'd agreed to join the little celebration that night.

The story Nicolette told the day she'd approached her after a math class their sophomore year was that she was from the northern wine region of France. Her directness had instantly made Cain wary. The unknown, especially in people, was something Dalton liked to preach about.

When Nicolette started talking about her family's wine business and how perhaps they could work together, Cain's defenses solidified. This was a potential ploy by the FBI to topple her family through what they saw as the weakest but closest link to Dalton. Cain knew all that, but when the fire was this beautiful, it was hard not to play.

"Would you care for another one?" Cain asked, taking the seat next to Nicolette. They'd flirted for years, but she'd never given in where Nicolette was concerned.

"I'd love another." Nicolette used her answer as an excuse to put her hand on the side of Cain's neck. "This might be the last treat you can give me," she said, her English flawless, but still tinged with a French accent.

"When do you head back?" The bartender nodded when Cain held up Nicolette's glass.

"After graduation my parents and I'll be on holiday here for two weeks, but after that we go home to our grapes." Nicolette rubbed Cain's neck gently a few times before removing her hand. "Will you miss me?"

"I'm sure the vineyard has a phone." Cain took a sip of the beer once the server opened it for her. "We'll keep in touch, and if I get some time off, France might be a good vacation spot."

"Paris is on everyone's wish list when looking for romance, but the north is as enticing, I think." Nicolette never lost eye contact with Cain as she lifted her fresh drink, running her tongue along her bottom lip after her sip in a way that made Cain fantasize about how it would feel on any part of her. "Do you consider yourself a romantic, Cain?"

"If you're talking about flowers and chocolates—no, I'm not."

The way Nicolette had turned in her seat gave them a little privacy, and the rest of their group left them to their talk for now. If Cain wanted safe, she'd end it there and concentrate her efforts on Lydia, the other female with them, since she knew exactly who she was and everything about her, including what it took to make her come so hard she'd do anything in return.

Tonight, though, wasn't about safe. Cain never ignored any of her father's advice, but she wanted to learn something on her own. If Nicolette, who from their first meeting had known everything about her as if she'd done extensive research, really was a trap, just how far was she willing to go to snare her? It'd be a good gauge for the future if the FBI thought all that was needed to cloud her judgment was a beautiful woman. The lesson she was most interested in now was if young eager agents did everything necessary to get the job done, or did they fuck for Uncle Sam if the prize was worthy enough of winning.

"Flowers you buy your mother, and chocolates you get for children," Nicolette said before draining her second drink. "Come with me and I'll explain my definition of romance."

Cain watched her climb the half flight of steps to the lobby before standing and motioning for Lou and Merrick to stay put. She followed Nicolette to the restrooms located past the empty ballrooms, and leaned against the wall when Nicolette locked the door behind her.

"We are young," Nicolette said, standing in front of her but not touching her. "For us romance isn't defined by such clichéd things, but simply by passion." The word *passion* sounded incredibly sexy with Nicolette's accent. "But perhaps you feel no passion when you look at me."

"Never underestimate what you make me feel whenever I see you," Cain said, not moving.

"Ah," Nicolette smiled, "you are waiting for me to make the first move. Interesting."

"Actually, I'm waiting to hear how you know so much about me." Cain followed the path of Nicolette's hand with her eyes but didn't stop her from untucking the front of her shirt. The feel of Nicolette's nails right above her navel made her abdominal muscles contract, and she momentarily lost concentration when Nicolette bent over and circled the same area with her tongue.

"My father told me after I said we'd met. You might not believe me, but we have much in common, as do our families."

Nicolette used only her index finger next to trace along the skin above her belt, but this time Cain locked eyes with her and placed her hand at the base of Nicolette's neck. "Was he doing a class project on immigrant Irish families?"

"Cain, you have nothing to fear from me or my father," Nicolette said, not appearing scared when Cain squeezed her neck enough that she stopped moving. "Our wine is very good, but quality costs money."

"Anything worth having usually does."

"Then you must know we, too, have figured out how to cut out the things that unfairly eat into our profits. I believe you know because it's the reason so many watch your family like the French authorities watch mine."

Cain had to give Nicolette credit in staying calm when she increased the pressure to what she knew was slightly painful. "This is an interesting seduction, and I don't think I got that part wrong."

"You wanted to know something, and I'm telling you."

"True, but why now? You've got two weeks in the States, and you pick now to bring this up? What exactly do you want?"

Nicolette laughed and flattened her hand on her abdomen. "Perhaps you aren't very experienced at this if you have to ask what *I'm* after."

"There's a difference between fucking and fucking around, so don't act cute," Cain said, letting go and moving away to tuck her shirt back in.

"My father wants to meet yours and discuss a deal that can be lucrative to both of them. It's why he's staying in the city after graduation." Nicolette pushed her hair behind her shoulders and took a deep breath. "That's his interests. Mine, though, are to stop our games and do something about the teasing we've done for too long. I have a great need to experience all I can before I go home, and you I desire."

"I'm Dalton Casey's daughter, not his secretary. If your father wants to talk to him, tell him to call his office." She unlocked the door and pulled it open. "We'll see about the rest."

Merrick and Lou were waiting close by and didn't say anything as she walked back to the bar. The others had settled their tabs and were ready to move on to some place with a little more action.

"I have to eat something first," Lydia said, accepting Cain's help with her coat. "If not, y'all will have to carry me home."

"Cain should treat since you got the best job," one of the guys said, making even Cain laugh.

To walk off their drinks, they followed Cain to Mr. B's restaurant after she promised to pick up the tab. When the hostess seated them, Nicolette sat at the other end of the table directly across from Cain. Their game hadn't ended, but Cain figured Nicolette was making her work for it instead of simply giving in. It was true that elusive things were more enticing when it came to the hunt, but in this chase she wasn't entirely sure who Nicolette considered the prey.

Their meal lasted close to three hours, and Cain enjoyed talking to her friends as they shared their future plans. None of them had such a detailed map of where they were headed as she did, but then the most peril the rest of them would be in was cheating a little on their taxes. Eventually taking control of her family's business brought dangers not only from those trying to lock them up forever, but from those who wanted to destroy them as a way to gain more power on the streets. She was ready for whatever came next and being Dalton's successor, she'd worked as hard to make him proud as she had for her diploma.

"Here's to everyone's success." Lydia raised her glass and made the toast after the waiter evenly portioned out the last of the wine.

"And happiness," Nicolette added, looking directly at Cain.

Cain acknowledged the comment with a slight nod and lifted her glass in Nicolette's direction before draining it. Nicolette smiled at her, then totally ignored her as their desserts arrived. As Cain slowly ate her bread pudding she felt like laughing, since now the parameters of the game were clear. She was the hunted, and Nicolette's strategy was to pull the trigger when she least expected it.

❖

The band playing at the Tropical Isle a half block off Bourbon was entertaining enough to keep them in there after leaving the restaurant. Cain had switched to water after the first drink, ignoring the teasing from the guys for being such a lightweight. In reality she could most probably outdrink them, but she never thought it was a talent to brag about, and she rarely lost control in such an open location.

Nicolette finally touched her again when the string of lively beach type songs gave way to "Red Red Wine." "Dance with me," Nicolette said, her accent more pronounced with the amount of alcohol she'd consumed.

"How about one dance, then I take you home?"

The makeshift dance floor was really an empty space between the high-topped tables and bar stools, but Nicolette didn't seem to mind as Cain stood and put her hands on Nicolette's hips. It was an invitation for Nicolette to get close enough to her that it appeared they were sharing her coat.

"If you want to take me home because you can't resist me one minute longer then we'll leave, but don't offer because you think I'm drunk."

"You're not?" Cain asked, leaning back to get a better look at Nicolette's glassy eyes.

"I told you what our family business is," Nicolette said, pouting. "It's not as potent as Jameson, but liquor is a family tradition for us, too."

"You make us both sound like such lushes." Cain kept her voice steady even though Nicolette had untucked her shirt in the back this time and was doing her best to get her hands into her pants.

"Saying what is true isn't an insult." Nicolette smiled up at her. "So if you're only playing with me, don't be afraid to say it. I'm interested but not desperate."

When Nicolette turned and left, the front of Cain's body felt cold, stunning her in place. She hadn't expected her teasing to push Nicolette into bolting, and she took off when she lost sight of her.

The crowd walking slowly down Bourbon was thicker than usual with all the family members in town for the various graduations taking place, but Cain was able to get a clear view in both directions. Nicolette was quick, but if she'd come this way she'd still be in sight, especially if she was trying to get around the sightseers.

"Cain," Merrick said when she turned and headed the opposite way.

"It's okay," she said, heading quickly down the street toward Jackson Square. "I've got an apology to give."

Lou and Merrick were right behind her, their footsteps easier to hear as the crowds of people thinned. It was the quiet of the area that allowed her to hear the beginning of a scream that quickly died away as if the person had been either hit or gagged. The sound stopped her and she put her hand up for Lou and Merrick to stay behind her.

Nicolette's rashness had landed her against a brick wall in an alley with more trash cans than working lights next to the doors that lined its length. It was obvious she'd been the one who'd screamed, and the knife the man was holding against her throat was as effective as a gag. Since Nicolette wasn't carrying anything and had left without her coat, Cain figured the scumbag was after something other than robbery. If that was true then she'd given him his wish, only her version of something else would leave a lasting impression.

"Get out of here if you don't want to get hurt."

Cain's first impression of the man when he grabbed Nicolette by the throat, pinning her in place so he could face her, was how big he was. He topped her six feet by a good four or five inches, but despite the knife he now pointed at her, she kept walking toward him. With only about five feet between them, she quickly noticed his expensive clothes and slicked-back hair, which made her think he was a man who enjoyed the image he found in any mirror.

"This is between me and her," the guy said, his words coming out slightly slurred.

"That's my date you're mistreating, so I'm going to disagree with you on everything you've said so far. This is actually between me and you, and if you don't get your hands off her it's you who's asking to get hurt."

"You work as a comedian around here?" He moved Nicolette so she was pressed against the front of his body. "If not you should, since you're such a riot."

"Let her go and I'll show you what a good time I can be." She spread her arms out and smiled.

Nicolette stood on her toes when he tightened his grip on her throat to lift her. Even in the low lighting Cain could see Nicolette's look of disgust when he licked from her chin to her ear before laughing at what Cain assumed was Nicolette's squirming. Nicolette stopped moving when his blade followed the same wet path in reverse, slicing into her skin from the middle of her cheek to her chin.

Cain was amazed Nicolette only whimpered, and she moved closer, not lowering her arms to keep all his attention on her. "You telling me a big guy like you can't get a date without that pretty knife?" she asked, ignoring for now the blood that dripped from Nicolette's face to the front of her black minidress, leaving what resembled dark maroon pearls above her breasts.

"Maybe I'm doing the Lord's work and teaching this whore His word."

"I can see you're a regular messiah," she said, locking eyes with Nicolette for a moment.

"Then get lost and leave us alone."

"You're here to preach, but I'm here for other reasons, so no can do, Reverend." She lowered her arms slowly, not wanting to startle the idiot into hurting Nicolette again.

"Let me guess, sinning is your specialty and you need to hear the message as well? Then stick around, because there's enough here for both of you."

"It's true I come from a long line of sinners, but it's not my specialty."

He moved his hand away from Nicolette so he could point the knife at Cain again. When he did, he also relaxed his hold around Nicolette's neck so that she was able to flatten her feet to the ground. It was enough of an opening for Cain to make her move.

She moved quickly to grab the hand he was holding the knife in, surprising him into widening his eyes and letting Nicolette go. Since she held his weapon hand with both of hers, he was able to land two hard punches to the side of her head. The idiot had made her ears ring but she wasn't about to let go and give him an opportunity to bury his blade anywhere in her. He was pulling hard to break her grip as he lifted his fist again, so Cain turned to press her back into him, using the strength in her legs to drive him and off balance.

When they fell together she heard Lou and Merrick run forward, but they didn't intervene. Any advantage he'd had because of his size had momentarily disappeared when his head hit the pavement with enough force to make his fingers relax so his knife fell next to them. The guy tried to recover and push her off to pick it up, but Cain reached it first.

"Stop trying to act like you can scare me. You don't have the guts," the guy said, laughing.

Cain was sure the hotshot carried the blade to intimidate women like Nicolette, but pointing something lethal at someone meant you'd reached the point where you were prepared to use it—at least in her world. His scream was louder than Nicolette's and his movements became frantic when she buried his knife in his hip to the hilt.

Before he could pull it out she twisted it, making him scream again. This seemed to drain the fight out of him, so she pulled the knife out and threw it toward Lou's feet. The guy stayed on his back, his eyes on the switchblade now open in her hand.

"You never did ask what my specialty is, Reverend," she said, placing the tip of her blade in the cleft in his chin. "Well?"

He tried to draw his head back, but only widened the cut on his face when she didn't let up. "What is it?"

"Crucifixion when the situation calls for it." She smiled as she said it and moved quickly away from him when she spotted his fist in her peripheral vision.

"You're lucky, but dead," he said as he came to a sitting position, wincing in obvious pain as he pressed his hand to his hip. The threat was laughable since he moved at a geriatric pace getting to his knees.

"What was it you said about comedians, Reverend?" The kick she delivered to the underside of his jaw sent him sideways into a pile of garbage bags. "The next time you think about taking something from a woman who isn't offering, I want you to think about the right side of your face," she told him as she brought him back to a sitting position, pulling him up by his hair.

"What do you mean?"

Like he had with Nicolette, Cain rested her knife right under his ear. "If I find out you ever try this again, I'll give you a matching scar on the left side." She drew her hand down, retracing what he'd done with his tongue.

He fell forward when she let his head go, holding his face as if he'd forgotten about the pain in his hip. In that position it was easy for Cain to take his wallet out of his back pocket. She laughed when she saw the family photo of this idiot with his wife and four children standing around him as he smiled and held a Bible against his chest. His hair was parted down the middle without the gel he'd slicked it back with that night, making him appear quite different.

"You really are a reverend, aren't you?" she asked, staring at the card in his walled that identified him as Reverend Jerome P. Smith of the Holy Briar of Christ Church, located in some northern town she'd never heard of.

"Please, I need help." His face was still down but Cain could tell he was crying.

"If you're talking about psychiatric help, I won't argue with you, but there's one thing before we get all those cuts taken care of."

"You're letting him go?" Nicolette asked in a way that made Cain think no wasn't the answer she was expecting.

"Not yet." Cain pushed Jerome over, and he didn't move when Lou pressed his gun to his forehead. "Merrick, find Jerome's phone for me, please."

"What for?" Jerome sounded more panicked than when she'd cut him.

"To see how bright you are." It was an older model, but Cain didn't have a problem scrolling through the list of contacts. "Home." She held it so he could see the screen. "Not smart at all for a womanizer like you, Jerome."

"You leave my family out of this."

"Or?" Cain asked, cocking her head slightly, interested in his answer.

"I'll pay you…whatever you want." Jerome seemed to tack on the incentive when she didn't jump at his first offer.

"This won't cost you much." A little boy answered the phone and screamed for his mother when she asked for Mrs. Smith, and the woman who came on didn't say much as Cain explained the situation.

"Do you think this girl will press charges, too?"

It wasn't often Cain was surprised, but the woman's question threw her. "It depends," she said, staring at Jerome. "This time the police didn't find him, I did." She ended the call and dropped Jerome's phone into her pocket along with his wallet. "You've done this before?" she asked Jerome, but he didn't answer.

"Cain," Nicolette said, moving to stand next to her. "If you don't mind, I'd like my father to handle this."

"That depends, too." Cain tilted Nicolette's head up to see the cut. It was deep enough to require stitches.

"On what?" Nicolette tried to smile when Cain gently pressed Lou's handkerchief to her face.

"On how your father handles things like this, and if my name will be mentioned, if the police will be involved. Not that I'm afraid of an investigation, but if that's what he's going to do, I'd rather tell the story than have someone do it for me."

"Police are the last people Papa will call."

Cain's French wasn't good enough to keep up with Nicolette's short but emotional call, but she offered Nicolette as much comfort as she could since she hadn't moved away from her. Nicolette's father, Michel Blanc, wasn't interested in any witnesses. Cain left Lou and Merrick behind until he arrived to collect Jerome. No police also meant no emergency room visit, so Cain took Nicolette to the Casey family doctor. He was waiting at his office with a plastic surgeon who used fifty-six small neat stitches to close Nicolette's wound.

Cain held Nicolette's hand until the doctor was finished, then took her back to the hotel in the Quarter where her family was staying. They'd made the short trip in silence and she'd put her arm around Nicolette when she'd leaned against her and pressed her lips to her forehead. There was no way to guess what Nicolette was thinking, but her thoughts centered on the possibility of her first impressions. If Nicolette was working undercover, she deserved a raise for what she'd gone through, because there was no way Jerome was part of the plan.

Michel was waiting in the lobby and immediately put his arms around Nicolette, looking at Cain as he held his daughter and spoke quietly to her in French. With his arm still around Nicolette, he asked Cain to join them upstairs, not commenting when Lou followed them into the elevator.

"My daughter's hurt, but the wound she's left with will heal," he said after Nicolette closed one of the suite doors to change out of the scrubs she'd left the doctor's office in. "The cut will heal much quicker and easier than what could've happened if you hadn't found her. That pain could've broken her."

"I'm sorry she was hurt at all, Mr. Blanc."

"You've nothing to apologize for," Michel said, putting his hands on her shoulders and kissing both her cheeks. "You protected what's most precious to me aside from my wife, and allowed me to give her an ending that'll keep Nicolette's nightmares away. For that, I owe you everything."

What he'd said gave her a clue as to what had happened to Jerome, but she only nodded before wishing him good-bye. The night had been bizarre enough and she was getting too tired to think clearly, so it was time to go.

Downstairs she was relieved to see her father waiting for her with her brother Billy, and instead of heading for the car, Dalton led them to the same bar where Cain had started her night. They were all quiet until the waiter set three whiskeys down in front of them.

"What lessons did you learn tonight, Derby?" Dalton asked in almost a whisper.

"It'll always be hard to know who to trust outside my family," she said as she twirled her glass on the bar. If the night was truly a trap, she'd failed in her father's eyes, but she didn't have it in her to leave Nicolette with that animal.

"True," Dalton said, putting his hand on the back of her neck as if to comfort her. "That's important to remember, but what you did made me proud of who you've become. A pretty face might've made you wary, but you didn't go backing away from getting rid of what makes children and lasses afraid of the dark. The world will try and paint you as the devil himself because of your name, but that doesn't mean you don't know the difference between right and wrong. Tonight you were on the side of the righteous."

"How would you paint me, Da?"

"I'm more known for weaving tales than drawing pictures, but I look at you and see a bit of your mother and a bit of meself. What that adds up to is someone who cares enough not to walk away from a fight when it needs fighting. That you got from your mum. The courage to stand up to an asshole bigger than you is something your mum would call foolish, but it does mean you're no different than any Casey who's come before you."

"We're a foolish bunch, then?"

"No," Nicolette said from behind them. She'd changed into a pair of jeans and a dark coat that made the white bandage on her face stand out. "Whatever you taught her about justice was something she took to heart, Mr. Casey," she said before she kissed Dalton's cheek. She moved to Cain and kissed her to show her appreciation. It was so passionate even with her wound to make Cain think of their earlier conversation about romance, and when their lips parted Dalton and Billy were gone. After caressing Cain's bottom lip with her finger, Nicolette stepped back and held her hand out to her. "Would you take a walk with me, then take me home?"

"Are you sure?"

"The darkness isn't something to fear because of you, so I'm positive."

Nicolette and her family left for home the day after graduation, but the story of what Cain had done spread to the other crime families. The lesson for them was Cain might've been someone they considered a devil in training, but in a dark alley facing a lunatic wanting to slice her into pieces, she'd earned their respect when she didn't hesitate in taking him on.

The others who took notice and realized what they faced were the FBI agents who'd matched wits with Dalton for so long. They'd rushed to the scene where the rumors said Cain had faced off with Nicolette's attacker, but there were no clues either of them had been in the now spotless alley. Jerome's wife reported him missing, but if the reverend had somehow been dispatched to a face-to-face performance review with his boss, only God knew—because the devil wasn't talking.

THE DARKEST NIGHT OF THE YEAR
VICTORIA A. BROWNWORTH

for I.D., *memento mori*

The duct tape is wound tight, like a bandage, mummifying the head from the hairline to just below the jaw. The body lies flat within the recesses of the dark, loamy pit, the delineation of arms, legs, torso all indistinct in the pre-dawn half-light. Clothing flows into the dirt—the sweater, trousers, scarf trailing like leaf matter or another set of veiny roots in the hole dug methodically, carefully, as if by a gardener.

In this light, little can be deciphered, little is distinct about the woman lying, now suffocated, in the neatly dug flower bed mimicking others at the edge of the small park. Closer examination later will reveal a ring—a gold band with a finely cut sapphire embedded in the center—on the left hand as well as a gold wristwatch, circa 1950, left wrist, a small Miraculous Medal, also gold, inscribed in Latin, hanging from a fine gold chain around the neck beneath the sweater, and a pair of simple round gold posts in each ear. The clothes will be found to be tailored; well-worn, but of good quality wool, with fine weaving. Dark crusts run circularly, where the now-dried blood had soaked all along the cuffs of the trousers and under the right arm of the sweater.

There are no shoes. The feet are bare and the soles have a series of round, red marks, some seeming to suppurate, even after death. The circular marks are paler at the outer ring, darker in the center; lividity intensifies this effect. Cigarette burns. About thirty in all. And around the ankles, small cuts, like razor marks, and traces of adhesive—more duct tape.

The duct tape around the head begins to unwind. Slowly at first, with the head rising, so that the effect—reddish brown hair flowing back and the tape unwinding—reminds Muriel of a painting by the French surrealist Magritte. The tape continues to unravel in a languorous swirl. Muriel looks closer and closer, waiting for the face to be revealed, but as the last bit of tape sweeps off and blows away into the intensifying wind around the floating body, Muriel sees that there is no face, that the face has come off onto the tape, skin flayed away from the bone, leaving nothing but a swollen pit of gore where the face—her mother's face—once was.

❖

The short, staccato shrieks, low and guttural, split the darkness as Muriel ejects from sleep, the dream of her mother's death surrounding her, a thick miasma threatening to suffocate her, just as her mother had been suffocated. *Suffocated.* Muriel cannot get away from this thought, cannot escape the images that come to her at the edge of sleep and even in full wakefulness: Her mother, tortured. Her mother, burned. Her mother, bound. Her mother, gagged. Her mother, suffocated. Muriel holds her breath several times a day, counting, and tries to imagine what it is to want to claw away one's own face just to get to the air, just to hold on to life. Muriel holds her breath—seconds, tries a minute, tries not to remember what the coroner said at the inquest, that suffocation is the most terrifying form of death after fire, that if her mother had been able to reach the tape around her face, if her hands had not been bound at the time of her death, she would likely have clawed away all the flesh of her face in an effort to remove the tape and breathe.

Muriel pushes the duvet off, pulls on the robe tossed beside her, gets out of bed, walks to the window and opens it wider. Every night since her mother's body was found three days after Christmas, Muriel has slept with the window open—December, January, February, March. Tonight, the air of a delayed London spring bites through her; she shivers involuntarily, pushes her hands deep into the Polartec pockets of her robe as she looks out over the little garden below her flat. Shadows creep and shift. Above, clouds drift over a barely discernable moon. Muriel would like to cry, or at least cry out. She would like to feel something other than dizzying horror, complicated remorse, and a deep, inchoate rage. She would like to reinvent another death for her mother, the mother with whom she was never close, with whom she had never quite been able to connect, even as a small child, but whom she nevertheless loved in the blind animal way that all children love their mothers. She would like, above all, to be able to delete the last thirty hours of her mother's life, to make them an unconscious blur—both for her mother and herself. Delete the hours in which her mother's house had been invaded, delete the hours in which her mother had been slashed and burned, tortured and buried—buried alive. The hours in which her mother had died and her aunt had, just barely, survived.

Muriel had lived in London for five years, doing art restoration at the Victoria and Albert Museum. It was the job she had worked toward for a decade, in a city she adored, at a museum where many of her former colleagues yearned to work. But the pay was painfully poor and the flat she shared with her lover, Liz, was too small and in a dodgy area near the Brixton Market. Muriel couldn't afford more than one flight back to the States a year to visit her mother and her other relatives back in the low, flat Kansas of her childhood. Kansas, the place she had flown away from three hours after she had graduated from college, never to return except for the annual visits, preferring to have her mother visit whatever East Coast city she was studying or working in before she moved to London.

Muriel and her mother had decided on a January visit this year. The terrorist warnings would lessen after the holidays and the flight would cost considerably less—a half-month's rent on the exorbitant flat less. Muriel's mother had promised to leave the tree up through Epiphany. They would celebrate Christmas then, like Russian Orthodox, instead of the Irish Catholics they were.

There had been no arguments, no recriminations. Muriel had agreed to work through the holidays at the museum, making the two-week trip to Kansas possible. And she had looked forward to seeing her mother. She really had.

But then… Then the calls had gone unanswered. She had rung and rung from Christmas Eve into Christmas morning until well into Christmas night. She had called her aunt, then, and her brother, as well. No one was home. She had expected that her aunt Jane would be with her mother—midnight Mass on Christmas Eve, followed by a Midwestern midday dinner on Christmas Day. Both widowed with their children far afield, Muriel's mother and Muriel's aunt—the wife of her mother's brother—frequently spent their holidays together, companionable as they had always been, liking each other's company more, Muriel believed, than they had ever liked that of their men.

Where are they? Muriel began to imagine car wrecks in sudden snow squalls; blizzards could blow up as fast as tornadoes this time of year and the sixty-something women, despite years of life in the bitter Kansas winters, had never mastered the art of driving in a storm.

On Boxing Day, Muriel tracked down her brother, Charlie, at his in-laws' in Oklahoma City. He, his wife Sharleen, and their two young children had driven out from Austin where Charlie taught history at the university. They weren't due in Kansas for another couple of days.

The conversation was brief and as usual, a little fraught. Charlie and Muriel had been estranged since she had told him, the night before she left Kansas on the eve of both her graduation and her twenty-first birthday, that she was going to New York to live with the woman, Liz, she had fallen in love with in her senior year of college. Liz, whom Charlie had asked out every time Muriel had brought her over to the house. Liz, the smart and sexy valedictorian of their class, specialist in Russian studies, mysterious and intriguing with her jet-black hair and eyes like coals. Liz, whom Muriel wished was with her now, rather than traveling through Russia on a fellowship that would keep her incommunicado except for occasional e-mails and even more rare cell phone calls through April. Liz—who Muriel knew, because Liz was her bedrock—who would somehow know how to find her mother or at least know how to keep Muriel from worry, if only she were here.

Muriel was never sure what it was Charlie resented most, that she got the girl he wanted instead of the one he settled for, or that she got to leave Kansas for good and he didn't, staying through grad school and beyond until he got the job at Austin. Charlie wished her a Merry Christmas and told her not to worry, that Mom was with Jane and they were both safe, he was sure. There hadn't been snow, in fact there had been a brief warm-up—unnaturally springlike for Christmas in their part of the world. He'd be there in two days, at the weekend, he'd call her and let her know everything was all right. Muriel could feel a tug of concern for his younger sister in his voice; momentary, brief, but she could hear it.

"Don't worry," he told her. But she was worried, nonetheless. In the end, Muriel had been right to be worried.

❖

Aunt Jane had arrived at Muriel's mother's house at nine o'clock on Christmas Eve. She had walked through the unlocked front door just as she had hundreds of times over the forty years she had been coming to the house to visit her sister-in-law and best friend, Irene. She had walked into an empty parlor and called up the stairs to her friend, *Merry Christmas, time for Mass*. But there had been no answer. No sounds at all, it seemed. Nothing to intimate that Irene was in the bathroom and just hadn't heard Jane.

Her foot was on the second step when Jane saw the wrapping paper just outside her periphery. It was in a ball on the floor where the hallway met the parlor, just below the stairs on which she now stood. A small trail of ribbon, then the big wad of crumpled paper. As if there had been visitors who had come early for their gifts and had left in a hurry.

Was it a sudden sense of dread or foreboding that made Jane back down the stairs and run toward the door? Was it the unconscious but clear sense that her well-ordered friend of forty years would never leave a scrap of paper on her floor, let alone this mass of wrapping and ribbon? Was it the eerie silence in the house that had always held some sound, even after the children had moved out and Dermott had died and even the dog was gone?

Jane hadn't known as she ran to her car and locked the doors behind her and drove to the police station across town that she had just escaped an excruciating death, a death she would have been unable to prevent her friend from experiencing, but which she at least would not now, herself, have to witness, before it was her own turn.

Menninger is a small replica of Topeka and lies just at the outskirts of the second-largest city in Kansas. In towns like these in the Midwestern plains states, most everyone knows everyone else or there is the sense that they should. When Jane walked into the Menninger police station at just past nine thirty on Christmas Eve, it didn't matter that she didn't know any of the men sitting around the big front desk eating Christmas cookies and listening to Frank Sinatra singing "Silent Night." They all looked as if they were cousins once removed and the desk sergeant came out to greet her and ask if he could help.

In small towns, missing persons reports or signs of trouble at a house where trouble never existed aren't dismissed for twenty-four or forty-eight hours, the way they are in big cities. Everyone knows what everyone else should be doing. And Sergeant Michaels and Officers Perez and McGee knew that widows in their sixties don't go missing on Christmas Eve when their family is coming by to take them to Mass.

It was Tony Perez who drove Jane Corrigan back to Irene Corrigan McManus's house, all the while hoping that this was indeed a false alarm and Mrs. McManus would be meeting them at the door with a warm cider and a plate of cookies and an admonishment to her friend for jumping to conclusions when she had only been in the basement looking for a particular Christmas ornament she had misplaced. But that thought receded when he asked Mrs. Corrigan to stay in his patrol car and he drew his weapon and walked gingerly through the still-unlocked front door.

The wrapping paper lay on the floor just as Mrs. Corrigan had described it. And there was a creepy quiet in the house that he had experienced before. The kind of quiet that goes with killing, except he didn't yet smell the death he feared was just past the kitchen or right up the stairs.

The kitchen was empty, but messy. Too messy for the kind of woman who kept a house like this neat and tidy little package. Chairs were pulled out from the table at odd angles and two beer bottles and a couple of half-drunk cups of coffee were scattered over the table top, where in the center lay an ashtray filled with two kinds of cigarettes, several lipsticked at the ends. The remains of a lunchmeat sandwich lay next to the ashtray right on the table, no plate, no napkin. Mrs. Corrigan was right; something was wrong here.

Perez stood at the bottom of the stairs feeling a dread similar to what Jane Corrigan had felt an hour before. He thought of his wife, Terri, and their baby, home with her parents on the kid's first Christmas Eve and made a quick sign of the cross before climbing the stairs, his gun cocked and outstretched before him.

The rooms were dark except for the bathroom where a fine spray of blood layered the gray tile floor just like artificial snow at the corners of the shop windows on Montrose Avenue. Between the tub and the toilet lay a washcloth soaked in blood.

Back at the car, Officer Perez asked Mrs. Corrigan if she could return to the station and make a statement. Jane didn't cry, but her eyes blurred for a moment. Mass would be starting in a few minutes and she would miss it for the first time since her first Holy Communion fifty-seven years ago. She would miss going with Irene for the first time in thirty-nine years and at that moment Jane knew that praying would not help. She would never see Irene again. And she might never be able to go to Mass again, once she knew what had become of her friend. She might just blame God for whatever hellish thing it was that had happened on this of all nights.

Irene Corrigan McManus had been doing dishes in her kitchen at eight thirty in the evening on December twenty-third, the longest—and thus darkest—night of the year, when the front door had opened. The tree was lit and the parlor was full of Christmas gifts for Jane, Muriel, Charlie and Sharleen, and of course, her grandchildren, Belinda and Will. Irene had grabbed a tea towel and walked smiling toward Jane only to find a boy and girl she had never seen before staring at her from the hallway.

Irene heard the knife before she saw it. Her father had worked cattle and she knew that sound of a switchblade clicking out from its sheath for all manner of unpleasantness. She had never liked the sound and right now it made her want to run, something she hadn't done in more than a decade. There was nowhere to go in the small house. No way to get to the back door before these tall, lithe young murderers had got hold of her and sliced at her sweater just below the armpit. Nowhere to go as the girl rummaged through the pantry closet and brought out duct tape and matches and the few beers she kept on hand for when Charlie came to visit, or Father Meehan. Nowhere to go as the tall, lanky boy with the sharp blue eyes leaned into her face and asked her for money, nowhere to go as the girl wound the tape around her wrists. They put the end of the tea towel in her mouth as they led her up the stairs and went from room to room searching for the money and jewelry she simply didn't have. There was the surprise iPod she had bought for Jane, wrapped under the tree, fully loaded with songs she knew her friend would love. The coin set for Will, who even at ten was a born collector. The gold filigree necklace with the three inset sapphires that had belonged to her husband's mother that she was giving to Muriel, also under the tree. But nothing else. Her TV—only 30 inches. Her DVR. No exciting new Blu-ray, just the cheapest on-sale no-name from Best Buy. Some other small appliances—microwave, coffeemaker, radio. Three hundred dollars for emergencies stashed in the top drawer of her dresser under her silk scarves. Her mother's silver server on the breakfront in the dining room.

After a few hours of swimming in and out of consciousness, of feeling her feet on fire, of lying in small pools of her own blood on the bathroom floor, Irene knew that money and jewelry and her eight-year-old car wouldn't be enough. Scott and Gina wanted to hurt someone, wanted to watch her suffer, wanted to spend their first Christmas together unwrapping other people's gifts and doing irrevocable damage. They had entered her house because the tree was lit, the gifts were wrapped, and the door had been open. But they had stayed well beyond two cups of coffee, a couple of sandwiches, a plate of Christmas cookies, and a few beers for something else, something so sinister Irene couldn't contemplate it. She could only pray. *Hard.*

The phone had rung and rung that morning while they hurt her over and over. Irene knew it was Muriel, Muriel who never remembered about time differences and was calling to wish her a Happy Christmas—she had stopped saying *Merry* once she moved to London—long before it was actually time. Muriel, whom Irene now knew she would never see again. Never have the opportunity to pass on that necklace, to say that she finally understood about Liz, to say that she knew they had never been what mothers and daughters are supposed to be to each other, but that she had loved her nonetheless, felt proud of her daughter who did a job she never fully understood, was always glad to see her, strong and fit and seemingly happy when she came to visit every year.

Irene was unconscious when Jane came through the front door on Christmas Eve, after twenty-four hours of torture and mayhem had suffused her house with a layering of evil that Muriel would later feel the second she walked through the door, ten days after her mother's murder. Irene was unconscious as she was dragged to her own car and shoved into the trunk, unconscious as the leggy blond girl wrapped the tape over her mouth and nose and eyes and ran out of tape before she got to Irene's throat. Irene was unconscious as her feet swelled from the cigarette burns and the razor cuts that Scott and Gina had taken turns inflicting, he looking bored and she just a little terrified as Scott crushed his hand over Irene's mouth when she screamed. Irene was unconscious as Scott neatly dug a pit just large enough to lay a hundred and twenty-seven pound, five-foot three-inch, sixty-seven-year-old woman at the end of the rhododendron garden in Menninger Park three blocks from the clinic where Irene had worked for the seventeen years since her husband, Dermott, had died suddenly of an aneurysm. Irene never knew the terror of being buried alive, for she was unconscious—yet still alive—when they laid her in what was to be her grave and tossed the dirt in after her. She never knew that it took seven full hours for her to slowly asphyxiate because of a small cigarette burn in the duct tape just below her left nostril allowing just a whiff of air, protracting her death.

❖

Muriel sat in her kitchen that was too bright in the manner of all English kitchens, drank a cup of strong black tea with just a hint of cream, no sugar, and tried not to think of suffocating. The newspaper was spread over the table: No murders, no tales of mayhem caught her eye. She had seen the papers after her mother's murder. Had read them over and over trying to get a sense of her mother's last hours, wanting to glean some clue about nineteen-year-old Scott Powell and eighteen-year-old Gina Tucci, both from Oklahoma City, who had gone on a crime spree in three small towns between theirs and her mother's. Scott, who had spent two years in juvenile detention for aggravated assault, having nearly beaten a fellow classmate to death with a baseball bat in a fight over a girl, and Gina, the special education student who had been in trouble over drugs and bad boys. Gina, with the beautiful waist-length blond hair and pretty, vacant expression, whom Scott had befriended in a court-mandated class for problem students a year before they decided to kill Muriel's mother and stab the man from whom they stole the car that took them out of Oklahoma City and into Menninger in time to destroy Christmas for Muriel, Jane, and Charlie for all time.

The sky was beginning to pinken beyond her kitchen window and Muriel rose to turn off the glaring kitchen light. She drank the last of her tea and rinsed the cup in the sink. Scott and Gina were apprehended two days after Irene Corrigan McManus was murdered, after Gina called the police from a convenience store outside Topeka because Scott had hit her, hard, and split her lip open for, Gina thought, no good reason. In the photograph in the Kansas papers, Gina was wearing the necklace belonging to Muriel's grandmother. Blood was splattered down the front of her low-cut white sweater and there were flecks of it across her cleavage, like dark red freckles. Muriel had been struck by how pretty Gina was, how very young she looked. It was difficult to imagine this pretty girl holding her cigarette to the sole of Muriel's mother's foot and watching while her boyfriend muffled her mother's screams. It was easier to believe such inexplicable violence of the sexy but mean-looking boy who glowered out from the page and who the papers noted had a predilection for violence, while the girl had never been in real trouble, just had never finished school past the ninth grade and had been involved in petty crimes before with boys not quite as sociopathic as this boy was. Muriel's aunt Jane had wanted the death penalty, but the youth of the two had been discussed during plea agreements. There had been no trial. Scott and Gina had pleaded guilty to second-degree murder which, given the plea, but with the aggravating circumstance of the torture, would offer them parole within the next two decades. Depending on how they spent their years in prison. Muriel was certain Powell would die there—either by the hand of another inmate not as fragile as her mother, or because he would kill again, even behind bars. She couldn't guess about the girl. The girl would befriend another female inmate as bad as the boys she'd been with up till now—Muriel knew this instinctively. Gina Tucci wasn't a girl who knew how to take care of herself. She needed another person to get through her days and nights. Some things are immutable. Her mother was dead, these two had killed her, and there was no payment, really. There were pleas and bargains; she imagined her mother had pleaded and bargained before her awful death. But there had been no mercy. And there would be none now.

Muriel hadn't wanted to think of them ever getting out, ever visiting someone else at Christmastime.

Muriel had flown to Kansas just as she had planned and had stood in her mother's living room looking at the Christmas tree, holding her breath until she had to gasp for air. She thought about the time it took for her mother to perish in the dark, cold ground. She thought about what it must have been like to be in one's grave and know it.

Charlie had sent Sharleen and the children back to Austin, and so Irene's son and daughter had spent a mostly silent night in their childhood home, neither even contemplating sleep, both sitting at the kitchen table taking turns holding their breath. At five in the morning, in silence, they had walked to Menninger Park and stood above the big hole, now surrounded by yellow crime tape, and looked down into the place they imagined their mother had viewed with abject terror before she was buried alive. Muriel had crouched down and touched the earth at the edge of the makeshift grave. It was hard and icy cold. She clawed a little at the earth with her bare fingers, clawed until the earth came loose in her hand, put the reddish dirt in her pocket, turned to see her brother, eyes glinting with unshed tears, looking at her with a fleeting look of horror. She looked down at her fingers; they were streaked with blood.

❖

Muriel waits at the airport gate at Gatwick, close as she can get in these days of heightened security, for Liz to come in from customs. She runs a hand through her russet hair so like her mother's had been and pulls her leather jacket tight around her, shifts back and forth on her feet. It is chill in the airport. It doesn't feel like spring, even for England. A rush of people—all carrying bags and bundles and the ubiquitous striped plastic valises—pours out from behind the customs barrier. In the melee, Muriel sees Liz, small and wiry, her black hair pulled tight off her face, big silver earrings slapping against her cheeks, a small tapestry bag in her right hand.

Liz sees Muriel and smiles, pushing a little harder through the crowd. Muriel walks right up to the gate, reaching out her arms for Liz.

"Poor darling," Liz murmurs into Muriel's hair as she envelops her in her strong arms, kissing first one cheek and then the other.

"Let's get you home." Liz locks her arm in Muriel's and leads them both toward the exit.

Through the airport windows Muriel looks out onto the suburban English landscape, out at the little tile-roofed houses linked together so much more tightly than those in Kansas. Muriel takes a deep breath and begins to count.

❖

Later, much later, Muriel lies in the dark, Liz's breathing soft and measured beside her. Muriel rises, walks to the window, looks out into the garden. In the dull and faded moonlight, she sees a dark hole off to the side, near a rhododendron. She squints her eyes, peers closer, her face fairly pressed against the window. In the half-light she spies a strip of gray blowing from below the shrubbery, from out of the hole she knows is there. Clouds pass over the moon and the garden is lit with silver. The shard blows again and Muriel can see pieces of flesh, red and white shreds, stuck to the tape. She opens her mouth to scream, then shuts it. Muriel presses her face hard against the glass, holds her breath until her heart slows and the window, blurred with grayish light, swims before her. She never feels the floor as she passes out, a little hiss of breath escaping her lips as she once again begins to breathe.

LOST
J.M. REDMANN

If I'd looked at the phone maybe I would have seen that it was a rattlesnake about to strike, but I didn't look, didn't even glance up from the computer screen, reached out and fumbled for the handset that even after five months, I still wasn't accustomed to.

I answered as I usually do when I didn't recognize the number, "M. Knight Agency."

"Michele?" But I knew the voice, dry as pious parchment.

"Aunt Greta?" I had—because I somehow imagined that my father would have wanted it—called her after Katrina. Her house hadn't flooded; she was fine save for the inconvenience of having to be away to avoid the mail disruption, long lines in groceries and the "new element" that had come to town—men of a different skin color helping to rebuild. She didn't ask how I'd done. I didn't want to tell her—we could barely discuss the weather politely—how could I convey losing the shipyard and house out in the bayous where I'd grown up? It was a brief conversation. I assumed that I would only talk to her again at some required family occasion, a wedding or funeral.

But it was her voice on the other end.

She didn't bother with pleasantries—perhaps thought I didn't deserve them. Or was aware enough that her asking how I was would be hypocrisy and she wasn't willing to inflict that on me.

"I need a favor," she said.

I'd never imagined hearing those words from her, so I could think of no reply.

She continued, "Bayard is lost. I need you to find him." There was a tremor in her voice, the only sign of emotion, of what she was feeling. Bayard was her oldest son. From my outside perspective, they were damaged people who used each other and called it love and affection. I called it need and greed.

I didn't say all the things I wanted to say, from the cliché of "good riddance to bad rubbish" to my true feelings of "may he rot in hell" to the sarcastic "I'm not the lost and found. Perhaps you should check ladies' lingerie."

It was six months after Katrina had washed away New Orleans; we were all rebuilding our lives, being kind because we needed kindness to survive.

I merely asked, "Lost? How?"

It was a sign of how lonely she was, the words poured out. Perhaps she thought she was talking to the phone in her hand, not to me. He had come with her after the storm had passed and people were allowed back in to check on the house he had grown up in and where she lived. Bayard had insisted that although it was all right, she couldn't stay there, not until things were better. Aunt Greta lived in the suburbs, where it hadn't flooded, but there was damage, loss of power. She didn't want to be a strong woman who made her own decisions, was happy to let her son dictate what she was to do. He found her a little place around Shreveport. He stayed with her, between jobs, and came down to fix up the house. He had been gone two weeks, told her he'd be back a week ago, had called to say that he was on his way. And that was the last she had heard from him.

She wanted me to find him, repeating the word "favor" to make it clear that this was not a paying job.

I agreed. It got her off the phone more quickly than arguing, although one of the last things I would have ever wanted to do was to look for my disgusting, arrogant cousin. But there had been a quiver in Aunt Greta's voice that I'd never heard before. She was alone in the world, having raised three children as self-absorbed as she was. Gus, her youngest, had moved out to Arizona years ago. Mary, her daughter, lived in Covington, on the north shore of Lake Pontchartrain, and never had time to drive over the twenty-four-mile Causeway unless she was shopping with her girlfriends or her husband was taking her out to a nice dinner in the French Quarter. Only Bayard had time to come around, mostly for a free meal, to have his laundry done, to crash when his latest girlfriend had thrown him out.

I do a lot of missing persons cases, especially now that so many people were missing from New Orleans. Aunt Greta hadn't asked and I hadn't told. She was clearly hoping that he'd somehow show up and everything would be as it was before. I knew that one of two things had happened to him: He was dead or he'd skipped town. Dead was clearly an answer she didn't want to hear, but if he'd left on his own—and cut himself off from her—that also wasn't going to be a happy end.

I looked at my desk. I was just finishing up the paperwork on several cases that I had closed, several others I was waiting on replies to inquiries, nothing was in the "need to do right now" category.

Aunt Greta would call again in a day or two, expecting miracles. There were none to be had, but at least I could have some answers. I sighed, put on my jacket, and headed for the house in Metairie.

I had lived there from the time I was ten, after my father was killed in a car wreck, until I'd left, when the clock struck midnight and I turned eighteen. Aunt Greta was cold and dutiful, Uncle Claude a blob in front of the TV, having lost too many arguments with his wife to try again, Bayard, Mary Grace, and to a lesser extent Gus, the real children, had been insistent on letting their interloper cousin know it. Bayard was the worst. The others were content to ignore me; he was five years older than I was and had uses for his young girl cousin.

It wasn't a pleasant memory. Instead I focused on what was outside the car's windows, searching for signs of reconstruction or dark water marks on untouched buildings and homes. I hadn't come this way in a while, probably several months. I'd returned in the fall, the October after the storm. Now it was spring, the trees attesting to the cycle of life, a delicate green erupting from their barren limbs. And like the trees, there was a slow rebirth of life—a water line power-washed away, trash stacked in piles by the curb, furniture being unloaded into a newly painted house.

I wasn't sure what I was going to find at the house. Maybe Bayard wanted to take a break from his clinging mother and had shacked up there with his latest floozy. He liked them young and stacked no matter how old and stooped he was. Intellectually I knew it was possible that he had been hurt or killed, but it didn't feel likely; he'd always been one of life's cockroaches, able to wriggle his way to survival. Finding him holed up there, one last blast of freedom, was where I'd put my money.

I hadn't been here since long before Katrina. Even this un-flooded block was different, trees torn down, roofs scalped by the wind. But also familiar, the houses the same pale yellow brick, one-story ranch, far enough away from each other so secrets and anguish didn't cross the hedges between properties.

The house didn't look lived in, lights off, although the power had long ago been restored here. The yard was unkempt, grass ragged, too high, weeds peeking through the azalea bushes that ringed the house. I had hoped that this would be no more than a quick drive out, a brief— very brief—exchange of me telling him to call his mother, and then it would be over. But Bayard wasn't the frugal type; he didn't turn off lights just because he wasn't home.

Even cockroaches eventually die, I told myself as I got out of my car. He was old enough and had both the genes and the lifestyle that a heart attack wasn't out of the question. He could be decomposing on the toilet, the girlie magazine on the floor, one hand rigor mortised around his now very limp member.

Trying to shake that image out of my head, I walked up the flagstone path.

It couldn't be that, I told myself; the lights would still be on, his car parked out front, if something like that had happened. It seemed that if he had been here, he had deliberately left.

I knocked on the door. No answer and more telling, no soft sounds of anyone in the house that I could discern. People may not open the door, but they usually either try to see who it is or move away so that they can't be seen by anyone peeking in, as I was now.

No lights, no movement, dust visible on the side table by the couch. I started to go around to the side window to get a different view, but a police car was slowly coming down the block.

Well, that didn't take long, I thought, digging in my pocket for my P.I. license. Even though it was broad daylight, I must have looked like a prowler—a middle-aged woman burglar—to someone on this block.

But the cop car cruised by me without a glance and pulled in front of a house three doors down.

I went around to the side windows, the ones that looked into the bedrooms. If this house had a tale to tell, it would be here. But it was the same old story. Mary Grace's old bedroom was held ready for her kids in case they came to visit, but there was dust on the toys, ones for a childhood a generation ago. Gus's had been converted to storage, as if he would never come back, and Bayard's was a mess, still his room, but nothing in it seemed recent, no dirty socks waiting for Aunt Greta to put in the laundry, no empty drink can waiting for her to take it to the trash, just the usual piles of junk. Her bedroom, at the back, was its usual neat and prim, not a wrinkle in the bedspread.

I heard a loud voice from down the block, where the police car had stopped.

"No, I'm not an idiot, I didn't forget and leave it open."

I hopped over the fence into the backyard, but the windows there revealed the same scene, a house that people lived in, but no one was home and no one appeared to have been here recently.

Only the garage had a different tale to tell.

Aunt Greta's car was parked there. She had mentioned that Bayard was using her car, since it was newer and in better condition than his and he was driving back and forth between Shreveport and New Orleans, about a five- or six-hour journey.

Bayard wasn't here, but the car he was driving was.

The house key was still in the same hiding place it had been for the last thirty years, a fake rock that was showing signs of aging that real rocks don't. I used it to let myself into the back door and from there went to the garage.

The backseat of the car held the usual jumble of fast food bags that I expected from Bayard. But the front seat was relatively clean, as if he had taken everything that was of use out of the car. The front garage door was down, not something that Bayard would bother with if he was coming in and out.

It was almost as if he didn't need the car anymore, but didn't want anyone to notice that it was still here.

I relocked the back door, hopped the fence again, and headed back to my car.

Down the block a man was in his front yard explaining something to the officer.

"I just bought it two months ago—"

The cop cut in, "Yes, sir, we'll be on the lookout, but honestly, it's probably in a chop shop by now." With that, he closed his notebook and headed back to his patrol car.

The man in the yard watched him drive away, so he didn't see me approach until I was about five feet away.

That P.I. license came in handy after all. I held it up as I said, "Excuse me, what happened here?"

He barely glanced at my badge, was happy enough to have someone listen to his tale of woe.

"My car was stolen. Out of my locked garage. Cop says I probably forgot to lock it, but no way. That baby was only two months old, I was still coddling her. Washed her every Saturday. Even in football season, she got her wash."

"When was your car stolen?"

"A week ago. Cops only now getting out here to take a report. Slow bastards." He added, "Pardon my French," as he remembered he was talking to a woman.

"What kind of car was it?"

"A 2006 red Porsche Boxster. Yeah, I know, go ahead and say it. Mid-life crisis. But I got the insurance money from a place we owned on the north shore. Wind. Probably a tornado. Not going to rebuild. So I got the sports car I've always been dreaming of. My wife even helped me pick it out—said if I'm going to be stepping out on her, might as well do it with something that won't give me the clap or ask for a fur coat." He shook his head ruefully.

"Do you have a spare key hidden anywhere on your property?" I asked.

He abruptly looked up at me. "Yeah, I mean, yeah, we all do around here. You think someone came out here and somehow found it?"

"When was the last time you moved it to a different location?"

"Moved it?" He thought for a moment before admitting, "It's been a while. Kids were in high school then. Now…they're both married with kids of their own."

"Would people around here know where your key would be?"

He wasn't a stupid man. "You think someone from here might have stolen my car? But we're all nice people, lived here for years. Besides, I'd kind of notice if a car exactly like mine showed up down the block."

"True, but someone else might have had their own mid-life crisis and decided that it was time to leave this nice neighborhood and thought taking off in a red Porsche would be a fun way to do it."

He just looked at me.

I asked, "You got the VIN?"

"Why?" he asked, but it was more curious that suspicious as he was heading into his garage and a stack of paperwork.

"My aunt Greta lives down there." I pointed in the direction of her house. "Her oldest son Bayard was checking on it. She hasn't heard from him in a week. Asked me to look into it."

"Yeah, I know him. We call him Mr. Moocher. He always invites himself over if he smells a barbeque. He seemed like a nice enough guy, bit of a loser, if you ask me. He should have married some plain Jane accountant, someone who'd support him, but he seemed to like the blond girls who expected him to buy the drinks. Disappeared a week ago, huh? Any idea where he is?" he asked as he wrote down the all the car numbers—VIN, license, registration—for me.

"Nope, not yet."

He sighed. "Damn, why couldn't I have at least held on to that car until my college reunion. Not much chance I'll get it back, right?"

I owed my cousin no favors. "Can't say. I don't know that he took it. Even if he did, if he was smart, he'd have gotten rid of it asap. But he's never been that smart before, so why should he start now? Plus, he's an amateur at disappearing. I'm a professional at finding people."

As I drove back to my office, I pondered the possibilities. Katrina had changed everything, disrupted all our lives. Some people were desperately trying to get back to what they had before. Others used the chaos to disappear. It was easy, claim that every single piece of paper you ever had was washed away. Find a new identity—you had the perfect alibi for the needed new copies of all those documents—and the perfect sob story to get people to eschew the usual checks and balances. Men running out on child support, women leaving abusive boyfriends. Always dreamed of California? Here I come.

People opened up their homes and their hearts. It was astonishing and humbling how kind strangers were. Everywhere I'd gone on my refugee road tour, people were generous and helpful. That kindness was a large part of how we got through the days, knowing that the bureaucratic blindness wasn't who most Americans were. Most of us were grateful, took what we truly needed and could never find the right words to say how thankful we were.

But there were others who took advantage.

Bayard?

Possible? You betcha. His mother had handed him everything, and he could never understand why life didn't continue to hand him what he wanted. He smiled and made jokes and expected that was enough to get him a good job and then a promotion at that job, and always had an excuse as to why that didn't work. Last I'd heard he was selling cars at a used car lot. But according to Aunt Greta, that job had disappeared with Katrina. Or at least that was what Bayard said.

Why not drive away in a nice Porsche and start somewhere new where nobody knew who you were and how many times you'd messed up your life?

No, this case would not be a quick drive by a house I never wanted to visit again. But the image of my asshole cousin handcuffed for grand theft auto was too good to pass up.

Time to drive back to my office and do the records search. Even at rush hour, traffic was still light driving back to the city—people were gone or had shifted out to the suburbs or north of the lake as they rebuilt. My late-morning drive back was positively serene, especially given that I was leaving the 'burbs behind. The "sliver by the river," where I both lived and where my office was, had not flooded. It was to that office and my computer I was headed.

Let's see what reasons Bayard might have had for deciding to run away with a red Porsche.

Reason number one was easy to find—child support. Bayard was the kind of pig who would expect that birth control was something for the woman to handle. The problem is if you like really young and stupid women, they're not always as conscientious about these things as they should be.

One Melva-Raylene Gautier seemed to fit in that category. She listed Bayard as the father of her three-year-old bouncing baby boy, and he was about two and a half years behind in his child support payments. A few phone calls and some flirting (with another woman) got me the info that Melva-Raylene had gotten tired of waiting and was taking Bayard to court. Her good fortune was that she lived out by the airport in the suburb of Kenner, so that meant all her court records were on the un-flooded side of the Seventeenth Street Canal and the trial date was coming up.

Reason number two appeared by midafternoon. I had used the court records to get places on employment. It was a long list. I went down it—phone disconnected; never heard of him; would only confirm he has worked there, no other information; records lost in the flooding; never heard of him; thought he'd been let go, but wasn't really sure, couldn't remember that far back; never heard of him (I was beginning to detect a scam—claim to work at a place you don't work so they can't garnish your wages) phone disconnected.

Then finally, "Yeah, him. You find him; I'll pay you if you let me know."

Alpha A Used Cars on Airline Highway. I was talking to Alpha Al himself. "He worked for you?" I confirmed.

"Yeah, slimy dog. If I could prove anything, I'd have a warrant for his arrest."

"What did he do? Allegedly?" I added, with enough sarcasm in the latter that Al couldn't miss it.

"We got through the storm real good, one sign come down and part of the roof over the employee bathroom leaked. A month ago, get a big shipment of cars—flooded cars meant people needed new cars—and come in on Monday morning to find out the place was looted. Not a break-down-the-gate type thing, but a someone who knew his way around kind of thing. Ten of the most expensive cars gone. Yeah, a window was broken, but most of the glass was on the outside, like someone broke it from inside to make it look like a break-in. The cabinet with the keys has crowbar marks, but it was unlocked, not busted open. All the money was gone, even the change pile on my desk. All my other guys arrive. Bayard shows up for two seconds, says he's gotta go take care of his mom up north and wouldn't be back. When I mention the thievery, first thing out of his mouth is an alibi, that he just got back in town, this was the first place he stopped. After he's hightailed it out, one of the other guys says that they'd met for beers the night before in a bar where they usually hang out.

"So either he did it or one of my current employees is a great liar and hasn't spent a dime of what he stole," Alpha Al finished.

"I'm assuming that you tried to contact him?"

"Oh, yeah, one day I told my girl to call him every half hour, use any and every phone she could get a hold of. He answered once, hung up when he realized it was us. Never answered again. Went by his listed address, they claim they never heard of him."

"How much did he hit you up for?"

"The cars alone were well over two hundred grand."

At retail used car price, I was betting.

He continued, "Plus the rest of the stuff he took, throw in another hundred grand."

"You kept around one hundred thousand dollars on the premises?" I asked. Maybe I should talk to Alpha Al about security.

He hesitated. "Uh, no, it was maybe ten K in cash."

I didn't say it, but even that was a lot of cash to keep around a business that usually operated on loans and credit. To prompt him, I said, "I'm not the cops. My only job here is to find this guy."

"I didn't know about it and it's stopped, but it seems that one of the guys was dealing a little weed on the side. He stashed it in a dead car out back. That disappeared."

Again, I didn't say it, but ninety thousand in drugs and money wasn't "dealing a little weed," it was big-time drug operation. However, I wasn't the cops, and this sounded like it could be reason number three why Bayard headed for the hills.

"So basically someone cleaned you out—and some of your sidelining employees pretty good?"

"Yeah, like I said, you find this guy, you let me know. I'll make it worth your while."

I left it as vague as I could, no promises to Alpha Al that I'd hand him Bayard's head on a stick. But I didn't rule it out either. Al's business seemed to be used cars and new drugs, using the former to launder money for the latter. It also explained why he hadn't reported it to the police. If he had Bayard arrested, Bayard could turn over the drug operation to the cops and he'd be the chopped liver to Alpha Al's sirloin as far as law enforcement was concerned.

I certainly wouldn't buy a car from him—hell, I wouldn't buy a car from anyone who'd hire Bayard—and even if it meant making some money on this, it didn't seem to be the kind of money I wanted to earn. But it was power, more leverage than I'd ever had over my asshole cousin. If he ever bothered me again, I could just mouth "Alpha Al" and get rid of him. Oh, yes, the colder the revenge, the sweeter the taste.

Just to cover all bases, I called Melva-Raylene, but she wasn't home or wasn't answering the phone. I didn't leave a message.

Then, because I'm a professional, I did the usual routine, called places like hospitals and police stations in all the parishes surrounding New Orleans—the ones that had functioning hospitals and police stations. No one with his name. I briefly considered that he might be using an alias, but if he was hurt—or dead—there was no reason to use a fake name. The fake name would be for the Bayard who had purloined a Porsche and pissed off a presumed drug dealer.

It seemed more than likely that Bayard had scrammed. I had the why, I didn't have the where. I sighed. Aunt Greta had bought a computer, more for him to use than her. I could go back to the ugly house—twice in one day—and see if he left any clues there.

My phone rang. Maybe it would be an excuse to avoid going out to the hideous house.

"Someone from this number called here," the voice said. It was a deep, cigarette and cheap whisky male voice.

"I don't think so," I said, not recognizing the voice or the number.

"I hit redial, so I think so. Who is this?" he demanded.

"This is a business," I answered. "Who am I speaking to?" I scrambled on my desk, looking over my notes to see if the number matched anything I'd scribbled down.

"What kind of business?"

Aha. Melva-Raylene. "We track missing people. We've been hired to look for a man by the name of Bayard Robedeaux…"

"That fucking rat-wad! How the fuck did you get this number while looking for that shit bag?"

"I looked up the court filings."

"You can't do that, they're private!"

"Legally not, unless it's sealed by a judge. Court records are public records."

"Oh." He seemed to be thinking this over. It was a slow process.

"I take it you do know who this is?"

"Not me, my girlfriend. Bastard knocked her up a while back and now he's not paying what he should. Wait, who did you say you were?"

"We didn't get that far. I'm a private detective and I was hired" (well, arm-twisted by a cadging relative) "to locate him. Any idea where he is?"

"Shit, if I knew that, he'd be rotting in a swamp by now."

Which wouldn't do much to get the back payments, but I didn't point that out.

"Any clue where he might have gone?"

"Shit, no, I never met the man. It was poor Melva-Raylene that got messed up with him."

"Could I talk to her?"

"Yeah, you can, but she's not here right now." A sly tone crept into his voice. "I could arrange for that to happen."

Lucky for me, his price was that we meet at a greasy grill out near where they lived and that it would be my treat. Lucky for him, that was about as high a price as I was willing to pay. I didn't think that I'd get much information about where Bayard might be, but I could get some more leverage and power. I would be able to rat out not only my obnoxious cousin to Alpha Al, but also Bubba Butch—probably not his real name, but close enough.

I glanced at my watch. Given how bad traffic was out in the suburbs, I had about enough time for a bathroom break and to leave a message at home that I might be a little late tonight.

And then I was on my way out to the land beyond the Orleans Parish line. The map should read, "here be dragons"—of the fast food, box store, commercial strip variety.

There were at least five motorcycles parked outside the place that Bubba Butch—I needed to stop thinking of him that way, lest I forget and actually call him that—had suggested. I drove a good block past it, turned around, and parked far enough away so that no one would easily match my car with my face at that bar. I could now watch the joint and make sure that all Bubba and Melva-Raylene wanted was a burger and some fries on someone else's dime.

But it was a quiet late afternoon, no sudden arrival of ten large men. At about five minutes past our appointed meeting time, a big guy and a little woman arrived. I gave them a minute or two, then followed them in.

A waft of artery-clogging grease greeted me as I entered the place. One table in back had the motorcycle gang gathered around it, but they seemed more intent on pouring the pitcher of beer than scoping out any new arrivals.

I approached the table with the man and woman.

"Melva-Raylene Gautier?" I asked.

She looked confused.

"You the person I talked to?" the man asked.

Melva-Raylene jumped in. "Oh, sorry, I'm not Gautier anymore. Now I'm Boudreaux. Mrs. Butch Boudreaux." She smiled shyly and put a hand on Butch's hand. I hate it when I'm this right about people. I didn't think my usual line would work here: "Butch? Isn't that a girl's name?" That seemed to only go over well in gay bars.

"Hi, thanks for meeting me," I said as I slid into a chair. I had to steel myself not to look down at the seat to check if anything was living there. Didn't want to insult their favorite eatery.

Butch was tall, wide, and deep, some of it muscle, some of it years of fried chicken. He still had a mullet haircut and one of those mustaches that wandered down his cheeks to meet up with his chin. The outdated hairstyle wasn't helped by the rapid surrender of everything on top. Either he never looked in the mirror or he liked what he saw.

Mevla Raylene was a good fifteen years his junior. If Bayard hadn't committed statutory rape when he'd gotten her pregnant, it was close. I hoped she and Butch didn't like doing it missionary style because she might have gotten lost underneath him. Her youth was accentuated by her petite stature and small-boned figure. She would probably look young at forty. And haggard at fifty when living with men like Butch finally caught up with her.

The waitress came by to take our order.

Butch got a pitcher of beer, with a quick look at me, to indicate that I was paying for it. Given the pitchers were three bucks here, I felt I could spring for it. He ordered for both of them, burger, fries, onion rings, and hush puppies. A lot of canola oil trees died for his sins.

I settled for some fries and a soda.

"Gotta eat for two now," he said, patting her belly. Then he poured her a beer.

It is not my job to discuss fetal alcohol syndrome, I told myself, suspecting that a lecture from me might not be the route to getting them to talk. But I didn't listen to that voice. "Is it a good idea to drink when you're pregnant? I think I read something about alcohol not being so hot for a developing baby."

"It's just beer," Bubba answered for her. "Besides, my mama drank like a fish every day of her life and it didn't hurt me none."

Sad to say, I wished that Bayard had done the right thing, been a daddy to his child, at least enough of a daddy to have taken the kid and dumped it on Aunt Greta to raise. As bad as she was, she wasn't this bad. But I was a private eye, not a social worker.

"When was the last time you saw Bayard?" I asked her.

"Just 'fore I got up with Butch here," she said, then hastily added, "Only about the money, honey. Nothin' else."

"How long have you been together?" I asked him. This was going to take a while if I had to ask his and hers questions.

"'Bout three or four months," he answered. "We're not really married yet, but we're gonna be just as soon as I can scrape together some dough to have a wedding good enough for my wife. That's why it'd be real nice to get all that money that rich asshole owes us."

Nope, wasn't going to touch that one with the longest pole I'd ever seen in my life. Ignoring his wedding plans based on her ex's money, I asked, "Where did you meet him?"

She scowled. I realized that was her thinking face. However, it seemed that her face muscles were working more than her brain. "Oh, that nice place on…what's the road that runs by the mall?"

"At a restaurant?"

"Yes."

I was hoping for a home address, but I couldn't be that lucky.

"When you were together, where did you meet?"

The short answer was cheap motels, the long answer was, "Romantic places like that hotel where that famous preacher man got caught with a prostitute. He liked to drive around until he found a place with vibrating beds, kinky stuff like that."

"Did you ever go anywhere, take a trip?"

The short answer was that they once went up to Baton Rouge to one of the cheap motels there. The long answer was…oh, never mind.

A mountain of grease was placed in front of us. Butch waved for another pitcher of beer.

According to her the only reason Bayard stayed in the area was because his mother needed him. I'd say the nouns were reversed, that he needed his mother, the money doled out from his father's large life insurance policy, her cooking, cleaning for him, and generally reflecting him at twice his size—no, this was Bayard—ten times his size. She thought he might have mentioned moving to Florida. Or maybe it was California. Some place where the sun was always shining.

I could confine my search to below the Mason-Dixon Line. That was helpful.

"Oh, yeah, there was one weird thing," Melva-Raylene said.

I waited for the long story.

"He said somethin' about having to get to the cemetery 'fore it closed. That last time I saw him. I was asking him when I'd get my money and I told him he could at least buy me somethin' to eat, but he said that he didn't have time, that he had to get out to the cemetery 'fore closing."

She stopped long enough to eat a hush puppy.

"Did he say which cemetery?"

"Don't remember," she said, chewing with her mouth open. "Just that he wanted to beat the rush hour and get there…"

"Before it closed," I finished for her so she could concentrate on her chewing.

I graciously offered the rest of my fries—I think I managed to eat two of them—to Butch and Melva-Raylene. I left two twenties on the table, more than enough to pay the bill, but there was at least one child at home and one on the way and maybe some of the change would be used for them.

I knew why Bayard would go to a cemetery. To find a grave of someone born around the time he was and who had died, so he could take that person's identity.

As I drove away from Kenner I considered—I could start a rock rolling—tell Aunt Greta about her grandchild, but couldn't see where it would end. Would she, could she, be of any help to this child? Or would it be a tug-of-war, with winning more important to both sides then the care of a kid? If they thought Bayard was rich, one look at the nice house of Aunt Greta's might cause them to leech onto her. Even if they were willing to give the kid up—and I'd bet that Butch would be willing to hand over another man's child for the right price—it wasn't likely that Bayard would be more of a father then he was now. That would leave the care of a toddler to Aunt Greta, and she wasn't young.

That could be hell for both of them—her tired and demanding rules to be obeyed and a kid who had the energy to outlast her in the daily battles.

The taste of revenge wasn't quite so sweet now, I thought as I walked to my car. I doubted that Butch would be able to live off whatever they were able to squeeze out of Bayard, but he was truly a weasel to slime out of supporting a kid he'd fathered. At least part of my revenge would be to right that wrong. And, then…just let everything else fall whatever way it would.

A glance at my watch told me that it was likely that the cemetery was, in Melva-Raylene's immortal words, "not yet closed." That was one of the reasons her stories were so long, she said the same thing over and over again.

It was a guess, but he was my cousin and, much as I didn't like him, I did know him. He was lazy. That meant he went to the closest cemetery, one near the house that I didn't really want to return to. Long shot, but maybe his laziness was to my advantage, he'd start nearest to where he parked his car and find one or two possible names. It was a nice afternoon and I was willing to try my odds before stopping again at that ugly house.

Metairie Cemetery was just off I-10 and, for Bayard's sake and mine, also close to Aunt Greta's house in Old Metairie. I'd give it about an hour; get some sunshine and vitamin D, so the afternoon wouldn't be a total waste.

But the gods of lost/skipped-town cousins were with me.

"That guy? Yeah, he was acting weird," the first groundskeeper I showed his picture to said.

"Weird? How?" It's important to ask incisive questions in the detective business.

"Wandering around, looking at grave markers, taking pictures on his cell phone of a few of them. Asked him if I could help him find someone and he got weasely on me, gave some story about being a photographer and wanting to take pictures of the graves before they got washed away. So I asked where his cameras were and he spun a story about them being stolen. He claimed to be from out of town, but with a New Orleans accent so thick, you could use it to make a roux."

I laughed as he expected me to; that was obviously a line he'd used before.

"I kept a good eye on him, let me tell you," he continued. "But he just wandered for a little while more, took a few more pictures and then left."

"Do you remember where he was looking?" I asked.

He pointed out the area. As I suspected, it was as close to the parking lot as it could be for him to find anything useful.

"You got any idea what he was doing?"

I told him.

"Damn. Some people got the nerve. Don't like him disturbing folks resting here. He a criminal or something?"

I didn't see any point in lying to the groundskeeper. "He owes some money, child support, and seems to have skipped out on it. I've been hired to find him."

"Damn. Thought there was something hinky about him. Guess I was right," he said as he walked with me to where he'd seen Bayard.

He helped me look once I told him what to search for.

We searched for about half an hour. The groundskeeper was pretty sure we'd covered the area where he'd seen Bayard. We came up with five possible names:

> Leslie Gruberston
> Melvin Weinberger
> Frankton V. Alzimer III
> Dirk Westen
> Alvin deLeaux

I thanked the groundskeeper for his help and headed back to my car. Before I started it, I looked over the list of names. Leslie could be used as a woman's name, so he wasn't likely to use that one. My cousin had many prejudices, one of them against the Jews taking over the world, so he probably wouldn't take the second name. The third was distinctive, probably too much so. Ah, number four. I'd bet Bayard wouldn't mind being a Dirk. Plus it was the shortest name and therefore the easiest to spell and remember. It's not a good thing to be unable to spell your own name.

The days were getting longer, so it was still light when I again arrived at that repulsive house. Still no lights on. No one home.

By now I was pretty sure that with Aunt Greta still up in

Shreveport and Bayard in either California or Florida—or maybe Texas or Arizona, some sunny state—there would be no one around to ask what I was doing here. Even though Aunt Greta had hired me—to do her a favor—I suspected that she wouldn't be happy at my snooping in her house. Which is why I wasn't going to ask her permission or tell her I did it.

I was hoping that Bayard was lazy and sloppy enough to have searched on the computer here for new places to live.

It was almost too easy. I was beginning to suspect that he was deliberately laying down a false trail to mislead me.

Except that he wouldn't have guessed that Aunt Greta might be desperate enough to find her oldest son to ask me to look for him. And he'd always made it clear that he thought I was stupid, that he was the clever one. He wasn't likely to think I would be smart enough to find him.

And if it had been anyone outside the family, it would have been much harder to trace him. Aunt Greta wouldn't have cooperated on letting someone into her house—like I was now.

Plus who would have guessed that his password was "freesafety" for his one moment of football glory, when as a second-string defensive player, a pass was tipped right into his hands and he managed to run it back for a touchdown.

That was my third attempt at his password; the first was his name, the second "password" and the third the charm.

So I was now sitting staring at his Internet searches in the days before he left.

South Florida. Fort Lauderdale, Miami.

I was ruthless. I went through his e-mails. He was corresponding with a twenty-something in Fort Lauderdale, spinning a tale of woe, destruction from Katrina, how he had pulled people off their roofs, seen bodies eaten by alligators (all this while driving Aunt Greta up to Shreveport two days before the storm hit). He'd lost his family, his sainted mother, and was all alone in the world. He wanted to go someplace safe—like the south Florida coast wasn't just waiting for a storm to sucker punch it.

He had researched short-term rentals in the Fort Lauderdale area, plus had listing for several apartments there as well. I printed out all the pages with the addresses on them. Once I was done, I turned off the computer and printer, wiped away my fingerprints—not likely that anyone would look, but better a suspiciously clean keyboard than evidence that I had technically broken and entered.

I didn't want to stay any longer than I had to. There were still too many memories in these walls. There would always be too many here. I hastily left, almost taking the spare key instead of hiding it back under the very fake rock.

Once I was in my car and heading for the sanctity of Orleans Parish, I contemplated my options. I had followed the data, not really thinking about where it would lead me. Aunt Greta hadn't asked me to uncover evidence that her son was a crook and could go to jail.

I could drop it and tell her I hadn't been able to find anything. Let him disappear. To a place where once he fell—and he would, the money wouldn't last forever—there would be no one there to catch him. Let Aunt Greta live with a hole in her life like she'd left me—telling my mother I had died because my mother wasn't what she considered a proper person.

Or I could turn what I knew over to the police—and Mr. Stolen Porsche, Alpha Al, and Butch the baby maker, let them become the furies of my revenge.

I could dump everything on Aunt Greta's lap; let her know her son had jettisoned her without a backward glance when he concluded he didn't need her anymore.

What I would do was go home, sleep on it, and hope that somehow an answer arrived in the night.

The answer arrived about midmorning the next day.

A client needed some majorly important documents delivered to Naples. Florida, not Italy. A quick look at a map told me that Naples was about a two-hour drive across the Everglades from Fort Lauderdale. I would leave tomorrow, and it was okay with them if I took an extra day or two once I had delivered the documents.

The phone rang and I didn't answer it. It was Aunt Greta. She left a message asking if I'd found Bayard yet. I waited until I was pretty sure she'd be out—she always did her errands after two in the afternoon—and called back. I was right, or lucky, and only had to leave a message, telling her that I hadn't located him just yet but had some very promising leads and I'd call her in a couple of days.

The rest of the day was spent getting ready to travel. I made arrangements to rent a car for a few days. My client was okay covering a night in Fort Lauderdale instead of Naples. I couldn't fly back the same day even if I wanted to, so that cost was built into his job. Far fewer planes came into New Orleans now, and if it wasn't a trip to Atlanta or Houston, the options were limited.

I made copies of everything I had on Bayard; I'd need the VIN should I stumble over a shiny red Porsche. Plus a couple more copies of his picture in case the police wanted several.

My plan was to fly into Naples, drop off the documents, then head east to Fort Lauderdale. If planes and traffic were kind, I'd be there by late afternoon. A quick check into my hotel, then prowl some of the addresses Bayard had left on his computer, just to see if I got lucky. In the morning, I'd find a wireless hotspot and do a run on the names he might be using; see if that netted me anything. If I had some leads I might stay an extra day and run them down; if not, I'd get a flight out the next day.

"Vengeance is mine," I murmured as I headed up the stairs at home.

"What did you say?" Cordelia, my partner, was home. Early for her.

As I came into the bedroom, I amended, "I was just musing on the ways karma comes around. You're home early."

She made a face. "I'm taking a quick nap. I agreed to cover for Lynn this evening."

"You're too kind," I said as I rummaged for the small duffel bag in the closet.

"She's taking next weekend for me." Many doctors hadn't come back after Katrina, so it was easy—sometimes too easy—for Cordelia to find work. "Are you going somewhere?" she asked.

"Courier. To Naples. Leaving tomorrow."

She glanced at the four pairs of underwear I was stuffing into the duffel.

"And…a little side trip." I told her about Aunt Greta's request.

"You're going to find your cousin?" she asked, her voice neutral, but her eyes showing worry.

I explained, "He's fled town, probably stole a nice new Porsche from a neighbor, skipped out on child support, and looted his last gainful employer. Plus abandoned his poor widowed mother. He doesn't want to be found. I'm going to find him." Then I added, "Or else he's dead and I need to find him so I can spit on his grave."

"I thought I heard you saying something about vengeance as you came up the stairs."

"Finally. I have power over him. This dish of revenge will be served well chilled."

"Oh, Micky," she said, "be careful what you ask for." She hugged me as if she could see a ghost that I couldn't, then said, "I do need to take a nap or I'll be useless tonight."

"I'll be quiet," I promised. Then added, "The weekend off…is for us to be together?"

"Yes," she said as she got in bed. "For us." Now she smiled at me.

"Good, I'd like that," I answered as I turned off the light to let her sleep.

The plane was on time, the rental car ready, the office to drop the documents easy to find, then I was leaving the palm trees of Naples to the ribbon of road through the Everglades.

It took me a little over two hours to get to Fort Lauderdale. I'd grown up in the old South, clapboard houses with shady overhanging trees. This was the new South, tall buildings all promising beach views or lagoon views, or some water somewhere views—"you can see your bathtub from the living room." It struck me as all plastic and concrete, and I felt older than every building in the city. Palm trees were planted evenly, clearly hauled in and put in their place rather than growing because nature dropped a random seed there.

I know I'm biased, but give me my old beat-up city with its history written in the old walls, cobblestoned streets, and oak tree roots winning against the sidewalks trying to contain them.

The hotel was easy to find. It had a view of one of the canals. After unpacking, I took the time to find the addresses Bayard had left on a map and plotted a route from the hotel past them all.

It's sad that I know my cousin so well, I thought as I cruised by the first address. He wouldn't live here. There was a store across the street with a name in Spanish and more than a smattering of people whose dark skin tones didn't come from the beach.

The second place was more promising, but I noticed a security cop out front. Big, black, and mean looking. His color might not stop Bayard—security was menial in his mind—but the scrutiny might. He wouldn't want someone observing his comings and goings.

The third place seemed a little downscale for his vanity. It was painted a festive pink but that didn't hide its cinder block construction. A small two-story row, with outside steps that led to a walkway that would be called a balcony in the real estate ads. If he was smart this was the kind of place he would stay. But an expensive red sports car would stick out. The parking ringed the outside, so I drove by both sides, but saw only beige or silver cars.

The next place was probably where he wanted to live, an expensive location right on the beach. The parking was hidden so I couldn't look for the telltale car, but I bet that it wasn't the kind of place that allowed just anyone to move in, especially someone with no job, no recommendations from previous landlords, and an oily manner.

The next two were also on the beach, also in the expensive category. An unctuous smile and a few months' rent weren't going to be enough to get him a place in either of those.

I had four more to go, but it was getting late; I hadn't eaten lunch and this driving around seemed pointless. He knew what he wanted, but he didn't seem to understand that he couldn't get there on the route he was traveling. These kinds of places were for doctors or lawyers or MBAs, people who spent time in school and worked hard so they could eventually get the place on the beach. His list was probably what he wanted, not what he could have. I'd do better going back to the hotel, firing up the computer and searching his bogus names. And eating lunch. He wasn't worth being hungry over.

The next to last one on the list was on the way back to the hotel, so I left the main artery to give it a pass. It was a new construction, but well landscaped so it didn't look like all the trees had been mowed down to make way for a building. There was a fairly large swimming pool. No red car. But in the balcony of the end apartment there were several empty beer bottles left sitting on the small table. Abita beer, a local New Orleans brand. Bayard liked his beer and was too lazy to pick up after himself.

But I was hungry and it was time to return to my old friend the computer and cease traveling for one day. And appease my grumbling stomach.

Lunch was good, a grilled grouper sandwich, but the computer was not friendly. It had been barely a week at most since he'd left town, of course he hadn't legally registered his car—I wondered if he even had insurance—or appeared on the voting roles or any other public record. Nothing for Dirk Westen or any of the other names he stole from graves. Bayard Robedeaux only appeared where it was likely to appear, back in New Orleans. The fruitless computer search took up the remainder of the waning afternoon.

If I was smart I would have just read a book, gone to bed, and caught the next plane out. But what we think we want and need to heal old wounds can blind us. I'd left Bayard to fate, left him to find his own destruction for too long. It was time for me to give him a justified push.

I left the hotel and drove back to the apartment complex with the empty beer bottles. The sun was setting, and darkness makes it easier to do a stakeout. I found a parking place on the road that was under a low-hanging branch, but gave me a decent view of the balcony and a sliver into the apartment.

And then I waited.

The TV shows only look glamorous because they edit out these parts, when the PI sits in her car for a couple of hours trying to not fall asleep.

It was three hours into my vigil when I heard the sound of a vehicle that wanted people to notice it.

A red sports car zoomed right by me. It was going too fast to notice me, sitting in my nondescript rental. It jerked to a halting stop at the turn into the apartment parking lot. Then lurched into a right turn.

"Someone doesn't know how to drive a stick shift very well," I murmured to myself.

Halting and jerking, the car pulled into the parking stop under the balcony with the beer bottles still reflecting the streetlight.

My cousin got out.

"You made it too easy," I said softly, although I didn't really mean it. He made it easy enough for me to win, and that was all that really counted.

From the passenger side, a young girl—woman, I guess, I was hoping that she was over eighteen, but it was hard to tell in the darkness—got out. She took a heavy grocery bag from the backseat, while Bayard managed to heft a six-pack of beer. Guess they ran out of Abitas.

"You got that, baby?" he said in his nasal voice. "Soon as my back is better, you know I'll do the heavy stuff."

She followed him into the entrance door and a few seconds later, the lights in the upstairs apartment came on.

No one came out to the balcony to clean off the beer bottles. Faintly in the background I heard a TV come on. They were probably in for the night.

I had a nice comfortable hotel room waiting for me, and a decent, albeit late, dinner. I could come by in the morning and finish this.

This is usually the point in the case when I relax, when I've found out what I need to know and it's mostly a matter of a few more inevitable steps. But I was far from calm as I drove away from his hideout.

"I've won," I chortled, pumping my fist at a red light. "I've won, you bastard. I'm never going to be your younger cousin again."

I didn't sleep well that night, imagining all the different ways this could end—he could fight back, but he wasn't in good shape. I went to the gym and had done karate long enough to have made it to brown belt. It would be satisfying to punch him. Or he could just give up; whimper as the cops led him away.

I woke early, at first light, and headed back his apartment. I had a few things I needed to check just to be sure. Highly unlikely, but maybe he had a different Porsche than the one stolen from his neighbor. If the VINs matched, I'd call the police and hand them a grand theft auto.

The streetlights had just gone off when I got there. It was a silent, misty morning, almost fog. Appropriate weather to catch a crook. I pulled into the apartment driveway, taking an open space in the outer ring of the parking lot about fifty feet away from the dew-covered red car. He'd know I was here soon enough, but I still had a few things to do. And I wanted to savor the moment.

I walked slowly, almost casually to where the alleged stolen car was parked. I glanced at the paperwork I was carrying in a folder. All the little string of facts that had brought me here. The idiot still had

Louisiana license plates on it. It wasn't the same tag as when it was stolen—I had that number written down—he had been smart enough to steal a license plate, but not smart enough to do it again once he got to Florida.

The VIN matched.

The outside door to the apartment opened.

I couldn't be sure, because I hadn't seen her very well in the darkness, but it looked like Bayard's latest girl toy.

"Nice car, isn't it?" she said, a slight Southern drawl in her voice.

"Very nice. Is it yours?"

"My boyfriend's."

"You're up early."

"The breakfast shift. You're up early yourself. You a line cook or something?" She seemed to realize that she was talking to a stranger, someone she knew nothing about. "You live here? I haven't seen you around."

"No, not a line cook, don't live here."

"So what are you doing here?" She was starting to get suspicious. "Checking out cars?"

She was young and she was about to learn one of life's unkind lessons. I would have preferred that she toddle off to work, but she seemed to sense that I was not here to do her any favors. If she called the police that might not be a bad outcome, but she would probably first run upstairs to Bayard, and the last thing I wanted was for him to get a chance to squeal out before anyone with arresting powers arrived.

"I don't steal cars. Especially ones already stolen."

As intended, that rocked her world. Her eyes opened wide. "Wha...?" But she couldn't think of a question to ask before I continued.

"I'm a private investigator." I pulled out my license and flashed it at her. "I was hired to find someone who vanished around the same time this car did." Then I brandished the picture of Bayard. "Have you ever seen this person around here?" I asked.

She gasped, the sputtered out, "That's Dirk. My boyfriend."

"Dirk Westen?" I asked.

"Yes."

"Dirk Westen died in 2003."

"What?" She's not the bad guy, I had to remind myself. She seemed so young, with a naïve openness that scoundrels like Bayard have been taking advantage of since we started walking upright.

"Dirk Westen is a name he stole from a grave. They were born in the same year. This way he could get a social security number. His real name is Bayard Robedeaux, he left New Orleans about two weeks ago, using his neighbor's fancy car as his ride. He left behind a not very happy former employer who was robbed, about three years of unpaid child support and—"

"This can't be real…is this one of them reality shows?"

"No," I said gently. "This is just real life. How did you meet him?"

"Online. We met online. One of those dating services. I didn't think anything would come of it. But he seemed so nice. He…wasn't pushy, but very attentive. He said he wanted to settle down, find a good girl and make a life. It sounded so nice. He was so nice," she repeated as if the word could make the ugliness go away. She bit her lip, her brow furrowed. Suddenly she said, "I got to go talk to him. He can explain this."

"Don't," I cautioned as I surreptitiously took my cell phone from my pocket. "You're okay now. You didn't know you were aiding a criminal. If you go talk to him, help him in any way, you become accessory to the crime. Don't go to jail over this." That was probably pushing it, but at the moment I needed her worried and confused, not ready to fight to the end for her man.

She bit her lip again.

I dialed the police. I turned away from her, trying to keep my voice low, so she wouldn't hear me turn her boyfriend into the authorities.

"I'm calling about a stolen car. I'm a private investigator and I was hired to check out a stolen Porsche. I've located it and now it's time to turn it over to you." I gave them the address.

When I turned back around, she was gone.

A light came on in the upstairs apartment.

I broke into a cold sweat—I wanted this too much, was caught between listening for the siren of the police and footsteps on the stairs. The silence was agonizing.

I glanced at my watch. Then looked at it closely to make sure it was still working.

Another minute ticked by and nothing happened.

Then footsteps on the stairs.

She came out first, still biting her lip, still looking worried.

He followed her, his face haggard with sleep and a dawning disbelief. He had thrown on jeans and a ratty T-shirt and was wearing pink flip-flops that were an inch too short for his feet. Probably mixed up his and hers in the dark.

First he looked at the car.

Then at me.

The seconds ticked before he finally spoke. "Micky? What are you doing here?"

"Your mama was worried about you. She called me, asked for a favor—like I owed any of you any favors."

"This is a joke, isn't it?"

"Aunt Greta called me, she asked me to find you."

He rubbed his eyes. "Oh, damn. Yeah, I'll call her in a little bit. Just been too busy." He started to head back into the apartment.

"And there's the matter of the stolen car, the break-in at Alpha Al's, and the child support," I shot at him.

"What the hell are you talking about? None of that's your business."

"I stumbled over them—and I do mean stumbled—since you did nothing to cover your tracks, trying to find you. As Aunt Greta requested."

"Okay, so you've found me. You've had your little fun, woke me up at the butt crack of dawn. It's too early to call Mama now, I'll do it later." He again turned away.

"Stolen car, looted workplace, child support. Those don't just go away."

He sighed audibly, letting me know that I was wasting his time. "Todd told me I could borrow his car—"

"Really? Wasn't what he told me."

"He must've forgot. Besides, he was always revving that thing up at all hours; no one on the block could sleep. I'm doing everyone a favor. I'll bring it back in a couple of days. I'll call him right after I call Mama, okay?"

"Child support?"

He shook his head angrily. "Wasn't my fault. Told her I didn't want kids. Forked out twenty dollars a month for her to buy things to take care of it. She tricked me, didn't take her pills and got pregnant. Thought I'd marry her. No way, José. I even offered to pay half the cost of getting rid of it. Next thing I know she's callin' sayin' I'm a daddy and I owe her money." He didn't give me a chance to say anything, rushing on, "And as for Al, the bastard cheated us every day I worked there. He'd skim off our commissions, forget to do paperwork, so we didn't get paid. I was just getting back the money he owed me."

"There's always an excuse for everything, isn't there?" I said.

"I'm tellin' the truth. I'm…" He was looking at something over my shoulder.

I turned to see the police car pulling into the parking lot.

He looked at me, then back at the cops, saying nothing as they parked right next to his stolen Porsche.

"You called the cops?" he hissed at me.

I saw fear in his eyes. Fear, uncertainty. And then desolation.

I had won.

"Yeah, I called the cops." I twisted away. He was no longer my cousin, instead a trapped animal about to be put in a cage.

I spoke briefly to the police officers, gave them the information about the stolen car. I didn't bother with the child support or Alpha Al's tale.

They handcuffed him, paying no attention to his claim repeated over and over that he had permission to use the car, his jeans sliding down his flabby butt, the pink flip-flops almost funny if he hadn't been so desperate.

His girlfriend ran upstairs and came rushing down with his real pair, putting them on him just as the cops had him in the backseat of their car. Then they shut the door and left.

She stood watching them leave, those ridiculous pink things in her hand, until there was nothing to see. Then she looked at me. "What am I gonna do?" She seemed bewildered, all alone in a parking lot in the early morning.

I had no answers for her save the usual clichés. Get her stuff out of the apartment, the police might come back and search. Find a friend who can be with her for a while. Don't get sucked into his mess.

But she didn't seem like she'd heard a word as she went back into the apartment, closing the door as quietly as she could.

I returned to my hotel and checked out, heading for the airport. I flew to Atlanta, then had to wait hours before I could get a flight back to New Orleans. It was a long, dreary day.

I'd won, hadn't I? So, why did I feel so lost? Because I'd learned that revenge isn't sweet; it's bitter and sour, relentless because it can never be undone.

CHASING ATHENA
DIANE ANDERSON-MINSHALL

When you think mean streets, you imagine the slums of New York or maybe L.A.'s South Central, places where law and order ceded to drug cartels and urban gangs long ago. You don't imagine the tree-lined boulevards of Portland, Oregon.

I've been a cop in Baltimore and private dick in the Big Apple and the Big Easy and they got nothing on this backwater burg, which the mayor's pitchmen like to call the City of Roses. I saw the lawlessness and corruption in post-Katrina New Orleans, a place where—for better or worse—everything goes, and still I was as surprised as anyone to discover that Portland had an even darker distinction. It has the dubious reputation of being a major port in the modern sex trade.

I just fished a dead hooker out of a Dumpster behind the Pussy Palladium, one of Portland's many strip clubs, and not a single patron seemed concerned. After gawking at the dead body, they disappeared back into the safety of the windowless club or fled to their SUVs and their banal suburban lives.

Surprisingly, Portland has more strip clubs per capita than any other city in the country. There's something for every taste. Like the chicks with the big balloons and blond ponies? Try Mary's. Want to see a contortionist with pierced labia and body ink that'd make a circus freak blush? Check out Club Devi8. Last year, some wank even made headlines by starting a vegan strip club—which led to far too many jokes about how there's no fur in that joint, if you know what I mean, heh heh heh. I've been to a shitload of titty bars, and I can tell you, none of the strippers have fur anymore. They're all shaved clean, like porn stars and pre-pubescent girls.

I've seen 'em all this year, so many palaces of pussy that I've started to feel like a gynecologist. You seen one hairless muff, you've seen 'em all. At this point, they mean nothing to me beyond professional curiosity. I'm just looking for one in particular.

The deal is, this fleece-clad strip club–loving town has an even seedier underbelly. It's the sex trafficking hot spot along the West Coast's I-5, corridor and while some of the local feminists consider their city's strip clubs are cool indicators of gender equality (at some of 'em you can find as many chicks throwing dollar bills on the stage as dudes), nobody likes the red light districts. A couple of years ago, the city tried to beautify the pros out of business by renaming one of their main thoroughfares, Eighty-second Street, the "Avenue of the Roses." Somehow the name change didn't drive business down, although locals now call the hookers "roses."

I'm looking for one of those roses now. One of the roses used to be my girl, and I'm determined to find her. I've already followed her trail across the country, and I won't stop looking until I find her. I'll look anywhere. Even in Dumpsters. Hence the reason I find myself fishing dead hookers out of Dumpsters and ditches and crack houses, even two thousand miles away from everything I know.

Let me take you back a beat. This is the oldest story in the book. Girl falls for girl, girl loses girl, girl goes crazy trying to find girl again. Except with a twist. Look, I'm a die-hard dyke and I'm good at my job, but I don't usually get the girl. I don't look like the broads on television, even the girls on the lesbian shows. I've sported the same cropped mullet since I started playing softball in ninth grade (the same year I fell for Eileen Delvecchio) and I've worn my high school letterman's jacket almost every day since I got it. I still strap my cell phone to my belt, and if I carry a bag at all, it's filled with a note pad, binoculars, bottled water, and PowerBars, not lipstick and a mini vibrator. I'm just an ordinary dyke and I know it.

But when I met Athena, she made me *feel l*ike the king of the fucking world. I guess that's how I ended up being the rube in my own story. I was in New Orleans for this PI convention, which sounds a lot sexier than it was. Mostly, it was me and a bunch of stiffs all trading barbs and jostling to the get the attention of insurance industry blowhards who usually get shitfaced and then assign out their biggest cases to a small roster of private investigation companies at the annual affair. It's hard to get those kind of gigs when you're on your own. I've been in the game a few years, ever since I left Baltimore Narcotics in search of a career path where I wouldn't have to fill out paperwork and get permission from my supervisors to so much as take a dump. Working for yourself is liberating. But it's a lot harder to pay the bills. So there I was in New Orleans, trying to pimp myself to one of these insurance reps so I can pay my mortgage.

Then Larry, this pharmaceutical investigator—who knew drug companies had their very own PIs, right?—Larry said we got to hit the titty bars on Bourbon Street. I'm not saying I don't like looking at T&A, especially when they're as buoyant as those on this chick at Big Dolly's, but the two-drink minimum meant throwing away twenty bucks on some swill called Cajun wine that tasted distinctly like cough syrup and Tabasco. My roll of one-dollar bills was rapidly depleted, and lap dances were totally out of my price range.

Plus, it didn't take long before I stopped thinking about tits and ass and starting thinking about the women swinging on the stripper poles. You know, about the dancers themselves, off the stage. Like: Does the redhead cowgirl have to leave her kids with a babysitter? Does the sexy construction worker spend all day at another job? Did the blonde in the schoolgirl outfit have a shitty childhood? And how could any of them possibly still be attracted to men after having to dance on their indiscriminate boners for eight hours, night after night? Had they all gone lesbo? I could swear I was getting a few lingering glances that were more than just delight at finding a woman among their clientele.

So I was sitting there, analyzing each broad's life like I was Dr. Phil, and after a while I just had to bolt. I took off, ran out onto Bourbon Street, mingled with the frat boys and drag queens and drank my way to Pat O'Brien's, a piano bar that a half-drunk hot dog vendor nearby assured me was a bit of a tourist trap but still "awfully fun."

Five minutes later, I saw a goddess, and my story is all down hill from there.

At Pat O's, dueling piano players take turn rousing the crowds with songs both regional like "Dixie" and what they probably call "adult contemporary" (though the latter seemed to be songs two or three decades old, like Billy Joel's "Piano Man"). The surly waiters served up these giant drinks called Hurricanes that tasted a little like Kool-Aid and rum while roving photographers snapped black-and-whites of tables full of idiots laughing, singing, and drinking. It seriously took all of one drink and two songs before I, too, was blitzed on the atmosphere, and before you know it I was singing the Alabama fight song (which I swear I don't know the words to) and I had become best buds with two babes from Ohio and a guy from Tennessee. It was the perfect release after a long day at the conference and a confusing night at the strip club.

Then I spotted this broad across the room, a perfect brunette version of Jessica Rabbit. She was the kind of woman for whom the descriptor va-va-voom was too tame. She was all angles and hips and curves you couldn't wait to climb and plant your flag on. The piano players switched their tune and the room began crooning a song by a local band, mellow and jazz, the beat of New Orleans.

I'll never forget it. The song and the way this woman moved with the music like the song was written especially for her. She was practically alone in the corner, I couldn't tell who she was with, perhaps with the three winsome ladies at the table behind her, but after watching her, mesmerized for three or four songs, I was encouraged by the Hurricanes to find out more.

"Hi," I yelled over the din. The word hung there, unanswered. The brunette continued to sway and the song came to a close. Still no response. I turned away, defeated. But just then she grabbed my hand and pulled me toward her.

"You just got here." She spoke with a throaty growl. It was the sexy kind of growl like Kathleen Turner.

"What?" I shouted, "I've been here for an hour!"

Her smile was like the rising sun. "No, I mean, you just got *here*. Don't go."

"Oh, sorry. I'm Parker."

"I like that. Parker." As my name rolled off her tongue, I immediately knew I never wanted another woman to say my name. My name would never sound as good coming out of another set of lips.

She told me her name, but she stayed an enigma for the next hour, even as I ordered more and more drinks and she continued dancing for me as if I were the only person in the room—which was so not true because the place was jam packed—and a photographer snapped our picture. Of course I bought it from him, even though it took my last twenty bucks to do so.

When I look at the picture now, I can see it clearly: I'm beaming and drunk and she looks like a woman haunted by a secret, but all I could see that night were those hazel eyes and big lips and all those angles and curves.

"Let's go," she said, grabbing my hand, not even pretending it was a question for me to answer. She knew me all of ninety minutes and assumed I'd follow her anywhere, which I would. Which I did. Which is how I got to Portland.

❖

We spent the next four days holed up at the Raven Hotel, a rather divey joint on St. Charles where the courtyard was filled with pros and the ground-floor diner was filled with cops. The nondescript room had a worn-out bed, clean linens, and little else, but I was so excited by marathon sex session that I didn't think to ask why she dragged me to this particular flophouse or why she seemed so at home with both the pros and the cops.

"Woman, you make me crazy," I moaned, flipping her on her stomach so I could kiss her lower back. I traced every curve from the nape of her neck—where a spiked gold star tattoo was fading fast—to her deliciously shapely ass. Even on day three or four, I couldn't get enough of her. I don't remember eating or drinking, though we surely must have; I just remember wanting to do nothing but make love to this broad the rest of my life.

"Tell me something about yourself."

She licked her lips and cocked her head at me. "Why? Are you bored with what we're doing now?" She moved her hand between my thighs without waiting for an answer, a moment of passion that now serves as a perfect example of how I could spend ninety-six hours with the same broad and learn so little about her.

She was a dancer, or an actress, or something like that. She was spending a month or two in New Orleans, then heading west, or north, or home—wherever that was I never heard. It was all so vague, but I was intoxicated with pussy and didn't even think there'd come a day where we stopped doing what we were doing. But it did.

On day five, the love affair ended. When I woke up sticky and dehydrated, Athena was gone and so were my wallet and cell phone.

Sitting on the toilet, I watched a lone cockroach scurry across the bathroom basin, no doubt on the way to a room where there was actual food to pilfer. I waited a while, making excuses: Maybe she took my wallet to get us beignets and coffee. Maybe she took my phone so she could call me at the hotel and tell me where she had gone. Maybe she was coming back.

She didn't.

The pockmarked boy behind the counter stared blankly at me. "Wait, what do you want?"

He couldn't grasp my query until I spoke to him like a six-year-old. "The woman who rented room forty-two, do you have *any* contact info? A phone number? She left but took my wallet." I was too frantic to be as mortified as I should be. I was still imagining a future in which she was kneeling above me, long hair falling across the sides of face, hot thighs spread before me like a—

"Hello!" The clerk shouted it like a question, breaking me from my reverie. Great, he finally talks and I nod off to fucking fantasyland.

"Sorry? What was that?" I pleaded.

"Look, lady, chicks like that come and go. They pay cash, stay a few hours, maybe a day or two. Get their mark on the hook, them take them for all they got. Don't usually see women johns, but hey, whatever floats your boat. It's the Big Easy, after all. You're lucky if all she took was your wallet." He ran his index finger across his jugular, "Coulda slit your throat."

With that he turned around and started placing sticky notes around his desk, a sign for me to move the hell on.

Maybe Athena was a dancer, a euphemism for stripper. But it was hard to believe she turned tricks, too. She certainly hadn't treated me like a john, and there hadn't been enough money in that wallet to pay for one night, much less four. But still, I wondered if the desk clerk could be right. Could Athena be a pro? What we'd had was special, wasn't it? If so, how could she just leave?

I left the Raven and walked, head down, hands in pockets, hoping the muggy Mississippi air would clear my head, wipe the cobwebs from my brain, and make this whole thing clear.

I'd like to say that was the end of it all: I somehow paid up with my own much nicer hotel and headed back to Brooklyn, leaving this broad and the lessons learned long behind me. But I can't. I stayed in New Orleans another week, tromping through every bar, cabaret, and strip club in the French Quarter, showing that black-and-white tourist photo from Pat O'Brien's to bartenders and door barkers and exotic dancers of both the male and female varieties, and a few who were clearly somewhere in between.

I spent hours on the phone calling my own cell number, hoping she'd finally answer. Why would she have taken my phone if she didn't intend to use it? I left messages that started out lucid and ended up in drunken rants begging her to come back, or at least call me.

Then one day I was talking to a buddy back home and she suggested I check my credit card to see if Athena had charged anything on it. I could have slapped myself. How could I call myself a PI? Only a woman obsessed would troll every sleazy bar in a city of one million but forget to just call the credit card company. By the time I did, Athena had left me a pedestrian but important record of her travels. There were purchases first in Baton Rouge, then Lafayette, Houston, Dallas, Albuquerque. She was moving west using my credit card. Instead of being pissed, I was relieved. I finally knew where she was. I finally had a connection with her. Maybe, I wondered, maybe she was using the card to stay in touch with me; maybe it was her way of leaving a trail of bread crumbs into the forest. With every purchase, I was one step closer to finding the woman who had become my all-consuming passion.

I kept telling people I was chasing this broad by necessity, but, really, how far does a normal person—even a fucking PI—go just to retrieve a wallet and a phone and maybe get a few answers about why she became a mark in the first place? The thing is, I couldn't believe I was a mark. I still don't. Maybe I started out a mark, but at the end of those four days, I don't think that's what I was. I think we had something. I felt it, she felt it. I don't know what spooked her, why she ran, but if I could just find her, hold her, I could figure it all out.

I got myself a new cell phone with a new number but kept the old one active, just in case she responded to one of my messages. Then I hit the road, always one state behind her, the credit card tab leading me to red light districts in half a dozen cities across the west. I showed that photo of us to the clerks at the adult toy store, massage parlor, liquor store, doughnut shop, and Laundromat near each location she stopped at. They always remembered her, the tall icy brunette with the hips and curves and overall va-va-voom. Who the hell was this woman and what the hell was she doing at these joints?

As soon as I got close, she was a ghost. Then my buddy Wyatt Turlington at Phoenix Vice called me with some news.

"We've got a dead hooker here, Parker, and I thought she might be your gal." Wyatt was always a straight shooter.

I felt my chest constrict and my throat close up. "No," I managed to squeak. "What makes you think it's the same broad?"

"She shares some of the identifiers with the woman you've described. And—well, I hate to break it to you this way, buddy, but she was in possession of your driver's license. We haven't been able to conclusively identify her, though. Could you come out and have a look, see if she's the girl you've been tracking?"

Wild bulls couldn't keep me away. As much as I didn't want to believe that she could be dead, I had to know for sure. I was on the road within minutes, and during the two-hour drive north to Phoenix, I vacillated between certainty that the corpse wasn't Athena and the certainty that the love of my life was lying on a medical examiner's slab.

By the time I made it to Wyatt's precinct, I was stone cold sober and all cried out.

Wyatt skipped greetings and dodged my first question. "Look, Parker, there's more to this story, but let's just see if this is your gal first." With that he led me down two flights of poorly maintained metal stairs to a frigid room filled with hospital gurneys seemingly floating on a concrete floor painted a putrid shade of gray. Pulling a small tab off the end of one gurney, Wyatt pulled back a sheet to expose a brunette corpse, still stunning even in death. Her hair was matted and her eyes whitened by the milky gauze of murder, but my pulse still quickened in recognition.

I've got an almost eidetic memory, a great skill for a PI and not so good for a girlfriend who remembers every fight and every injustice like it was yesterday. But today, looking at the brunette on the slab, I'm taken right back to Pat O'Brien's, to that night I first laid eyes on her. The corpse was one of the broads who was with Athena that night, the three seated behind her, who I thought might have been with her. They were all pretty, well built, dark haired, but not worth much of my attention other than to wonder if they knew Athena or not. Now I had my answer to that query but so many more questions were at my door.

"It's not her, Wyatt, but she was with Athena that night at the bar," I explained. "I don't know her name, though, I just know they were together. What can you tell me?"

"I think it's time for lunch. Meet me at the Hooters right down the street. We'll talk." With that he was off, and I glanced at this mystery woman one more time before turning tail and making my way to a restaurant I loathed in order to get possible info on a dead woman who might have known the woman I loved. What are the odds?

"The wings are great here," Wyatt said, ordering a couple dozen from a perky blond waitress while thumbing through an already dog-eared onionskin folder.

"Yes, I'm sure that's why you come here." I was snarky but not out of place. Hell, I just spent a month in the kind of titty bars that made Hooters look like Sunday church in comparison.

"So, tell me what you know," Wyatt urged. I laid out the whole embarrassing fiasco, including the four days in bed, the cross country search, the women in the bar. To his credit, he didn't needle me about chasing a broad cross-country or essentially funding her trip. But he looked concerned.

"We found this gal behind a truck stop Dumpster. The truckers had seen her alive not fifteen minutes before, so we assume she was working the joint, and someone didn't like the cover charge and did a dump and dash."

"Fifteen minutes, that's not a lot of time," I pondered out loud.

"Yeah, but wait, there's more," Wyatt continued conspiratorially. "We did some digging, and turns out there was another hooker killed in Fort Worth last week, same MO, the broads even look the same. It's too early to say we have a serial because this is just two and, you know, plenty of junkie hookers turn up dead every day in this country."

It was true. Serial killers often preyed on sex workers, and even as we spoke the newspapers were awash with gruesome stories from Philadelphia's Kensington Strangler—just one of many such murderers on the loose at any given time.

"What did the cops in Fort Worth say about *their* vic? Did anyone see her? Any relation to this girl? Any leads on a suspect?" I was full of questions, even though I foresaw his reply.

"Look, Parker, I know you're chasing a dame and that's all well and good, but I'm not sure if this is going to help or not. The uniforms in Fort Worth didn't seem like they were going to spend too much time on this one. The cop I talked to called it a NHI case. They don't know her, they think one less junkie whore on the street, less problems for them."

I'd heard cops in New York use the acronym NHI—no human involved—when talking about murdered street workers, but it still riled me every time I heard it.

"Those fucking lazy bastards," I roared.

"I know, man, I know." Wyatt tried to calm me.

"Do they even know if the broad in Texas was using?"

"Tox screen came back positive for ketamine, nothing else." He knew what I was thinking.

"Horse tranquilizers?"

"Usually it's teenagers we find using K, but it's pretty easy to get on the street."

"What about the vic in your morgue?"

"Waiting on tox." Toxicology reports can take days. I had no idea how fast Phoenix crime analysis labs worked.

Wyatt filled me in on the rest of the details he knew. The truck stop, no witnesses, the weapon a simple garrote, milky white eyes, no other trace so far. Then he brought out a photo of Texas and I blanched. I knew that face.

"Oh my God. I saw her, too." I blurted it, lost in thought.

"What? When? Where?" Wyatt was impatient.

"In New Orleans. Same place as the woman in your morgue. They were both at the table at Pat O's behind the woman I'm chasing, behind Athena. At the bar, the bar I told you about, where everyone was singing. Athena was singing and dancing and she wasn't really interacting with these two girls, but she was right next to them so she might have been with them. Now that you've connected them to some of the stuff Athena stole from me, I guess there's no other explanation."

Wyatt pondered. "Sounds right. So what are we thinking? Your girl Athena killing off her friends? Or someone hunting them all down?"

"I can't imagine her as a killer," I admitted.

He nodded. "Still, we've got a professional interest in your girl now, too."

❖

By the time I woke up the next day, Wyatt had pulled the LUDs on my old cell phone number, and his team had begun tracing calls to see if they could find a way to track down Athena. In his mind, she was now a potential suspect, or at the least a possible witness. If the girls were dosed with ketamine, a woman could easily strangle them. But why would she? I just didn't see it. More likely, she was in danger. Either way, I wasn't saddled with paperwork and forensics, so I promised to keep him posted on any new info and headed out of Phoenix. I hadn't told Wyatt that a new charge had showed up on my credit card that very morning, so last he knew, Athena was in Santa Barbara—but she wasn't. She was now in Portland, Oregon, and that's where I headed. Wyatt would be pissed when he found out, but I had to get to her first, keep her safe.

The drive passed quickly. I kept thinking about the cases I'd worked back in Baltimore. I'd been assigned a shitload of dead prostitutes and yeah, I probably didn't labor as hard as I could have. The brass doesn't push hard on pros and the newspapers don't care as much about victims who aren't cute, white, and eight years old. Hookers on the street aren't like they are in movies; half them are using drugs to keep tricking, to keep the disgust of what they have to do out of their minds. Some of the girls on the street are twelve years old, seen an eight-year-old once in fact, and you can round 'em up but if you can't fix their lives, they'll just be back on the street the next day, taking five bucks for a blow job just so they can score a tiny dash of blow themselves. It's no secret most big cities have predators working the red light districts. If there are three hundred serial killers in the U.S. at any given minute, I can tell you most of them are hunting in the areas where down-on-their luck broads are turning tricks.

By the time I made it to Portland's "Avenue of the Roses," I was seeing ghosts of my own. All the working women I've turned a blind eye to, even those lanky young things I was watching at the titty bars the night I met Athena. Who loved those women? Who looked after those women? Who cared when they were dead next to a truck stop Dumpster?

It's been weeks since I made it to Portland's east side, a

neighborhood in which one avenue alone offers twenty blocks of strip clubs, massage parlors, porn shops, shower shows, and even one joint advertising live lingerie modeling—for men only, of course. Average folk in SUVs and hybrid cars whiz by this "Avenue of the Roses" as barely dressed women flit in and out of these T&A joints. Some clubs only offer pulchritudinous broads dancing in the nude, but at many a pocketful of cash will get you an around-the-world with the dame of your choice. Women whose youth is long gone, thanks to hard work or the quick ravages of meth, can't get into spots with overhead, so you'll see them trolling around the bus stops and lone fast food joint. The cops here are friendly but overwhelmed.

"I'm not sure I can help you, but I'll check our case files to see if anything matches the Phoenix case," a short, portly uniformed gent told me. After sitting in the station lobby for thirty minutes, a fatter, older man, a captain, ushered me back to a private conference room. Or maybe it was an interrogation room, I wasn't sure.

"Tell me what you're doing in my town, Ms…" He left it to me to fill in my name.

"It's Parker. I was on the job ten years in Baltimore, so I know the drill. Can we just skip to the punch?"

He shrugged. "Our CI is from Baltimore, Carol Wakefield—maybe you knew her." He was testing me.

"You mean *Karen* Wakefield? Yeah, good broad, knew her well." That was an understatement, but I didn't want to give this jackass my history of one-night stands just to pass his test.

"Listen, here's the drill. I'm a private investigator." I paused to show him my license and concealed weapons permits before I continued. "I'm working a missing persons case. The trail led me here to Portland. Along the way, I've also discovered that there seems to be some connection between my missing person and two homicide cases—one out of Phoenix, Arizona, and one in Fort Worth, Texas. I don't know what the connection is, and I've already shared what I know with law enforcement of those municipalities. The trail has gotten me here, but now I'm stumped."

He laughed. "Well, that's fitting, seeing how Portland's nicknamed Stump Town." He chewed on the inside of his cheek. "What's your relationship to this missing person?"

Pissed that he'd joke around when two women were dead and I

was afraid the love of my life might be next, I retorted quickly, "It's a case I'm working." He didn't need to know I was in love with Athena. As far as he needed to know, I got a client looking for her missing kid.

He pulled out two photos, both of stunning young women, long dark hair, each beautiful except for her milky white eyes, translucent skin, and faint garrote marks. "You recognize these women?"

I shook my head, confused. Two more dead women? What did they have to do with Athena?

"Listen Ms...Parker, this doesn't leave this room, got it?" I nodded. "We've got two homicides here in Portland that match the DBs in Arizona and Texas. You're telling me you know a potential witness. The thing is, you're the only one who seems to have seen her, you're the only person who the cops know had any knowledge of these women. You seem to be the only link between these four murdered women. See where I'm going here?"

"No. Wait. You thinking I'm a suspect? That I'm driving across the fucking country killing hookers?" I chortled as loud as I could. "I'm pretty sure I don't fit your profile, Captain." Aside from a few notable exceptions, women weren't serial killers. With that explosion of anger I turned and walked away, my hands still balled in fists of rage. Damn him. Damn Athena. Damn this city.

"Wait!" It was Karen Wakefield. Great. A reunion. "Parker, wait."

"Hey, doll. I just heard you were here." My rage was subsiding, but I still wasn't feeling like playing reunion with Karen.

"Look, Parker, I heard what's going on. I don't know about this woman you're looking for, and I know you aren't a killer. *Please*, you couldn't even spank me." She winked at me.

The obvious inappropriateness of her comment, smack in the middle of the police station, made me laugh unexpectedly.

She smiled. "It's good to see you again, Parker. But you got to know, this is a different city, about as different from Baltimore as you can get." Karen rushed alongside me as I kept walking. "Portland is a dichotomy. Everyone's progressive. Damn sure they'll go to bat over an endangered bird or a stolen compost bin. But nobody thinks twice about having to step over these homeless street urchins sleeping on the sidewalk downtown."

"Yeah, I noticed a lot of kids on the streets here." I encouraged her to continue.

"Folks here brag about a public policy that allows so many strip clubs to flourish, but do nothing about being one of the sex trafficking capitals of the country. It's not just the runaways getting sold off as sex slaves anymore, it's ordinary kids from the suburbs. Underage sex trafficking is happening here right down on Stark Street."

I was curious. "How do they get these girls into the game? They drugging or abducting them or what?"

"Some are abducted, some are runaways. They just did a study that found it took only fifteen minutes from the time a runaway arrives in Portland to the first time they are approached by someone who plans to victimize them. A lot of times the first contact is by someone who seems trustworthy, a person who just wants to help. Or sometimes it'll even be a pimp who will 'date' a girl—sometimes we're talking ten-year-olds—and then start telling her if she loved him she'd have sex with his friends. By that point she's hooked, usually within the first month the pimp is moving her up Interstate 5 to Seattle or down to Los Angeles."

"Why are you telling me this?"

"A lot of times they use older women to bring in the girls, show 'em the ropes. She's usually a pro, has been through it herself, still works but curries some favor—or avoids some beatings—by bringing in new girls, too. Maybe your missing person is a recruiter?"

I must have looked as clueless as I felt because Karen leaned closer and continued.

"Recruiters help bring girls into the life. I thought your person might be involved because they've linked our homicides with those other two homicides in Phoenix and Fort Worth, and we can confirm at least three of the women were forced into sexual servitude for a group of Ukrainian pimps. All had nicknames, they'd all been branded—well, tattooed by a group called the Stolichnaya Boys. Do you know about them?"

"Yes, the girls are called the Stoli stable. I read that article in the *Times*. They turn out the women along trade routes, sending them out at truck stops and porn stores mostly along I-5 on the West Coast and I-10 across the South, right?"

She nodded. She continued while I digested way too much

information about sex trafficking on the West Coast, the victims whose birth names *have* been discovered (one from Portland and the woman in Fort Worth), the Eastern European prostitution trade, and so much more. She swore me to secrecy, then divulged what linked the dead women besides me (and the fact that they all look similar and were offed in the same way). Each woman had a tattoo on her neck, a gold star with a spike. Just like Athena.

By the time she was done, I was filled with many more questions. But the portly cop came running over.

"Karen, we've got a possible dead body in a Dumpster out on Eighty-second." Ah, there's that "Avenue of Roses" again.

Our conversation abruptly ended. Karen put her business card in my hands and darted out the door. Remembering that I'm a detective by trade, not *just* some fool being led around by her crotch, I followed their squad car from Stark to Eighty-second, jumping out without closing the door as we stopped at the Pussy Palladium. I ran to the Dumpster behind the joint that had already attracted a tiny crowd of scantily clad women and nervous, half-erect but fully clothed men. Karen and Mr. Portly were on my heels yelling at the crowd—me included—to back the fuck up from the dimly lit metal can, but not before I had a chance to see her.

She was all curves and angles, and even in death, she was gorgeous. It was Athena. My chase was over. I had finally found her. And I was too late. She was gone. My legs went weak. I felt like all my structure had disappeared, my bones melting away until I nothing but a paper doll blowing in the wind.

I reached out to brush the chestnut hair from her angelic face.

Karen grabbed my hand and pulled me back. Her fingers on my skin were like a slap across the face. But I couldn't help but look back at Athena's dead eyes. And then I gasped. It wasn't her. It wasn't really Athena after all. The differences were slight, but they were there. The two weren't close enough to be identical twins, but definitely sisters, the way genes could recycle the same looks even years apart. Upon second glance, the dead girl was younger, much younger than the woman I spent four passion-filled days with.

I was so overwhelmed with relief until guilt rushed in afterward. How could I be glad it was this girl whose life was snuffed out instead of Athena's? But in that instant I'd gone from seeing a beloved woman to just another murder victim. Still, I wanted Karen to roll her over so I could see if she had a spiked star, too, so I could see if she was part of the pattern. Maybe there would be something about this new corpse that would finally reveal the complete puzzle and how these dead girls were connected to my missing lover.

I didn't get the chance to see what Karen might discover, because Mr. Portly had moved me and the others too far back to see.

Athena was my only anchor to this town, but she'd become a ghost. Any time I thought I was getting close, something else threw me off her trail. I wondered if she was running from me, if I was the thing pushing her to move from one town to another, until she'd ended up here in Portland. Maybe I was just inept as a detective. Either way, this was the closest I'd been. With a dead girl who looked like Athena's younger clone.

It had to mean something. It had to be more than just an empty lead. While a growing number of cops worked the corpse and the scene, I slipped inside the Pussy Palladium. A blonde with an artificial tan and a big rack was writhing on stage to an old Whitesnake song, so I pushed the photo of Athena and me at Pat O's in front of the few remaining patrons. Anxious stares turned to pure avoidance, but more than a couple men pointed out toward the Dumpster. No shit, Sherlock. You'd think these guys would notice a ten-year age difference, but hell, I probably hadn't paid that much attention to the faces of strippers before either. Until I started hunting one.

"Who's the girl in the Dumpster?" I overheard one of the uniforms questioning a bartender.

"Aphrodite. Swore that was her real name. She only worked here a couple a days. I don't know nothing else." He sounded earnest. "She was just up on stage like an hour ago, I swear. I didn't even see her leave. She's still, I mean, she *was* still supposed to be in here doing private dances."

"You got paperwork on her? I-9 form? Social security number?"

"Sorry, but we're cash only until the girls work a few weeks. We legally don't have to. And most newbies don't stick it out past the first week."

"You sure she's even eighteen?" It's no secret a lot of girls get on stage long before they're legal. The question caused the bartender to look instantly uncomfortable.

"Shit yeah, man! Our boss runs a legal business here. All the girls have to show their IDs before we hire them. We keep copies on file, and you can check any of them, just ask the girls to show you." He paused, lowering the register of his voice so heads turning his way would look back at the stage. "I want to help, I do, but I ain't got much to say. She just showed up two days ago, but she wasn't half-bad. Boss gave her a couple of shifts this week. She was quiet, kept to herself. Seemed a bit nervous about the crowd today, but that's normal for newbies. She did two songs, went backstage, and then next thing I know one of the other girls starts screaming outside."

Since there was no smoking allowed in the club, dancers and patrons both went out behind the Dumpster for a cig. I figure that's probably where patrons get BJs from the girls willing to do extras—even if the bartender insisted the Palladium wasn't "that kind of place." Anyway, one of the girls on a smoke break took a look inside the Dumpster, saw Aphrodite, and screamed.

By the time I got back to my hotel parking lot, I'd spent hours with Karen, having coffee and comparing notes. The dead girl in the Dumpster did, indeed, have a gold star with a spike between her shoulders. Some of the clubgoers said she offered them extras, so the cops thought she was a pro. The fact that she looked like Athena—a woman whom only I have seen, though I did at least show Karen the photo so she doesn't think I'm crazy—didn't go into the homicide report because Karen said it "wasn't clearly evidence" of anything.

As soon as I walked into my slightly musty hotel room, I could tell something was different. It was a smell that I recognized. Then I flipped the light and saw her. In person. The woman I had been chasing for weeks now had come to me.

"Athena?" I don't know why I stood frozen, questioning. I had seen so many doppelgängers of this broad, I didn't trust my own gut anymore.

"Hi, baby." The throaty voice, the lips made for loving, it was her.

She didn't say anything else, but she moved toward me and I couldn't help but take her into my arms and kiss her as desperately as

I did that first night in New Orleans. At this moment, the stolen wallet, the dead hookers, all the time and money I spent following her just fell to the wayside. I could put that all out of my mind for a few minutes of unbridled passion. Make that more than a few minutes. She pushed me on to my unmade bed, straddling my waist and removing her shirt. I started to lose control, so I flipped her over before my crotch did the thinking.

"Wait, what the fuck, lady? You need to slow down and tell me what the hell is going on."

"Please, just wait." She reached for me, kissing my neck, my face. "I need you. I need this."

I kissed her back, pushing her hands to her sides and moving my face over her breasts.

"No, now," I said—to myself as much as to her. "You take my wallet, my phone, leave without a word, I chase you across the country and in your wake are four dead broads, two of which I saw you with. Are you a prostitute? Why did you play me? What's going on?"

"I didn't play you. You knew what you were getting into." She was teary but defiant. The woman I loved.

"If that's what you think, lady, they better check you for a fucking heartbeat. I had a life, I had a job. I dropped everything for you."

"I didn't ask you to." She rolled over, maintaining eye contact but moving away from me, and hugged herself self-consciously.

"I know. We had something, didn't we? Or was I just a mark?" I wasn't sure I wanted to hear the answer.

She shook her head. "You weren't a mark. You were a surprise. A lovely surprise."

I grabbed her hand and pulled her closer. I wanted to make love but instead I held her closely and listened as she began to tell me her story. The long, complicated story that I could never have imagined. When Athena was nineteen years old, her car broke down near a shopping center in Seattle. A couple offered her a ride back to her dorm, and since there was a woman there, she thought she was safe. But as soon as she was in the car, she realized something was terribly wrong. They didn't take her to her home; they blindfolded her, took her purse and phone, and drove her to a house with ten twin beds, eight other girls, two vicious-looking hounds, and three silent but mean-looking men. The first day the man who had driven the car beat her, but on the second day he was nice, cleaning her wounds and letting her sleep in his bed with the television, instead of the twin beds where all the other girls slept. The woman that had been in the car with her was called his number one bitch, but they were all his girlfriends, it would seem. They all called him Daddy, their boyfriend. Some, like Athena, were lesbian before they got to the house, but after he beat and raped them, he would turn them out to do tricks. There was never talk of being gay after the first week of beatings.

The muscle-bound watchmen guarded them constantly, preventing any escape attempts. If the girls were working a hotel or truck stop, there was always a watcher nearby. They were moved at night from one house to the next, after a while losing touch with where they were or even what day it was. If a woman complained, she was beaten badly and sometimes taken away, never to be seen again by the other girls. The man they called Daddy (the bodyguards called him Dimitri) developed a fondness for Athena, and soon she was appointed his number one bitch. She tried to keep her spirit alive, keep remembering who she was even after she was renamed.

"I just kept trying to find a way to escape, but every time I was caught I was beaten even worse." Athena was dry-eyed but sympathetic in her accounting. "When Dimitri fixated on me it got easier, sort of." She still turned tricks and was raped by Dimitri, but she got more perks at home than the other girls, more freedom. Eventually, she was allowed to make a phone call home, but by then her mother and little sister had moved and she didn't know where to find them. She felt lost and alone and ruined, but still she tried to keep her spirits alive by dreaming of life outside of Stoli stable.

She noticed something eerie, too. The more Dimitri obsessed over Athena, the more the other girls he brought in started to look like her. Soon the whole stable was made up of all brunettes, curvy and tall, with long hair and big eyes. Some women were forced to get surgery, breast implants or nose jobs, but even then they didn't escape, she said. No doubt, Dimitri had doctors and surgeons in his pocket or on his client list.

"Once a woman's spirit is broken, she'll never leave. You can leave the door open and car running and she'll stay there at the house. It's how it is, usually."

I was stunned by the story. It was so outrageous, but my gut said to believe her. Which made me sad for this woman in front of me, spending maybe ten years as a sexual hostage, a battered woman cut off from everything in her life.

"So, New Orleans—"

She cut me off. "I was on the job. I was there with three newer girls, all of us looking for clients. Our chaperone was busy watching the new girls since I'm trusted, well, was trusted by Dimitri. I've been his head bitch for almost a decade now."

Shit. A decade of turning tricks. This is not the kind of broad you take home to mother, but still I wanted her with my whole being. I don't care how many men she had to sleep with, I know what I felt was real.

"Was I a mark, then? Or was it real? I knew we had something. Or are you really a good actress?" I vacillated between anger and compassion.

"You were a surprise, a wonderful, wonderful surprise," she repeated again, cracking the first smile I had seen from all night. "I've never tricked a woman alone, but I just felt you looking at me and really seeing the real me. I thought maybe we'd have fun, and I'd get some cash and that'd be it. But after that first night I knew I could never go back to Dimitri. So I stayed with you as long as I could, then I took your wallet and phone and just ran."

"The girls that were with you, did they know?"

"No, as far as they knew I was with a john. Then when I got to Portland, I called the only number I had—Sarah Martin, of the girls who used to be in the stable, used to be called Artemis—we all were given Greek names. Anyway, her parents got her out with some expert who retrieves people in cults. She left me their phone number and I kept it with me all the time, just in case. She helped me get in touch with a battered women's underground network here and I've been hiding here since then."

Sarah Martin was one of the dead girls in Portland. Athena didn't know this yet, didn't know about the murdered women from the truck stops or the Pussy Palladium either. I pulled out the photos I had, every vic except the last, and watched her break down in loud squalls. They were all Stoli girls, all forced to prostitute in exchange for living. If you could call what they were doing "living."

After she calmed herself, Athena looked perplexed. "If he's killed five girls, and I'm gone, there's only two more girls left in the stable.

Why would he…is he killing off the whole stable? Or replacing us? I don't understand."

I didn't have the answers. It baffled me, too. But I wasn't nearly as afraid of Dimitri as she was. He hadn't broken my spirit, and I desperately wanted to nail the bastard. It was suddenly about more than just Athena. "Athena, I need you to trust me. I need to call a friend."

❖

Karen was as flummoxed by Athena's story as I was. She knew Dimitri, had caught a case where he had beaten and raped a fourteen-year-old. When the girl moved out of town and refused to testify, no doubt too terrified to do so, the DA dropped the charges. Karen was still bitter about the dismissal, in part because she had been the first person to talk with the girl and still remembered the haunted look in her blackened eyes.

Athena told Karen everything she could about the last ten years, the people, places, the women who had gone missing from the stable house. Often she only remembered the pseudonyms that Dimitri had assigned them—Delia, Xena, Zoey, Aphrodite, Alexa, Tianna. Karen showed her the photos of the dead women, to identify them as well. But when she got to the last one, the girl at Pussy Palladium, Athena blanched. Ashen-faced, she began to sob, saying, "No, no, no," over and over again.

I put my arm around her, and she melted into my shoulder, sobbing for what seemed an eternity. Finally she spoke: "That's my sister. My real sister. I don't know how he got her, but I'd recognize her anywhere."

"Are you sure?" Karen pressed. "It's been a long time since you've seen her. Couldn't this be another girl with plastic surgery to look like you?"

"No. I'd know," Athena paused, briefly giving in to hope. "Well, maybe. But I don't think so. Please, can I see her?"

❖

Athena and I spent the next two weeks holed up in my room at the hotel. We spent most of our time fucking, re-enacting those few crazy wonderful days in New Orleans. Any time I tried to get her to talk seriously, she'd pull me back into bed, wrap her gloriously long legs around me, and put her mouth someplace—any place—that made me forget my own name, much less anything else that was even less fundamental to my life.

"Where do you want to go? You know, when this is all done?" I nudged Athena to talk about our future, to make plans for how we'd mesh our lives now that we'd been through so much.

"I don't know, babe. We'll see." I gleaned that "we'll see" was somewhat of a motto for Athena, a live-in-the-moment ethos that had gotten her through a decade of hell. In mere days I had mastered the art of patience, learning never to push too hard for answers that Athena simply wasn't prepared to offer up. I had a house in Brooklyn, a girlfriend in Portland, and a career in need of a cash infusion. But as long as I had Athena, I could go anywhere that made her happy.

"Maybe the beach somewhere. Or a nice little house in the country where we could settle down. You could go back to your real name even. Nobody would ever know anything about your background." I offered up ideas because I couldn't stop coming up with them.

She pulled me close again, the hips and curves and angles closing in on me, and whispered into my ear before she bit it gently. "We'll see."

❖

Arresting Dimitri Chekov was easier for Karen Wakefield and her colleagues than anyone ever expected. Athena, whose real name, it turned out, was Jennifer Jessup, gave her so much information she was able to get someone to infiltrate the perv's inner circle.

While Athena and I were canoodling across town, their sting operation had moved along swiftly, and before we even realized they had acted, I got a call from Karen.

"We nailed him," she said triumphantly. We had been in bed snuggling all morning when I got the call. I relayed the news and Athena beamed. "Want to come down to the station so I can tell you all the gory details?"

Looking between the cell and Athena made the decision even harder, but I'd set this whole thing in motion, I wanted to thank Karen in person for following it through. The best part of it all was that now Athena and I could be together, no Dimitri, no sex work, no obstacles to our love. I wanted to grab her and run off to Casablanca—or wherever private dicks and lady vamps now ran off to. Instead I threw on a Steelers cap, a henley shirt, and a clean pair of jeans; an off-duty outfit that Karen no doubt had seen before.

"Want to go with me?" I pointed at Athena, though I already knew the answer.

Athena shook her head, smiling seductively. She was staying put. No doubt that meant I would be rushing back to bed as soon as earthly possible.

❖

Karen Wakefield was a brassy broad, but she was built like a brick shithouse. She was no doubt the sexiest criminal investigator I've ever seen. Even though she sported a button-down oxford shirt with one too many buttons undone to be considered workplace-friendly, I was able to ignore her advances because I had a goddess at home. Well, in my hotel room bed, that is. Soon she'd be at home with me. Wherever home was these days. We still hadn't talked about the next step, both of us so focused on getting her out of Dimitri's grasp we'd failed to discuss much of anything beyond that. We did find time to make love, of course.

Now I was so wrapped up thinking about the road ahead and having more sex that I almost missed Karen's triumphant spiel.

"Hey, you there?" Karen snapped—her voice and her fingers—in my direction.

"Yeah, sorry, my mind is multitasking apparently," I admitted, trying to look sheepish. "Tell me what's up."

"First, the good news. The girl in the morgue—it's not Athena's sister. It's Candace Marshall, a seventeen-year-old from Boise. She just went missing a month and a half ago from Lloyd Center Mall; apparently an ice skater, was there for some sort of competition." Portland's beloved Lloyd Center offered one of the few ice skating rinks in the Northwest. Tanya Harding, the disgraced former champion skater, grew up skating laps there. I couldn't imagine a safer place to send your kid.

"Did she look like that when she was abducted?" I remember how unnerved I was looking into that Dumpster, the resemblance to Athena so uncanny.

Karen shook her head. "This one wasn't even a natural brunette. Her eyes were already similar but the ME said she'd had lots of injectable fillers in her face, lip augmentation, cheek implants, a nose job."

"You said she'd only been missing six weeks." It was a statement, but I said it as though there was a question mark at the end. "How…"

Karen interjected. "Yeah, I know, it's fucking crazy. The ME says the surgeries happened the first week she was missing. Another disgusting tidbit: All the murdered women had botulism toxin in their jaws and throats."

I stared blankly, trying to grasp what that meant.

"Oh…Botox injections in their jaws." I began to understand. Forced Botox in the jaw as a precurser to other forced things in the mouth. "Gross."

"Yeah," she agreed.

After we serpentined our way to a small hazy room in the back of the station, Karen swore me to secrecy.

"Pinky swear, boss," I said, which made us both smile.

Karen hit Play on small silver DVD player and suddenly I was seeing Dimitri Chekov for the first time. He was fresh-faced, not unattractive, faintly familiar, and he looked about fifteen years younger than I knew he had to be. Perhaps having a stable of women doing all the work for you keeps a pimp young. If I passed him on the street, I'd probably mistake him for the Olympic ice skater from Russia, Evgeni Plushenko. I wonder if that's what Candace Marshall saw, too.

It wasn't *Citizen Kane*, but the slightly grainy video captured Dimitri's seduction techniques. In this case, that involved simply offering wine coolers and weed to an undercover cop who looked all of fourteen. She also captured his wrath when she tried to get away from the bastard. In short order, the undercover girl, er, woman, started to plead: "I gotta go home, my mom will get worried." She looked genuinely panicked. I'm betting that although she was wired and had ample backup, the undercover was as terrified as Athena or Candace or all those girls who Dimitri seduced and turned out with beatings in between.

Karen cut off the video, but the impact was clear.

"We got him dead to rights," she said. "They're arraigning him today on multiple charges of kidnapping, child sex trafficking, forcible rape, sexual assault, fraud, and murder two. It's enough to keep him in prison for many lifetimes."

I was so relieved, I think I actually exhaled audibly when she finished the list of charges.

Turned out the flophouse where he was keeping the two remaining women from his stable was rife with DNA evidence linking him to crimes in California, Texas, Arizona, and three other states—crimes the cops hadn't even known about. The women were mute at first, but once they realized Dimitri and his muscle men were going away for a long, long time, the women opened up about the treatment they had undergone. They also explained what the last few months, after Athena had escaped, had been like.

"Both of the women—well, girls, really, because the two still alive were both still teenagers—but both of them had been attacked with regularity in the last month. Punched, kicked, choked. They said Dimitri was increasingly paranoid, so they were chained up a lot more than they had been before Athena escaped. He also became obsessed with finding Athena and with replacing her."

"Did they both look like Athena, too?"

"No," Karen said. "One was a blonde, actually, but they both had had lip injections, so we're thinking he just had yet to get to them."

What I didn't understand still was why there were dead women in multiple states, why they had been killed, even why Dimitri was forcing surgery on some women but not others. Karen seemed to read my mind.

"The DA still has to try the case, and if for some reason he's acquitted, your friend Wyatt is ready to extradite the bastard," she said. "But Dimitri is already trying to cut a deal, offering up bigger perverts in the slave trade. DA's not going to deal, but they're milking it. Seems that Dimitri was tracking Athena the way you were, and he blamed girls who had been at the club with her. He'd hit a city, torture one for information on where exactly she was, and when that failed—because they didn't actually know anything—he killed her as a lesson to the others. When he got to Portland, it was fairly easy to track down Sarah Martin, who actually did know something, but apparently even though he tortured her for hours, she never gave up where Athena was."

But Candace Marshall didn't even know Athena. "Did Candace Marshall, Aphrodite, did she try to escape? Is that why she was killed?"

"No, he had her working at the club with a bodyguard to diversify. But by the time Candace was scooped up, Dimitri had already spiraled out of control, and she was just killed for not being Athena. He had clearly devolved so much at the end, I won't be surprised if his attorney files for an diminished capacity defense."

"Let's hope that doesn't happen," I said.

Diminished capacity, insanity defense aside, no doubt, Dimitri and his cronies were going away for a very long time, which made both of us very, very happy.

I couldn't wait to tell Athena about all of it: the arrests, the rescued girls, that she could start planning that family reunion with her mother and sister. Best of all, the future we could have now without having to look over our shoulders, without having to run from city to city.

I drove back to the hotel, so flush with excitement that I was singing along to a song on the radio, something I hadn't done since my teens. I was a woman in love, a woman who was finally free to be with the woman I loved, the woman I fought for and rescued. I was a chivalrous champion of good over evil and I was going to walk up one flight of stairs to my gorgeous reward.

There was no pot of gold at the end of my rainbow, though. The room was silent and nearly empty, save a handwritten note on the bed. I started to tremble, tearing up before I even read the damn thing.

Dear Parker,

I know you won't believe this, but honestly, you never were a mark. You were my lovely surprise not just because I enjoyed fucking you—something I didn't think I could do ever again—but because you saved me from Dimitri. You will always be my knight in shining armor and for that I'll be eternally grateful. But I'm not the girl you want me to be, either. I will never be happy on a beach or in a little farmhouse or even in your Brooklyn flat. I'm not your girlfriend, I'm definitely not wife material. I'll never be kept again—by man or woman. Please don't follow me this time. But do know you'll always have a place in my heart.

Always, Athena.

Too bad I had my wallet and cell phone with me this time.

LUCKY THIRTEEN
ANNE LAUGHLIN

S ara was nearly out the door of her office when the phone rang. She didn't want to answer it. Desperately did not want to answer it. The day had been full of property showings to disinterested buyers, listing appointments with angry sellers. The collapse of the real estate market had taken almost every bit of fun out of the business. It had also taken away a lot of her income. She had to pick up the call.

"Crane Realty. This is Sara."

"Sara, my name is Tammy Sanders. I'm a friend of a friend of past clients of yours?"

That's better, thought Sara. Referrals from past clients were the best kind of business to have. Maybe something good would come of the day after all.

"Wonderful," Sara said. "Which clients were they?"

"I'm afraid I don't know them. Our mutual friend gave me your name."

Sara sat at her desk and pulled a pad toward her. "The important thing is they referred you. Tell me what I can do for you."

"I'm moving to town soon and wanted to start looking at some houses. I'm not giving you any notice, I'm afraid. I'll be in town for the day tomorrow, but back for a longer stay next weekend."

Sara fought the exhaustion falling over her. She'd have to scramble to put a schedule together. What she wanted was a bath and her book. If she were being honest, what she wanted was a bath, a book, and a drink. But everyone seemed to say that the drink wasn't an option for her anymore, and most of the time she agreed. Just not all of the time.

"That is short notice, but I'll see what I can do."

"I totally understand. There's only one property I'd like to try to see tomorrow. I saw it online and it looks perfect. We can do more when I return next week."

At least she's reasonable, Sara thought. She woke her computer and logged on to the MLS.

"That shouldn't be a problem. What's the address?"

The address Tammy gave her was a property just outside town. Sara scanned the listing sheet and saw that it sat on a five-acre lot. The photo showed an old and run-down house, but the price was attractive.

"Looks like it's on a beautiful piece of land, very isolated," Sara said.

"Yeah, the house is a mess from the looks of it, but otherwise it's perfect. Isolated is just what I want."

Sara got Tammy's contact information and they arranged to meet at 4:30 at the property.

When they rang off, she entered Tammy's information into her smartphone. If Tammy turned out to be a buyer who actually bought, Sara's year would at least end on a positive note.

❖

After a long soak in the tub, Sara stared into the bathroom mirror as she dried off. She was slender through the arms and legs, but a paunch had attached itself to her middle and seemed to defy any reasonable attempt to get rid of it. It marked her as middle-aged, as surely as did her graying hair and disturbing hormonal fluctuations. Her lover, Ellen, used her belly as a pillow when they watched TV together. She used it as a tray when they ate in bed. And when they made love, she kissed it all over as if it were a exquisitely sensitive erogenous zone, which in fact it was turning out to be. Even if she'd rather do without it, Sara couldn't deny that her extra padding had proved very useful.

With a cup of tea in hand, she crawled into her bed and stared across the large king mattress. Ellen had urged her to go big when it was time to get a new bed, and Sara couldn't decide whether she regretted the decision or not. With Ellen in the bed it made a wonderful and spacious playground. Without her, it seemed to cruelly call attention to the fact that Ellen was elsewhere. The only woman Sara wanted in her bed was Ellen. Unfortunately, Ellen had several other lovers. She was a very popular person. If Sara regretted anything at all, it was agreeing so readily to Ellen's idea of a relationship, which seemed just fine when Sara was so hazed by pheromones she would have agreed to remove some body parts just to relieve others. Now she knew the situation simply made her feel depressed, but to protest it would mean losing Ellen. Inertia had settled into her bones.

❖

With a good night's sleep and gorgeous fall weather, Sara cruised through her Sunday appointments. She'd successfully gotten hold of the listing agent for the house they were to see at 4:30, and the code to the lockbox was written on her hand. She drove south of town and then headed west off the main road, climbing a steep hill toward the property. The houses here were far from one another, separated by woods that were just past their peak fall colors. Many of the homes had not changed hands for decades. Some were in good repair, others close to ramshackle. When Sara pulled into the drive of the house for sale, she saw it fell somewhere in between. The yard didn't have the debris that some others had, but the house itself was sad looking. Its wood siding badly needed paint, the roof was missing shingles, and several of the windows were boarded up. She knew from the listing agent that it was vacant and rarely shown. She could see why.

She was just opening the lockbox to retrieve the keys when a car pulled up behind hers. Sara watched as a tall, angular woman got out of the Ford sedan and walked toward her. Her hair was tied back in a tight ponytail and she wore a mauve sweat suit. She looked younger than Sara, but not by much. The most noticeable thing about her looks was the huge pair of horn-rimmed glasses she wore, dwarfing her plain face. What might look hip on someone else was disastrous for this woman.

"You must be Tammy," Sara said, extending her hand.

"So good to meet you," Tammy said. She seemed a little reluctant to shake hands, pulling away quickly. "I really appreciate you setting this up."

"It was no problem. The agent was thrilled we wanted to see it."

As Sara unlocked the door she saw Tammy take out a small bottle of hand sanitizer and quickly rub her hands with it. Her heart sank a little. Neurotic was not what she wanted to see in a buyer. She left the key in the lock and walked into the house ahead of Tammy, flipping on lights, slightly surprised that the electricity was still on. The house was chilly and smelled of mold.

"Obviously this place needs a ton of work, which you probably know from the online photos," Sara said.

Tammy moved closer to Sara and stared into her face. "You look familiar to me. Is there any chance we've met before?"

Sara doubted she'd forget those glasses. "I don't think so. Especially since you don't live here."

"But I used to. I don't look familiar to you?"

"I'm afraid not."

Sara broke the eye contact and moved toward the kitchen. "Let's take a look at the rest of the house."

It took just minutes to work their way from the attic down to the basement. The bones of the house were good, but everything in it was old and falling apart. The smell in the basement spoke of repeated drenchings, but other than an elaborate workbench built along one wall, it was empty and relatively clean. The cement floor was dry, but the drywall was speckled with mold.

Tammy stood staring at her. She had some strands of hair in her mouth, sucking on them. She removed them to speak.

"I think I love it. What do you think?"

"It depends what you're willing to sign up for. If you don't mind the work, it's a great place. Let's take a look at the furnace."

Sara led her to the rear of the basement where a separate room held the utilities. Just as she leaned over to open the electrical panel she felt a stabbing pain in her neck. And she knew nothing more.

❖

When Sara woke she found herself back in the main room of the basement, on the floor and tied by the wrists to the wooden workbench. Duct tape bound her ankles together. Her head felt cottony on the inside, but her skull felt like someone was pressing on it with a vise. It was like the worst hangover she ever had, which was saying something. She'd had bone-crushing hangovers, so ill that almost anyone not used to them would have been convinced they were dying. Sara, being quite accustomed to feeling wretched, would heave her way through the workday, refusing to acknowledge how bad her drinking had become. But she was sober now, she reminded herself. This time she hadn't found trouble. Trouble, or something worse, had found her.

She raised her head and took in the room. It was harshly lit by several overhead fluorescents, the green tint they cast making her feel queasier. She must have been given an injection of some sort. If she'd been hit on the head she knew she'd feel something different than this, more pain and less confusion. There was no sign of Tammy, other than her tote bag sitting along the wall opposite Sara. Next to the bag was Sara's phone. She didn't see her car keys.

The wrist bindings were tight, holding her arms up and behind her, crucifix style. The plastic ties holding her wrists were threaded through bolts in the wood of the bench. It seemed unlikely the bolts would have been conveniently there for Tammy to use, which meant she had brought them along. Sara noticed the bits of sawdust around the base of the bolts. Tammy must have used a drill to bore holes, an idea that seemed to switch on the terror she'd been too groggy to feel.

She could move her legs from side to side and bend her knees, but that wouldn't do her much good. The windows in the room were boarded up. She screamed with no real hope that anyone would hear her. This wasn't a neighborhood where people took evening strolls. They didn't walk their dogs, they just opened the door and let them out. Tammy had picked her place carefully.

As her brain began to clear she thought about who might know she was here. The listing agent for the house would be calling her the next day to see if Sara had any feedback for her on the showing, but she wouldn't bother before then and wouldn't think twice if Sara didn't return her call. There was no one in her office with whom she shared her schedule, and the appointment wouldn't show up on her office computer. She kept everything on her smartphone. Ellen was in New York with one of her paramours, a woman a lot younger, richer, and sexier than Sara. For all she knew, Ellen might never call her again.

It took the absurdity of the situation for Sara to realize how alone she was. She'd lost all her friends by the time she bottomed out on alcohol. Apparently, she'd forgotten to make new ones. She almost felt glad that Tammy's bag was in the room. At least that meant she was coming back.

She heard the door slam upstairs and her heart jumped. She began to pray that the end would come quickly. She feared torture more than anything. If she'd been a member of the French Resistance and Tammy of the Gestapo, Sara would already have retrieved the cyanide capsule from her molar and swallowed it. Two seconds with the thumb screws and she knew she'd rat out her whole cell. She realized her situation was worse than if she had been a freedom fighter caught by the enemy. She had nothing to give, nothing to exchange for her life. She had no idea who Tammy was or why she was holding her.

The stairs creaked as Tammy came down. She had a wide smile on her face and she looked relaxed and somewhat triumphant, like she'd just gotten a big promotion or won a prize. Sara supposed she was the prize, though she couldn't begin to fathom why.

"I hope you're comfortable," Tammy said. She didn't seem to be kidding. She was holding a grocery bag, which she placed on the floor next to her tote. She slithered down the wall and sat with her knees hugged to her chest. "This house really is perfect."

"Listen, I don't know what this is about, but you have to let me go. If you do, I promise I won't tell anyone about this."

Tammy reached into her tote bag and brought out a cloth, which she unwrapped in her lap. She picked up an automatic pistol with a long silencer attached and shot a bullet on either side of Sara's head. It happened before Sara even realized Tammy had a gun in her hand. The *pffft* of each bullet was instantly followed by an explosion of wood behind her. A shard caught her forehead and blood started to run down her face. She felt her bladder let go.

"That will be the end of your talking. Do not open your mouth unless I give you permission. Do you understand?"

Sara was frozen, unable to take in what had happened. She felt her eyes nearly bulging out of her head, locked onto Tammy's calm ones. Tammy didn't look crazy or like the sort of person who would enjoy terrorizing someone. She looked like everyone and no one.

"Now, I'm starving. Excuse me while I eat."

Tammy took some items out of the grocery bag and made a ham sandwich. She wore latex gloves while she did so and kept them on while she ate. In between bites she prattled on.

"I got some stuff for sandwiches and fruit and water and some cookies. I'm an Oreo girl myself."

"Who the hell are you!" Sara burst out. Tammy kept her sandwich in one hand and picked up the gun with the other. She shot to the right of Sara's head, closer this time than the last. More wood blew apart and she felt a large splinter hit behind her left ear. It stayed there, sticking out of her neck like a needle.

"If you open your mouth again, one of these bullets goes into your leg."

Tammy finished her sandwich and put her trash neatly into the grocery bag. Her legs came back to her chest with her arms wrapped around them, the gun close enough to hand. She stared intently at Sara.

"Of course I know you, Sara. I would hardly go through this kind of trouble over someone I'd never met. In fact, I'd say we know each other in a very intimate way. But apparently, you plan to keep pretending you don't know who I am."

Sara felt another sinking feeling in her gut, one that was more than a little familiar. It was familiar to all blackout drinkers, those times when someone felt compelled to tell her in detail what she'd done the night before and had not the least recollection of. Painful, awful moments that simply made her pick up another drink. She was familiar with the feeling, but she still didn't remember Tammy.

"It was a little over a year ago when I met you at JJ's. You walked in at about ten and I knew right away you were the one for me. Not just for that night, but The One. The one forever. You may think that is a little hard to believe, love at first sight and all that. But I didn't have a doubt in the world. Your hair was longer then, and you wore a very slick coat with a snapped-up collar and I thought you were the most beautiful woman I'd ever seen."

JJ's had been Sara's regular bar, the only gay bar in town. Its clientele was generally younger than Sara, but that was true at most taverns, except for the ones where the die-hard alcoholics went to die. She only went to those places when she wanted complete anonymity. At JJ's the bartenders and most of the regulars still liked her. She felt at home there. Of course, when she made the mistake, as she quite often did, of sleeping with one of the regulars, or worse, their girlfriends, there was drama aplenty. But that seemed normal. No big deal. She tried to limit sex to newcomers to the bar, and there were always plenty of those. At least she knew that Tammy wasn't a regular there. She hadn't been in a blackout all the time.

Tammy drank some water and continued. "You took the bar stool next to mine and I thought right away that you liked me. You said hello and then started talking to the bartender. I remember that my heart was racing. That had never happened to me before. It was like God had put you right next to me and all I had to do was take hold."

Sara realized that Tammy was talking about a time just before she went into rehab. She had been a complete mess. Sallow, smelly, unable to function without a drink in her hand, and then it was a relative sort of functioning. Her odds of successfully picking up anyone at that point were close to zero. She would have slept with a man had one shown any interest in her. No doubt Tammy appeared as a goddess to her that night. She knew how her mind operated then, if you could call it that. If anyone showed interest in her it meant she wasn't as bad as she thought she was, and she clung to that like a life preserver in a cold, dark ocean. And within seconds of that gratitude she'd adopt a cocky attitude, as if she were God's gift herself. It was dizzying how rapidly her mind could blanket reality with her own version of the truth.

"We got to talking and you told hysterical stories about your real estate experiences. You asked about me and seemed to really listen. You bought me drinks. We stayed until closing time and that's when you reached for my hand and asked me where I lived. I'd been about to make a move, but the fact that you beat me to it just confirmed what I already knew. You were the one. It wasn't just me thinking it. We walked over to my apartment."

Tammy drank more water. Sara was thirsty, but that was nothing compared to the discomfort she felt in her arms. She kept moving her butt around, trying to relieve some of the pressure on her shoulders. Tammy picked up the gun and aimed it at her.

"Stay still. I want you to concentrate."

Sara opened her mouth to say something and Tammy shot to the left side of her head. More of the workbench exploded. Then she kept talking as if nothing had happened.

"When we got to my place you immediately took me into your arms and gave me the most soulful kiss I've ever had. We didn't talk. You just led me into the bedroom and made love to me in a way I'd never known. I knew I was in love. And you seemed so happy, so sweet."

This is what used to get Sara in so much trouble. She had a tremendous capacity for alcohol. She could drink for ten hours and not appear drunk to anyone but herself. She could act almost like a normal human being, but it was really some alter ego that had taken over her body. Her real self was already passed out, waiting for morning when she could start all over again. It was that alter ego that thought everything was fine and carried on acting like an ass. The discomfort Sara felt was not just in her shoulders. She ached for all she had done, all the life she'd wasted.

"I woke the next morning and you were gone. It was only seven o'clock, so I don't think you needed to rush out to an appointment. You just left me without saying good-bye. I didn't like that. Didn't think it was right, but I was willing to give you the benefit of the doubt. Maybe you'd tried to say good-bye and I just didn't wake up. I'd had quite a bit to drink, after all. But that's when I began to discover that you were really like all the others.

"You probably want to know what others I'm talking about. I'll just ask the question for you. All the others like you who feel it's okay to play with my feelings. Who flirt with me, fuck me, and then treat me like a piece of shit."

Sara could see the shift in Tammy's mood, from a sort of sweet nostalgia into rage. There was nothing she could do to help herself. She was terrified that if she opened her mouth to talk, Tammy would shoot her. She tried to compose her expression into one of empathy or regret, but that was hard enough for her to do under normal circumstances. Now it was simply impossible. She looked down, avoiding Tammy's glare. She saw the blood on her blouse and the stain on the cement where she'd wet herself. She'd lost feeling in her hands, and the rest of her was freezing. She knew she wasn't going to live through this.

"Look at me," Tammy said. Her high voice had become raspy and desperate. When Sara looked up she saw a steady hand pointing the gun at her head, but Tammy's face was twisted and painful looking, as if a thousand words and feelings were trying to fight their way out. She reached for her bottle of water and drank slowly, breathing deeply as she put it back by her side. She kept the gun trained on Sara. Minutes passed and Sara could see Tammy become calmer. Thank God.

"Somewhere along the line people have forgotten how to act decently to one another. I expected more from women, but I see now that was naïve. For instance, I didn't expect that you'd avoid me the way you did after the night we made love. I went to JJ's every night for a week and you never showed up. The bartender said she didn't know where you were, but I could tell she was just covering for you. I left a note for you with my phone number, but you never bothered to call me."

That must have been when I went into rehab, Sara thought. There was never a time she didn't go into JJ's for a whole week. Impossible. If she stayed at home one evening a week she thought she was a paragon of virtue. And by some miracle, she'd not been back to JJ's since. A whole year now. Though if someone had put a drink to her lips as she sat tied up and sitting in a puddle of her own urine, she doubted she'd struggle much.

"I left town for a new job shortly after that. When I came back during the summer for a visit I saw you at the farmers market, wandering around with a basket on your arm, looking a little sad. I wanted to hate you, but my heart leapt in the same way it had when I first met you and I knew that I should try again. There had to be a reason you'd abandoned me last year."

Tammy put the end of her ponytail back in her mouth, staring down the barrel of her gun at Sara. She remained silent for another few minutes, an agonizingly long time during which Sara started praying. She knew it was a foxhole prayer, that it wasn't how you were supposed to connect to whoever it was she was praying to. But she wasn't asking for a new car or a girlfriend. Her life hung on how Tammy worked out whatever was in her crazy brain. A little intervention was needed. She remembered the woman at the farmers market, but would never have connected her to the woman across from her now.

"I approached you as you were looking over some tomatoes and you smiled when I called your name and asked how you were. But your eyes were blank. You denied knowing who I am, but kept being terribly polite about it. When I reminded you that we had slept together and shouldn't you be decent enough to acknowledge that, you just turned your back on me and left."

Sara desperately wanted to tell Tammy that none of it had anything to do with her. She didn't doubt that Tammy was telling her the truth about what happened that night. She hadn't turned away from her at the market because she lacked respect for Tammy. She fled because she still couldn't face the things she'd done. She remembered getting home from there and desperately wanting a drink. She didn't leave her house for two days.

It was the drinking, she wanted to say. But that might just have the effect of making Tammy feel even less significant than she already seemed to. Learning that Sara only slept with her because she was dead drunk wasn't likely to lessen her anger. And Sara also feared that if she tried to say anything at all she'd be shot.

"I have to say that I was crushed. You aren't worth it, of course, but I did really love you. I know I wasn't wrong about how you felt about me that night, but apparently it's easy for you to throw away an experience like that. Apparently it's easy for a lot of people. But that day at the farmers market was a turning point for me. Do you want to know how?"

Sara nodded, half expecting another bullet to whiz by in response. But the gun now lay still on Tammy's lap.

"I decided to take action. I made my list and started going through it, and that's kept me busy until now. You're the last on my list."

Oh, fuck, Sara thought. "Please let me talk to you," she said. "I know we can work this out."

Tammy picked the gun up and shot the tip of Sara's right ring finger off. Sara screamed and thrashed and somehow managed to drive the little stick of wood farther into her neck. Then she started sobbing.

"Please," Sara gasped.

Tammy shot the tip of her middle finger off.

"Actually, that was the finger I'd been aiming for, so thanks for being idiot enough to not follow my instructions. It gave me another shot."

The blood was streaming down Sara's hand, dripping onto the cement floor next to her. Her hands were still numb and she didn't feel the wounds as much as she'd expect. But she threw up anyway.

"The brilliance of the list," Tammy continued, unperturbed, "is that for the first time I was totally in control of my relationship with women. No more waiting to see if they'd be nice to me, if I'd be treated with respect. Each woman on the list has been a shit to me. I've made twelve trips to houses like this, spread all over the country, in all the towns I've lived in the past twenty years."

Sara looked at her beseechingly.

"Yes, I've made twelve trips, and all twelve women are dead. You're lucky thirteen."

Tammy pulled some keys from her pocket and put them by Sara's phone on the floor next to her.

"So, here's the deal. I've put both our cars in the garage and turned out all the lights upstairs. I don't suppose anyone from around here is going to notice anything different about the place, not so's they'd investigate. And here's the key to the house. I shut the lockbox, so if any other agent comes by she won't be able to get in. That's unlikely, though, don't you think? This dump has been on the market forever. I think that makes us safe here for a while."

Jesus. Did that mean she was going to be here, alive, listening to Tammy and having pieces of her shot off as the days dragged on? Her mind was whirling out of control, trying to think what to do. She didn't want to die.

"With the other women I said my piece and then shot them. It wasn't a big deal. Nothing dramatic or prolonged. They knew what they did to me and what their punishment was. I told them up front that I'd be killing them. Frankly it was a little anticlimactic. But you've always been different. You were the one I wanted the most. Unlike with the others, I was only with you the one time, but it somehow meant more."

Tammy sighed and looked a little sad.

"It's nice to sit here talking to you. I don't hate you, just so you know. A lot of the anger seems to have left me. But I can't very well let you escape when the other twelve didn't, can I? I mean, if it hadn't been for you, I probably wouldn't have ever drawn up the list. Fair's fair, after all."

Sara hung her head again. In her terror she hadn't stopped to think that were it not for her own actions with Tammy, the other twelve women might not have died. For a moment she welcomed the idea of death. Quickly, like the others.

"I can practically see the thoughts unraveling in your brain, Sara, but you shouldn't bother trying to figure out how you're going to get out of this. You're not. And now it's time to draw this to a close."

Sara squeezed her eyes shut, waiting for the sound of the gun, the end of her life, the stupid, crazy end to the life she thought she was just starting to live over again. When she heard the gun go off her heart stopped, and then it began again with the next beat. She opened her eyes to see Tammy slumped over, the gun now on the cement floor, the blood running down her face from the wound in her right temple.

The keys, the tools, the phone, the food and the water. Every means of freedom or sustenance lay ten feet away. With her hands and feet bound, they could have been ten inches away and just as useless. She knew she had no options. She was the lucky thirteenth.

FEEDBACK
LINDY CAMERON

The airboat splashed to a stop outside the dilapidated facade of 223 Collins Street. I hadn't said a word but the pilot had rightly figured this was the place to drop me. Even without the five cops providing crowd control on the dock out front, *I* knew it was the right place, too, coz I'd been here before. I also knew I was about to face one of those dreaded moments when the victim at the scene was someone with whom I'd been acquainted.

I powered up my anti-grav pod, hauled myself into the seat and strapped in. The idiots loitering in the drizzle hoping to catch a glimpse of something dead really pissed me off. I made a close calculation and just cleared the heads of the nearest onlookers. I did shout "look out," so it wasn't entirely my fault that half of them ended up face-down on the wet promenade.

"Thought they revoked your licence for that thing," Officer Jordan said.

"Just a wild rumour," I said over my shoulder as I hovered towards the lifts.

"Another one?" She smiled. "Lifts aren't working. Chief said use the fire stairs."

Oh great. I leant forward to check for downward traffic before I began my ascent. The tightly angled stairwells in these late–nineteenth-century buildings were not designed for anti-grav manoeuvring; in fact, they wouldn't be much use in a fire. At least they'd only burn down to water-level these days. Aggie and I—yeah, my inanimate anti-grav pod *does* have a name—made our way up to what had once been the nineteenth floor, but was now the fourteenth above high-tide canal level.

The fire door at the top opened directly into the warehouse space of Napper Trading, which overflowed the entire 15,000 squares. Rows of metal shelving stretched in every direction piled with terminals, naru-engine parts, jakka tools, odd pieces of weaponry and satellite components, cranial fittings, vintage hologram projectors, service bots, vid-screens, and even antique radio and TV parts. The reception area was an old Teflon desk with a metre of clear space around it.

"What's the deal?" I asked the officer who was ferreting in the apparent havoc.

"Place has been ransacked," she said. "I'm looking for clues."

"Wouldn't bother," I said. "This place *always* looks like a lunatic looking for a whippet screw went through at warp speed. Where's…"

"Chief's in the back with the Cutter and the deader." She pointed.

"The chief? He *never* leaves HQ."

"Reckon this case has connections that require his physical participation."

I hovered in the direction of the chief, the coroner and the body, keeping to the dead centre of the aisles in case I brought a century's worth of recycled tech down on my head.

The sound of Chief Bascome's gravelly voice biting off orders prompted two medtechs to scuttle out of the corner office, as if keeping their skin intact depended only on getting out of his reach. This was strange indeed. In six years I hadn't known him to leave HQ, let alone attend a crime scene.

"You're scaring the children, Chief," I said from the doorway to the room where Chief Bascome was leaning over the corpse that lay in the crash chair, and Dr Huang Delta Anne was crawling round the floor.

"Where in Hades have you been?" he bellowed.

"Having my toenails buffed."

The chief gave me the once-over, from my head to where my feet would be if I had any, and snorted: "And my cat has joined the space cadets."

I ignored the dig. The casual observer might think the old man didn't like me, but in truth the chief loves me like a daughter—okay, like the daughter he never wanted, but he loves me nonetheless.

"Why are *you* so grouchy? After all, that's *my* uncle you're prodding." I floated over to take a look.

"Jimmy Strong's long past caring; and I didn't think you'd give a damn," he stated.

"True." I looked down at the deceased. Jimmy wasn't really my uncle—that being a scientific impossibility—but he *had* co-habited with my aunt Juno for five years until last summer. She'd insisted I call him Uncle, a request I avoided by not calling him anything at all. Poor stupid bastard. He hadn't been good for much when he was alive, and now he was good for nothing at all. Judging from the muscle spasm in the face that contained his vacant eyes, even his brain would be rejected by the organ banks.

"Where's he been?" I asked, removing the burnt-out lead from the socket behind his ear.

Delta Anne got to her feet. "No idea. The external black box is scrambled." She handed me the matchbox-sized Data Locator Unit that, in situations *not* like this, records a trawler's route and flags the cords of places they wish to return to. "All I can do now is tell you what killed him."

"That's obvious," I remarked. "The real question is why."

"Take a guess," the chief said. "Stupid jerk—wrong place—wrong time."

"That's why we have to ask why," I said. "Jimmy didn't go trawling, Chief. The man had a phobia about cyspace. He dealt every kind of tech, but only ever hardware. And look at this jack." I indicated the dodgy skull socket. "This is a bad pirate job. It's not even fitted properly. Some backyard tech implanted this in such a hurry it's amazing Jimmy didn't have a stroke on the way home."

The chief looked hopeful. "This might be a stroke?"

"No way," Delta Anne stated. "This is murder. Capra is going to have to find out where he's been."

I smiled joylessly. Capra, that's me. Agent Capra Jane—cybercop, attached to the Southern Indian-Pacific Corps, headquartered in Melbourne City. I trawl the mean streets of Cy-city and the other virtual resorts—the ones that ordinary beat cops fear to tread. And that doesn't mean *they're* gutless and I'm some kind of hero. Far from it. In fact, even *I'd* agree that statement says a boat-load about common sense versus foolhardiness. They have it—common sense, that is—and I, well I basically don't *give* a shit.

I removed and studied the other end of the lead that had introduced

Dr Death to Jimmy's cerebellum. It couldn't have been just inexperience that made him incapable of protecting himself against the surge that effectively desiccated his brain.

I glanced at the vibrating plasma-phone in my forearm. It was my mother's ID; the one with her "urgent" face. As her idea of imperative differed greatly from mine, I figured she could wait. I opened Aggie's tool kit instead.

Delta Anne was right—the black box was cactus; but at least it hadn't fused to Jimmy's Terminal Interface. Once I cleaned out the charred wiring in the TI's input socket, I'd be able to jack in and use my own sensorpad to search the TI's internal black box. I could trace where Jimmy had gone trawling—or, at least, where he'd last been.

"Capra Jane?" the chief said.

"Why are you here?" I asked him. "Since when do you even leave your office?"

The chief ignored me. "Just do a prelim scout for now, CJ. You'll have a partner on this case."

"Oh no, you know that always ends badly, Chief."

"Part of the exchange deal with the Space League. We *all* get to pull duty with the RSL."

"*Returned* Spacers," I said in horror.

Pouting seemed like the best response, but I controlled myself. "There are only ever two reasons for space jockeys to be classified 'returned.' Either they've been sectioned-out coz they're psycho from space fever, *or* they're old codgers who might not last the next voyage."

I snapped a surge protector into the socket I'd cleaned. It wouldn't save me from a direct hit but it'd give me a few seconds' grace to get out *if* I saw an attack coming. I opened Aggie's deck to reveal the tools of my trade: the left-hand keypad, calibrated precisely to the measured speed and dexterity of my fingers; the cylindrical joystick, connected to my control-deck by a long flex-wire; and, finally, a set of state-of-the-art, three-point tracer leads.

I logged in with my left hand, then removed my hat and fitted the second point of the tracer lead to the skull socket over my right ear. I palmed the joystick, picked up the free end of the tracer lead, leant forward and jacked into the terminal.

Jimmy Strong's office and its occupants dissolved around me as I made contact with the cyber matrix. It's never a good idea to keep your eyes open when the connection is made, coz the shift in perception is kind of like stripping away the reality of your existence.

But if you *do*, the rush out the other side is exhilarating.

The tracer program began its hunt for the entry or exit trail of the previous user, while I swerved bodiless against the precipitous transparent walls of information that surrounded me and progressed forever outwards in every direction.

Waiting for entry induces a nausea that makes mentally pacing this void unpleasant. None of this is necessary if you know where you're going, or what you want to access, but when you're tracking someone else, this is invariably how you have to start. And the wait depends on the skill of the previous user. An expert who doesn't want to be followed can keep you out for several minutes and then lay false trails all over the matrix. But idiots like Jimmy can keep you at bay for longer simply coz they have no idea what they're doing, so there's no logic to follow.

I received the sensory shove that indicated re-entry and surged up and over—these being relative terms—the splendid purple rim of the DaerinCorp Research Foundation's feeder link and into the record banks of their research division.

Shit, Jimmy, what were you up to? I followed his trail, which paused at the towering data stacks of DaerinCorp's Future Projects Division, which, not surprisingly, he'd been unable to get into. Even *I* don't have clearance for that level access, despite my badge and closer family ties to Daerin's board of directors.

An odd shimmer below caught my attention. It appeared someone else had piggybacked on Jimmy's poorly executed hack. I wondered if the hitch had been intentional or the trawler had just been passing and decided to latch on. I slowed my onward motion to try and make out the tag name but couldn't quite…*Whoa!*

A virtual quiver in the matrix at my back sent an orgasmic frisson curling into my brain.

Nice—but, naturally, I spun around.

Nothing and no one. Not that I could see anyway.

I could, however, sense someone laughing.

I returned to the original trail but suddenly everything went black. This was followed by a rippling sensation and the realisation that the mid-section of Jimmy's trail had been fried, and his last port of call was about to cross paths with my current position.

Twin moons glowed overhead, the sound of smooth reko-jazz filled my ears and a neon sign ahead blinked: "Beer, Boys and Babes."

Downside?

The usual moment of rational dislocation was replaced by the familiar, as the holographic-construct of Cy-city's shanty town folded around me.

What the hell were you doing here, Jimmy Strong? Back in the real-world my left hand worked the keypad to access one of my avatar cloaks. Form—mine—materialised out of the matrix and I found myself standing in one of the maze of back alleys near the notorious Pit Club.

"About time," growled a metal-plated Neanderthal who was aiming a Rat Gun at me.

I flung myself sideways, tucked myself into a roll to get my feet under me, then hit the ground running—I *love* running—around the nearest corner and out of immediate harm's way; while my real fingers, in that other reality, flew across the sensorpad searching for an exit. I found it, reached for the terminal connection point, and jacked out so suddenly that I flipped backwards across Jimmy's office.

While I waited for the interference in my brain to clear I realised that someone was swearing up a storm. I opened my eyes to find myself upturned and hovering over a sprawled Chief of Police.

"That was a stupid place to stand," I said, drifting away so I had a clear area in which to turn right way up. The motion, combined with perception-residue from the trawl, had a hokey affect on my vision. Still upside down, the shadows in the far corner of the room seemed to be alive with…with deeper shadows.

Ack! I haven't done this flipping nonsense for years. Used to happen all the time when I first acquired Aggie. Caused me a great deal of aggravation—hence, the best reason for her name.

"Why'd you come out so fast?" the chief asked. "You were screaming blue murder."

"A reject from a horror vid tried to take me out with a Rat Gun," I said. "Think he was waiting in case Jimmy came back. Or maybe for whoever came in after Jimmy was shot."

"Your uncle was shot?"

"Yes and no, Chief," I said.

"Well there's no sign of a struggle," he said. "So he must've known who did this."

"Why?"

"For the killer to be here and walk right up to him…"

"He wasn't killed here," Delta Anne said.

"What, so this is a body dump?"

"No. It was feedback." Delta Anne turned Jimmy's head indelicately to reveal the scorched flashpoint round the socket.

"So his socket blew a fuse?"

"Not exactly," said Delta Anne. "This *is* more like a powder-burn from close proximity to a weapon."

The chief looked exasperated.

"The doc means Jimmy was here, when he was killed elsewhere," I said.

"Feedback," Delta Anne said again.

"A Rat Gun," I elaborated.

"Knew I should've retired last month," the chief said. "Now, about your new partner, Capra…"

"Not gonna happen, Chief," I said, distracted again by the weird shift in the shadow that shrouded the back of the room. I shook my head.

"No choice, CJ. This comes from High Command. Five Spacers have been missing for nearly two months and, according to their envoy, *their* case leads to your uncle."

I laughed. Jimmy Strong dealt with crooks—it's why the thing with Aunt Juno was doomed—but he wasn't himself a bad guy.

"You find that amusing?" The shade within the darkness spoke for the first time.

"Yep," I acknowledged, then turned back to the chief. "Let me guess. Secret Agent Shadow here is from the League of Space Loons. Chief, you know they have, *had* a gripe with Jimmy coz he whistleblew their smuggling racket."

"I'm not *with* the Returned Spacers League."

The chief looked like he was about to enjoy something way too much. "Agent Capra Jane," he said, "meet Captain Zanzibar Black—of HomeWorld Security." He indicated the shadow that was stepping out of the inky-dark, still morphing into something tangible. Literally. Not that the chief saw the transformation. His eyes were on me for some reason; and my eyes clearly needed testing coz I was seeing things…

Oh.

And crap! My world tilted as the darkest of hours-past engulfed my soul with *all* their reality: the nightmares, the peace, and the fabulous imaginings.

I'd long ago chucked the deluding meds that had made me relive the too-real bad, while yearning for the clearly impossible. The constant mind-shift from blood-spattered trenches to an irresistible beguine, from the pits of hell to a dance of sheer reckless joy, had been way too much.

"CJ? You okay?"

Frak'n hell—flashbacks are a bitch! I hadn't had one for seven years; until this slight shift in perception, this trick of the limited light had turned a ghostly shade to a shimmer of such beguiling colour…

Maybe my implant needs realignment.

"Capra Jane!"

"Yes, Chief," I said, blinking to refocus on the now completely corporeal HomeWorld rep.

Oh my!

Captain Black: eyes—green or blue, or green; hair—short and blood-red; mouth—perfect.

Zanzibar Black: sex on two long, *long* leather-clad legs.

"You sure?" He patted my arm.

"Yes. Chief. I'm sure."

"That wasn't quite the reaction I was anticipating."

"*Why* were you expecting anything?" I glared at him and collected my senses before turning to the Amazonian spook from Espionage HQ. "Here are you—who. Why?"

"That's more like it," the chief said.

I ignored him and raise my eyebrows at Captain Black, waiting; as if I'd made perfect sense.

She had the grace to simply answer, "The late Mr Strong met with two of the missing Spacers."

"Returned Spacers came to Jimmy all the time to catch up on the history they'd missed while out beyond the Belt. He's the only merchant in the Free Zones who dealt the old tech. I assume they were cleanskins."

"Yes. But only the men came to Mr Strong."

"Well yes, of course," I said. "The women from the Jump Ships have no need. It's only the men who are banned from implants."

Zanzibar Black shrugged—eloquently.

How was that even possible?

"In between meeting the Spacers and them going missing, Mr Strong also made contact with a Judah Plenty."

Uh-oh. I always knew that connection was gonna bite Jimmy on the arse. I steered my pod over to the bank of computers, hovered higher, retrieved a framed vid-image, and handed it to Black. "They were in the same unit in the Border War."

"I'm aware of that." She glanced at the faded picture of Jimmy and his mates with the low-rider tank they'd liberated from the Raven Brigades. "But as you know, Agent Capra, *ex*-pilot Judah Plenty is now a known slave trader."

I looked Zanzibar Black up and down, slowly—mostly because the view was great—before nodding. "If he's so *known*, Captain Black, why haven't your lot shut him down?"

"Please, call me Zan," she said—for no good reason at all. "Plenty's connections have been…"

"Let me guess. Plenty useful to HomeWorld Security," I finished for her. I was trying valiantly to *appear* interested in late-Jimmy, bad-Judah, lost-Spacers or anything, while an aural flashback this time—a soft whispering of my name—began liberating my libido from its four-year hibernation.

The chief cleared his throat. "CJ, return to HQ and report to Chief Jayla Ellen so she can intro your new partner."

"What?" I looked from the chief to… "Aren't *you* my partner, Captain Black? Zan."

"No. A Returned Spacer, one Milo Decker, will do the field work with you. He *is* a League member, and a cleanskin, just like those who are missing."

"Oh." *Damn.*

The chief waved his data-strap over my touchscreen and Aggie thrummed to attract my attention. I read, aloud, all about my newest liability. "Ensign Milo Decker. Stellar cartographer. Born Geelong, January 4, 2040. Shit!"

"What?" he asked.

"This bloke's nearly ninety!"

"Technically he's only eighty-seven," Zanzibar Black said.

"Is that a problem?" The chief flexed his eighty-three-year-old muscles in some kind of strange manly pose—which did not a thing for me.

"No, Chief, unless it's combined with a lifetime in those Jump Ships flashing around the galaxy at fifty times the speed of light, exploring new worlds and fighting the Sakaas for the mineral rights to every asteroid they pass.

"Those spacers, especially the old codgers, have big trouble re-assimilating. This I know from personal experience. My great aunt Marin drove us batty every time she came home, just on leave, until she discovered the jetcar circuit. And she's only sixty-six. And *this* one," I protested, "this one will be old *and* whacko. Sixty-eight years in the Space League and the guy's still an ensign!"

"He might surprise you," Captain Black said.

"Don't like surprises," I snarled; but not at her.

I glared at the chief, who cajoled, "Hey, he's healthy. There aren't that many of us left. You should be nicer to us."

"Why? You blokes brought the shit on yourselves."

I began securing my gear, until two other things occurred to me: Zanzibar Black was also a cleanskin; and therefore, "Is this Spacer of yours bait?" I asked.

"Of course not, Capra Jane. And yes, I, too, am tech-free." As she ran her hands through her hair in demonstration, my skin tingled with way more than lust. It was almost an erotic prompt or sensual proposal.

Bloody hell—these weren't flashbacks. Well, not all of them.

The damn woman was a telepath.

No, Capra Jane. It's not that simple. Look at me.

Okay. So although I "heard" that in my head, and knew without doubt that no one in this room had "spoken" those words, I did as I was asked. I looked at Zanzibar Black…and marvelled at the truth.

I am Beninzay. A second-generation hybrid.

While Zan was having a quiet little chat with my mind, the oblivious chief was searching his pockets. That means she…*you, that means you can also turn invisible.*

I felt rather than heard her laugh—and it was a joyous thing.

It's camouflage, Capra, not invisibility. But we do have skills that even urban myth hasn't dreamt up yet.

"CJ, go back to work."

"Right. Yes, Chief."

Later, Capra Jane.

I didn't want to "think" anything revealing; well, than I already had—*bugger*—so I just left.

It took me ten minutes to get back to SIP Corps HQ, but an hour later I was still hovering around the chief's forty-fourth-floor office. On my own. Bored out of my brain.

Report to the chief, the chief had said. Problem was, Chief Bascome's new Co-Director of Operations was nowhere to be found. And there's only so much you can do in someone's space without resorting to hacking their Terminal. I'd already gone through her drawers.

Sure Chief Jayla's office—in one of the causeways built back in 2051 between the Eureka and Southern Cross Towers—had a great panorama; but it was no more spectacular than the view from my apartment. Hers took in the Great Southern Harbour, which comprised old Port Phillip Bay, the tidal flow of the Yarra River—the lower reaches of which still flowed under there somewhere—and the multitude of inner waterways that formed our island city. Mine overlooked the canals that threaded what had long ago been the streets of Melbourne City. Whatever the view, it was a bloody lot of water.

"Ah, Agent Capra."

Finally! I directed Aggie to face the side door, through which Chief Rho Jayla Ellen had entered her own office. At thirty-seven she was the youngest SIP agent ever to take the Corps' top job, and therefore one of the Southern Hemisphere's highest command positions. She deserved it, and even Chief Bascome admitted she was damn good at "their" job. The fifty-year age difference between the two chiefs was seen as a good thing by all who gave those things any thought. Not that the old man had a choice. All positions of any import held by men across the

Southern Indian–Pacific had to be shared by the Alpha-Omegas. The Clan could hold solo positions, but the boys had to share. And there was no use complaining; it was all their own fault.

Chief Jayla tossed me a coffee tube, then thwarted any possible complaint on my part. "Your new partner is a done deal, Agent Capra."

I sighed and cracked my tube. Instantly hot coffee fizzed as its perfect aroma jazzed my nostrils. I took a sip. "But an *old* codger?"

She shrugged. "HomeWorld Security's choice."

"So where is he?"

"He entered HQ about forty minutes ago. Probably sorting gear."

"He's an eighty-seven-year-old ensign. He's probably lost."

"Go find him, then, so he can help you find your uncle's killer."

"He's *not* my uncle." I smiled. I got as far as the open main door before she finally stated the bloody obvious. I manoeuvred to face her.

"You realise that HomeWorld Security's interest makes this more than a simple murder."

"No such thing as a simple murder, Chief. Even a snap domestic homicide carries a shitload of baggage."

"But this could prove delicate."

I laughed. "You realise I don't do delicate, Chief. I don't care about the politics; don't really even give a shit about Jimmy Strong. I just do the job and go home."

"Denial might be why you're so good at your job."

Denial? "You trying to shrink me, Chief?"

"I wouldn't dare. I've read your file, Agent Capra. I know why you are…you."

I seriously doubt that. "Yeah? We should compare notes some time."

"Over dinner?"

Oh *great*! The new chief was flirting with me. When I smiled—a yes and no—an uncomfortable prickle scrambled up my spine, as if Aggie had sparked me right through my coccyx. I backed out of the office and into something that shouldn't have impeded my exit.

I turned to find one of the finest specimens of manhood I'd ever seen, sprawled on his back in a silk Jimani suit. Not *my* type at all, in any sense—but definitely beautiful. And despite a strangeness about him, I contemplated taking him home for my mother.

This was the second bloke Aggie had flattened today, though; maybe she'd developed a thing against minority groups. Speaking of which, I realised Chief Bascome was also in the passageway, loitering and laughing.

"That better not be directed at me, Chief."

"I'm laughing at your old codger," he said, pointing at, "Milo Decker."

"What," I began, and then ran out of ideas.

"To allay your fears about my ability to assimilate, I do not suffer from space fever or any other stress-induced syndrome and I've never been on a Jump Ship," Decker announced.

"I apprised him of your concerns," the chief mocked. I scowled at him.

"But yes, Agent Capra, I *was* born in 2040 and I *have* been in space for sixty-eight years, although for me it was more like five."

Oh—frakn—no.

"I was part of the original Australian Probe Ship Mission."

"Give me strength!" I begged. "How long have you been back?"

It hit me then, that what was stranger than the thing I'd half noticed earlier—that Handsome had a full head of hair and no implants—was the fact that this cleanskin was so young.

No, take that back. The huge oddity was the fact that he was a *man* so young.

"One month," he was saying.

I turned on the chief and snarled, "You assigning me a techno-retard as a partner?"

"Calm down. He'll catch on quick."

"Realise I sound like a walking cliché, Chief," I began.

"I don't mean to be offensive, Agent Capra," Decker interrupted, "but I doubt you could be a walking anything."

Valuable commodity he might be, but Ensign Decker had just demanded an arse-kicking. I pinned him to the wall before he realised I'd moved. "Your file says you're eighty-seven years old, Decker," I said quietly. "What's your calculation?"

"Twenty-three," he stammered.

"Good, so by anyone's calendar, you're old enough to know that it's unacceptable to say what you just said."

"Yes, Agent. But you called *me* retarded."

"Technologically retarded is what I said. That referred to an educational inadequacy, *not* your physical appearance. Did not call you brainless, did I?"

"No," he replied.

"Then do not ever point out that I am legless. Got it?"

He nodded.

"Good," I said, and hovered off down the hall. "You coming?"

Twenty minutes later I was sitting in my office crash chair, hot-wiring the lead wire from an elderly virtual reality helmet into my TI so I could piggy-back *Ensign* Decker into Cy-city.

"So, we're going inside the computer?" he said.

"No. We're going to use the Terminal Interface to hitch a ride into the matrix of cyberspace and go anywhere we like."

"Except we don't leave this room."

"Of course not," I replied.

"I'm having trouble with this."

"They must have had some kind of cyber tech sixty-eight years ago."

"I'm sure *they* did," Decker replied. "But my experience was limited to what was relevant to my training. Preparation for my voyage began when I was six. It was a combo of survival skills and firearm drills, plus advanced biology and stellar cartography. My only personal interest at the time was archaeology." He shrugged. "I wanted to explore the old San Francisco ruins."

I raised my eyebrows. "Gone now."

"Yeah," Decker grumbled. "Guess I'll have to learn to pilot a sub to realise that dream."

"Okay, so that was then," I said, handing him the helmet. "What's stopped you since?"

Decker smiled. "Since? Agent Capra, you forget that by my body clock I was only gone for five years—during which time I mapped the Margolin quadrant and the entire sector between Allyo and Jajaray."

"That's quite a bit of space." I was genuinely impressed. "But I can't process that you're a twenty-three-year-old who's been alive for eighty-seven years. Travelling at light speed always *was* beyond my understanding."

"Try going offworld for five years and returning to find your little sister's a great-grandmother," he said. "I was eighteen when the

Australian Mission left Earth. Our Light Ship was at the cutting edge of state-of-the-art; we were *so* advanced we were still science fiction.

"By travelling *at* the speed of light, months as you know them passed like days for us. Our voyage lasted five years; but decades went by back here. We thought we'd been contacted by an advanced alien culture when we came across a Jump Ship on our way home. Those things travel at up to six *billion* kilometres a second. They can flip to Titan and be home for dinner. We felt like dinosaurs."

"Well, prepare your dino balls for another future shock, kid," I said.

Decker looked nervous and pointed at my vid-screen. "And there's really a city in there."

"Not in there," I corrected him. "And not even—more logically—in the bio-cell vault, which is in *there*." I stroked the translucent purple interface deck that shielded the banks of neural gel-cells and my nano-tech maintenance crew.

"Cyspace is out there; *every*where in *non*-space." I waved my hands in the general direction of nowhere in particular, trying to find words for a concept that was incomprehensible—until you'd seen it.

"It's an artificial alternate universe. And yes there are *cities* there. Our beat is Cy-city or, more often, Downside, a sprawling shantytown of cabo halls, blues bars, data saloons, and holo-brothels. It's in a hundred back alleys off the old Information Superhighway."

Decker looked like he was in pain.

"It's like *imagining* information. Parts of cyberspace are still just stacks of data or ribbons of info; at least that's what it looks like when you're trawling. When you access something specific, however, you can actually see it. Although what it *looks* like depends on how it was stored in the first place. Much of the old stuff is just dry, endless reams of figures, words, or images—some flat, some 3-D, some holo-fabrications. Like what you'd see on your vid-screen or projected via a holo-imager.

"More recent or imaginative info is like a full-on interactive vid. You *can* view it unplugged, but when you jack *into* cyspace, through a Navigation Controller like CC-Fly or ParaWeb, then you see and feel that information as a version of reality.

"For example, the stuff you charted on your voyage would appear, all around you, exactly as *you* saw it, and logged it, in person out there." I waved in the direction of outer space, realising I was giving Decker directions to the same "nowhere in particular" that I'd called cyberspace.

"You don't see it with your eyes, though, right?" Decker said.

"Well, *I* don't," I said, "coz my skull implant is connected directly to my brain's visual cortex. You, however, will be seeing things the old-fashioned way, coz you have to receive the data via the visor. Assume you've at least used one of these before."

He rammed the thing on his head. "For games."

"Games?"

"We each have our own skills," Decker stated. "While you've been scragging this inorganic ersatz universe, I've been flipping through the real thing cataloguing star systems and making contact with new species."

"Okay, game boy, this works the same. Images and sound get delivered via the visor and, just as you once believed you were in the crew lounge on Asimov Base, or fighting the Granks in a space battle, now you will *know* you're in Cy-city.

"The cities in cyspace are way more than virtual reality; they are, in a sense, virtually real. It's the ultimate head-trip coz you're not confined by a program that generates a game. You can go anywhere that information is stored, and *everywhere* you go takes you somewhere else, even if it's just back to the *central* matrix, which is a misnomer coz it's not *at* the centre, and there's actually more than one of them. Cyberspace is like real space; it has no centre, no edges, and no top or bottom—*and* it's an expanding universe."

"But it's not real." Decker was still unsure.

I laughed. "No, it's not real. But *real* is a relative term, just like time and space. You of all people should understand that."

Decker grunted. "So how can you *be* a cybercop?"

"Why you'd *want* to be one is a better question," I said. "When people started spending half their lives in cyspace, for recreation, knowledge exchange, propaganda, or profit, some bright spark came up with the idea of creating virtual spaces where trawlers could meet—anonymously, by using avatars."

Decker shrugged. "You mean you could lie."

"Yes, you could lie. You could *be* anybody or thing you wanted—including yourself. You could reveal the you that had zilch to do with an ugly face or a lack of arms, or *any* real-world signifiers that supposedly *describe* you but really just label you as a mottle-skinned, bi-gendered accountant.

"Then a pair of tech-heads co-named Breckinridge Fink took the virtual notion, juiced it with imagination, and made it tangible. They established ParaWeb and turned parts of cyberspace into permanent holographic constructs of the landscape of the cyber matrix.

"Breckinridge Fink built Downside, Cy-city, and BerinSpace but it was only a dash before competing NavCons and matrix architects went on-line. Suddenly there were trade regions, cities, and resorts like CaraBazaar and ParisBo. They're still amazing amalgams of ultra-tech and unfettered creativity, where blissful paradise meets darkest nightmare in the same scape, and where the avenues and edifices are blended fact and fiction. It's a wondrous hybrid of myth and common reality."

"I'm waiting for the but," Decker said as I leant over to adjust the audio flaps on his helmet.

"But it is beset, naturally, by that parasitic by-product of all human endeavours."

"What's that?"

"Crime," I snarled. "And more varieties of it than you'd ever think possible. I might be a cybercop, but when I enter cyspace I'm going where there is *no law*. My badge, your new badge, no badge, same thing. The *rules*, such as they are, are loosely *guided* by a century-old free-market code of honour that is just that: an honourable, civilised kind of thinking. And 'thinking' is the only *truly* operative word, concept and act in the whole of cyspace. It's a region that works cleanly and honestly—in its intentions.

"Bad elements, however, turn up wherever there's a buck to be made or a drek to push around, so we are tolerated coz we proved ourselves to be useful. But until the NavCons ask for an official SIP Corps presence, we're merely bounty hunters or secret agents, using cyspace just like everyone else does, to get or pass info. Don't be fooled, though; it's as dangerous for cops in cyspace as it is on any streetside posting."

I jacked Decker's tracer lead into my TI deck to check the calibration. I hadn't used something as hokey as a VR helmet in decades.

"When you enter any cyspace city or resort," I continued, "you sling on a Cloak, or adopt an avatar, of anything you like. While there you can eat, drink, talk, or listen to a rantan band; you can have mind-blowing sex in a holo-brothel, without risk of disease; you can even pick a fight and have the crap beaten out of you if that's your quirk.

"If you've got an implant, like mine, you'll actually *feel* and taste it all. Your avatar will bleed and bruise, but the experience leaves no mark on your real body at home in its crash chair. But, coz your brain *thinks* it's real, your endorphins get triggered, your adrenaline pumps, and up goes your blood pressure. If your heart can't take it, your brain will shut it down. If your *mind* can't take it, then there's a tank-load of cybertherapists listed in the Yellow Files."

Decker shifted uncomfortably in his seat.

"You *should* be nervous, Decker. Life is strange enough out here, but our beat trawls the seriously weird. Have I put you off yet? Or are you going to lower your visor and take a look for yourself? Make up your mind, Ensign Decker, coz *I'm* going now."

The noise that followed me into the matrix told me Decker was right behind me. He sounded like he'd been thrown out of Jump Ship that was still warping through space.

"Fraaakn-ell!"

My left hand keyed in the cords for Downside, and as the public entry point for the town materialised around us, I accessed my Cloak and chose an appropriate avatar for my new partner.

"Turbo*shit*, what a charge!" Decker exclaimed.

The permanently rain-slicked main street reflected the neon-lit, forever night-time world of Downside. Tonight, that being a relative term, the footpaths of Bernezlee Alley were crowded with trawlers of every description, and there was music, conversations, arguments, and laughter spilling from every establishment down the strip.

"Close your mouth, Decker, you look like an idiot, particularly considering how you're dressed."

He looked down, then swivelled to catch his reflection in a window. He had to search for himself coz the person who looked back *at* him was not only barely dressed, but didn't look a bit *like* him.

"What is this?" he demanded.

"Apollo," I replied. "Thought you'd look good in a toga."

"Yeah?" he snarled. "Well, I like your *legs*, Agent Capra, but who are you supposed to be?"

"Incognito! As are you, *Ensign* Apollo," I responded tartly.

Whatever Cloak I adopt, and this time I'd chosen a fem-punk variation, I *always* grant myself killer legs, so I decided against punching Decker in the mouth for mentioning them again. I headed off down Bernezlee towards the Bender. A sleazy nightclub was always the place to start.

"There's one thing I still don't understand." Decker trailed after me.

"Just one?" I reacted involuntarily to the vibration of my plasma-phone. I raised my real arm long enough to hear my mother snapping: "Jane, this really is urgent," then waved the call off.

"If you can get beat up here and there's no mark on your real body, how was Strong killed here?"

"There's a wicked illegal little device called a Rat Gun that gives a badarse electric shock or, if it hits *just* the right spot, a synaptic power surge. If a drek with one of those takes a dislike, you're fried toast in seconds. The last thing you'd ever see, while lying in a Downside gutter, is *these* neon lights. But your body, and a skull full of soup or dust, will be found in your crash chair at home still jacked into your terminal. Just like Jimmy."

"Do these murders *ever* get solved?" Decker asked.

I thumbed myself. "Best cleanup rate in the Corps. Hope you not gonna ruin my record, *Ensign*."

"Hope you're not gonna spend our entire partnership being patronising," Decker remarked amiably.

Five minutes later we were sconced in a Bender booth, waiting for a drink and listening to a very bad rantan artiste.

"What *is* he trying to do?" Decker asked.

"*Can't* do it, that's his problem."

"Is it supposed to be music?"

"You sound like my mother. Yes, this *is* supposed to be music. Not this bloke, though; he should be refried."

A five-note chime announced the return of our bartend Beano, a snake-skinned rogue who growled at Decker, "Sit back, mavrak."

"Right*o*," Decker snarled back.

I glared at Decker, then smiled at Beano. "He's a virgin," I apologised.

Beano grunted: "K'n tourists," and slid back to the bar.

"What's with him or whatever that was?"

"He's a bartend. It's his prerogative to be mean as batshit—if he wants."

Decker tasted his burly and curled his lip. "Seems pointless if you can't taste it."

"Pointless to you, maybe." I shrugged. "Tastes vivid to me, like riko juice and deepsouth bourbon."

I scanned the patrons for the tag-signs of my snitches. The crowd this night was a spicy mix of mean-faced dealers, xotic-limbed hosties looking to score, club ragers, and chronic barflies. The latter were lazy dreks who'd missed the point of trawling and only ever came to drink and ogle.

"Incognito?"

"What?" I asked.

"Sorry. I didn't know what to call you," Decker said.

"Incognito's good," I smiled. "Did you want to call me something for a reason?"

"Yeah. I was wondering *how* you lost your legs. Bascome said it was in the Border War, but..." Decker recognised my expression for what it was. He took a breath and pressed on regardless. "It's just that I don't know anything about that conflict, not having been here and all. It must have been hell to deal with, I mean..."

"The war or the legs?" I squinted at him. I had no intention of letting him off the hook for asking such a personal question so soon in our relationship. It didn't matter that I felt remarkably comfortable with this young man. I rarely took to anyone quickly, but Decker possessed a strangely intimate quality. Either that or I was drunk.

"Both, I guess," he muttered. "I mean, how do you deal with a physical loss like that? And, um, what I *did* hear about the northern trenches was...scarifying."

Poor bastard still had a lot to learn about social etiquette, so I gave him a point for refusing to *pretend* he was sorry about broaching an inappropriate subject.

"The legs thing is *not* a subject for today, Decker. Okay? S'pose it *is* a good bar story—how I lost them in a swivel grenade blast—but there's nothing you *need* to know about that. And what you might *want* to know is a matter of public record. Go look it up. Also, I have no intention of helping you comprehend a near decade of bloody warfare by letting you inside my head."

Decker's Apollo-visage smiled a genuine apology; so I smiled back.

"Besides, my ringside account wouldn't give you an objective view. You'd just get my anger, my gunsight, and my nightmares. And believe me, you don't want to know about my nightmares."

Or my escape. That incredible dance on the edge of utter abandon. I took a swig of burly. I hadn't told a soul about that imagined passion with my exotic lover. Weird that it was the second time today, and the first time in years, it had come to mind. The memory felt like a coiled snake of pure elation had shifted in my chest.

"History is never objective," Decker said. "It's always written by the…"

"The winners, I know. And we were the winners, so from me you'd get double-subjective, coz personally I think we should've walled the Raven Brigades into their precious enclaves afterwards. They're a scourge, liable for more life damage on this planet than any other group since humans first stood upright and worked out how to whack someone else over the head with a rock."

"Easy to say with hindsight," Decker nodded. "But back before the Raven Corporation was so blatantly manipulative, they—"

I snorted. "Rackers! You *do* need a history lesson, Decker. Manipulative is how Raven Corp began; genocidal is how its brigades ended up. That we didn't know about it for half a century just shows how deceitful they were. But let's start with the World War, precipitated by the fuel crisis… Oh, but you were here in 2047, weren't you? So you'd remember—bad war, good result; coz it led to the International Power Pact."

"I was seven." Decker grinned.

"Oh, reality check," I groaned. "I wasn't even born then, and now I'm ten years older than you. Okay, so as a kid you were oblivious to the rumour, later proven, that the fuel crisis was facilitated by the Raven Corporation.

"Then, after you left earth, the United Nations' Eugenics Moratorium was abandoned after a decade of legal stoushes over the 'right to free trade' bankrupted the UN. The resulting Gene Trade Disputes, while an obvious outcome of an economic system with no controls, were just legal money-spinning clashes of ego and marketing between the world's largest gene-makers like the US Genofactory, EuroGene, and Raven Corp.

"But, having opened the market to free trade, these egos then tried to control it, but buggered themselves by not noticing the emergence of an international black market, orchestrated by the secret Raven Corp Brigades.

"The once morally respectable Gene Trade took a backseat to the truly free but illegal street trade. And in a decline reminiscent of the previous century's drug wars, the gene trade soon degenerated into armed skirmishes, then major border conflicts, and finally the full-blown Gene War of 2060.

"The latter made the Gene Traders, especially Raven Corp, rich beyond belief, but even their wealth couldn't protect them when one of their own, that lunatic Ferry Barcolin, let loose the Mantaray retrovirus in 2063. And you *do* know the result of that, Decker, coz of what you are now you're home.

"But," I continued, making the most of the soapbox I hadn't intended to climb on, "out of every parcel of man-made shit—and I used the word *man* quite deliberately—comes something good; and in 2067 we got the very best that civilised human beings could come up with: the Alpha-Omega Accord.

"The AOA enabled First Contact, the Interplanetary Exchange, unprecedented techno-progress, world peace until—and again after—the seven-year Border War; which was, of course, initiated by feral remnants of the Raven Brigades.

"These are the bare dry facts, Decker, and all a matter of historical record. You want colour? Go to the holomuseum. Maybe if you stick around long enough I'll tell you my legs story. Until then it's personal, and it's history—much like my actual legs."

Decker looked like I'd beaten him around the face with an old-fashioned encyclopaedia; and then he smiled. No idea why that delighted me as much as it did. It was very disturbing.

"It was Second Contact," he said.

"What?"

"Your wonderful Alpha-Omega Accord enabled Second Contact. Our Probe Ship made First Contact. We traded with the Creons, lived with the Benin, hired several Avanirs as pilots."

"That may well be, Ensign—but if the Jump Ships hadn't found your vessel out there beyond the Belt, we'd never have known what you did or who you met."

Decker smiled again. "Except for the strange stories those other spacefarers would've told about our passage."

I shrugged. "True. But right now—apart from warning you that one of my way-weird snitches is about to join us—there's only two stories we need to know about each other in order to bond. And they are that *you* are one of only four thousand human males on this planet with viable sperm; and *I* am Lambda Capra Jane of the Alpha-Omega Clan."

My snitch was a tech-trader called Zippo Farqar. Tonight his avatar was a scaly humanoid with antlers and piercings. He sat, I ordered him a stinger, he sniffed at Decker.

"Weird one, this."

"True," I agreed.

"No. I mean frak'n weird," Zippo insisted.

"How do you recognise each other if you're always switching avatars?" Decker asked.

Zippo sniffed again. "Pheromones."

I grabbed Zippo's antler but addressed Decker. "Every trawler has a batch of tags, separate people-specific codes we can exchange. I enter Downside with my Farqar-tag switched on. If he's in, and wants to meet, he finds me. Or vice versa. If incognito is preferred, the tags stay off or ignored."

"Ah, she's a cleanskin," Zippo said, running a talon across Decker's hand.

The reaction was instant, and bone-crushing. Zippo nursed three fingers.

"Impulse control not your thing?" I asked my new partner.

"Do I *look* like a she?" Decker asked.

"Don't be ridiculous," I said. "Downside is the great lie, remember."

"Want my intel, or not?" Zippo asked.

"Want." I nodded.

"Okay. Uncle J came Downside three times. Or three times shared his tags."

"I gave Zippo the master ID to Jimmy's tags," I explained to Decker.

"First time, he asked all around for word on stem factories, organ harvests, and gene therapy."

"What the frak for?" That made no sense. Jimmy cared bugger-all for anything but hard-tech.

Zippo shrugged. "Second, he got took to a Zen-den down Styx Alley."

"Which one?" I asked, giving Decker the "later" signal before he asked the obvious.

"Triple 6. Run by Charon Marx."

"What did Jimmy want?"

"Charon wouldn't say. Third visit, Jimmy gets turfed from Triple 6, goes troppo on Styx, and is rat-gunned and dies a click away by the flagpole on the Crop. Though no one saw nothin'."

"Of course not."

"This next is for your ears only." Zippo waved a dismissive finger.

"Decker, go wait outside while I pay my dues."

When we were alone Zippo said, "Didn't think you'd want this shared with your weird frak'n girly-boy-Apollo. Intel threw up a connect to your Juno." He raised his hand. "I *know* they had a thing, CJ. It was a threat against her."

I stood. "Jimmy would never harm aunt Juno."

"No, he was Downside doing *whatever* coz of the threat."

Jimmy playing hero? That didn't gel either.

"What's with the *she* refs to my Apollo?"

"I thought you, of all dyksters, would have sniffed to that one."

"I was with Decker when *he* cloaked. I chose his avatar."

Zippo touched his nose. "I told you, CJ—pheromones."

"Dream on. The person who masters original-trawler scent will be rich indeed."

He smiled. "You know I'm a real-world Pharma. I've almost perfected it."

"Almost is the word, Zippo. Come see me, real-world, when you perfect at least a valid gender ID. I might bankroll you."

I rejoined the buff Milo "Apollo" Decker outside.

"Secrets?" he said.

"Maybe."

I led the way to the seamier, nastier realm of Downside, the quarter known as Hangman's Crop. We threaded our way between street vendors—hawking everything from food and microchips to T-shirts and banzai—and entered Crop Plaza. Trawling there—where Bernezlee Drag met Pyramid Way and the five Cracker Alleys—was a circus of freaky avatars trying to outdo each other with visible weirdness or strange behaviour. And Decker, still the dopey tourist, kept bumping into them.

"Watch it, jerkman!" snarled a three-foot Kewpie doll. With chainsaw teeth.

Decker recoiled, then snorted.

Please don't laugh, Decker. I grabbed his arm in the same moment that mine—back in my rack—had been touched, reassuringly.

"The green Kewpie," I said, yanking Apollo Decker from trouble, "could be an amped-up gym-jock. While lugnuts there," I pointed to a scarified ogre, "is probably a schoolgirl."

"The lie thing again." Decker smiled.

"Yup." Despite feeling strangely turned on by—I've *no idea* what—I clasped Decker's forearm and headed for the flagpole at the centre of Hangman's Crop.

"What are you looking for?" Decker asked as I scoured the area.

"This is where Jimmy bought it."

There was no such thing as a crime scene in cyspace, no way to collect forensic evidence, and, as Zippo said, "no one saw nothin'."

"And?" Decker said, sussing I was clueless.

"Doesn't make sense that Jimmy died here. The feral with the Rat Gun was down an alley near the Pit Club."

"Could he have made it here and then died?"

"Technically no. If a Rat Gun kills you, which it did Jimmy, then you die where you're hit. Unless where I entered on his trail was the last moments of his life, not the end. I had to run; maybe he did, too."

"You look excited." Decker sounded surprised.

"Graffiti! Look for a message." I turned to the closest walls.

"You're joking!" Decker's reaction was understandable given Downside's exterior walls were an ever-evolving canvas of doodles, scribbles, and the rare masterpiece.

"Incognito," Decker called.

"Yeah?" *Whoa!* An unconventional thrill surfed my brain. Decker's fingers—back in my office—were on my arm again.

"Stop that," I snarled. "I don't do boys."

"Sorry. But remember I can't feel stuff in here like you can."

"Doesn't mean you get to real-world touch me. What do you want?"

He was on his knees, pointing at the flagpole's base. "Did you say your Alpha-Omega honorific was 'Lambda'?"

I joined him on the ground. "Oh, Jimmy, you clever, stupid bastard."

My left office-hand took a snapshot of Jimmy's graffiti. It was a small rough circle containing the letters λCJ, the words *Daerin Juno*, and the scrawl *37.48 144.57 libr.*

"Damn. Zippo was right."

"About what?" Decker asked.

"Jimmy's being here was connected to my aunt. Come on."

We headed into Chin Sha's Emporium, zigzagged a multitude of tables laden with exotic curios, to the entrances of the five notorious Cracker Alleys. I pointed and named them for Decker: "Acheron, Erebus, and Tartarus; Hades—location of the Pit Club; and Styx—which is where we're going. Welcome to, Hell Ensign Apollo; try not to draw attention to yourself."

Decker gestured at his pecs and barely-there toga.

"It's attitude not avatar that gets you noticed down here," I said and waded into the ankle-deep fog that forever-curled above the flagstones of the sharply angled Styx Alley. We followed a centaur along its twists and turns until he slipped into Black Persephone's Tavern. I then calculated the best route to the Zen-den enclave.

"You were going to elaborate about these Zen places," Decker said.

"Ah, yeah." I frowned. "They're like last decade's oxygen, b-boy, or porn bars," I began, then recalled Decker hadn't been on Earth last decade. "A Zen-den is this century's hookah bar or opium den, where people zone on whatever floats their boat. Some dens have virtual reality pods; others are hands-on S&M joints, fight rings, or saunas. Drugs, sport, or sex—pretty much covers everything."

"Isn't VR superfluous in a virtual world?"

"I guess; never really thought about it." I stopped before a red door bearing a large brass 666, but had to grab Decker by his toga and yank him back to me. I rang the bell, an eyelevel door slot slid back, and a foul-smelling voice demanded the password.

"Frakn hell," Decker swore, "how are we…"

The door opened.

I laughed and pushed my partner into the haze and heavy-metal thump of the Triple 6 before the door drek changed his mind.

"I can't touch *you*, but obviously you can drag and shove me on a whim," Decker complained. The hand that Apollo the avatar placed in the small of my back, was matched by Decker's real one.

I glared at him. "Do that again and I *will* break your fingers." I scoped for the Boss of 666. The place was kitted out like Valhalla—all stone, shields, and animal hides—but with demon heads on pikes and human torsos roasting over braziers. Wenches of indeterminate sexes delivered ale mugs to patrons at pitted log tables in barred booths.

"Popular joint," Decker shouted.

"His joint," I said, nodding at the towering mish-mash of scary mythic beings who sat on his skull throne on the dais above "Hades Gates."

"Charon Marx?" Decker verified.

"Real-world Bruce May," I said. "He is such a poser!"

"He's not alone," Decker said, running to keep up with me.

I knew the trolls and ogres loitering below the dais were Charon's goons, employed to keep the hoi polloi at bay. Also knew the only way to the top of any pile is on the backs of those you step on. So that's the route I took.

I barely touched the first five trolls, but they ended face-first on a beer-soaked floor rug. I felled a gnarly ogre on the second step with groin kick and another with an elbow to his throat, and then literally used them as a stepping stones to the top.

No idea where Decker was in 666, but beside me in my office there were noises suggesting he was being thumped or was choking in disbelief. No one else in the Hall paid much attention—except Charon

Marx himself, who'd leapt into a defensive squat on his menacing throne.

"Step away from my man!" It was a Cyclops—with huge bare breasts.

I was still laughing after my spinning back kick laid her out at the foot of Charon's high chair. *I love my legs!*

I leapt up beside the God of 666 and whispered, "Hey, Bruce."

"Oh crap, CJ!"

"Come on, mate," I cajoled. "Buy me a drink."

Moments later Decker and I were sconced in Charon's private suite chatting about old times.

"So tell me why you threw a punter into the alley about eighteen hours ago…"

Charon gave his best Overlord laugh. "Don't know why the last five scrags were bounced, CJ, let alone yesterday's—"

"To get chased and rat-gunned—to death," I finished.

"Oh. Him."

"Yeah, him. My uncle Jimmy."

"Uh-oh." Charon's avatar morphed from the Hellgod of Supreme Ugly to a face and figure only a smidge removed from the original Bruce May—or at least the one I'd met in the flesh five years ago. This avatar was bald, thin, and ancient, but still oozing his trademark androgynous sex appeal.

Decker must have sensed a bit of reality had arrived in the Triple 6, coz he grabbed my real-world arm again. I didn't raz him this time because Bruce really was almost a collector's item.

"Hang on." Bruce frowned. "You can't have an uncle. It's genetically…"

"Impossible, I know, Bruce. But he and one of my Matriarchs had a thing, so he's almost family."

"Don't call me Bruce, you know I hate it, CJ."

"Why was he here yesterday?" Decker was finally doing the cop thing.

I patted his real-hand encouragingly; then stopped immediately as that same damned-exquisite vibration flooded the parts of me that Zanzibar Black had switched on earlier. A burning urge to track her down and give her a piece of my…*everything* made no sense at all. And then…

Frakn hell; again?

"You okay?" Decker whispered in my real ear, while his Apollo-avatar faced the still-talking Charon. I made mine get up and pace the den.

"First, I didn't know the man," Charon stated. "He got ejected from my premises after a scuffle. Second, I vestigated after I heard he got fried and—*still* didn't know the man—but Ragnor said he'd been here once before wearing a different Cloak."

"A scuffle? Really, Bruce? Sorry, Charon."

"Okay. A bloodbath brawl."

"Jimmy was fighting?"

"Didn't say that, CJ; said there was a brawl. Ragnor reported the now-fried pirate, er, your uncle, was in it; but it more happened around him. And maybe to him."

"He got beat up in your establishment, so you threw *him* out?" Decker said.

"Threw them both out."

"Two people had a bloodbath?" I said. "Was Jimmy cage fighting?"

"Course not, CJ. Was obvious to a gnat the bloke was a Startup."

"A what?" Decker asked.

"Fresh meat," Charon said. "Like you. All wooden and such."

Apollo glanced down at his perfect form and then at me, and acknowledged, "Attitude not avatar."

Charon poured three cups of mead and pushed ours over. "Didn't know he was the same bloke till hours later."

"What same bloke?" I asked.

"Same bloke as the one asking me about the Liebestraum Institute."

"You said you didn't know him, *Bruce*."

"Oh. Right." Charon downed half his drink. "I met him the time before, when he was a ninja and asked for an audience. With me, I mean."

"You personally? Why?" I asked.

"Man wanted to know shit about organs."

Well, that gelled with Zippo's intel. "And stem factories?"

"No, just organs. Oh, and juice banks."

"Why ask you that?" Decker asked.

"Don't he know who I am?" Charon looked hurt.

"People forget, mate." I shrugged. "Since you've moved in here, there's a generation never heard of you."

Decker's hand was back on my arm as Apollo gave me a quick glance. Charon didn't need to know that my partner was both too young *and* too old to have ever heard of the Liebestraum Institute, let alone Bruce May and his cohorts.

Although, strangely, I got the sense that he had. And that he knew… Decker removed his hand.

Okay. Knew what? I was starting to wonder if I hadn't been tagged by that bloody Rat Gun. Obviously not enough to kill—unless this really was hell—but maybe a blast-residue had followed me out of Jimmy's terminal. It would certainly explain the flashbacks and the inappropriately heightened libido and—*that, too, dammit*—that sense that someone was laughing at me.

"CJ? You okay?" I looked up to find that Bruce had resumed a smaller version of his Charon Marx avatar. Probably so he could sulk discreetly about being a long-forgotten rock star.

"What could *you* tell him about the Institute?" Decker asked.

Now, you see…very odd question. I looked at my partner, who was clearly avoiding eye contact. Given everything else he hadn't known today, his question should've been: *what* is the Liebestraum Institute.

"I live there, man," Charon said, as if the whole world should damn well remember that.

"I don't understand," Decker said.

"Charon, or rather Bruce and a motley collection of entertainers—"

"Motley?" Charon objected.

"Pooled their substantial fortunes to fund the Dreamscape Wing of the Liebestraum. It was then opened to anyone—who could afford it—to take up permanent residence, rather than, you know, *die*."

"Your tone suggests disapproval, CJ," Bruce said.

"Talk to me when it's available to all on UniCare and I might be less subjective in my opinion about who gets to die or not, *Bruce*."

Decker tapped the table. "Dreamscape Wing; organ harvests?"

I looked at my partner again. Ensign Clueless had suddenly become Detective Impatient. What's more, he continued to avoid eye contact.

"We have one thousand three hundred and forty-one Dreamers residing in the Dreamscape Wing," Charon began.

"Who exist on life support, in induced comas, while living permanently in Cy-city," I finished.

That made Decker look at me. "Living in here."

"Will you show him, mate?" I asked the Undead Host of the Triple 6.

Without a word, Bruce May allowed his Charon Marx avatar to morph from the achingly handsome Rock God who'd been lead singer of Scattered Heads sixty years ago. Then on through the gracefully aging legendary lead of Fraught, to the avatar he shown us moments before, to—and I felt Decker's shock, beside me in my office—the total reality of the wizened and barely recognisable comatose shell that he was now.

Although this avatar was looking at us with Bruce's eyes, I knew that back in the Dreamscape Wing, his eyes—like those of the other 1,340 Dreamers—were closed, permanently.

"Remember I said some of the Zen-dens had virtual reality pods?"

Decker nodded.

"Well, one good use for them would be for Dreamers like Bruce."

"Except *I* don't use the pods." A scowling Charon was back with us.

"I know, mate. Explain to Decker how the Dreamers get a different reality from the average Pod people."

Charon got to his feet and beckoned. "Come with; I'll show him."

Decker and I fell in behind a regular-human sized Charon Marx and wended our way through the dance crowd in his great hall, to Hades Gates beneath his throne. The music dwindled to silence the moment we descended the nine steps to Charon's suite of Zen-dens.

I'd been down here many times and knew the Triple 6 layout, so I kept half my attention on my partner's reaction to his newest frontier.

"So, Startup," Charon addressed Decker, "Bruce May exists at the Liebestraum but I, Charon Marx, live here. Close to five hundred other Dreamers live in Downside or other parts of Cy-City; the remainder live in CaraBazaar, SanFran, or Hawksnest; and a great many of them circulate throughout the zones.

"Triple 6 is my joint. I am the architect, builder, and lord of all I survey. I frakn love this place. And coz I choose to recognise *this* as my world, I've never felt the need for extra virtual reality. Although I often relax in my Zen-dens, like this one." Charon opened a set of double doors to a sandy arena with a martial arts deck where a bloody fight was in progress.

We continued down the hall. "And this one." Charon brushed his hand over a panel that turned the stone wall translucent, to reveal a Roman orgy in full swing.

"A thousand of my regular clientele—tourists I mean, not residents—take the Plunge, that extra trip into deeper VR, maybe a couple of times a year. But some of the Liebestraum Dreamers do it weekly, or even daily, because by doing so and then returning to their Downside homes, they reckon life in here feels more real."

Charon had stopped again, this time at the balcony that overlooked the four hundred VR pods—rows and rows of arm-chair or bed booths, stretching into the distance. He peered at the panel of stats he'd conjured on the wall beside him.

"Got a hundred and twenty-three Dreamers and seventy-three tourists in at the moment."

"What has all this got to do with our dead man and organ harvests?" Decker said.

"And the juice banks remember," Charon said. "That's what he took most interest in after he'd seen my Abandon Pods."

"What?" Decker and I said in unison. I added, "So you brought Jimmy Strong down here, too?"

"If, CJ, you're asking did I personally bring a ninja calling himself Dweedack down here, then yes. He wanted to know if any clients other than Dreamers stayed for extra-long periods."

I poked Charon in his oversized bronze chest. "Please don't tell me you call them Abandon Pods coz they forget to leave, or you abandon them coz they don't pay?"

"I am deeply offended, CJ. Leaving non-paying customers in situ is not good business. I can't rent out occupied space. I use Ragnor's bone-breaking skills for that."

"Who the hell is Ragnor?" Decker was either playing bad cop to my good, or he was genuinely aggravated.

"She's my wife, Startup," Charon snarled, as "Bruce" added a fleeting doubling of his avatar's size to tower over "Apollo." "She was on the dais with me earlier."

Apollo-Decker stood his ground. "You mean the one-eyed, triple-breasted leviathan that Agent Capra knocked out with one kick?"

"Yes, her." Charon laughed heartily. "I told Ninja Dweedack that only the Abandon Pods were addictive enough to hook people into protracted sessions. Why? They're called Abandon Pods coz most feature hard-core sex programs, or other adrenaline-endorphin raising adventures. Either way, they're designed to get your juices flowing."

"Ah, hence the juice banks reference," Decker said.

This time I joined Charon in the exaggerated laughing.

"What?" Decker asked.

"Juice banks are sperm banks," I managed to say. "Their contemporary existence is the stuff of urban myth, of course. But until mid-last century they were nearly as common as blood and stem-cell banks."

Decker's real-hand, clasping my forearm, this time conveyed an unmistakable sense of foreboding. It was shaking.

"What is it?" I asked him.

"Charon," he said, "what exactly did Jimmy see down here and, specifically, what did he ask you?"

"He saw everything you've seen, plus the Abandon Pods. Come with." Charon took the wide circular staircase down to the Pod Deck.

"And you just showed him, Charon?" I asked.

"CJ, when will you learn, I don't do favours. Except for you. The ninja paid for a personally guided tour. Paid well enough for me to let him scope some of the Plungers."

"So much for privacy," I noted. "*What* did he ask about organ harvests?"

Charon tapped at the plasma screen on his left palm. The VR Pods began moving around the cavernous space, jostling gently for position.

"Ninja Dweedack asked if the black market in cloned organs still existed. I said of course it did. Dumb frakn question really."

"Cloned organs, not harvests?" I said.

Charon rolled his shoulders. "I *now* surmise he wasn't interested in organs at all. After I explained the nature of most of the Abandon Pods, his quizzing became precise, and turned quite earnestly to the subject of juice banks. You with us on that subject now, Startup?"

"Yes," Decker sighed.

"When we got to this very spot here, he wanted to know if any new Plungers, say in the last two months, had been introduced to Hades Gates *by* someone. Especially if the *same* someone intro'd more than one."

"And?" I asked as Charon suddenly seemed distracted by the tango his pods were doing. "Sorry, I'm calculating. Step back a bit, please."

Decker and I did as we were told.

"And when I checked," Charon consulted his plasma again, "I found that thirty-three Trawlers had been 'treated' to first-time Plunges by friends, but only five had been intro'd by the same friend. But not all together. Each of their first visits were a few days apart. After a week, the same someone—a drek Ragnor later ID'd as Belbo Armitage— escorted them in together, like they were regular old-world bucks. The five have since been here like clockwork: three days in Abandon, two days gone, back again for three, et cetera, for a total ranging fifty-two to fifty-nine days."

"And Jimmy's juice bank questions?" I asked.

"Your 'ninja uncle' seemed convinced the banks were a reality and that I *must* know their real-world location."

"Why?" Decker asked.

"Because of the five Plungers, I think," Charon said. "But as I told him, over and over, there's no point in juice banks when the produce is forty-five years beyond its use-by date."

Oh frak. I glanced at Apollo-Decker, who'd clearly seen the same light.

"Here they are," Charon announced as a group of pods pulled to a stop before us.

Decker and I stepped in to take a look at "the five Plungers" as the realisation of what was most likely happening to the missing Spacers hit home. I was swamped by a tsunami of anguish and distress; of almost...*oh help, unbearable grief.*

But not mine.

Not my grief. What the hell?

I grabbed hold of Apollo's arm to see if the misery emanating from the pods was affecting him, too. In the same nanosec that he resisted my attempt to make him face me, I remembered he couldn't *feel* anything in here.

Real-world Decker then snatched his hand from my arm, and Apollo...disappeared.

"That," Charon pointed to the empty space, "is exactly what your Uncle Ninja Dweedack did."

"I don't get it," I said—to both Charon in Downside and Decker in my office.

Only Charon bothered to answer. "Ragnor said that when your uncle came back as *Pirate* Dweedack he met with Belbo Armitage, the Plunger's escort. Then the brawl started and they were thrown out."

I inspected the Plungers again. They were all wearing simple masquerade masks—the most basic of avatar cloaks—which meant they really looked just like the blokes in the Pods. I took a better look at the one Apollo had been checking...out.

It was, it looked like...

I reached out, removed the mask, then shook my head. It didn't help. For the second time today I was gazing down at one of the finest specimens of manhood I'd ever seen.

The young man in this particular Abandon Pod was Ensign Milo Decker.

As my office-hands performed vital logging-out procedures, my fem-punk avatar waved good-bye to Charon Marx. The real-world materialised around me and I swung Aggie around to find out how the hell anyone could be in two—no, who knew how many—places at once.

My freshly minted partner was lying on the floor. Again. Only this time he seemed to be out cold. Probably hadn't accounted for the lack of space between my terminal and the wall behind when he backed out of Downside so fast. Obviously yanked the VR helmet off and smacked his head into the wall.

None of which explained the fact that Milo Decker and his spiffy Jumani suit were shimmering—I squinted—no, phasing in and out of focus.

I stared at my own hands, then the wall.

Not shimmering.

I directed Aggie down to the floor but still couldn't reach him coz my anti-grav unit was in the way. I unbuckled and heaved myself over the edge to lie on the floor beside the definitely phasing Decker.

I poked him. The shimmering stopped. Then started again.

I patted Decker's cheek. He grabbed my hand *and* stopped shimmering.

"Who the frak *are* you?" I asked.

He blinked. "Who do I look like?"

"You look like the bloke in the Pod back there."

"Really?" he frowned, then hauled me across his body and held me there.

I struggled for three seconds until I registered that the person below me was now morphing like a changing avatar. Decker became Bruce May became—*bloody hell, me*—then Decker again.

This was simply not possible in the real world.

"It's coz I hit my head," whoever-it-was beneath me said.

No, clearly I had died earlier today. And this was my hell, forever caught nowhere at all.

Capra Jane.

Ooh peace. Oh that's nice.

Look at me, Capra Jane.

I did as I was told because now the morpher looked like that delicious Captain Zanzibar Black, and she was doing that talking in my head thing again.

Jane, remember. It's time to come back to me.

Well! With an invitation like that, how could I *not* let this brilliant hallucination kiss me like her life depended on it?

The sound of distant gunfire, exploding shells, and screeching Atter-jets filled my mind. No, not my mind; it was outside, scragging the air around me and tainting it with noxious fumes.

Where was I again?

I shifted on the makeshift hospital bed and my blood chilled me to the core.

"Major Capra, wake up." I did, so Dr Black kindly held my hand.

Not again.

It's okay, my love. You're not really there.

Fresh air, music. A deep throbbing tango; just like sex on legs. Don't have legs.

Jane, concentrate. On me.

I was now kissing Zanzibar Black like *my* life depended on it. And clearly it did, coz nothing could feel this good and not be intrinsic to my very existence.

Her tongue was in my mouth. Mine was in hers. I was never going to let her go, ever again.

And then I did.

Just to check which part of my fractured existence I was in at the moment.

Yes, I am real.

Zanzibar Black was lying on my office floor, under me. We had been kissing each other.

And now I felt *completely foolish.*

I rolled away from her and sat up, shaking my head in an effort to say: *I. am. so. sorry.*

What for?

"Speak," I said. "Who the frak are you?"

She smiled and—*my insides melted*—said, "Zanzibar Black, just as your chief introduced us earlier."

I scowled at her. "My other chief intro'd my new partner as Ensign Milo Decker. But he was in Downside and, and now it seems I've…"

"Been with me all along. Sorry." Captain Black got to her feet. "I'm going to check out Jimmy's lead."

She walked out my office.

Just like that.

What? Did you forget I can't just follow you? I mind-shouted, in the hope she'd hear me. She did.

I'm sure you'll catch up, Jane.

Jane? What's with the Jane nonsense?

I rolled over and into Aggie, hovered back up to my terminal, and began an intel-hunt on Captain Zanzibar Black. Only family called me Jane, dammit. Family and lovers. And actual "lovers," *not* two-minute stands.

Why on earth, while kissing a woman I'd met today, had my strongest feeling been not to let her leave me again? Actually that was the strongest *emotion*, in my chest and mind; the earth-shattering feeling was in a whole other place.

Concentrate.

I brought up the image I'd taken of Jimmy's graffiti and stared at it, while my terminal did its own analysis.

λCJ

Daerin Juno

37.48 144.57 libr

Okay. λCJ equals Lambda Capra Jane; easy. Daerin Juno? Was that simply a ref to Aunt Juno being on the Board of the DaerinCorp Research Foundation, or an actual clue? Jimmy's final route into Downside had been via Daerin's data stacks; specifically their Future Projects Division.

But what could any of this have to do with Juno herself? What would be enough to prompt Jimmy Strong to turn into the most unlikely of heroes to protect her?

And why would Captain Black, a spook from HomeWorld Security, impersonate a missing Spacer? Coz it was obvious—well, *now* it was—that Milo Decker and the other four of Charon's five Plungers were indeed the missing Spacers.

If Jimmy had also been searching for them *and* asking about juice bars, then Charon's offhand remark about use-by dates was the crux of this whole mystery. My "partner" obviously had the same revelation about the value of "viable" juice in an age when the expiry date of genetically useful men was nearly half a century gone.

Dammit. I'd even reminded Decker—or Zanzibar—myself that he was one of only four thousand humans in existence with functioning sperm.

My terminal chimed, so I glanced down at Aggie's screen.

Zanzibar Black: Beninzay, female, born Benin, 2068; father Benin, mother Beninzay. Ranks/designations: current—Captain, HomeWorld Security; previous—Medical Officer-Surgeon, Benin MedCentre, Battalion Field Hospitals on Western Front, Sydney and Auckland, North Border.

Bloody hell. Captain Black. Dr Black. North Border Field Hospital. I checked the date of her deployment there.

2116. Eleven years ago.

The year I lost my legs in the northern trenches. No evac for three months from that stinking on-border field hospital. Stranded, in a mostly drug-induced fog, dancing a beguine with the imaginary love of my life. Or so I thought.

I headed out of my office to find out if Chief Bascome had thought to pin the usual visitor's trackerbot on our mysterious bloody HomeWorld spook, so I could track her down and...

My plasma-phone vibrated with my mother's urgent ID again. I'd put her off too many times, so I forced a smile and raised my wrist so we could see each other. I also took the lift to the next floor.

"Finally! I've been calling for hours."

"I'm kinda busy, Mum."

"I know, Jane. You're investigating your uncle's murder."

"He's *not* my uncle."

"He most surely is today, Jane. He was helping your aunt."

"You knew about this?" I snapped.

"No. I just knew he was helping." My mother—the queen of deniability. "Not that his endeavours actually helped. She's been kidnapped."

"What?" I hovered out of the lift and headed for the chiefs' wing.

"Juno—my sister, your aunt—has been kidnapped."

"Why didn't you call the cops, Mum?"

"I did. You didn't answer," she snapped, scowling like *all of this* was my fault.

"There *are* other cops...forget it. How do you know? Is there a ransom demand?"

"I was with her when they snatched her from the Daimaru Flywalk. Three men in masks pushed me over, dragged her into a scootercab, and made off with her."

"Okay, Mum. I'm on it now." I waved the call off and opened the chief's door without knocking. He and Chief Jayla Ellen were sharing a meal.

"Sorry, Chiefs, but I hope you pinned Captain Black. I need to know her current location, now."

Chief Bascome knew when urgent meant yesterday. He turned to his terminal. "Sending you the cords," he said.

"Have you found the missing men, Agent Capra?"

"Almost, Chief Jayla. I think they're being... Actually I'm not sure what you'd call it. I suspect they're being held captive, probably together, while as avatars they're regularly taken to a hardcore porn suite in Downside for the purposes of arousal. So they can be milked."

The chiefs blinked at me and then stared at each other.

"I'll leave you to think about that then, shall I?" I reverse-hovered to the door. "Oh yes. One other thing: the President has been kidnapped."

I was already in the lift by the time both chiefs rushed in the hall demanding more info.

"Later," I waved. Aggie was screening the results of my analysis requests. It seemed *37.48 144.57 libr* was the latitude and longitude of Melbourne's old, very old, Library, which explained why Zan Black's trackerbot placed her on Swanston Canal heading north.

I emerged from SIP HQ, zipped onto the nearest police airboat, and asked the pilot to take Russell Canal to La Trobe. The only part of the Victorian Library building that was still above water at high tide was its massive copper-green dome and one upper level, which constituted nearly half its original above-street-level height.

It was 6.20 p.m., Melbourne's nightlights were on, a storm was brewing southwest of the city, and the tide was about to come back in. I knew this coz, as the airboat approached one of our few almost remaining truly historic city landmarks, I could see the extra floor that was exposed every low tide.

I directed my pilot to the pedestrian Skywalk that ran around the dome and off in several directions to connect with the others that spider-webbed the city. The statuesque Beninzay who stood at the apex seemed to be waiting for me.

I joined Captain Zanzibar Black on the high deck that overlooked the dome's oculus. The five-metre-wide skylight provided an eerie glimpse into the partially illuminated interior: thirty-five metres down to the dry top-most gallery level that ran around the octagonal space.

"It's quite incredible," Zan noted.

"Yeah," I agreed. "When the tide returns, that second level down will be back underwater, though. At the moment it's a good thirty metres deep over the dome room's floor, which is another level above the old street."

"Bloody weather," Zan said, then turned to me. "What took you so long?"

"You left me on my arse on the office floor. Then I had to report to the chiefs."

"Right," Zan noted, as if we always talked this way. "Do you think my boys are in there?"

"Probably; and I think whoever's got them also kidnapped my aunt Juno today."

"The President? Damn. What is her connection to all this?"

"Something to do with DaerinCorp's future projects I think. I hope she'll be able to tell us. Shall we suss this joint?"

"After you, Capra Jane."

Call me Jane.

Okay, my love.

There was no time to sort our history out now. I pointed Zan to the ladder and hovered beside her as we descended to the concealed service entrance at the base of the dome. My SIP universal passcode gave us immediate access and we slipped into the upper gallery.

There were arguing voices echoing across the thirty-five-metre diameter, which made it hard to pinpoint their exact location but, as one, Zan and I pointed to the same spot.

"Why did you camouflage, if that's the right word, yourself as Milo Decker?" I whispered.

"So you would give a damn about what happened to him."

"What made you think I wouldn't care about these Spacers?"

And, yes, I am offended.

Zan smiled at me. "You haven't cared about anything much for a decade, Jane." She headed clockwise through the annulus, the walkway between the concentric walls of the gallery levels, with me right behind her.

"That's not true," I said.

She turned and raised an eyebrow.

"Okay. So what? You're right. I don't give a shit about anything much."

"Are you worried about Milo now?"

I squinted at her. "Maybe. It depends how much of that performance you gave was even him."

"Oh, it was him," Zan said. "That's the gift of the Beninzay. With basic information, we can camouflage as anyone. If we've met them, it's even easier. I was as much Milo Decker as he is. It's not sustainable, of course, and it *is* only a superficial personality reproduction."

The argument we'd been approaching stopped suddenly—as if the two men had perhaps heard us. It was a momentary hiatus, followed by the sound of smashing furniture.

Captain Black and I drew our weapons and covered the remaining distance at speed; she ran the eighty metres or so around the annulus, I dropped over the nearest balcony and hovered across the gap. We entered what turned out to be the scene of the crime at the same moment.

Two men were having a full-on fist fight; pushing, shoving, and smacking each other senseless. Another bloke was watching them go at it. No one paid us any attention.

The man spectating was Belbo Armitage.

To the right was a row of maybe forty hospital beds, each with people hooked up to the most basic life-support equipment. To the left, tied by the waist to a chair but drinking a beer, was Aunt Juno.

One of the fighters sent the other sliding face-first across the floor. He came to an unconscious stop at Zan's feet.

"Shit, where'd you two come from?" Armitage fumbled around the table next to him.

"Move again and I *will* shoot you," I said.

Zan crossed the room, grabbed and threw his semi-auto against the wall, and punched him in face.

"Jane darling, how nice of you to come rescue me."

I shook my head. "I didn't know I even had to do that until half an hour ago, Juno." I hovered over, took a laserknife from Aggie's toolkit, and cut her free.

When I turned back Zan was going patient to patient, looking for her Spacers. No, it was more than that: she was looking for a certain Spacer.

"Juno, what the hell is this really about? I mean apart from the produce collection that's going on."

Aunt Juno held my hand as we walked the line of hospital beds. "All of these men number among the four thousand," she said.

"That much we figured."

"Judging by their ages, most are original Earthers resistant to the Mj21 Virus," Juno said.

That made sense. The first twenty beds, according to info scrawled on the wall behind, held men aged from sixty-two to eighty. They were all so emaciated, though, it was hard to tell. None looked half as good as Bruce May and the comatose Dreamers I'd seen at the Liebestraum, only thirteen of whom were resistant.

"They're not gonna survive this, *whatever* it is, are they, Juno?" I said.

"No, my dear. Maintaining their lives was unimportant to that villainous excuse for a scientist over there." She pointed at the bleeding Belbo Armitage. "Not even the younger ones further down the room will recover enough for their lives to have meaning. This procedure is killing, has, effectively killed them."

"But…why?" I asked.

"DaerinCorp have been trying for decades to find a cure for the Mantaray retrovirus. Armitage, who I may well execute before we leave this room, worked in our labs until six months ago. He thought he could get Jimmy to break into the Daerin banks to steal the latest breakthroughs to use in his own cloning research.

"Jimmy tried once, because he believed Belbo would assassinate me if he didn't, but realised it was beyond him. So he came to me and we set about finding out exactly what Belbo was up to. It's just terrible that it got Jimmy killed."

I squeezed Juno's hand, but the wash of sorrow that suddenly flooded my senses came not from her, but from Zan at the far end of the room. I went straight to her.

Milo Decker, or what was left of him, was holding Zan's hand. She wiped at the tears trickling down his sunken cheeks, and he opened his eyes.

Again I felt an anguish and heartache that—this time—also brought to mind a day long gone. The day, now real to me, that Zan left me in that field hospital. Left me to the care of others, to return home to the troubles brewing on her own world.

I knew she wouldn't leave this young man. But I also knew he was not going to live to know that.

Are you sure?

The question my mind heard, was for Decker. He blinked, licked his lips, and blinked again.

Zan glanced at me. "Yes, that's her," she said aloud.

Decker smiled, barely.

Zan leant forward, kissed his forehead and—before I could do anything to stop her—put her gun to Decker's head and pulled the trigger.

"What the frak?" I dragged her away from the bedside. She let me do it and then crumpled to the floor.

For the second time today I set Aggie down on the floor and threw myself out.

Zan allowed me to hold her and we sat rocking for a moment.

"I really don't understand," I whispered. "Why camouflage as him and then do that?"

Zan held me at arm's length as her blue-green-blue eyes searched mine. "Do you care that he's dead?"

Stupid question! "Yes, Zan. I liked him; you, him a lot. I really do care."

"I needed to reach you. Make you care again." She smiled wanly. "He was my grandfather."

"Oh dear," said Juno.

Zan glanced at her then back at me. "It was three years ago, for him, on that Probe Ship; fifty-eight years ago for my grandmother. Milo Decker and Zanzi Aru were famous in the history of everything as the first Benin-Human coupling.

"I came back to Earth for him. And for you," she said.

Zan got to her feet, then bent and lifted me back into Aggie. And I let her, which was something I'd never allowed anyone else to do.

CONTRIBUTORS

DIANE ANDERSON-MINSHALL is an author, journalist, magazine editor, celebrity skirt chaser, media personality, and one hell of a good lay. She's author of an award-winning detective series (*Blind Faith, Blind Curves,* and *Blind Leap*) as well as the Lambda-shortlisted thriller *Punishment With Kisses.* She's appeared in several anthologies including *Bitchfest* and *Body Outlaws* as well as numerous media outlets(from *Femme Fatale* to NPR, *The New York Times* and the TV series *Secret Lives of Women),* and as the longtime editor in chief of *Curve* magazine she inspired a fictional character on *The L Word's* fourth season.

VICTORIA A. BROWNWORTH is the Lambda Award–winning author and editor of nearly thirty books. She was the book critic for the Baltimore Sun for seventeen years and her writing has appeared in the *New York Times, Village Voice, Chicago Sun-Times, Miami Herald, Philadelphia Inquirer, Los Angeles Times, PW,* the *Advocate, OUT,* and *Curve,* among others. She has been an editor for several major publishing houses. She teaches writing at the University of the Arts in Philadelphia. In 2010 she founded Tiny Satchel Press, an independent publisher of young adult books geared toward multicultural and LGBTQ-inclusive writing.

LINDY CAMERON writes both crime fact and fiction, and is a co-convenor of Sisters in Crime Australia. She is author of the Kit O'Malley lesbian PI trilogy (*Blood Guilt, Bleeding Hearts,* and *Thicker than Water,* all Bywater Books, USA) and the archaeological adventure *Golden Relic.* Her latest book, *Redback* (Clan Destine Press), is the first in a new adventure series featuring Commander Bryn Gideon and her team of Australian retrieval agents. Lindy is co-author with her sister Fin J. Ross of the true crime *Killer in the Family,* and with her friend Ruth Wykes of *Women Who Kill.* www.clandestinepress.com.au.

JEANE HARRIS is Professor of English at Arkansas State University. She is author of the novels *Delia Ironfoot*, *A Grave Opening*, *The Magnolia Conspiracy*, and *Black Iris*.

Award-winning author CLIFFORD HENDERSON lives and plays in Santa Cruz, California, where she and her partner of nineteen years run The Fun Institute, a school of improv and solo performance. In their classes and workshops, people learn to access and express the myriad of characters itching to get out. She is the author of novels *The Middle of Somewhere*, *Spanking New*, and *Maye's Request*. Her other passions include gardening and twisting herself into weird yoga poses. Contact Clifford at www.cliffordhenderson.net.

MIRANDA KENT writes short stories and novels for young adults. She is the author of the Madison McKenna mystery series, including *Solitary Confinement*. Kent mentors children in the inner city and does writing classes with middle school kids. "Some Kind of Killing" is excerpted from her upcoming novel, *The Things Inside*.

LORI L. LAKE is the author of eight novels and two books of short stories and the editor of two anthologies. She is a 2007 recipient of the Alice B. Reader Appreciation Award, a 2005 Lambda Literary finalist in the anthology category, and winner of the 2007 Ann Bannon Award and a Golden Crown "Goldie" for *Snow Moon Rising*. Lori lived in Minnesota for twenty-six years, but recently relocated to Portland, Oregon. When she's not writing, she's at the local movie house or curled up in a chair reading. She's currently working on the fourth novel in the Gun series. For more information, see her website at www.lorillake.com.

ANNE LAUGHLIN is the author of *Veritas*, which won a 2010 Goldie award in the mystery category. Her short stories have appeared in anthologies from Cleis Press, Alyson Books, Bold Strokes Books, and others. In 2008 Anne was named an Emerging Writer Fellow by the Lambda Literary Foundation, and in 2009 she was accepted into a writing residency at the Ragdale Foundation. Anne is currently working on her next mystery/suspense novel for BSB. She lives in Chicago with her partner, Linda.

LAURA LIPPMAN is the author of ten Tess Monaghan novels, including *Baltimore Blues*, *The Sugar House*, and *Another Thing to Fall;* five stand-alone novels, including *Every Secret Thing*, *To the Power of Three*, *What the Dead Know*, and *Life Sentences*; and one short story collection, *Hardly Knew Her.* She is also the editor of another short story collection, *Baltimore Noir.* Lippman has won numerous awards for her work, including the Edgar, Quill, Anthony, Nero Wolfe, Agatha, Gumshoe, Barry, and Macavity. Her most recent stand-alone, *I'd Know You Anywhere*, is a finalist for the Edgar Award for Best Mystery of 2010, and her most recent Tess Monaghan novel, *The Girl in the Green Raincoat*, is a *New York Times* bestseller.

J.M. REDMANN has published six novels featuring New Orleans PI Micky Knight. Her latest is *Water Mark*. Two of her books, *The Intersection of Law & Desire* and *Death of a Dying Man*, have won Lambda Literary Awards; all but her first book have been shortlisted. *Law & Desire* was an Editor's Choice of the *San Francisco Chronicle* and a recommended holiday book by Maureen Corrigan of NPR's *Fresh Air*. Redmann currently lives in New Orleans, at the edge of the area that flooded. Her website is jmredmann.com.

KENDRA SENNETT prefers short stories, but spends most of her time at a day job writing grants and reports. Her stories have been published in anthologies such as *Hot Ticket*, *Uniform Sex*, and *Electric*. Currently she is working on a novel, which she hopes to have out in 2012. She is not a social worker, just in case you were wondering, and wishes to thank her cat Stalker for having so far not yet tripped her on the stairs.

CARSEN TAITE works by day (and sometimes night) as a criminal defense attorney in Dallas, Texas. Though her day job is often stranger than fiction, she can't seem to get enough and spends much of her free time plotting stories. She is the author of five novels: *truelesbianlove. com*, *It Should be a Crime* (a 2010 Lambda Literary Award finalist), *Do Not Disturb*, *Nothing but the Truth*, and *The Best Defense*, all published by Bold Strokes Books. Learn more at www.carsentaite.com.

ALI VALI is the author of the Devil series, which includes *The Devil Inside*, *The Devil Unleashed*, *Deal With the Devil*, and the recently released *The Devil Be Damned*. Her stand-alone novels are *Carly's Sound*, *Second Season*, the Lambda Literary Award finalist *Calling the Dead*, and *Blue Skies*. Ali has also contributed to numerous anthologies, with her latest short story appearing in Bold Strokes' *Breathless: Tales of Celebration*. Ali is originally from Cuba and now lives outside New Orleans with her partner of twenty-six years. When she isn't writing, she works in the nonprofit sector. Ali is one of the 2011 Alice B. Readers Appreciation Award winners.

About the Editors

J.M. REDMANN has written six novels, all featuring New Orleans private detective Michele "Micky" Knight. The fourth, *Lost Daughters*, was originally published by W.W. Norton. Her third book, *The Intersection Of Law & Desire*, won a Lambda Literary Award, as well as being an Editor's Choice of the *San Francisco Chronicle* and featured on NPR's *Fresh Air*. *Lost Daughters* and *Deaths Of Jocasta* were also nominated for Lambda Literary Awards. Her books have been translated into German, Spanish, Dutch, and Norwegian. She currently lives in New Orleans, just at the edge of the flooded area.

GREG HERREN is a New Orleans–based author and editor. Former editor of *Lambda Book Report*, he is also a co-founder of the Saints and Sinners Literary Festival, which takes place in New Orleans every May. He is the author of ten novels, including the Lambda Literary Award–winning *Murder in the Rue Chartres*, called by the *New Orleans Times-Picayune* "the most honest depiction of life in post-Katrina New Orleans published thus far." He co-edited *Love, Bourbon Street: Reflections on New Orleans*, which also won the Lambda Literary Award. He has published over fifty short stories in markets as varied as *Ellery Queen's Mystery Magazine* to the critically acclaimed anthology *New Orleans Noir* to various websites, literary magazines, and anthologies. His erotica anthology *FRATSEX* is the all-time best-selling title for Insightoutbooks. Under his pseudonym Todd Gregory, he published the bestselling erotic novel *Every Frat Boy Wants It* and the erotic anthologies *His Underwear* and *Rough Trade*.

A longtime resident of New Orleans, Greg was a fitness columnist and book reviewer for *Window Media* for over four years, publishing in the LGBT newspapers *IMPACT News*, *Southern Voice*, and *Houston Voice*. He served a term on the Board of Directors for the National Stonewall Democrats and served on the founding committee of the Louisiana Stonewall Democrats. He is currently employed as a public health researcher for the NO/AIDS Task Force.

Books Available From Bold Strokes Books

Harmony by Karis Walsh. When Brook Stanton meets a beautiful musician who threatens the security of her conventional, predetermined future, will she take a chance on finding the harmony only love creates? (978-1-60282-237-5)

Nightrise by Nell Stark and Trinity Tam. In the third book in the everafter series, when Valentine Darrow loses her soul, Alexa must cross continents to find a way to save her. (978-1-60282-238-2)

Men of the Mean Streets, edited by Greg Herren and J.M. Redmann. Dark tales of amorality and criminality by some of the top authors of gay mysteries. (978-1-60282-240-5)

Firestorm by Radclyffe. Firefighter paramedic Mallory "Ice" James isn't happy when the undisciplined Jac Russo joins her command, but lust isn't something either can control—and they soon discover ice burns as fiercely as flame. (978-1-60282-232-0)

The Best Defense by Carsen Taite. When socialite Aimee Howard hires former homicide detective Skye Keaton to find her missing niece, she vows not to mix business with pleasure, but she soon finds Skye hard to resist. (978-1-60282-233-7)

After the Fall by Robin Summers. When the plague destroys most of humanity, Taylor Stone thinks there's nothing left to live for, until she meets Kate, a woman who makes her realize love is still alive and makes her dream of a future she thought was no longer possible. (978-1-60282-234-4)

Accidents Never Happen by David-Matthew Barnes. From the moment Albert and Joey meet by chance beneath a train track on a street in Chicago, a domino effect is triggered, setting off a chain reaction of murder and tragedy. (978-1-60282-235-1)

In Plain View by Shane Allison. Best-selling gay erotica authors create the stories of sex and desire modern readers crave. (978-1-60282-236-8)